THE STAR
BEYOND TOMORROW

Vincent Havelund

iUniverse, Inc.
New York   Bloomington

iUniverse books may be ordered through booksellers or by contacting:

iUniverse
1663 Liberty Drive
Bloomington, IN 47403
www.iuniverse.com
1-800-Authors (1-800-288-4677)

Because of the dynamic nature of the Internet, any Web addresses or links contained in
this book may have changed since publication and may no longer be valid. The views
expressed in this work are solely those of the author and do not necessarily reflect the
views of the publisher, and the publisher hereby disclaims any responsibility for them.

ISBN: 978-1-4401-9574-7 (sc)
ISBN: 978-1-4401-9575-4 (ebook)

Printed in the United States of America

iUniverse rev. date: 03/11/2010

Introduction:

This book is a fictionalized account of planets in different solar systems to our own, which is dominated by one planet that is far more advanced than the others. This leading planet has defeated the tyranny of distance in space travel and there are many ways in which it is way ahead of all of the other planets in technology and medical services. It is a planet that has been under development for many more millennia than any of the other ten planets, its laws are controversial but have been proven by the test of time, and however there are glaring problems.

The biggest one is the age for retirement which is 260 YOA and the average age lived is 300 years, but it is the highly advanced medical technology that keeps people able to live and work that long. The problem is that many people don't want to live and work that long; so that when the allotted working life is over many choose just to die from just being tired of living. Meantime the state has had its people working to their maximum capability until they are allowed by their age to retire; they may not by law retire earlier.

Earth was the first planet found, but is considered too far behind the others in every way to qualify as a member of the Federation of Planets; rather it is given the status of a protectorate of the leading planet Orbsey, and has its own special place within the group.

The reader must discern the similarities between the story of the highly advanced planets and the actuality of life on earth 2,000 years later. The story is based on the discovery of several new Planets and the interaction between the new comers and the people on the Planets from which the highly developed major planet is setting up small colonies within their own territory.

This account is fast moving often funny, sometimes tragic, and other times just a difference between the citizens of ten different planets. Naturally all have different ways, but the ones we are going to be dealing with are the colonies set up on Orbsey for observation purposes. When the colonies are complete they are a very diverse lot, all with different ideas, but planet earth is the most backward of them all, but one of the main character is an earthling and the earth colonies are favored for this and several other reasons.

Author's Profile

The writer was born in NZ on Oct 25ᵗʰ 1935 and lived there until August 1970. He came to Australia before there was the need for a passport between the two countries.

He has worked in many industries as a Professional Public Officer for small companies for many years in both Australia and NZ? In his early days that position entitled him to represent his client companies, at the Australian Tax Office and in the Equity Court of NSW? The Laws are now changed as the Legal Profession objected to that area of Law allowing none accredited practitioners to do legal work, which seems quite fair in retrospect? The writer did take accounting as a young man, but did not sit the final exams.

The areas of work that was undertaken has been numerous and created quite an interesting background, he has worked in many different industries over the last almost fifty five years? In NZ he owned and developed a very big wholesale meat company which failed for personal reasons after initial great success. It was at the time the biggest privately owned meat company in NZ; the loss when the companies as a group failed was large, financially and personally.

The industries he has had interests in were: Mixed dairy farming, Meat, Timber Soft and Hardwood, Fat Lamb Export, Heavy Interstate Transport, Mushroom Farming, Truck Stops and Restaurants, Professional Public Officer, (Australia only) International Finance in USA, London, Sao Paulo Brazil, Vienna etc; Shearing (NZ Only) Union Rep (NZ only) Canning of Tuna Fish, (Fiji only) Property Development, etc. The above interests are the source of the many short stories Vincent has written, from Humorous & Timid to Serious the vein is always, quick snatches of a very diverse life all in camera?

Chapter 1/

Orbsey a Star
in the Distant Heavens:

O VER 2,000 YEARS AGO at about the time of the birth of Christ in a distant galaxy, on a planet "Orbsey" very much bigger than earth, but whose people were in many respects similar. The Scientists started sending out probes, searching for a world in a solar system that was capable of maintaining life similar to their own.

Their own planet was peaceful all wars had been stopped or forcefully cancelled out many years ago but their ambitions had extended far, and now they wanted to know are there others out there like us, and if there are can we communicate with them. Many probes had been sent out but none had been successful, then on behalf of a radio based quest a famous scientist reported a solar system had been found from which definite signs of life had been heard.

The site from where the radio signals were sent were not too far distant and research was being pursued to get confirmation of its existence, and whether the radio signals had been deliberately sent; by intelligent beings capable of understanding they were sending the messages. The big question was where they also trying to find any sign of intelligent life, because if they had there must be an advanced intelligence involved.

From then several years had gone by during which more probes were sent out and had reported back, the information the Scientists wanted. It had been found that the planet was in many respects a complete replica of the Planet Orbsey except they had only one Sun and one Moon. On the contrary Orbsey moved in a planetary system that had three Sun's and Orbsey itself had several Moons, their own system including ten member planets. All of the member planets revolved around the various Suns within their own solar systems. Orbsey was almost double the size of the Planet Earth and had a highly developed population of almost 16 billion people.

The Orbsey population size had been controlled for many years, and peace had also been normal for a long time. The people had millennia before settled all differences and the planet Orbsey lived in harmony, controlled by one big central Govt and with six different almost equal (numerically) groups all represented within the central Govt. There had been a serious overpopulation on Orbsey until they had begun to increase the natural life span of its peoples and then control the rate of birth, the results had been spectacular and now with the life span greatly expanded there was no aging problems.

All military action had ceased millenniums ago when a method had been found that nullified all weapons of war, even hand guns had been abolished. Only pistols for sporting purposes were still allowed and they could not fire bullets, these were confined to none destructive laser beams. A method had been created whereby no weapons of any level of destruction could be used for any purpose and the police used the stun guns only against criminals.

The people were much the same in appearance as the people from earth, but the method of communication had many centuries before changed to thought only, the only thing they had to do was think of someone and they were in instant touch. All food was ingested by simply thinking of what they wanted to eat and the food intake was immediate through the thought process, as a result over many years they had gradually lost their mouths and were now quite comfortable without them, and really had no use for them except perhaps to make a noise at a sporting event.

Any illnesses could be corrected by the simple process of replacement of the parts that were sick or weak, as a result their heads were a little bigger than earthlings, but they had no ears they weren't needed so again had been lost over the centuries. All other parts were still the same as earthlings, legs, arms, hands, torso etc.

It had not been general knowledge what the Scientific Community had had been doing, because they had wanted to keep the discovery secret, until they could be certain about what they had found. At the early stage the only contact had been by radio, but now more information had been confirmed, by way of a huge telescope system in orbit over Orbsey, all of their scientific hopes had been confirmed.

When the news finally broke there was great excitement, they had even found an area on this Earth that was only lightly inhabited, within a huge area of sea and comprising several Islands, one that was very large and another with two Islands but quite small and lots of smaller islands on the outer peripheral.

There were huge expectations, finally they had found a land mass similar to Orbsey but a lot smaller, inhabited by people that looked very similar to their own, but very backward in dress and development for example the only mode of transport was horse drawn.

A great council special meeting had been held and the reports from the Scientists had been examined. The delegates had as usual met by cyber link and the decision to send out stronger probes to search out the chance to set up a settlement and maybe colonize the area that was seen as being unsettled, except by a very few of the new worlds peoples. There were other big landmasses but these appeared to be occupied far more densely, whereas the future for them to settle in this area seemed logical considering the very few inhabitants there appeared to be.

It had been decided to send a spacecraft big enough to carry about 2,000 settlers to this world, which from the scientists they found was named earth by the local peoples. There were no problems expected and certainly the new settler's would have more than adequate knowledge to be safe in this new world. They would carry no weapons for any type of destruction, but they did carry the technology to neutralize all war machines sent against them, for their society it was simple to cancel out the power of any explosive weapons of any caliber.

The space freighter would carry a landing vehicle for use by the settlers and the mother craft would be put into permanent orbit around earth so they could return home at any time they wanted, the only condition being there must be at least a minimum load for the space freighter.

ORBSEY BIG BROTHER OF PLANET EARTH:

Orbsey the Planet is twice the size of Planet Earth and in an adjacent Solar System! The Planet has a surface area of 1.2 Billion Square Kms, within which there are twelve continents with close to one billion populations each and another 30 independent small countries dotted around the Orbsey globe. Within the big continents there are over 300 independent small countries each with their own national integrity but dependent on central associations. These central associations each provide a population to the independent groups of three free trading groups, into an approximate division of four billion people. The small Island countries come together as one group with another four billion people to represent. The ability of the individual Govts to influence the Central Govt in Cordiance is all relative the idea is to give every citizen of Orbsey an equal vote that is meaningful when they reach full voting age.

The voting for the representatives to the Central Parliament is every five years with a rotational retirement after three terms or fifteen years if one survives that long, and there is an upper house to keep the lower house in check. One cannot run for parliament in any constituency until reaching the final work term which is normally at approximately 174 YOA, but one may run in the elections for their first term before that age in order to actually enter Parliament at the minimum age. The voting process for all levels of Govt is by thought control, when first elected to Parliament it is compulsory to give permission for ones votes to be registered via ones thoughts on any given subject. One is able to control ones thoughts, but if this is done during a vote, it is a criminal act subject to a heavy penalty.

There are major parties that form their own chorum, but the voting is first past the post and then the parties negotiate to form the Govt, with full voting rights to all elected delegates.

Orbseyns Great Parliament, is the controlling body situated in Cordiance, and with final say over a fixed agenda, Medical, Food, Homes, Transport, Clothing and Footwear, White goods, the intent being that there are no homeless or Orbseyns that are unable to support themselves, any unfortunates that fall through the cracks must be picked up by their own countries and cared for at the cost of the central parliament.

There is no govt control of vital resources such as fishing and other luxury items, these delicacies are left for the private economy as are many other delicacies such as artificial meat and vegetables etc. These products are still processed for the thought feeding process but, the taste is refined and separated for the connoisseurs of such fine food, but one has to be rich to be able to afford such luxuries.

The Law encapsulating Police, Lawyers and Courts are very pro active and move very fast, there are no jails, but there is a tightly administrated system of control if convicted of any criminal offence. There are capital offences that means quick death if found guilty, and the police ability to find guilty parties is very high, if a person has been executed for false evidence and that is subsequently proved, all guilty parties are quickly executed. Capital offences are Murder, Rape, Pedophilia, and all sexual aberrations. The reason the punishment is so severe is because all such crimes are committed by persons who have the right to declare their various problem and can be fixed up without cost quickly and easily with very little interruption in their lives.

All other crimes the punishment is to be put on a special watch machine and to be forced make recompense to the state for all court costs and accumulated extra costs. This also involves the working off of the debts and repayment to the victims of such crime. When the payments are all made the criminal is fully restored to society and all of the beneficial rights of a citizen of Orbsey.

Social welfare there is none, any citizens unable to work must present for medical rehabilitation and they will be fully fit again within a week, there is no unemployment. Deterioration in health through age is also curable, but stops at the acceptable average age limit. Cure at any age can still be acquired but only through private resources the Govt has done its job, by ensuring every citizen reaches the average age limit, but normally there's another 50 years of good living if you have been a saver and can pay, for all of the luxuries you might like in old age

There is no tax but all consumer goods have a consumer tax added, this includes all material to produce everything that is controlled by the Central Parliament for processing etc.

The flora and Fauna suffered badly in the early period about five millennia previously, but had all been restored by the Scientists many centuries ago, now the original growth had all been restored. The forests had also all been restored with native trees being forbidden to be cut down; only soft quick growing trees are allowed to be cut and milled. Such exotic timbers are used only on the houses of the wealthy that type of material being very expensive.

White goods are available also through the two systems and only the wealthy being able to afford the architecturally designed products, the entire govt guarantee products are mass produced in enormous quantities as are all common consumer goods.

The ideas behind the Govt controls are to ensure that all are fed clothed and housed to an equal level they may rise above that level, but they not become slaves to debt. All may have a commonly produced car, but again that's the norm for all, any may rise above that and enjoy the fruits of their labor. The catch being they are limited as to how much they can leave to individual beneficiaries etc.

Orbsey had many Millennia ago been a world of wars and killing on an enormous scale, the death and cost of wars had been crazy the planet couldn't develop. They first got to a very high technical achievement level that threatened to destroy the planet and that's when changes started. The scientists discovered ways to nullify explosive materials of all types, and this controlled the fear of total destruction.

Then small weapons were banned and scale of production was lost so again these were stopped. The laws were legislated that unilaterally condemned certain crimes these were universally implemented and the many draconian punishments were imposed the intent being used to stop rising serious crime.

When then the Central Parliament loaded up the repayment system of punishment for small crime gradually even petty crime was on the wane. Then when the quick police response and legal conviction were sped up so high the damping down of crime was what got criminals to change their lifestyles. There is still a lot of blue and white collar crime in Orbsey but very much on the wane, which is why they are still trying to control all crime, by improving always police efficiency.

They have robot police but don't use them against the general populace; they hadn't been deployed for hundreds of years.

A new world a new home.

The new settlers had been treated so that they all had a mouth and ears, there was only one thing they were all quite brown by skin color, but they soon found there were many skin colors on earth. They could now talk and eat like the earthlings but their heads were just a little bigger. Taken casually it was difficult to tell the difference between Earthlings and Orbseyns.

The big launch off day had arrived and the chosen settlers for the new world had been taken aboard, and prepared for the flight, this wasn't difficult because for years daily intergalactic flights had been available at quite nominal costs so many people were used to being prepared for these flights, although never before had there been specific destinations to visit another planet, it wasn't unusual for private flights to visit one of the moons. The cargo vessel had been loaded with all of the necessary equipment to set up the new colony.

A site had been chosen in the middle of the huge Island now known to be named in the center of Australia. It was known that gold was highly valued by the earthlings so big quantities of gold and other precious metals were on board so that any land they wanted they could buy. Australia was the chosen site, but if they were rejected they could easily return home, on board the vessels that would be hovering in the stratosphere. Although the distance between the worlds was vast millions of light years, the tyranny of distance had been conquered many years ago and the travel time would be no longer than 168 hours at the most. On arrival the fleet would go into slow orbit around earth while an advance party would land, and if they could set up negotiations to buy land in the vast unoccupied desert.

Once negotiations to buy had been completed another advance group would land with the transfer vessels and unload the modules that would make living conditions quite normal on the desert sands. They would also land their equipment that would close down any weapons big or small that may be aimed at their new homes.

The home materials would also be unloaded but the control of the colony, once it had been constructed would be up to the leaders of the new colonists, they would have complete control including behavior anyone misbehaving would be held with laser shackles on board the craft circling above.

There was great excitement aboard the fleet which was now in orbit, and soon they expected reports back from the advance parties, to advise that they could now land on their new land, they were in for a rude shock.

It was after their scouts arrived in the deserts of Australia and they had made the first contact that, they begun to understand what it was like to be back in an ancient culture.

The first meeting was with a group of Aborigines, and it was easy to communicate, all they had to do was listen and their thoughts translated immediately, then to talk back they had an internal ability to be able to converse in any language that they heard being spoken.

They found the people very friendly and nice but extremely backward and natural! Because the climate was so hot they wore few clothes and had no knowledge of the outside world. Although they seemed to live a happy and carefree life, it was clear they must be short lived and had to keep moving to gather food, with women doing much of the work, and the men moving always out front hunting for food and in charge of the community.

There was no objection to the newcomers setting up a colony, and they weren't interested in gold, they didn't see any use for something they couldn't eat or wear. On the other hand any ornaments they could wear or at least things with a practical use would be welcomed. When asked who owned the land they seemed to be at a loss to understand the word owned, they had no conception of any one belonging to the tribe owning anything, the colonists were welcome to come live and enjoy.

The fleet was well aware of what was happening at all times because of their level of communication being so high, and all of the colonists were in agreement they wanted to land and set up a temporary home but use the time to search the world for where they would want to settle down permanently. They had small craft that could be used to search the entire new world if they wanted, and it seemed right to start where they were accepted. This would allow them to acclimatize themselves and then seek to spread out, if they indeed wanted to and if the new environment wasn't to their liking they could just pack up and go home, without any regrets. It was certain that when they got home they would be welcomed as heroes, who had visited a new world; all would be well they would all have homes again even if not the ones they had left behind.

The transfer to the earth was easy; they had a fleet of small craft which were used to land first the Colonists and then the equipment. The leaders of the group then set about to set up the homes and a dome was set up over the entire encampment to protect them from any strange phenomena that they may find. Food supplies were available in over abundance, and the desert sands would quickly be made viable for growing their needs, then immediately processing them to their own method of sustenance.

Within two weeks there was a flourishing Colony, the Aborigines could not be found they obviously had neither interest nor curiosity with their new visitors. This was not the case with the newcomers, they were intensely interested in their new neighbors and had hoped they would come and visit. It was to be almost six months before the same group of earth people once again appeared, but still showed little interest in what was going on, in the new encampment. The leaders of the new Colony had to chase up the Aborigines to try and at least strike up some type of acceptance. It was the children that first got together, the colony had about fifty youngsters aged from five to ten YOA they soon met up with and created the first integration something their parents had been unable to achieve.

In the meantime the small craft had been being used to investigate the new world, but they had done so without revealing themselves. Firstly they found this world was very sparsely inhabited and was extremely warlike. They found all manner of differences there were some even darker than themselves, others that had different shaped eyes and a yellowish skin, others that were light skinned in color and with multi colored hair, still others that seemed to be the same color as themselves. The one thing they all had in common was the ease in which they killed each other, the men seemed to take a savage delight in death, but this was anathema to the Orbseyns, in their eyes these people were extremely barbaric and not the type they would want to live with at this stage, or without in some way quietening them down. Since this was beyond their capacity to achieve and there was no taste for killing among themselves this aspect of the local peoples were considered very negatively.

It was decided that some of the men among the new colonists would spend time in differing countries to get a real understanding of this new world, only by actually living among earthlings did the leaders think they could find out if it was possible to integrate among the earth's population.

The following teams were sent out: China a team of six, Rome six, India six, German Barbarians six, The Americas six, New Zealand two, Australia four, and the Pacific Rim countries six.

This part of the book is about the efforts these people made to find a place to integrate and settle down. The intent was to help modernize this world and introduce a new advanced culture.

All of the groups had left at once; the Orbseyns had the technology to change their appearance to what was needed. It was automatic that when the groups arrived at their destination they would take on the characteristics of the people they were with, but they could change to whatever they wanted at any time. All of the groups had been left at their various destinations and they had to be picked up again from wherever they were in six months, only then would the decision be made where they would live, or in fact if they would even stay.

The group to check out China had arrived and quickly settled down in their new society, they soon found it was one in which the common people had little or no rights and life was very cheap. The leaders could kill the commoners with little reason, it only required for some little mistake to be made and one could be decapitated instantly. It didn't take the Orbseyns long to decide this wasn't a place for them to settle, because the type of warfare being waged couldn't be controlled by their anti war devices. They were horrified at what they were seeing but where stuck there for the six months period.

They decided to spend the entire time just travelling through the country, they needed no food still being linked to their food at the base in the Australian desert, all they had to do was think of food and it was there. As they travelled throughout China they found out just how big the country was, but they had several bigger back in Orbsey. The peasants had to work hard and most of what was produced was taken by the elite for their own use. There were no discernable rights allocated to the peasants and if they were wanted for the military they were simply taken and training started immediately. The better or middle classes if that could be assessed as so, were taken for the cavalry and the peasants were simply drafted into the infantry.

Iron had just been invented and they were building bridges strong enough to carry vehicles, they had the wheelbarrow and had just invented paper, as well as explosives which the Orbseyns could neutralize.

As the travelled the country they met with and stayed in the homes of many of the local people, whom they found the people as wonderful and friendly. At one village in which they stayed there was an extremely beautiful young girl of 18 YOA and one of the Orbseyns a young man of some thirty YOA was very attracted to her. The age difference was irrelevant since the average age for their race was well in excess of 250 years; one was only breeding aged by time they reached 120 years.

The young man's name here on earth was Orlos; he was single and had his parents and one brother back in Orbsey, only two children were allowed per couple back there, one between 100-150 YOA and another between the ages of 150-200 YOA, so his brother was 120 YOA and he was 30 YOA.

Orlos was falling in love with the Chinese girl Li Sun but his team was trying to keep them apart there could be a tragedy in the making.

The girl Li Sun was committed to be married to an older man chosen by her parents, and the arrival and attentions of a handsome young man was well received by her, but rejected by her parents. Of course they had no idea how young Orlos really was but he looked in earth terms to be about 20 YOA whereas the man she was committed to was in his sixties, a grand old age even then. There was no reason the pair couldn't match up, but the group was well aware they may not be staying, and although Li Sun could be taken with them it didn't seem wise to encourage the two especially Orlos, since he was aware of the problem. The group had been there a week and the young couple was becoming more and more enamored of each other much to the annoyance of the girl's parents and her old paramour, things were getting decidedly hostile. The group Leader then decided it was time to move on, but the young couple took matters into their own hands and ran away together.

Of course Orlos couldn't get away he was tied to the group through thought connection, but the girl was lost to her parents and her husband to be, she would never be accepted in marriage, it was a cultural stalemate. A very substantial dowry had been paid and that now all had to be repaid immediately, but much of the money had been used up for the wedding. It was a very dangerous situation until the group leader stepped in and paid the frustrated groom in full.

The group left and were joined by the young couple, but now Li Sun had to be told the truth which wasn't easy, because she now understood she had pledged herself to an Alien not one of the planet earth peoples. She was at first terrified, but Orlos reassured her he would never leave her and if they went back to Orbsey she would be able to go with them.

Many centuries previously the marriage ceremony had been forsaken on Orbsey, the procedure now was simple a couple claimed a mate and they were together for as long as they were happy. Either one could give the other a note of intent to end the agreement and move on to whatever situation they may choose for their future.

They could not however engage in conjugal sex without first giving notice of intent to leave their current partner. The rate of marital breakup was very low and most stayed together for their very long lifetimes, there were many rules however before a young couple could be accepted by Orbseyn society as a pair

Because the young couple had eloped together as far as the group was concerned they were committed to each other, no thought had yet been given of what would happen if the Colony never eventuated and they all went home. The leader of the China group now decided belatedly they would split up and travel in pairs with Orlos and a team mate making up a three some with Li Sun present.

ORLOS & LI SUN:

When we left Orbsey I had no thoughts of meeting a girl and falling in love, but the minute I first laid eyes on Li Sun I knew she was the girl I wanted. I knew it was unfair for me to take too much interest in her because we might not be staying, and I knew that from what we had seen so far this most probably wouldn't be the planet for us to settle in, they were way to backward a civilization for us to live in permanently. The total lack of any decent level of sophistication was way below what we were used to, and the lack of respect for life was to us appalling, already most of my companions were expressing reserves.

The first day I spoke to Li it was like listening to a beautiful bird. I could only manage a smile and a simple "hello how are you today?" and I stuttered that out like a child.

Li also was very shy and could barely stutter out a "Hello I am well thank you"

Gradually as we were able to see each other even if only out of the corners of our eyes we both managed to sneak a smile at each other and whenever we did I felt giddy all over, she was so gorgeous and petite, all I had ever dreamed of for my mate. For the first few days I completely forgot we were on a strange planet, and when I remembered I was devastated.

It was obvious we both wanted to talk together but how was the problem to be resolved, one day we were lucky and met in the pergola on the outside of her home and had the chance for our first real conversation.

I spoke first and said, "I have so wanted to be able to talk to you alone, how you are getting on please?" in the friendliest manner I could.

"I am quite well and how long are you and your group going to stay with us?" she asked.

I had no time to be backward so I said, "not very long sadly, but I should like to get to know you is that possible? I am very attracted to you and have you in my thoughts all of the time." I said with as friendly a smile as I could.

"Yes I would so love to talk to you I also haven't been able to get you out of my thoughts since I first saw you, but I am pledged to another and my parents have already got the dowry so it's very difficult, but I would still like to talk alone with you, my intended husband is older than my father, and I am terrified for my future," Li Said with a wistful look on her face.

We agreed to meet that night at midnight when everyone would be asleep, and when I left her I was so excited the several hours of waiting seemed like years to me.

On the dot of midnight I was waiting for Li, she was a little late and I was getting anxious when suddenly out of the dark she slipped into the pergola and we were together alone at last.

We were both very nervous and I was the first to regain my composure, so I said to her, "hello Li I was getting worried thinking you couldn't come now you are here I am delighted".

"If I could have I would have been here hours ago, but my parents are suspicious and have put a guardian to watch me, I had to wait for her to go asleep I am here now, but if they catch me there will be real trouble. I have been betrothed to a man older than my Father and we are to be married within a fortnight, but I am terrified and really feel it's best for me to run away?"

"Is there nothing else you can do because for me it was love at first sight, may I step in and ask for your hand in marriage?"

"No my father would be furious and there has been a big dowry paid, he has spent most of it on the wedding and would be in trouble if the marriage didn't go ahead," Li said with a sad smile.

"That's not a problem my group could pay of your fathers debt would that fix it for us?" Orlos asked anxiously.

"No it wouldn't!" said a saddened Li, "the honor of my Father would be compromised and he would be furious," Li said with a gentle smile.

"Well" said Orlos, "I am in love with you and if it comes to the final reckoning will you elope with me, and we will make our way back to my people. But you must be careful because with my people we have to be sure of what we are doing and there are difficulties which I will tell you about later. Perhaps it's best if we meet again tomorrow night and I will check things out with my group leader is that alright?" I asked Li anxiously.

"That will be fine yes I will be here at the same time tomorrow, but we must be quick because the marriage is to be soon then it will be too late, I shall be taken away and locked up until the first baby is born," Li said with a sad little smile.

We parted with a quick hug, and both of us promised to meet the next night at the same time.

The next evening we met as agreed and this time Li was there first, but I was very soon after and we started to talk seriously immediately.

"I have spoken to our group leader and your father will be paid the dowry money immediately, but our leader isn't so pleased with the idea, because we don't really know each other, and they think it's too quick. They have also reminded me that we are very different and you may not like to come to our country which is far, far away." I said very nervously.

I knew that if she knew we were really Aliens from another world she would be very frightened and might change her mind, but I had reasoned that her situation marrying a man, to her, who was so old would be worse than with us. I was absolutely certain of my love for Li I knew how I felt, we Orbseyns were known for being very quick at making these types of decisions, but then sticking to it for life.

Li was shaking a bit but said with a determined lift of her head, "I love you and I have done since the first time I saw you across the room with your party, I want to come with you no matter where or how far away we will be going. I know it's unusual to feel so strongly at first glance, but I know my love for you is real, what is important is knowing if you feel the same for me?"

"I have no doubt at all that what I feel for you is true love and we will live our entire life together, there will be hard times but that's usual and shouldn't stop us!" I said with a total belief in my words.

We made arrangements that the following night we would meet again, but this time we would elope. We also agreed that we wouldn't make love until we had really been blessed in a marriage type ceremony acceptable to my own people.

The following night we met as agreed and left immediately, we were both nervous but both fully certain of our feelings for each other, and so our journey into a long tumultuous life had begun. But we never wavered from that very first night on earth when we met and talked then ran away together. We have as far as I am concerned had a wonderful life. Li and I became faithful partners, and I have always been as happy as on that night we first eloped and spent our entire lives as one at that same level of contentment.

EARTH

The Colonists had realized the sheer size of Australia was such that it needed a team of six not four, the size plus the apparent small population meant the party would split up into pairs and be picked up from where ever they were at the end of six months. The first party headed North to what in the future would become the Northern Territory. They would then turn East and travel down to future Brisbane. the Other headed down to Sth Australia and then would travel up to the Western area, the last two headed South to what would one day be Melbourne and would travel North up to the future Sydney.

The ones that went North were staggered by the sheer size of everything, the landscape was unblemished except for a few Aboriginal camps, but the locals were not particularly friendly just indifferent, they didn't seem to care one way or the other what the visitors did on their land. They did get caught in the big wet, but with the facilities they had there was little problem. They came across a big rock (Uluru) but apart from a quick look around kept going, they had no concept of danger or getting lost in dangerous situations. Their navigational systems were so far advanced even on what earth would have in the 21st century that there was just no danger. They travelled up to Darwin and then started down to Townsville on the East Coast heading towards Brisbane; they were having a great trip and were impressed that there seemed to be no fighting amongst the Aborigines. The various Colonist teams were in constant communication via thought processes; this kept them aware of the savagery being witnessed by the other teams that were on the other side of the world.

The team that had headed west was interested in the topography, and they were aware of the rich deposits of Iron Ore and other minerals as they travelled, this country they knew would be a wealthy one even if it had been on the Planet Orbsey.

The team that was travelling up the East Coast of the country became aware that this area seemed to be agriculturally the richest in the country and in time would probably be the most densely populated, of the entire country. If they allowed for the dryness of the continent it was a beautiful area, but would need some very hard work to develop the Continent into an agricultural one around the coasts then a mineral producing country in the arid area.

It was very obvious the present inhabitants wouldn't develop the country they obviously lacked the drive necessary to use the opportunities that were there to be taken. It had been quickly obvious the coastal areas were fertile and would be productive at some time in the distant future, but the center of the country would lag far behind, until the real value of Australia's heart land could be understood and capitalized on.

The big difference the colonists saw and respected was the Aboriginals of Australia were not killing and murdering each other as they found in other parts of the world.

ROME.

The team that went to Rome shared out the Roman Empire and the various areas of Europe one pair started in Spain and travelled up through future countries such as Germany, France and the lowlands, the other pair started in India and travelled up into Egypt as their final goal. The last pair started in Rome and travelled outwards to various parts of the Roman Empire including Greece and up through Hungary etc. The one thing the three teams had noticed in common was that this area was really in a state of constant war, and the forced subjugation of the Nations by one type of Republic, and even that one was struggling to find a balance, its leader Julius Caesar had just been murdered, and his adopted Son had taken his place. The Orbseyns had spent time in Rome before splitting up into three groups; their impression of this supreme western Capital was poor in the extreme.

The city was host to many different travelers and permanent residents many of whom were in some way involved with the military. They witnessed an event in the main stadium with Gladiators fighting to the death which to some degree was acceptable, but the feeding of criminals to hungry lions etc they found totally barbaric. The very poor living conditions and the infanticide of baby girls was intolerable, the fact that so many men were killed in battle which made girl baby's if kept alive, becoming too high a ratio of the population.

The housing was poor and the sanitary system only really catered to the wealthy people, these fortunate's they found enjoyed a very luxurious standard of living. The only mode of transport was by horse drawn vehicles, horseback or just by walking; they were to find the conditions in Rome were far better than some of the countries that were part on the Roman Empire.

They then split up two going off to Egypt, another two went to Spain and the final two went to Constantinople, all travelled on horseback.

EGYPT.

This country they found as quite advanced compared to standards they had seen so far, but they were still unimpressed. The wealthy lived in great splendor while the laboring classes were really only bonded slaves, the money spent by the Pharaohs' on their own eternal future life seemed to be a little over the top, and the forced labor with poor return was hard to understand. The enormous stacks of stone as burial places seemed over the top to the Orbseyns, but compared to a lot of other countries so far visited the people were quite well treated.

The control of the people by priests playing on the superstitions of the uneducated if it wasn't so pitiful would have been to the visitors rather funny. These priests seemed to have more control than the Pharaohs, but it just seemed like a lot of mumbo jumbo all mixed up to hold the people in bondage, and the method was very successful.

The source of life was the river they had named mother Nile and the annual flooding and silting of the soil was why Egypt was such a fruit bowl, but they had been defeated and virtually been in bondage since the time of Alexander the Greek.

He had built a great new city Alexandria and one of his generals had founded the present Ptolemy Dynasty his descendants, Cleopatra and her brother was still the joint Pharaohs of Egypt.

SPAIN FRANCE AND PORTUGAL

These future countries were still in the formative stage, the former Carthage had been the centre of trade for many countries, but since that country had been completely destroyed by the Roman Legions those countries had become more attached to the Roman Empire. At present they were being occasionally invaded by the German Barbarians, but they had only small populations. The

German Barbarians they met they found to be a smelly but handsome people, who were fantastic fighters and when they weren't fighting they were making babies, those were the two favorite pastimes enjoyed by both men and women. The war and killing seemed to them natural, but at times they did a bit of growing of food for consumption, the trouble was the weather was cold and hard, so many of the efforts to grow food were frustrated by the cold. This being the reality these Germanic Tribes was really wanderers moving from place to place living off the efforts of others as they confiscated all vegetables and animals for eating they came across as they moved from place to place.

Their nomadic ways were exacerbated by the natural vigor of a people that lived in the cold climate that was a natural weather pattern in that western part of the world. At many times they subsisted and those were the times they went looking for new homes, in new areas, but since they were nomadic they never stayed long enough to start developing and improving by their own effort they far preferred war and living on the efforts of others.

Spain was one area that certain tribes of Aryan Barbarians actually started to settle, but this is a country that will develop into a superior economy and will in the future have a real part to play in the development of this Planet Earth. The same comments applied to France and other adjacent areas that were still not in the process of real development.

THE AMERICAN CONTINENT:

The south of this area was where the first two of the group was let off their transport in what would become Central America the next two were dropped off in what would become Canada, the last two were dropped off in what would become Argentina.

The group that travelled by foot down through the vastness of Canada into the top end of the future USA found native tribes who were a beautiful friendly people happy in their own style of living and keen to learn off their visitors. Many happy hours were spent with the many different peoples but the populations were very small by number of what would be needed for real development.

The natives were light brown in color and had a big variety of dialects all of which the visitors could understand.

The areas in the Mexican area down the South had hosted high levels of civilization, but the two main cultures the Orbseyns found sickening and because of the sacrifices to Gods once again were deemed as the manipulation of the people by priests and others so that they were pleased to leave and forget that continent even though they seemed to have developed an advanced level of understanding. As far as the Alien visitors were concerned planet earth was just a barbarous world and could not be a part of a highly advanced world such as Orbsey was.

INDIA:

This country was obviously a subcontinent that hosted a big variety of religions, but was a really colorful one that would one day have a huge population. This was even now an advanced culture but not in a technological sense.

India has been repeatedly invaded over the years by many different peoples including repeatedly by the Chinese, Alexander the Great conquered part of India after fighting his way over the Himalayas. The country although it was huge didn't appear as if it was one that could host a colony of aliens, because of the huge internal difference in the natural population.

India had a lot of different religions but the main ones were at that time Buddhist, Muslim, and Hindus. The background was far too old fashioned for the Orbseyns they could see no attraction to India.

NEW ZEALAND:

The two Colonists who went to NZ found a country that was almost uninhabited, there were a few Natives but like the Aborigines of Australia they weren't much interested in their visitors. Compared to Australia the climate was very cold and wet, the natives called themselves Moriories and were quite passive by nature. The entire landscape was heavily covered in forest and bush scrub, and the biggest bird the visitors had ever seen lived in the forest. It was a giant and stood about 12 feet high at the head when standing upright.

Starting at the bottom of the country and travelling by foot right to the top the scenery was beautiful, there was very little wild life if any, but the plumage and singing of the native birds were fantastic. The Mountain Peaks in the Sth as they travelled North were like visions of Icy splendor rising out of the mists in the mornings and then clearing around 10.00 am to beautiful days. The beauty of the fjords and the waterfalls coming up the West Coast was a sight to behold unspoiled by earthlings of any type.

It was when they got up to the top of the North near the end of their stay that they made a wonderful discovery. The scenery had been wonderful all of the way and the birds more abundant and bursting with song than in the South, but except for one major mountain there wasn't as much the majestic scenery they had seen on the way up to the North. The bush and rivers were perhaps more beautiful than the Sth but in a different way, the fertility of the soil was very obvious and there were far more of the gigantic Moa's to be seen.

It was when they got well up the Nth Island they discovered the enormous trees (Kauri) huge straight hardwood stretching with gigantic trunks clear of branches fifty meters high. Only at the tops were there any branches with leaves, so that the bush appeared to be just a mass of these huge trees all reaching to the stars. The surrounding ground at the base of the trunks was all clear; obviously the giants took all moisture to sustain them in spite of the constant rain that fell almost daily. One of the travelers noticed that when he notched one of the trees it started to bleed a yellow resin. They tested the resin with heat and found that provided they applied the heat before the resin touched the soil, it hardened and became solid gold, this was quite interesting and they reported their tests later on their return, so that their discovery had great effect in the areas future. In certain parts of planet earth gold was highly prized and quite accidentally it was gold that from the start created a greater affinity between Orbseyns and Earthlings.

One night while they were camping at the base of the trees they could hear a rustling down at the base and they found that hard to understand, until they realized it was the trees talking to each other. Because Orbseyns had the ability to understand any language they realized if they listened carefully they could hear and understand what those mighty trees were saying. They suddenly understood they were listening to the spirits of the Kauri trees, telling each other how strangers had come who understood the blood of the trees could if properly treated be turned to gold. When suddenly the Orbseyns started to talk back to the tree spirits there was for a few seconds of startled silence, before they began to rustle at a very high tempo, the Orbseyns understood immediately the great trees were laughing.

As the rustling lowered they started once again to talk, "how is it that you strangers understand us when we are talking they asked, we and our ancestors have been growing here for 500,000 years but no one has passed by who understands us?

"Well we are from another planet a long way from earth and we have the gift of understanding all languages as well as being able to speak and language we hear, so we have no problem in understanding you and being able to talk to you."

The rest of the time they were at that spot the team from Orbsey learned more about Mother Earth than the rest of the expedition combined. The spirits explained they were well able to travel anywhere they pleased and because they were thousands of years old they knew more about this planet than anyone else. The only other life on earth as old as them (except stone) with other great trees certain parts of earth and they met quite regularly to laugh and play whenever they felt so inclined, but normally once a year at least.

The tree spirits explained they could manifest into any beings they wished but didn't bother unless they needed to because all people and animals were so short lived they had little knowledge. But sometimes a person may pass by who had been reborn many times then they were wise and could understand the trees. Just to prove the point some of the trees manifested the

By the end of their trip they had been unable to make any friends with the few local peoples, whenever they found a village or camp site the occupants showed little interest in striking up a friendly conversation, so they didn't pursue any further attempts to get to know them. At the very top of the Island looking out over the ocean the site was as good as any they had seen on their entire journey, but it was almost time to be picked up and returned to the Australian base.

All of the travelers were back in Australia now and in general found Planet Earth although very attractive not much of a world on which to base a sophisticated colony. It was felt that this planet was very backward and in some places still practiced human sacrifice to obscene Gods. The recommendation was that they should go home to Orbsey as quickly as possible!

ORBSEY BIG BROTHER OF PLANET EARTH:

Orbsey the Planet is twice the size of Planet Earth and in an adjacent Solar System! The Planet has a surface area of 1.2 Billion Square Kms, within which there are twelve continents with close to one billion populations each and another 30 independent small countries dotted around the Orbsey globe. Within the big continents there are over 300 independent small countries each with their own national integrity but dependent on central associations. These central associations each provide a population to the independent groups of three free trading groups, into an approximate division of four billion people. The small Island countries come together as one group with another four billion people to represent. The ability of the individual Govts to influence the Central Govt in Cordiance is all relative the idea is to give every citizen of Orbsey an equal vote that is meaningful when they reach full voting age.

The voting for the representatives to the Central Parliament is every five years with a rotational retirement after three terms or fifteen years if one survives that long, and there is an upper house to keep the lower house in check. One cannot run for parliament in any constituency until reaching the final work term which is normally at approximately 174 YOA, but one may run in the elections for their first term before that age in order to actually enter Parliament at the minimum age. The voting process for all levels of Govt is by thought control, when first elected to Parliament it is compulsory to give permission for ones votes to be registered via ones thoughts on any given subject. One is able to control ones thoughts, but if this is done during a vote, it is a criminal act subject to a heavy penalty.

There are major parties that form their own chorum, but the voting is first past the post and then the parties negotiate to form the Govt, with full voting rights to all elected delegates.

Orbseyns Great Parliament, is the controlling body situated in Cordiance, and with final say over a fixed agenda, Medical, Food, Homes, Transport, Clothing and Footwear, White goods, the intent being that there are no homeless or Orbseyns that are unable to support themselves, any unfortunates that fall through the cracks must be picked up by their own countries and cared for at the cost of the central parliament.

There is no govt control of vital resources such as fishing and other luxury items, these delicacies are left for the private economy as are many other delicacies such as artificial meat and vegetables etc. These products are still processed for the thought feeding process but, the taste is refined and separated for the connoisseurs of such fine food, but one has to be rich to be able to afford such luxury.

The Law encapsulating Police, Lawyers and Courts are very pro active and move very fast, there are no jails, but there is a tightly administrated system of control if convicted of any criminal offence. There are capital offences that means quick death if found guilty, and the police ability to find guilty parties is very high, if a person has been executed for false evidence and that is subsequently proved, all guilty parties are quickly executed. Capital offences are Murder, Rape, Pedophilia, and all sexual aberrations. The reason the punishment is so severe is because all such crimes are committed by persons who have the right to declare their various problem and can be fixed up without cost quickly and easily with very little interruption in their lives.

All other crimes the punishment is to be put on a special watch machine and to be forced make recompense to the state for all court costs and accumulated extra costs. This also involves the working off of the debts and repayment to the victims of such crime. When the payments are all made the criminal is fully restored to society and all of the beneficial rights of a citizen of Orbsey.

Social welfare there is none, any citizens unable to work must present for medical rehabilitation and they will be fully fit again within a week, there is no unemployment. Deterioration in health through age is also curable, but stops at the acceptable average age limit. Cure at any age can still be acquired but only through private resources the Govt has done its job, by ensuring every citizen reaches the average age limit, but normally there's another 50 years of good living if you have been a saver and can pay, for all of the luxuries you might like in your old age.

There is no tax but all consumer goods have a consumer tax added, this includes all material to produce everything that is controlled by the Central Parliament for processing etc.

The flora and Fauna suffered badly in the early period about five millennia previously, but had all been restored by the Scientists many centuries ago, now the original growth had all been restored. The forests had also all been restored with native trees being forbidden to be cut down; only soft quick growing trees are allowed to be cut and milled. Such exotic timbers are used only on the houses of the wealthy that type of material being very expensive.

White goods are available also through the two systems and only the wealthy being able to afford the architecturally designed products, the entire govt guarantee products are mass produced in enormous quantities as are all common consumer goods.

The ideas behind the Govt controls are to ensure that all are fed clothed and housed to an equal level they may rise above that level, but they must not become slaves to debt. All may have a commonly produced car, but again that's the norm for all, any may rise above that and enjoy the fruits of their labor. The catch being they are limited as to how much they can leave to individual beneficiaries etc.

Orbsey had many Millennia ago been a world of wars and killing on an enormous scale, the death and cost of wars had been crazy the planet couldn't develop. They first got to a very high technical achievement level that threatened to destroy the planet and that's when changes started. The scientists discovered ways to nullify explosive materials of all types, and this controlled the fear of total destruction. Then small weapons were banned and scale of production was lost so again these were stopped. The laws were legislated that unilaterally condemned certain crimes these were universally implemented and the many draconian punishments were imposed the intent being used to stop rising serious crime.

When then the Central Parliament loaded up the repayment system of punishment for small crime gradually even petty crime was on the wane. Then when the quick police response and legal conviction were sped up so high the damping down of crime was what got criminals to change their lifestyles. There is still a lot of blue and white collar crime in Orbsey but very much on the wane, which is why they are still trying to control all crime, by improving always police efficiency.

They have robot police but don't use them against the general populace; they hadn't been deployed for hundreds of years.

Chapter 2/

A new world a new home.

T HE NEW SETTLERS HAD been treated so that they all had a mouth and
ears, there was only one thing they were all quite brown by skin color,
but they soon found there were many skin colors on earth. They could
now talk and eat like the earthlings but their heads were just a little bigger.
Taken casually it was difficult to tell the difference between Earthlings and
Orbseyns.

The big launch off day had arrived and the chosen settlers for the new
world had been taken aboard, and prepared for the flight, this wasn't difficult
because for years daily intergalactic flights had been available at quite nominal
costs so many people were used to being prepared for these flights, although
never before had there been specific destinations to visit another planet, it
wasn't unusual for private flights to visit one of the moons. The cargo vessel
had been loaded with all of the necessary equipment to set up the new
colony.

A site had been chosen in the middle of the huge Island now known
to be named in the center of Australia. It was known that gold was highly
valued by the earthlings so big quantities of gold and other precious metals
were on board so that any land they wanted they could buy. Australia was
the chosen site, but if they were rejected they could easily return home, on
board the vessels that would be hovering in the stratosphere. Although the
distance between the worlds was vast millions of light years, the tyranny of
distance had been conquered many years ago and the travel time would be
no longer than 168 hours at the most. On arrival the fleet would go into slow
orbit around earth while an advance party would land, and if they could set
up negotiations to buy land in the vast unoccupied desert.

Once negotiations to buy had been completed another advance group would land with the transfer vessels and unload the modules that would make living conditions quite normal on the desert sands. They would also land their equipment that would close down any weapons big or small that may be aimed at their new home.

The home materials would also be unloaded but the control of the colony, once it had been constructed would be up to the leaders of the new colonists, they would have complete control including behavior anyone misbehaving would be held with laser shackles on board the craft circling above.

There was great excitement aboard the fleet which was now in orbit, and soon they expected reports back from the advance parties, to advise that they could now land on their new land, they were in for a rude shock.

It was after their scouts arrived in the deserts of Australia and they had made the first contact that, they begun to understand what it was like to be back in an ancient culture.

The first meeting was with a group of Aborigines, and it was easy to communicate, all they had to do was listen and their thoughts translated immediately, then to talk back they had an internal ability to be able to converse in any language that they heard being spoken.

They found the people very friendly and nice but extremely backward and natural! Because the climate was so hot they wore few clothes and had no knowledge of the outside world. Although they seemed to live a happy and carefree life, it was clear they must be short lived and had to keep moving to gather food, with women doing much of the work, and the men moving always out front hunting for food and in charge of the community.

There was no objection to the newcomers setting up a colony, but they weren't interested in gold, they didn't see any use for something they couldn't eat or wear. On the other hand any ornaments they could wear or at least things with a practical use would be welcomed. When asked who owned the land they seemed to be at a loss to understand the word owned, they had no conception of any one belonging to the tribe owning anything, the colonists were welcome to come live and enjoy.

The fleet was well aware of what was happening at all times because of their level of communication being so high, and all of the colonists were in agreement they wanted to land and set up a temporary home but use the time to search the world for where they would want to settle down permanently. They had small craft that could be used to search the entire new world if they wanted, and it seemed right to start where they were accepted. This would allow them to acclimatize themselves and then seek to spread out, if they indeed wanted to and if the new environment wasn't to their liking they could just pack up and go home, without any regrets. It was certain that when they got home they would be welcomed as heroes, who had visited a new world;

all would be well they would all have homes again even if not the ones they had left behind.

The transfer to the earth was easy; they had a fleet of small craft which were used to land first the Colonists and then the equipment. The leaders of the group then set about to set up the homes and a dome was set up over the entire encampment to protect them from any strange phenomena that they may find. Food supplies were available in over abundance, and the desert sands would quickly be made viable for growing their needs, then immediately processing them to their own method of sustenance.

Within two weeks there was a flourishing Colony, the Aborigines could not be found they obviously had neither interest nor curiosity with their new visitors. This was not the case with the newcomers, they were intensely interested in their new neighbors and had hoped they would come and visit. It was to be almost six months before the same group of earth people once again appeared, but still showed little interest in what was going on, in the new encampment. The leaders of the new Colony had to chase up the Aborigines to try and at least strike up some type of acceptance. It was the children that first got together, the colony had about fifty youngsters aged from five to ten YOA they soon met up with and created the first integration something their parents had been unable to achieve.

In the meantime the small craft had been being used to investigate the new world, but they had done so without revealing themselves. Firstly they found this world was very sparsely inhabited and was extremely warlike. They found all manner of differences there were some even darker than themselves, others that had different shaped eyes and a yellowish skin, others that were light skinned in color and with multi colored hair, still others that seemed to be the same color as themselves. The one thing they all had in common was the ease in which they killed each other, the men seemed to take a savage delight in death, but this was anathema to the Orbseyns, in their eyes these people were extremely barbaric and not the type they would want to live with at this stage, or without in some way quietening them down. Since this was beyond their capacity to achieve and there was no taste for killing among themselves this aspect of the local peoples were considered very negatively.

It was decided that some of the men among the new colonists would spend time in differing countries to get a real understanding of this new world, only by actually living among earthlings did the leaders think they could find out if it was possible to integrate among the earth's population.

The following teams were sent out: China a team of six, Rome six, India six, German Barbarians six, The Americas six, New Zealand two, Australia four, and the Pacific Rim countries six.

The next part of this book is about the efforts these people made to find a place to integrate and settle down.

GOING HOME TO ORBSEY:

All of the groups that had gone out to get a thorough knowledge of the planet earth were back in the desert with the Colonists. While they had been away a nice development had been built up, a very nice place for the group to live at, but now it was time to decide, were they going to settle or was it best to go home.

A full meeting was called off the Colonists and as usual was very orderly, as was normal for these people. Each of the groups that had gone out had reported in sequence of their experiences and observations of what they had seen, except for New Zealand, Australia, and North America which were all virtually uninhabited except sparsely of native tribes the groups were very unimpressed. The main members of the groups that had gone to Rome, China, Russia and the surrounding territories were unequivocal; this world in general was too backward for Orbseyns to set up a colony in. The Leaders in the various countries were obsessed with war and the blood lust was extreme. These war conditions had been brought under control several millenniums ago in Orbsey, but the weapons of war on earth were so obsolete that they couldn't be controlled. One couldn't stop men from taking sharpened swords getting on the back of a horse and killing each other even on Orbsey this type of activity couldn't be controlled, but their the people had long since lost that lust of battle.

When the Orbseyns had been in the position to blow their own world up they had first found a way to control all weapons of mass destruction, and all stockpiles had been destroyed. Gradually the banning of militaristic weapons had stopped all fighting of any consequence on their planet. Finally the destruction and creation of laws prohibiting hand guns of any kind for anyone; with heavy penalties for any persons found in possession of small weapons. It had taken several centuries but in the end all weapons of death had vanished from existence, the sales had become so poor and penalties so high that businesses found it commercially silly to produce weapons, of any type. Death with deadly weapons was almost unknown on the big planet Orbsey, but isolated instances did occur. The perpetrators were always quickly found and punished.

After all of the questions had been asked by those who hadn't been out with the exploratory groups, a vote had been put and it was decided to abandon the attempt to set up a colony on planet earth. It was recommended that instead of a colony a small group of around 100 should be sent to Egypt and changed over every two years. This program should continue indefinitely just so there was a continuing connection and at some time in the future maybe a colony could be set up.

This recommendation was accepted as reasonable and there was an immediate acceptance by 100 single men to stay for the two years, after every two years they were to be replaced.

The vote had been strongly in favor of the decisions, on the grounds of the earth's not being ready for the sophistication that the Orbseyns, would bring with them and too much damages would be caused. It was decided the damage would be not only on the human population but on the eco systems as well. It was well known that Orbsey was a modern civilization, but its modernization had been created with a big loss in other areas such as, Flora and Fauna, Animals and Birds as well as the creatures of the sea.

In spite of the big advances in technology Orbsey was a planet that was more developed to the need of their human like species, there were wilderness areas etc.

The packing in readiness to leave for home was quickly accomplished, and the schedule was that they would be leaving in a week.

LI SUN.

Things had happened so quickly for me it was terrifying; I had now found the man I loved more strongly than life itself was taking me to another world, another dimension. When I had first found Orlos was an alien it hadn't crossed my mind he would want to take me away to his world, but now it was a reality and it was due to happen in a week.

The people in the colony had been so loving and had accepted me without reservation, and I soon found it was so easy to be one of them, and my love for Orlos had grown stronger than ever if that was possible. Orlos had been so strong and understanding and had never wavered in the slightest in his insistence of the depth of his love for me, so really this is about our love and how it would be in his world. But we were living in our own world of love, I couldn't help but wonder; after all I am Chinese, and we have always been a pragmatic race.

Anyhow Orlos has convinced me we should go back to Orbsey together and make our life together there, and we would have a long happy one. He has said the average life span on the entire Planet is at present 250 years and by time our span is up it will be at least 300 years according to their medical profession. He has told me the marital system as we know it doesn't exist, but that the percentage of couples breaking up is less than 10% and his family has never had a separation over several millenniums.

The preparation to leave was advancing rapidly, and the shuttles had ferried most of the equipment to the space ships, waiting and ready for the launch into the stratosphere. Since I was the only earthling travelling my Orbseyns friends were reassuring me that all would be fine, and since they all knew that Orlos loved me unreservedly there would be no real trouble for us, except adjusting to my new home.

I had been living with friends of Orlos and on our last night before we left, we spent the evening together. Apparently the Leaders would have liked to have said good bye to the Aboriginals, but they couldn't be found so the formalities were forgotten.

When Orlos came to me he said, "Well my Darling we leave tomorrow for our freighter ship are you scared? Believe me there is no need to be, the only thing that worries me is that our civilization is so far ahead of this one on earth, you may be overwhelmed".

"Yes I am nervous, it's a big step but far better than my Father was going to condemn me to, you and your friends have been so good to me, that I have no fear. I will be glad to arrive, but it will be strange to live with a people with no ears or mouths, but it will only take a short time to get used to that situation. Will they want to take of my mouth and ears? I asked.

Orlos laughed, "No they won't want that, with us native Orbseyns it happened naturally over thousands of years, and to make you feel comfortable I will keep my mouth and ears. Your life expectancy will be the same as other Orbseyns and we won't have our first child until you are about 120-150 YOA. We natives of Orbsey aren't as obsessed with sex as the people on earth are, we have many more things to keep us together than wanting to be in bed all of the time. In fact compared to earthlings we are very weak in the sex area. Does that worry you? He asked me with a concerned smile.

"No not at all when I think of that old man forcing himself onto me and then having a baby by him I feel positively sick. It would be far better for me to remain a virgin for the rest of my life, that's really not a problem, but at the right time I will come to you gladly and with the full bloom of our love for each other." I said shyly.

We had a wonderful evening together laughing and then enjoying our evening with our friends. We were due to embark our shuttle at 8.00 am the following morning and there was an air of excitement among us all, even Orlos and I were highly excited.

That night it was impossible to sleep all my childhood memories kept coming back, it had been such a happy time, my parents had been successful traders, but suddenly things went bad and Father finished up in heavy debt to the old man. Then suddenly the old man made my father an offer to forgive the debt and as well pay a handsome dowry, but in return he was to be given me as his latest wife. I was horrified, he was a really ugly old man it was inconceivable to have to go to his bed, but a deal was struck and I was to have no choice.

Then one day these six men arrived at our village and suddenly I spied Orlos, and my heart started to thump in my chest, it was as if my breath had been knocked out of my lungs and I was gasping for air. At the same time it was obvious he had seen me because his reaction was as strong as my own, he looked at me our eyes locked and that was it love at first sight.

Now here I was on my last evening on earth, in the morning we would be gone and I would never see the planet earth again, but I really didn't care. Wherever my beloved Orlos was I wanted to be, and if he had said we may die on this trip there was no doubt in my mind I would still go with him, and if die we must so long as we were together that was fine by me.

At 7.00 am sharp the shuttle arrived and we were ready to start loading ourselves into the passenger cabins, there was nobody to help us we all knew what we had to do. At 8.00 am exactly the shuttle took off and within an hour we were all seated aboard that huge freighter, all ready to go.

Orlos had told me that a lot of the power was generated by thought and we all had to concentrate on the journey, but especially at take off. What was required of every passenger was they imagined ourselves back in Orbsey and that we imagined our crafts journey being of weeks or 168 hours duration. It would mean we would pass from one solar system to another immediately, and then the rest of the flight in the Orbsey solar system would be what took the time.

Orlos had gone to a lot of trouble to explain how their scientists centuries before had finally defeated the tyranny of distance, and how they could pass our craft from galaxy to the other effortlessly with the power of controlled thought. It was for this reason they were now sending out many space probes and had found Planet Earth then had hoped to plant a colony there. This effort had failed, but only for the time being at some point in future, when earth had further developed out of the Barbarian age, another attempt would be made, but next time far more investigation through manned probes would be carried out. Although Orlos explained that to me in great detail it was too much for me to comprehend, but now it was the reality forcing knowledge on me.

During the entire week we were in transit until our arrival over Orbsey the journey was very pleasant. We could move around the huge spaceship at will, and there were all sorts of organized activities for the passengers. The passenger cabins were so well insulated there was no sensation of travelling at such a high speed which we were, we felt as if we were just smoothly moving through space.

Back home in China the fastest we ever moved was on a horse, which girls were rarely allowed to ride anyhow, now here we were gliding along and acting as if we were sitting in a comfortable lounge room. The games and things to do were so many and so varied, I could never have imagined such things exist, and everyone was always so friendly especially towards Orlos and I, it was a wonderful trip.

Before we realized it our arrival over the Inter Galactic Space Terminal was announced, Orlos told me we would soon be allowed to disembark and then would trans-ship to his own home country and city. We could see excited crowds waving on the tarmac, as our spaceship gently landed as on a cushion of air, it was hard to believe we were on the ground it was such a soft maneuver. My fellow travelers gave a wave in the cabin, and there was a huge wave of approval among the crowds waiting for us.

My first glimpse of the people through the cabin windows gave me a shock it was so strange seeing them all with no mouths or ears, for a few seconds a shudder of revulsion went through my body, but the firm grip of Orlos around my waist reassured me everything was fine.

Then we were disembarked and I was in my new home, the Planet Orbsey! My future was now sealed there really was no going back, but I knew instinctively I would never want to leave, and so it proved to be this really was my land for the future, but it was a very quiet land indeed.

The Parents and Brother of Orlos were there to meet us, and they were so pleased to see their Son and Brother once again. Obviously I was the person of interest an earthling was among them, and for this reason many of them gathered around to look at me, but they soon lost interest as they couldn't see much difference between me and themselves. I felt a little intimidated at first, but they were so nice, that I soon felt very comfortable with them all; the only thing was that Orleb the Brother of Orlos was over sixty years older. To me that felt so strange I who had thought of the old man who had been chosen for my husband at sixty was repulsive, but this man was ninety YOA and looked no more than a quite a young man would look back in my home village.

We had to take a flight from where we had landed to another country which was over 20,000 earth miles away, but the flight only took one hour and even the embarking and disembarking only meant a total of 2 hours for the entire journey. After we had landed we took a type of home air shuttle service that picked us and several other families up, and within fifteen minutes we were home. The home to me was bewildering, it seemed small outside but inside was huge, I was quite lost. I shall not try to describe it until I have settled down it's all just a little too much to take in.

During the first few days there were several things I quickly noticed, the first was that the days were long and the nights very short. At most stages of the day there were two Suns in the sky and at others only one! At night and visible also during the day there were several moons rotating in the heavens, because the nights were so short moons were in the sky night and day, so that the heavens always seemed to be lit brightly night or day. The full day was 32 hours, but the hours seemed to be a bit longer than on earth, night was only 10 hours so the day was 22 hours. The temperatures seemed to be very much the same as it had been in my own country of Central China, but it was more constant and there were very few clouds ever in the sky.

Orlos was with me all of the time until I had settled down and got comfortable with my new home, but the rest of the family had to work although to me even that was strange. They each had an office in the house and spent all of their working life at home, Orleb was an architect of some type, his Father was a professor of history and lectured to students, and their Mother was a Professor of home economics and also lectured to students via some type of system I could not yet understand. Orlos when he started again was a student of history and would study under his father and several other lecturers via this strange communication I didn't yet understand, but it all seemed so exciting. I asked Orlos what I would be able to do once I had become adjusted to my new home, and he laughed politely.

"Well you will start school via the internet and will study at home. When you have passed the exams up to the accepted University level then you will be on the same type of system as me, but you will choose what subjects you want to take. Like Mother for example she is an expert on home economics, and that is a compulsory subject for all young people before they can take a mate and live together as a couple. There are other compulsory subjects that you will learn the basics of before you get to University, which is when the serious learning begins. But don't worry my Love you will get special attention so that you can catch up to your own age group," he said with a gentle laugh.

"Oh I love it here already and I want to start this learning course as quickly as I can, if that's what we must do before we can live together that's fine, just let me start as soon as possible. I had already received the gift of languages and communication by way of thoughts, but it was hard to get used to.

It was still hard for me to remember there was no need to talk, I could now pass and receive communication just by thinking of a person and they would appear just as soon as they could in my mind and on my console that we all carried everywhere.

In many ways my new life was very frightening there just seemed so much to learn and so little time to do it in, I so loved my Orlos, but it seemed we would have to wait forever before we could be together. Then to top off all that learning we had to have a home of our own before we could be together, it was strictly forbidden that we could live together in the home of Orloses parents we had to have a home of our own. Transport wasn't a problem, there were air shuttles everywhere and we could move around easily without having our own Aerocar, but there was usually at least one of these vehicles at each home.

Orlos was like me and anxious to be together, but no exception to the rules could be allowed, mainly because his parents as two academics were very strict and they would never consider breaking the laws in any way. Not the Orlos and I wanted to do the wrong thing it was just that it seemed as if it would be years before we could be together. We were allowed to go out together, and it was so nice to find they still did old fashioned things like dancing, and playing sports for the Amateur and the Professional sports persons. It was a so different than it had been at home in China, but very soon I had begun to enjoy it just as much as we had playing our own games at home.

When I had first seen moving pictures on the main wall of our home it had been a shock, I had seen them when we had first landed in Orbsey at the terminals, but hadn't thought to see them at home as well. There was all sorts of stories and if we wanted we could watch the news all day, but really after a while it all got to be too much for me and rather boring. I needed to do something that would help me to be less overwhelmed, everything seemed so huge, apparently Orbsey was twice the size of Planet Earth with probably ten times at least bigger population, and the countries were also very large compared to those on earth. I had only been away from my parent's home for less than two months, but now my world had become so big I had come from a small village in China now here I was in a big country on Orbsey. Our state was named Cordiance' and has a population of nearly two billion individuals, more than the entire population of Planet Earth.

Orlos and I went out often together, but his education lessons daily were intensive especially since we wanted to be together, and after a month just getting acclimatized to my new life, Orloses Mother Jerrianda and his Father Orlosa decided it was time for me to start my education so the time of just thinking about my old home was over, now it was time to learn how to be an Orbseyn.

My first lesson was fairly basic as could be expected, but gradually we got to more interesting subjects that I could understand quite easily.

I learned that the planet Orbsey had been settled for over ten millennia and that the current people had originally been from all different cultures much like earth. The planet had a total Population of over 16 billion inhabitants, the land mass is 40% and the water consisted of 60% of which over 25% of that was fresh water.

The rain is controlled by the weather bureau and is directed to the areas that are scheduled for rain as needed. Fresh water is controlled in the international water banks and doled out to the consumers as needed, and sewerage is collected and processed into drinking water and manure for the rural farms from which the food banks are fed. The food banks are there to spread the food in the amounts needed, anybody who wants more than their allocation has to pay the difference, but there is no difficulty with getting extra although very few ask for more.

Originally the different countries were made up of a variety of national races, but as the millennia went by and the countries interbred then the whole of Orbsey became as one, all one color and shape with obesity conquered. Gradually the mouth and ears of most people became redundant so that in time these facilities became redundant on most people and gradually grew out over the years. The most difficult thing I had to overcome was getting to know other Orbseyns, because ours was an academic household everybody worked from home and there were little chances to know others. We went to clubs and sports clubs but even so we didn't mix much Orlos seemed to be at a loss in the company of his fellow citizens. As far as he was concerned we had each other he had no need for anyone else, but I enjoyed company as we learned how to interact socially.

Although it didn't mean much to me the early lessons included the geography of the different countries around Orbsey. There are 12 major continents with average populations of around 1 billion each then another 4 billion were living in small island countries that bought the population up to a little over 16 billion in total.

Unlike Planet Earth there are no ice caps on the top or bottom (North or South Poles) of Orbsey and the suns cast late shadow on the Planet which seemed to mean there was no time to sleep, but just like earth they sleep about 8 hours per day.

There is crime and sexual attacks here but fairly well controlled by the police, and there is no portraying simulated sex on the home media systems so that no unnecessary sex is seen on the shows that are freely available to all. All of this stuff was really unknown to me, we had nothing like this in our village, when it got dark at home in China it was time to go to bed, but here we often sit up late watching shows but its often late in the day when sunlight is finished and early when it gets light again.

Orlos and I had received a request to attend a seminar about our journey to the Planet Earth, I was asked to attend as an honored Earthling who had decided to come to Orbsey to live, and if possible to give my feelings about being here and how I had been treated since my arrival.

Orlos was keen to attend, but for myself although I was happy to go with him I wasn't inclined to be giving any opinions, because it was far too early and as yet there was little I know about my new home. I wanted Orlos to explain I had come because I wanted to be with him and now I was here it was a wonderful place, far better than my home on earth which seemed to be so backward compared to what I had seen here so far. Orlos and his family were so understanding and suggested that I give permission for my thoughts to be read, and a simulated statement would be given that was exactly as I felt, but this couldn't be done without permission. I gave written permission and this was what was read out, my new family explained it was a criminal offence to take thoughts without permission and that I could if I wanted actually block my thoughts out, but that nobody could change their thoughts so as to deceive somebody.

ORLOS:

The decision to return to Orbsey was a disappointment to me, I had hoped we would stay on Planet Earth to start a new Colony and help this world to develop, but my Peers were very sure this world was too undeveloped and our presence would be destructive. My love and pride in Li had got stronger and stronger as she faced up to our Alien presence and to her, our strange ways from the time we got aboard the recovery vessel, and we were taken back to our small settlement.

All of the Orbseyns at the settlement were curious at first to meet this Earthling, but that curiosity soon abated and we just settled in. Li stayed with a group of my friends and I stayed with another group, but by day we spent all of our time together. Our mutual trust had grown into a wonderful friendship as well as us being very much in love, but although we no longer had an established wedding ceremony on Orbsey, there were still a lot of things we had to achieve before we could live together. It was presumed the rules would still apply even if we stayed on earth and we would have to fulfill the usual obligations, before we could live together. Sex wasn't forbidden, but I had lived very strictly to my parent's ways and for us it was forbidden until we had met all other obligations, one of which was to have our own home, this may be a little more difficult here on earth.

The decision to return to Orbsey wasn't unexpected to us, but I could see it was quite a shock to Li she took it very well and never lost her ready smile, I could see though she may have shed a few tears when she was alone. Our flights back to our home in Cordiance were uneventful, and the meeting with my family was a happy one, but it was easy to see they were curious to meet Li. It was naturally a bit tense disembarking at the Intergalactic Terminal which was only ever used for joy flights into space, by many of us that just wanted the thrill of space travel; it was really very cheap but usually reserved for those with a clear imagination of what they wanted. The joy flights were very popular and hundreds of interstellar flights left daily and perhaps one or two Intergalactic flights also left each day.

The sight of so many faces all with neither mouth nor ears must have been intimidating for Li, but she never hesitated and retained that smile all of the time. She was a bit tense at meeting my family but that soon passed and we were very quickly back at our home in Cordiance 0000,455, this was how we named all of the districts in the different countries by numbers. There was no change to this system no matter what country or state you came from.

My family was full of thoughts to us and since Li had already become used to inter thought communication, there were no problems for everybody to get to know each other; by the time we had arrived home the flow of thoughts was easy and happy. As is usual in Orbsey my family, they indicated strong support for my loved one Li, she was fully accepted.

LIFE ON ORBSEY: ORLEB:

The news that the Colonists were coming home wasn't a surprise, we had heard from the Scientists that the new found life sustaining World was still very much undeveloped and they knew there was a good chance this first effort would have to be aborted quite quickly. Our Mother in particular was ecstatic she had never wanted Orlos to go on this, to her, mad mission in the first place, and when we heard he was bringing back an earthling to be his future partner we were intrigued.

There had never been any worry about the Intergalactic travel such journeys into Space had been available as Joy flights for hundreds of years. Incontinent travel was almost no different than getting in an Aerocar and taking a quick journey anywhere on our Planet Orbsey.

I had been almost 60 YOA when Orlos was born and as is usual on our planet the Siblings are rarely close, because of the age differences. Mother and Father now each close to 185 YOA and looking forward to retirement the acceptable age being 210, but this was expected to be extended soon as the average age was now up to 300 and the working age expected to be increased to 260 YOA. My parents were strongly objecting to the increase in their working life, they had both worked from the age of 30 so it was a lot of years, they just felt 250 was too high.

We were all expected to work for 180 years before we retired and during that time we were to have four different careers, each of 45 years duration.

For me my second career was getting close to over, and I had chosen to do Civil Administration as my next Career, my first had been as a Civil Draught person it was expected that the careers one chose during one's life should be compatible, so that as little training as possible had to be undergone when one changed over, from one career to the next. Since we were a family of academics we were all able to work at home, but that was optional it was quite permissible to find work to which we had to travel to an office daily, it was very simple to do this if that's what one preferred.

Orlos had been training for a legal life so he would be expected once he had finished his training to first go into the a Police Career, and he would spend the first stage of his Career in the Uniform Police, the next would be Plain Clothes Police, then as a Lawyer and Barrister, and finally to either as a judge or a Politician. It would depend on ones record where one finished up and just how well one had performed their duties as to how high one rose on the way through in each career, just how good that final career would be. Mother and Father were both on their last careers, but if the new law was passed then they would have to spend another one before they could retire.

The method of reward for work done on Orbsey was by a system of credits, and these credits could be accumulated and used as required, credits could be used to buy anything but every Orbseyn on starting work received 100,000 credits into an account, these credits could only be used to buy a Home and an Aerocar which if one only wanted the average home and Aerocar would take all of one's credits. Ones monthly credits could be used for whatever was required for all and every service one wanted including daily sustenance and all services, but all and anything that is required to live a decent life requires very few credits. However all extras such as an extra nice home or fancy Aerocar took up a lot of credits, which must be available in ones account at time of purchase, because there is no trading or borrowing of credits. Our parents cannot donate to us any of their credits, nor could we borrow any off any organization, credits are a Government function and there are no variations allowed.

Our society has been for many years sectionalized and effective throughout the entire Planet the economy has for many years been tax free for all who live on Govt sponsored credits and we all have that right.

The private economy is fully financed initially by Govt credits, the system is a little like the public economy in that the initial credits for business is supplied by application to the dept. of business, but must trade in private credits, so that all private trade is controlled by credit banks, but the banks can only control the credit flow, they do not issue or lend credits only the Govt may supply new credits. New credits can only be obtained by proving the business is a/ being managed properly, b/ needs the new credits to expand trade c/ has the need to acquire and raise stock levels to levels compatible with the commonly roll over rate of similar type business as gazetted etc'.

There is no such thing as interest rate being charged, but private credits are transferable, extra trade credits earned by any business big or small must be shared with the workers and may be converted to Govt credits by those workers. Any business big or small may distribute excess credits to workers or management as decided by the Board of Directors, but the level of the distribution must be pro rata to the individual's contribution to the earning of those aforesaid credits.

There is a major grouping of the 1/ Academics, 2/Professions, 3/ Govt Employees, 4/ Trades, 5/ Business and the 6/ the laboring classes. These groups break down to hundreds of other classes as decided by the various workers unions. All Orbseyns are classified first at birth and then at age thirty the year they are first expected to start work. There are exceptions for special projects when time is allowed, this for example would apply to all who had been selected to be possible Colonists on planet earth, they were given gratis credits on their return to Orbsey. There are no taxes on Orbsey but there are consumption taxes, all consumption carries a price in a credit that includes a fee to the Govt; which uses the credits for all of its costs. Private business is highly encouraged and the State never interferes in how a business is run, and since there are no taxes there is no need for tax returns nor any other Govt control, because ultimately all private credits must get converted by the Govt somewhere along the way, and in this way controls are inevitable. Entrepreneurs are encouraged and many Govt incentives are given! All profits can be kept, but if wanting to say upgrade a house, then one would have to convert some of one's own private credits to Govt credits to be able to have the credit to pay for that new upgraded home, the same applies to Aerocars. Homes, Food, Clothing, Footwear, Law and Medical are strictly Govt controlled; these products must be acquired by way of Govt credits.

There are few hospitals on Orbsey, because private practice is encouraged, and General Practitioner can replace body parts, heart lungs etc but not brains, these are still managed in special hospitals that only do work on the head ie eyes, nose, brain, cranium, tongue etc; but such hospitals are owned and operated by the specialists.

Money related crime on Orbsey doesn't exist because there is no way the credits can be transferred, even the origins of private credits have to be confirmed and proved before being able to convert to govt credits. There is a lot of other crime, fighting and destroying private property is common, dissenting to govt laws being enacted causes many problems, petty theft is really bad etc. Sex crimes are unusual on Orbsey because any rapist found guilty is immediately turned into a eunuch, and sexual perversion such as same gender sex, pedophilia etc is treated medically as soon as found and rectified, there is no appeal once found guilty of any sexual perversion whatsoever the medical changes are automatic and cannot be stopped.

Orbsey has for over two millennia had all of its citizens being of one race, the inter breeding had accomplished that naturally there had been no laws put in place to force that issue it had just gradually happened. The foods that were ingested by way of thought were all artificially flavored, but there were menus that supplied the genuine product at high prices supplied by private restaurants and roadside, same with clothes but all types of consumer goods were available with private credits.

The Orbseyn form of Govt could be considered a Capitalistic Egalitarian one, in that the Central Govt funded the first home and vehicle, when a couple comes together with the intent to stay together. They must stay that way for five years if they want to split up they cannot until the term is served and the home and vehicle must be returned, no further assistance is given to either party if they should set up a new relationship. From the time they split up the couple are put off any form of Govt assistance such as Home, Vehicle, Food, Clothing, Medical Credits etc; they must go on private credits and they rarely manage to return to the Govt system. They must still convert their private credits to Govt credits, for their consumer goods and they can only redeem their situation by depositing 100,000 credits to their Govt account and then they will be restored completely to the system.

There was no real military on Orbsey, but the Police Force does enforce all Govt policy over the entire Planet, Cordiance was the biggest and major Country within which the Orbsey Central Govt was stationed.

There was a two level form of Govt for all countries with a population under 100 million citizens, for countries with a population of 100 million and over the system was a three level format.

The two level forms allowed for Central and National Govt, with the State Govt running all of the Govt Programs not run from the Center of Govt. With the three levels Govt; there was an added Govt of the people, which dealt with the National Govt which in turn dealt with the Central Govt. Elections were held every five years on a revolving basis with a Triumvirate of equal powers at the top of the Central Govt; each person was elected once and stood for reelection once every fifteen years, this meant there was a new member of the Triumvirate once every five years. Each country sent to the Central Govt one member for every 100,000,000 persons that were registered in the country they were from. Because the voting age started from age 30 and there were 12 billion registered voters, so the Central Govt had 1,200 members.

Each individual country had its own Govt and they were responsible to keep the Highways and Flyways clear and under control. The administration of Justice, plus the Central Govt Courts were held at the Central Govt Courts and were all heard in the Central Courts, to attend was as simple as boarding a flight on an Aero-bus the longest time taken from the farthest country was one hour. All of the problems of travel had been removed from the Orbseyn way of life. In the big countries that had the three levels of Govt there was a type of people Govt that were there to keep the State Govt aware of the people needs they didn't run any type of controls, their position was purely one in an advisory capacity.

The main point of Orbseyn economic policy was to keep the capitalistic drive and creativity and to subdue govt so that it was a pass by point for credit flows and the Planet had only one system with an automatic simple control of all credits. Simply put all credits had to flow through the Govt system then all credits would be used by the govt to settle all credits due from various sources. For example the methodology of feeding the Planet was developed by the food Industry in tandem with the medical Profession, meaning the systems were actually owned by those two groups. The industry produced the material and processed it to the status of food etc and then the Medical Profession had the responsibility to control the methods of consumption, all the Govt did was to pass the credits due to the industry.

This method was used for the main consumer products namely, White Goods, Clothes, Footwear, Medical Costs, all other products were direct trade but using converted credits from Public to Govt credits, then all payments were passed through the govt agency. The payments made on behalf of the consumer had an add on cost that included the handling fee which was essentially a consumer tax. The population were all treated the same because all started of equal with a 100,000 consumer credit for a home and a vehicle, it created the base for the egalitarian state. There was no reason not to sell the assets so granted by the state, but if in so doing the couple finished up with nothing they would be passed into a govt controlled home and wouldn't have a vehicle.

They would be expected to work and rehabilitate themselves but they would get no help on the way, if they did manage to get back on their feet they would simply be reinstated, if not they would simply be put on simple govt work for the rest of their lives. The credits they were entitled to would be used to keep them; sickness wasn't an issue because all medical conditions were under control.

There were animal parks all over the Planet and each country had the responsibility to have large areas set aside for wild animals and Flora and Fauna. There was little agriculture, all protein was created by the medical scientists and domestic animals weren't kept for killing and processing for food. There was a huge variety of animals kept as pets and there were many hobby farms just for this purpose, as there were also for all Flora and Fauna that had been kept from the old world before Orbsey became so sophisticated.

There were very strict laws to ensure that animals were well cared for, many creatures were still being bred that had survived for many millions of years.

Sport was a major industry and elite athletes were treated with great respect, but they were still controlled within the spectrum of the govt credits system, adulation from the masses was fine but excessive credits weren't acceptable. The abuse of athletes by producers etc was strictly controlled, and they were locked into the system of credits, but the creativity wasn't in any way hindered promoters were treated with the equal respect as their protégés.

Each country has retained their natural culture, the assimilation of the races has been achieved by inter marriage over several millennia. Only after this long period all of the original indigenous races looked alike and had the appearance of one single race, now there is an Orbseyn culture of which all are proud but also an indigenous culture of which the countries are equally proud.

Business citizens were allowed to accumulate as much credits as they wanted, the problem came for them in their Wills, there was no such things as Family Trusts nor other devices to avoid how the credits could be distributed after death. There was a maximum that could be left to a single beneficiary, but one could name any number of them, if there was any credits left over they must go to some charity and the must be settled within 30 days of the funeral or the entire estate would be transferred to the Govt.

THE FUTURE OF THE FAMILY:

At a family gathering it was revealed that Orlos would get a credit of 6 months for the period he had been away from Orbsey, and he would continue his education that would now have about 12 months to complete as an engineer. Li had received a tertiary grant and had been allocated to a first legal career starting with the uniform police force, her education would start immediately and she was the only one in the home who had to work away from the home her education was to be one of on patrol duty and daily seminars at the police college..

There was 30 days to appeal the positions for both Li and Orlos, if no appeal was received both would have to start within 30 days., at that stage they would be eligible for the credits grant and could have their own home and Aerocar. Both Orlos and Li had agreed to the grant and the terms offered so no letter of appeal was sent.

Orlos now explained to Li, they would have to wait until she had finished her education and both were actually working, so the better she did with her schooling the sooner they could be together and in the Orbseyn belief of good society committed to each other. With the family of Orlos this was a family ritual and had been so for at least millennia, on both sides of their family tree, neither Li nor Orlos would dream of breaking that important family thread.

Now that Li knew her future she was very happy, she still thought periodically of her home and family, but the specter of that ugly old man interfering with her body soon dispelled any longings for home, she knew she had been blessed and had a wonderful family now.

The day to start her education had arrived and it was time to go out on her own, Orlos took her to the police college and told her to send him a thought message when she was ready to come home and he would pick her up.

When Li entered the college grounds and then entered the office, it was as if she was just another old student coming back from a vacation. She was immediately escorted to the Masters office and he took her to the classrooms immediately. She was introduced to her tutor and the other students, as the earthling who had come to settle in their neighborhood and had been allocated to be one of their fellow trainees. There was a little curiosity after all she was from a different planet, and had ears and a mouth which to them looked a little strange, but apart from that she was no different and they soon forgot her being a stranger and just treated her as one of their own.

The lectures that first day were over 8 hours by length of time including a break of 30 minutes every two hours. Then after that there was another six hours including breaks spent as a trainee on patrol, it was only then that Li started to see the real Orbseyns at work and play.

The patrols where staggered with vehicles leaving every hour on the hour, the first call they got was to a break in at a Jewelers store. They were alerted and on the scene within five minutes but the culprits were well gone; within minutes all of the information at the site had been processed and sent to the Plain Clothes Division.

The next call was to a rape, the same procedure and again within minutes the data had been sent to the plain clothes team.

This continued for the rest of her day and then she was finished and Orlos was there to pick her up. Li was so happy she had loved every minute of her day, and couldn't stop remembering and passing her memories to any in the family who cared to tune in to her thoughts. Orlos was delighted because Li had enjoyed herself so much. He then started to share his thoughts that it was nice to be back at where he had left off and most of his old buddies were still there and keen to share his thoughts on Planet Earth. Later that night when Orlos had gone home and Li was in bed she once again sank into a reverie, of remembering especially her beloved Mum and her siblings none of whom she would ever forget, even after they were long dead, even her Father was in her thoughts, she knew he had done the only thing he could do in the sad circumstances he had got into.

Because Li loved her education time went quickly for her, the years seemed to fly by. First Orlos had passed all of his exams and now it was up to Li as soon as she was finished her exams they could finally be together. They were both proving to be fairly strong sexually and the restraints were becoming hard to contain, but they had honored Orlos parents and strictly abstained. To achieve this chastity they had refrained from being alone in compromising situations, and had refrained from too much contact such as dancing etc anything that put them to close together was not to be allowed by their own choice.

Li was doing well and her actual Orbseyn age had now been calculated and she was now 24YOA and had been in the country for four years, she was in every respect now an Orbseyn in fact as well as in her heart, she really loved her new world, family and Orlos as well as her education it was all really wonderful the little girl from China was at home in every way.

The education she had been getting gave her a full view of Orbseyn society; she could see the wealthy and those that would be wealthy. There was the criminals that really couldn't help themselves and were truly victims of the own poor mental level. There were the average people that just couldn't help but get into trouble and have to pay the penalty for their own cupidity; there were so many forms of crime that Li just couldn't believe what she was learning.

Gradually she was sitting and passing her exams she thrived on every test they gave her, she was already three years ahead of where she was expected to be, the family were all delighted with their new daughter and sister to be, they were not to know the natural acuity of her forebears.

Li had become a type of teachers pet really they loved her at the police college, and were fascinated by their earthling student, who supposedly came from a backward culture yet found the Orbseyn education so simple.

Out on the road on patrols in the prowling Aerocars she was again very popular with her quick grasp of the job frequent comments were made about her rising very quickly through the ranks and achieving high command in the police force. All had predicted she would be one of the highest ranked females ever in the force, and achieving that stature during her career and retaining her personal popularity was her own perceived goal.

For herself Li quickly demonstrated just how ambitious she was, her personality was fully controlled, but at the same time always looking for way to improve herself. The physical regime in the force, Li in spite of being small proved she could take the training and lead the way when leadership was needed; she was in every way an Orbseyn in spite of still having a nose and ears.

When she had occasion to arrest vagrants of whatever type they were always intrigued at how funny to them she looked, many were the laughs she shared with her workmates as the crims stared at her in wonder and to some, even fear._One afternoon Li was making an arrest a very large person who didn't like being stopped by somebody who he thought was deformed, he went to strike Li with his great big fists, suddenly he had been flipped on his back and shaking his head in horror. Li's tutor in the vehicle just stood and roared with laughter while the bully shook his head in shock, he stood up looked at Li in disbelief and stuck out his arms for the electronic shackles, two hours later he was still shaking his head in disbelief.

When Li sat for her license to control and drive/fly an Aerocar, she passed first time tested so from then on she was allowed to be in charge of the patrol vehicle she was out with, and the tutors were always glad of the rest. Li passed her final exams at the age of 26 four years quicker than was normal; she was now a fully qualified police person in the state of Cordiance on the planet Orbsey the first earthling to be so honored. Her Family was very proud finally Li & Orlos were fully qualified for the starting 100,000 credits and the right to have their own home and vehicle. The young couple was so excited finally they would be as one in a home of their own on, the waiting was almost over and they both had their careers well underway.

The system of creating a situation whereby starting up govt credits are handed out to the citizens subject to certain conditions is meant to eliminate debt, and in so doing eliminate the danger that Orbsey World Citizens could be protected from slavery to debt. By opening one's life with a home and a vehicle the intent is to avoid its people starting life in debt and therefore in slavery to the lender, and so far it had been very successful. It has not only stabilized debt but also reduced failures within the couples who can start life without the pressures that were once a part on the economy.

The funding of small to medium sized business and the support for growth is also designed to eliminate debt from the money lenders; the govt wants to see its citizens free of all financial entanglements that can create financial slavery. So far it seems to be working but it's a mammoth job that is still being put in place, changes are being made as problems are found. Like all things theory is great but the next stage is the reality, it was tried first for twenty years in the smallest country then slowly developed until the system had been fully implemented. There are still problems that come up but they are all based around the sheer size of the program, the intent is right and has been proved, the administration is still being implemented.

The Central Parliament has implemented the structure and passed the first stage down to the consolidated groups, the groups in turn have passed them down to the individual countries to force the implementation. So far the system is taking root and in spite of fraud and start up problems is gradually working, it won't be 100% in place until an entire new population is born when the system started ages, and all who qualify for the 100,000 govt credit contribution.

The business world has been revolutionized as debt is cancelled out with govt credits and production starts to flow unhindered by stress for business people as they grow their businesses. Another 100 years will find the system fully in place on Orbsey and the entire population freed from debt, by govt contribution, these are none recourse contributions never to be repaid unless for family break down or criminal activities.

The banking system has become administrators for the govt; and the govts are barred from any commercial activities unless specifically ordered from the Central Parliament, for some natural disaster etc.

Distribution has been beaten by the method of part processing on production before the products are sent off for final process and converting to whatever system for which each product is designed, ie food is final processed within each country then beamed into a central grid for distribution via the thought demands. Private product is distributed by a private grid that is strictly for products being bought within the private economy.

The reliance on the Cyber system is enormous but the power of thought has been harnessed as the main power source to ensure the computer powered back up is always in place. The attacks on the system have been very persistent as criminals have tried to break into the system and fraudulently tried to beat the system. The stealing of the finished products proliferated very successfully for years, as the difficulties were so hard to solve, then when the system was up and operational they criminal element try to divert the credits through fraudulent claims, this also worked for a while but was gradually controlled. The attacks on business to force credits to be paid out without any rights were also another problem now beaten.

Finally alone together:

Selecting a home was pretty easy these after all were cheap first home owner's property as was the vehicle, all mass produced well made in Cordiance. They now had enough credits left over to furnish their home they were ready for life as a couple. Li and Orlos had been together for 8 years nearly all on the planet Orbsey, and now it was time they were recognized to have the status of adults now and would be given the grant for life as it was called. Although there was no form of marriage on the planet, each family had their own traditions and the family Orlosa certainly had its long traditions, the youngsters never left home without a celebration and they were expected to be virgins when the happy leave time arrived. If they weren't then there was no celebration they simply left and they were dropped from the family tree, the idea being to keep the tree pure to family tradition.

The celebration for Li and Orlos was going to be huge, the name wasn't what kept the line alive it was the bloodline. All of the population had only one name and the Fathers name was the line name ie this family was the family Orlosa, The family name for Li and Orlos would be Orlos, but all by blood followed the tradition down through the millennia.

The celebration was in full swing and the family bloodlines were all represented, Li was dazzled by the size of her family and was happier than ever, after the main celebrations were over. The blood Patriarch got up and gave a great thought welcome to Li who really would inject new blood as he succinctly thought it would bedazzle all of the other blood lines of whatever stature it would be millennia before it would happen again. Then Orlosa spoke of their pride in their earthling daughter, after that they all danced the night away, many got drunk as they filled themselves with alcoholic thoughts of booze, and it was a great day and night.

The next day the young couple shifted into their home and at last they were together. Both were Virgins and not so sure of what they were to do, they had had all of the lessons, but now it was time for the real thing. That first night was very difficult for them both, but having broken their Virginity, they both decided they liked this sex game, and they found they could practice all they wanted to; neither of them would be fertile until they were 120 YOA and that was over 90 years away, there would be plenty of practice before then.

On the first night Orlos found it difficult to get an erection he was scared witless, then when he did finally rise to the occasion he couldn't get into Li because she had just dried up in fright. Several hours after starting to try they succeeded but it wasn't so great at that point, but the next time same night it was easier, but by then they were both sore, Li internally and Orlos though his penis was a flame.

After the next night trying again to get it right it was a lot easier for both of them, but after a week they were quite the experts.

Li and Orlos were really in their own private version of heaven, the years of abstinence which they didn't really understand anyhow until they finally did get together was time well spent. They adored each other and their honeymoon lasted for many years, they never seemed to tire of sharing each other's body and when 90 years later their first child was born she was the true fruit of her parents love for each other. Still that was a long way in the future for now it was just them by themselves and they ate of the fruit liberally. For the first five years they spent all free time in bed practicing at how to make babies, both found it to be a wonderful pastime and they only had to have a spell period once a month, which really was just as well else they would have both faded away to walking shadows.

Orlos was now involved in the construction industry as a major construction engineer, and he was known as that fellow with the foreign wife, who made him inordinately happy; he loved it knowing that his wife was different.

On the other hand Li's workmates had forgotten she was an earthling and truly loved her and her dedication to her work and her fellow workers, she would do anything for her colleagues take the extra shift, wait back for someone running late, and nothing was a problem. Even as she was lifted rapidly through the ranks they never demurred and were happy for the little earthling who was so small yet so capable. There had been many times when she had arrested big angry men but had to pacify them before they would do what she wanted, but it was never a problem big or small they all finished up groveling on their backs, much to the amusement of Li's male colleagues.

The one thing Li found hard to get used to was never having to cook and clean for her man, it was all done automatically by a house robot which was more intelligent than many of the crims Li had to deal with daily. It was a net 12 hour day allowing for breaks, but the pace was constant, there were a hell of a lot of crims living in Cordiance and they seemed to just keep rolling through. Because of thought control and the controls available to stop a prisoner telling lies the flow through the courts etc was very quick and there was no time wasting, from arrest to court and sentence took no more than two days. The free labor supplied by the criminal section of Orbseyn society was a big contribution to the state budget.

The percentage of crimes solved was close to 60% within a few days of the crime committed, but over the longer period of 30 days the arrest rate was went up to almost 90% so that crime didn't really pay on Orbseyn, the performance in all of the States was just as high. White collar crime was a lot different, these types of criminals were left to plain clothes, but they were very smart and only the best in the police force where kept aside to deal with them.

One day Li came into work and found a very dismal situation in the usually cheery Police Station two of her colleagues had been abducted and the note received was that they were to be killed and their bodies destroyed by fire unless certain conditions were met. This was a serious threat there was no way the medical fraternity could restore ashes and bring the men back to life, there was no doubt the threats were genuine because if caught the culprits if caught would be executed within days, so the situation was serious.

Because the captives were from Li's precinct they had the right to try and get their friends back, but the ransom conditions were so onerous it was doubtful if the Chief Justice would meet the terms set out so all would die, the crooks and their captives.

Knowing she was so small that the criminals would never take her for a police rep Li without permission managed to find her way to where the hide out and enter without suspicion. To Orbseyns who didn't know her she looked deformed and a bit of a joke, but she had her laser stun gun and her own lethal hands which the abductors weren't aware of. After getting into the hideaway quite openly she made herself at home acting the part of a deformed clown, and soon had the crims in thoughts of laughter. The prisoners who knew her were astonished here she was playing the clown, what was she going to do; they looked at each other in wonder and watched.

There were three crims all as nervous as could be they knew what they had done was a capital offence so Li's antics was breaking down the fear that was pervading the room. When she had gained their confidence and they weren't being so watchful suddenly Li went into action, within the space of a few minutes she had stunned with her laser two of the crims and disarmed the other by flipping him on his back. It all happened so fast the prisoners were astonished; suddenly they were free and had three prisoners. When all arrived at their station there was a gasp of surprise this little woman had overpowered three real thugs on her own she was an instant hero, from then her journey to the top was unstoppable.

Orlos had been retained to do the engineering design for a new building that was to be 140 stories high and he loved the challenge. His Father was a close friend of the developer and had put in a good word for his Son, but when he got the contract Father and Son were both delighted, it would keep Orlos working for 3 years or more. Because it was a private contract Orlos would earn a lot of private credits, there was no govt credit control on this work.

The credits for work performance were not high working for the govt, the private sector was far more attractive, but since eventually all private credits had to be converted to Govt credits so Orlos was in the position that he needed advice on how to contract his work. All that needed to be done was to send the data to a business consultant and then meet with them by thought process. The expert suggested he should set himself up as an independent, and write the contract in his own name rather than as a govt employee. This he did and was pleasantly surprised at how well he would be remunerated as a self employed contractor. The young couple was indeed both doing well at their chosen professions.

The young couple were now on their own and rapidly setting up a circle of friends of their own, most in different professions, but mainly academics or older friends reaching the top of their careers and who were very respected in Cordiance Society. As was quite normal the couples would come together and enjoyed each other's company, often for many hours in the evenings and long weekends. The Orbseyn work week was four days at work or study and another four days work free. Since the normal days work was 14 hours the normal week was 56 hours, but balanced by the next four day weekend.

The work week was however revolved, one group of the people worked permanently on one cycle, another group worked the other, and this meant that industry etc was always working. However in reality there was four cycles so that the world of Orbsey works 28 of the 32 hours working 28 hours per day and has a down time of four hours. This is the daily time for the cleaning and maintenance teams to be working, but this is normally done by retirees or workers that want to make some extra Govt credits. Not all of the States had the same routine, but 90% of the population worked to the routine herein set out, the other 10% were artisans that were free to do whatever they wanted, as in fact all of the peoples were, but it was mostly the art world that cared to do their own thing at all times.

When relaxing often stories were told of their work, and one evening the following story was told with much hilarity within the couples as they listened. The story was told by a Legal worker who had reached a high level in his chosen vocation.

A young man a lawyer by profession wanted to become a developer of Real Estate, but he wasn't interested in starting at the bottom, he wanted to use his legal knowledge to climb rapidly into being a big player in that industry.

First he searched out properties of a decent size and earning a surplus in trade credits and after negotiating prices he then set out option terms, which would come to the call at the same time by date and hour.

The option term was 90 days and time of day was 13 hours which was one hour before the change of shift.

Then having got a lot of Properties under legal options he set about raising the credits that he needed knowing that he couldn't go into debt, so he had to have buyers with trade credits to settle. The law is explicit when the time for settlement arrives it must be done by the one clerk in the registration office and if that clerk cannot complete the documents they must be rolled over and the terms of the option started all over again. Neither the Vendor nor the buyer may withdraw if the option holder had committed to complete by agreeing to the settlement.

This lawyer had acquired 20 options on major developments and he had set them at a time that the stamp duties office wouldn't be able to complete more than one maybe two contracts. Effectively he had got himself delayed settlements by time the 20 were settled of almost 36 months, by which time he would be well able to settle all contracts himself. When the time came for settlement both sides presented themselves, but when the advisors for the vendors asked how many settlements where due our hero said why twenty is there a problem? There was an immediate outburst of rage, this they claimed is a trick and you have done this deliberately.

Not so he replied I am not a property lawyer I didn't know how long settlements take.

Quite so said the clerk he has never had a settlement before, but the law applies, what I have done by time I finish work is what will be processed this time around. Now leave me be and taking the first contract he was only able to complete that one, and half of the next so the balance of them had to be rolled over until the next time.

There was uproar and an immediate application was listed with the equity court for the next day. The next day as required the equity judge said he would need time to examine all of the implications he would give a decision the next day. The next day he was very explicit the law was fair, the buyer was now committed to a real contract, but all of the terms still stood.

The lawyer had got himself 20 major properties for which he had heaps of time to find investors who had surplus Govt credits. The whole party exploded into thoughts of admiration, what a smart move they all said, he was best as an Entrepreneur, he needed to change his vocation.

Chapter 3/
The eye in the sky.

THE SPY IN THE sky control of the population was one that Li had only just come to grips with; much to her amazement she found that 95% of the people were all recorded on the data base and the ones that weren't were just not worth bothering about.

Li was shocked at the amount of control that spy in the sky had, there was literally hundreds of thousands of cameras all reporting back to the eye in the sky, and even all of the leaders were subject to that control It wasn't a matter of any instructions being issued to that spy it had all of the legal controls and it had the practical understanding of anything and everything that was happening. Li quickly learned that that eye was the real ruler of Orbsey. All of the people were totally controlled and this included the plebiscite leaders, if and when one died he was merely replaced until the elections and then only those with impeccable records according to the eye were eligible to contest the elections. The plebiscite members were men who had reached their last term of work and they were appointed to that post, it wasn't ever by popular choice. Li had begun to understand the reality of life on Orbsey at was good while young but the aged struggled to keep up to the harsh demands. When she had first heard the age average on Orbsey she had thought how wonderful, but then she began to see how tired the parents of Orlos were and their constant wish to be able to retire in peace. The sorrow in their eyes when the age work average was lifted by forty five years showed it was a terrible disappointment to them both.

Then short of committing suicide there was no way out, because no matter what the medical profession could keep you alive fit and well up to the last term, but the tiredness of mind couldn't be overcome. Even after 300 YOA if one was so inclined life could go on, but there was very few that even made it to the 300 let alone living any longer, once the govt stopped forcing the medical people to keep people going at the end of the last term many just sat back and waited to die. The Eye over viewed all of life, work, relaxation, having babies, work performance everything, mind there was the good side of it all too. There was little abuse of wives and children by recalcitrant males, because they were soon bought to order by the eye, and punishment was swift and harsh, the same applied to any female abusers and there were quite a few.

The entire planet of Orbsey was the same, many years before the Eye there had been different races from different countries, but marriage or a type union between the young of each country had greatly increased. The advent of a superior travel system became so cheap and easy that it wasn't long before the young thought very little of shifting to a different country and settling down. Then with the advent of the Eye, racial disharmony was banished forever because anyone found guilty of creating such problems were charged with serious disturbance of the peace and branded as trouble makers. Auto theft was another crime that was now to dangerous even to think about the eye seemed to be able to read the mind of thieves and stealing of any type was quickly brought to justice by the police with a lot of help from the Eye.

Even career criminals had a tough time getting through the system because they had to prove the source of their income which was very hard to do with the Eye constantly keeping everybody under surveillance. Whenever a crime of any sort was committed the police would text a message away and within a few minutes receive back the name of all possible culprits that were in the area at the times given, nine times out of ten a catch would be made and the case before the courts the next day.

Li had begun to wonder who actually ran the planet was it the elected officials or was it that all Seeing Eye in the sky that seemed to know everything.

Then when the parents of Orlos had finally finished their last term Li and Orlos went to visit them and were amazed at how worn out and tired they both were, it was no surprise they just wanted to pass away in peace with no more medicine keeping them working. Sure enough within a month they had both passed away and finally looked as if they were at rest.

Li began to work out her own future as a servant of the eye! At 120 YOA she would be able to have her first child, and then at 150 YOA her second would be allowed. After that she would have to work for another over 100 years, my goodness she felt tired just at the thought, and she was only 100 YOA so it must be tough doing that last stretch.

LIVING IN CORDIANCE ORBSEY.

Li and Orlos had now both completed their first careers and both had achieved high honors, Li had graduated top out of 250,000 who had completed the course with her. Her colleagues were proud of her on her last day the precinct had set up enormous banners proclaiming their affection for the little earthling who had stolen their hearts. The next step was into plain clothes within the quick reaction division. This meant they got the smaller style petty criminals which had an average find and convict time of three days. Li had done quite well in accumulating quite a sound surplus in Govt credits, but the remuneration was after all stuck in the usual credit control system, she had earned nowhere near as much as Orlos. Orlos had also graduated high and had now moved on to the architectural side of high rise engineering, he was self employed and had accumulated a large surplus in Govt credits.

They had now the surplus in credits to look for a better home and could become a two vehicle couple, which they did with two better quality Aerocars, the one they had was handed back to the Govt for recycling and their full credits for the vehicle was reinstated.

After they had found a new home, they handed in the keys for the old one to the Govt including the furniture they had bought, the original 100,000 Govt Credits were restored, and the home was either passed on to another new owner or recycled to the system it was irrelevant, there was no loss to anyone.

Li and Orlos now moved into a new home that cost them 200,000 Govt Credits and with furniture, white goods and two new vehicles had spent over 250,000 credits and still had a healthy surplus in Govt Credits. Orlos now talked to Li about his ambition to create a construction company and to license his business to become a real estate developer on the construction of high rise homes under semi contract to the State Govt. His goal was to build the complexes and to have them as investments owned by themselves and other friends who had surplus credits they wanted to use up.

Li was so happy with her own career she gave it little thought, but agreed immediately to Orlos doing whatever it was he wanted. But Orlos had never shown himself as an astute trader he had been successful as a subcontractor, but that didn't involve risk. It was the developer who took all of the risks now Orlos would be taking the chances it was a completely different world, one that can bring heartache or pleasure, but to the unskilled often heartache.

Li now doing plain clothes petty crime found it was still easy and again quickly flourished as she had in the uniform police. It wasn't long before she was just as admired and respected her rescue of the two policemen had never been forgotten, and she was loved by her colleagues. It wasn't very long before she was getting promoted and soon found herself working in the hard crime arena, one that would really test her skills and nerve, now she was into murder, rape, violence of every type and it wasn't a pretty world. In spite of being so high tech Cordiance had it all in abundance, criminals who never seemed to learn were always being found. Li was to learn some vicious lessons over the coming years as indeed was Orlos; they were now part of the real world one that can be very hard and unforgiving a high tech paradise.

Li had been promoted to the serious crime division; the elevation was based purely on her performance in uniform and plain clothes Petty Crime. She had received three promotions within 10 years and now at the age of 83 she wasn't even up to the middle of her new career and looked as if she would go to the top before she was 95 YOA.

One of the first serious crimes she had received and solved was high level fraud and she had proved her ability with numbers as well as her many other attributes. A larger style company had been accused of enticing people to invest their surplus govt or private credits in a scheme to promote the purchase of production rights for a new health product. The company had claimed the rights for the product, and an agreement to sell through the private thought food delivery system. But shortly after the credits had been taken in claims of fraud were made against the promoter of the scheme.

The case was put onto Li's work list and she was quick to respond. The promoter produced reports and claimed options, all seemed reasonable and should be able to do what was claimed, but suddenly Li could see a hole in the claims made, but it wasn't easy to prove. Very carefully she indicated she thought the proposals were possibly ok, but in fact she was getting a police employed forensic accountant to check the projections. It was quickly seen that the claims were in error, but it would be hard to prove, so Li had to set up a trap for the very glib promoter. She set up a very subtle trap and within two days the wily fellow was caught and on his way to a future working for the Govt.

Her next case was a serious murder which seemed to suggest a serial killer, who in spite of the high tech police weapons had been able to avoid capture, but when caught he/she would be executed promptly. There had been a rampage of killing but all in the state of Cordiance, and narrowed down to Li's precinct area. There had been over thirty women killed and raped over a period of 5 years, and it was thought it must be someone with a police background because they appeared to have a sound knowledge of the detection methods used and avoided all of the traps. Li spent days and many hours following all of the threads she could find, and finally she thought she had a trace, but she needed some bait and there was only herself she could and would commit to the danger.

Having set the trap and walking into the bait position she had to wait to see if the rat would bite, finally after three days there was a tentative nibble, but it was really very tentative. The rat smelled the bait and liked it but wasn't yet ready to bite, plenty of smelling but no bite. Using the analogy of cheese she placed out a stronger cheese but still the rat was only smelling still no bite, and every day became more dangerous for Li her nerves were starting to fray. But she still persisted and again strengthened the cheese, finally a bite, but what a bite.

She had been taken for a whore and suddenly she was invited to a very interesting party, now setting up a backup she went and was invited by a very suave looking character to have a little exercise, again she accepted even though she had been laughed at because of her nose and ears, the risks were now very high.

Suddenly she was attacked with the perpetrator being first after sex, which would be followed by death of this her attacker boasted. He also knew he had the famous Earthling and she was a high ranking police officer, this seemed to urge him on to greater dreams of what he intended to do. He had restricted his thoughts to Li but foolishly forgot she could redirect his thoughts through her own, and that she could signal the danger and the time to attack. Suddenly the serial rapist/killer moved to molest her, but he hadn't known of her notoriety in attack suddenly like so many others he was cringing on the floor in fright and she had him secured by laser handcuffs, he was dead within five days.

Li's success rate just soared, but unbeknown to her Orlos was on his way to big trouble. He had moved ahead and won a development on the usual terms of funding part Govt and part Private, but sadly he was a great engineer but a less than accomplished developer. It was soon obvious he had under quoted for the development, and the govt under no circumstances would raise the price they would pay for the finished product.

As with all developers he had set his targets markets etc with the govt as a back stop for sales if needed, he had done all of that work very well and accurately, but he had committed the ultimate folly. He had badly under costed the development and now his projected losses were very heavy, in fact he would finish up bankrupt unless he could find a way out of his predicament.

DISASTER:

Li had been so immersed in her own work she didn't notice how her mate was sinking into negativity, hers was nothing but success and she thought Orlos was the same. Sadly the day wasn't far off when he would be the target of attention from one of her colleagues. Foolishly Orlos turned to downgrading the quality of the material he was using on his development, it wasn't a criminal action unless he didn't specify on his specifications what he had done, that's where he went astray he didn't follow the right proto cols and got caught. The development was over 80% finished when the down grade was found and a real uproar developed, it involved police and forensic accountants who led to serious problems being found and charges would be laid.

Out of the blue one of Li's colleagues had to tell her that her mate would probably be charged for fraud and he would be in severe trouble with the courts. The charges wouldn't have been referred to Li anyhow it wasn't serious enough to reach her level, but she was devastated how could her beloved Orlos have got into trouble. Then when she started to think she realized all of the signs were there but she had been so wrapped up in herself she hadn't reacted and was truly ashamed of herself, her old Chinese background was still with her. She was so deeply in love with Orlos that she had queried nothing he had been doing, nor tried in any way to help him, but there was nothing she could now do just let the law take its course.

Within three days Orlos had been found guilty and been ordered to pay the state an enormous amount of compensation credits his development had been downgraded to govt only stock.

The shame for the family was severe but that wasn't held against Orlos, his job now was to fight his way back and repay the state the credits he owed. Li had been affected very little she was tough and took their fall from grace stoically, but Orlos wasn't so easy to adjust, he had disgraced his family and the more they stood by him the worse he felt, he gradually sank into a miasma of self pity. Li was at her wits end what was she to do? She went home to her In Laws but they too were unable to advise what to do, it seemed they would have to insist he take medical treatment to heal his problems such as depression. They hated to bring up the subject with Orlos all they did know was he could be cured with treatment, but it would be at the hospital that specialized with problems of the brain, and that would be hard to convince him to do, but it must be done and as quickly as possible.

Li felt she must start to try and encourage her mate to lift himself up, she felt if he could be convinced they could get out of their mess quite quickly, he would become enthusiastic again and they could work off the debt together. There was now a debt of 2 million credits to be repaid, quite a staggering sum when Li only earned 20k in credits pa and the most Orlos could earn would be 35k pa. After all costs they could perhaps pay off 30K per year, until Li's next promotion which would give them another 10K pa there was at least 50 years of working for the Govt not a very pleasant thought.

Orlos could have a higher paid position than Li because he could work in the private sector, but he would now have to apply for work or enter govt employ. This would mean he would only have the same income as Li which would reduce the repayment of credits and would take much longer to fully settle the debt. After he had taken treatment at the hospital he had recovered, but he still hadn't lost the urge to be a self employed developer, or at least as a high rise engineer. Orlos had changed, not in his love for Li but in his attitude to their friends and family, it was as if he blamed everyone for his failure except himself, gradually his attitude began to affect Li and her rapid rise started to falter as she worried about Orlos.

Their world was falling into turmoil, Orlos had a job with a private developer; but he couldn't forget his lost dreams of becoming a major developer. From once being a happy carefree person he had become morose and petulant, Li was at her wits end, there were plenty of friends male and female at work, but none could give her the comfort of her once fabulous marriage; she gradually sank into a mess, of so many memories, from their meeting in China to their journey together. She had loved her Orlos from the time she had first seen him and still did, it would never change, but she was worried about him as he seemed to struggle under the cloud of his mistake, what if anything could she do was there anything? By the time they were out of debt it would be time to have their first child, she would go to the clinic and she would be prepared for childbirth.

STARTING AFRESH:

Returning home one day Li was surprised to find Orlos waiting for her with a visitor, a friend from his work she didn't know. Orlos was very excited and on introducing the visitor, it was clear why, this person owned the business he was working for he was an experienced developer.

Orlos then asked if Li remembered the report from the team that had gone to New Zealand.

"Why yes I remember that well why do you ask?"Li asked.

"Do you remember one of the important discoveries they made near the end of their journey and the sample they bought back?" Orlos asked with rising excitement obvious in his thoughts.

"Well yes they discovered how to get pure gold from the sap of the huge trees they found, yes I remember that's why they didn't want to come back, they wanted to stay and collect gold," replied Li with a smile. "but what has that got to do with us now that's way back on earth not much we can do about it from here is there?" Li asked.

"Well I have kept a copy of those reports and I know all about how they processed that gold, now Coreum here is a developer and he is interested in putting a consortium together to visit planet earth and get a load of gold and bring back it back home. We would also like to try and find some earthlings who would like to emigrate here in Cordiance, and set up a tiny colony here. The idea is to get the Govt to subsidize the flight of the biggest freighter we have, and bring back the gold and about 1,000 Earthlings.

You would need to get leave to come with us so as to demonstrate to your fellow beings they will be safe with us and that you are indeed the first interplanetary expat. Who has been here for over 50 years will you do it. We are to share half of any profits from the trip and Coreum will be coming with us, this would more than pay of my debt to the Govt and we would be free again. But more importantly it would be great to go back again, we could even visit your home so what do you think?" asked Orlos both men looked very excited waiting for her answer.

Li was excited herself but she didn't allow her feeling to show instead she asked, "Why don't you get the trip and everything arranged and approved first, if the numbers and the govt guarantees look right I think it will be fine. First get it set up then we will know it's real and I will gladly say yes, but until then it's just a dream".

Both of the males let out a sigh of excitement and relief, they had thought Li might not want to make such a trip, but her love for Orlos was so strong she would try anything to get him out of trouble.

As usual on Orbsey everything moved very quickly, within a week Coreum had the cost and terms for the trip to use the biggest Space Ship in the fleet, plus one small Cruiser for the International travel on Planet Earth. The state had also agreed to subsidize the trip if they bought any immigrants to settle on Orbsey, this was a great chance for the State and they would very much like to set up an Intergalactic Colony the first on record. As for the harvesting of gold that wasn't so important on Orbsey, there was a good value on the mineral, but it was suggested the promoters might like to sell the gold to the Egyptians since they seemed almost obsessed with that mineral. The problem was how the Egyptians were going to pay for the gold, they didn't have anything that was wanted on Orbsey and the Space Ship was expected to be full of immigrants, how the problem could be solved was a puzzle.

Li had checked out the materials used in Orbsey for clothes and had discovered they had no silk, she suggested they bring back a load of silk and spices, and that the immigrants should include experts who knew how to work with silk. If possible they should try to bring back with them the silkworms and thus set up a new industry on Orbsey, and have the experts to really make it work, her Chinese pragmatism was coming out even after all of the years. Sadly she realized that all of her sibling and her parents would have by now died of old age, because she was now in Earths terms over ninety YOA.

Finally Coreum had all of the numbers in and he confirmed the project would be a success. The project with govt help was viable, and would make a surplus of millions in govt credits because the state had agreed to underwrite the project. If the gold couldn't be used for trade on Earth then they were to bring it all home and it would be credited at the value of gold on Orbsey. The value of the proposed colony of earthlings was considered to be very high, so that even if they only bought back 100 earthlings the govt would be satisfied.

After all of the information had been collated and filed Li took it to the police forensic lab to have all of the details checked. It was returned with a very good result as to cost and feasibility, it was only then she sat down with Orlos and Coreum for a final meeting to finalize the terms of a contract to be drawn up between the two parties. Li and Orlos were to own one share and Coreum would own the other share. Within 32 hours after the meeting the final contracts had been signed and the expedition to Plane Earth was a reality.

Now there was a surge of excitement Li was busy arranging an extended furlough of 6 months, Orlos was finishing up his job and handing back what he had been doing and Coreum was putting his business in order for the period he would be away.

The Space Freighter had been loaded and a cruiser was sitting nicely in the hold, it would not be bought back to Orbsey but put in permanent orbit around earth which could last for fifty tears, if it wasn't reclaimed in that time it would simply disintegrate and become space junk.

The freighter had been fitted with living accommodation for 1200 coming back, with the facilities to put them all into an unconscious state; so there could be no problem with frightened and rebellious earthlings. There would be no harm done at any stage to the hoped for new earth colony on Orbsey, but the safety of the mission had to be ensured and if that meant the new travelers had to be put to sleep it would be done but with every precaution for their comfort. The number of earthling they wanted to bring back to Orbsey was, 150 Chinese, 150, English, 150 Germans, 150 Indians, 150 Sth Americans, 150 Africans 150 Egyptians, 150 American Indians, 50 Australians, a total of 1250 plus any children who were part of any family groups, the more the better. The Earthling's are to be treated with the greatest respect, but they were going to be forced new settlers for Orbsey on that they had no option.

The Space Freighter was ready to launch now at any time, but Li wanted a last round of checks before they took off and they found one problem. Since a lot of the power to move from one Galaxy to the other was thought powered how they were going to get such a big freighter through with only 10 persons on board. Then coming back the earthlings could hardly be expected to provide thought power so how again were they to move from one Galaxy to the other. This wasn't really a problem, but it would change the cost dynamic for the Govt, that extra cost had to be approved and it was necessary to install another piece of equipment to facilitate the use of stored thought power. It was an embarrassment to the Scientists that such a fundamental mistake had been made, but to Li just another example of how thorough she was in everything she did.

The Launch to Planet Earth.

The take off was smooth and easy not much different than a normal international flight, it is like rising on a cushion of air, but when reaching above the gravitational pull of Orbsey is when the real flight begins. Suddenly without apparent disturbance the Spacecraft was in the Planet Earths Galaxy and the real flight was underway, but again there was no sense of the enormous speed generated. They were very quickly moving back in time, but none including the Pilots were aware of anything, many light years backward had been traversed over the entire trip on earth it was the year 90 AD when they arrived, they had left in approximately 5 AD but the actual difference from Planet to Planet was millions of Light years difference.

The intricacies of Interplanetary travel and the tyranny of time had been defeated centuries ago on the planet Orbsey. All on board now settled down for the week's journey to Planet Earth, there was plenty to keep all types amused, but for Li and Orlos it was a time for memories shared so lovingly, they clung to each other the whole way. As they relaxed aboard an empty huge Space Craft, it was like going back in time, but now they were mated so they had a second honeymoon, both wished it would never end, but sadly all good things must end and it did oh so quickly.

Quite suddenly the Captain announced, well folks we are here, it will soon be time to launch the cruiser, myself and most of the crew will stay aboard to check everything is fine for the trip home. The Cruiser has two travel jets aboard with the same controls as an Aerocar on Orbsey; these are at the disposal of your team leaders. We will have one here, but that is only for use if you need it, then you must call for it to be sent down. The Cruiser will return to us, the mother ship automatically just press the homing button that's all you need to do. There are also two Aerocars aboard each cruiser that you can keep with you down there for local travel, but you will have to keep them hidden if you keep them with you, we leave that decision up to you.

When you have cargo to be sent to back let us know and we will send down the cruiser, it will pick up and return your passengers for the trip home. We have two medical specialists on board who will if necessary anesthetize the earthlings until you return, then you will look at them and may in consultation with me revive any you think can travel with us, the rest will be left to sleep until we get home. If you have too many immigrants for the cruiser to carry and take with us, we can just beam them straight up and sedate them on the way.

As you know this is a private trip so when you leave us you are on your own, but we are here to help if necessary, once back on board you will again be in the crew and my safety umbrella, until then good luck and we on board hope the goals of your trip is fully successful.

The cruiser was ready to go destination Central Australia, the disembarkation hold was opened and they glided free safely and within 30minutes were again landed on Terra Australis.

The first day was spent just orientating to the earth's slightly weaker gravitational pull but the next day it was time to start work. The team of four going to New Zealand had the coordinates and would take one of the Aerocars, the others would travel on the other Aerocar, but would only stay there long enough to see the team settled then they would fly direct to Egypt. All of the travelers had been treated so they had mouths and ears and looked just like earthling with slightly bigger heads for which they would never be noticed. The trip to New Zealand took 45 minutes and they had found the gigantic trees in minutes. They landed and as expected the area had no signs of life the area was completely deserted, just as Australia had been when they landed.

They spent a day there following through the instructions that had been left by the previous Orbseyn group, and were quickly all set up to heat the mineral gold just as quickly as they could farm the trees. It was exciting to notch the trees at several points around the trunks and watch the flow of the gold colored extract, exactly as the reports they had said it would. Collecting the resin and then heating them into ingot shaped containers, it was obvious that one tonne of gold could be collected easily in no more than three days, so the target was increased to four tons of gold within three weeks. Meantime the other craft was off to Egypt.

The trip to Egypt took them almost three hours but now the speed could be felt these vehicles weren't meant for this type of work, but the performance was still formidable. Outside of Egypt the vessel was hidden they took on the appearance of the local people and entered the capital Alexandria quietly; they wanted to see the Pharaoh and abduct twenty of their civilians. The visit to the Pharaoh wasn't easy to arrange they had to change into being aristocrats, but once they had done that it was easy. The offer to sell three tonnes of gold was enthusiastically accepted provided the source could be proved, but then the problem was how they were to be paid, not only for the gold but he secret of where the gold was to be found. What could an ancient culture provide

Orbseyns there could only be trade goods, but what goods did they have that Orbsey could use up.

The start could be the supply of 150 people from the areas as listed; these must know they were going to a new culture as new settlers. A team of experts were needed to grow mulberry trees and silk worms for a new industry on Orbsey. Silk wasn't available on Orbsey and the cloth had been found and inspected by the Coreum and Orlos both agreed such beautiful clothe would be very popular in their country. Families with children were preferred for the new colony, and since the Govt would reimburse them on a headage basis, it seemed they would be best to take more colonists for the immigrants wanted by the Govt and the silk for private industry.

The information on how to find and process the gold would be handed over when the new immigrants were made available, Trans shipped to Australia at Egyptian cost. What was being given to the Egyptians was not of great value to the Orbseyns, but to the earthlings had great value. It was left to Li to value what they were getting, in exchange for what they were trading and after reflection she said, 'If we take back one tonne of gold and 1250 immigrants for an earthling colony in Cordiance it will be a very valuable and profitable cargo that's what we need to do and thus stop trying to find other products when it was almost impossible. The only products Earth really has is immigrants so the more they could take the better, a check with the mother ship confirmed 1200 plus children, but all would have to be kept unconscious, that would be too many to be left conscious they may run riot in fright.

The problem was for the Egyptian Pharaoh was to get the immigrants to Australia it would take months and a fleet of Carthaginian boats into an area that was unknown to them. The team had offered to take the Pharaoh to have a look at the gold producing trees, but to do so they had to reveal a little about themselves. At the end when everything was ready the Cruiser would be called in to take Pharaoh and his court to New Zealand, part of the deal was that the Orbseyns would never again harvest gold, but they may come back for more immigrants. It had been agreed the immigrants would be beamed up to the cargo ship and sedated on the way up; this made it far easier for the Egyptians to reach the delivery points.

Finally the agreement was approved, 1200 plus children immigrants, and the silk etc in return for 3 tonne of gold and the secret of how to find the gold trees.

CHAPTER 4
NEW IMMIGRANTS

THE RUNNERS WERE SENT out to collect the people required for the immigration to Orbsey, and arrangements were ready to have them beamed up to the Mother Ship but it would take too much of the stored energy so the cruiser would have to be sent. But how would the people be transferred even to the Cruiser it was a real problem, these people may panic when they got sight of the strange vehicle; there would be a problem to get them aboard. The cruiser could carry up to 250 people at a time, there was no alternative, they would have to be put to sleep as soon as they were embarked which in itself was a big job.

When reaching the Mother Ship they would have to be carried on board and put into their lay back seats for takeoff that was going to be far too difficult. Finally it was decided they would have to be sedated just enough to sooth their fears, and then once they were aboard the Mother Ship they would be kept quiet just enough so they could be lectured by Li. Because she was herself an Earthling it would calm them down and the message would kept up until arrival. The authorities would be asked to clear the terminal of all Orbseyns before the ship was disembarked so the new immigrants wouldn't be frightened. It had been agreed that any immigrants that couldn't settle in Orbsey would be sent back after 10 years and released near their old home.

Finally everything was in place the new immigrants were being assembled as close as possible to the ratios asked for except the Australians it was decided to leave them out, their culture was just so ancient the shock would be too much and they would never be able to settle on Orbsey. It was time to order down the Cruiser to transport Pharaoh and his assistants to New Zealand to witness the gold being harvested. Orlos and Coreum had decided this was a highly commercial opportunity and if the Earthlings settled well on Orbsey they would apply to the Govt to return with a fleet big enough to take at least 22000 new settlers back.

If the settlers they were taking now failed to settle they would have to be bought back at Govt cost! They decided to get two of their staff to stay on earth and prepare at least 22,000 Earthlings for the next trip. It was felt with that number they would then have a viable colony on Orbsey, and they could trained to one day in the future send some of their young back to help develop their own Mother Earth. The main goal would be to train earth to exist without wars, and get rid of all weapons of death, as had been done on Orbsey. One day they hoped earth and Orbsey may be planets working together both with advanced technology, but only if peace prevailed. It was impossible to eradicate crime the only thing that could be done was to control it as much as possible.

The cruiser was now hovering high over Egypt ready to come in to receive the Pharaoh and his group of about 40 people and all was set to leave the next morning. The group including Pharaoh and his wife had been well versed on what was to happen, and they were to meet the Cruiser alone with as few observers as possible. The group in New Zealand knew of the group's arrival and was ready to load four tonne of gold onto the ship as soon as they arrived. The embarking and disembarking was very easy, the Egyptians were very nervous at first but as soon as they were underway they settled down. The high speed of the Cruiser meant they were ready to land in NZ one hour after liftoff in Egypt.

After they had disembarked at the site of the trees and had seen how the gold was harvested, all of the Egyptians clapped their hands in glee at the sight of the 3 tonne of gold they were to receive for the immigrants they were to supply, but they had no idea the people were going to another planet. On the arrival back in Egypt Pharaoh was asked how two men would be treated if they were left in Egypt until the return of the fleet for more Immigrants possibly 22,000 of them in several years time. He was most amenable to the idea and promised the men would be kept as special envoys with access to the Pharaoh whenever they felt they needed his help.

The new immigrants had been assembled before Pharaoh and told they should have no fear, and that he himself had already taken a trip on the strange machine and seen wonderful things in a far off land. The people cheered their ruler, but some from far off were still anxious, but when Li stepped forward and told them she had lived with the strangers for many years all became quiet and expressed that they were all ready to leave in the strange boat that floated through the air.

The Cruiser had loaded half of the immigrants on board and had left for the Space ship to unload them and the 1 tonne of gold going to Orbsey. Before they took off they were all given a powerful sedative that would keep them quiet for 40 days, by which time they would have landed in Orbsey. While the first load was being embarked onto the Mother ship there was a final meeting between Orlos Coreum and Li, and Pharaoh and his courtiers, they promised they wanted 22,000 more settlers any that were unhappy would be bought back. Meanwhile the two men who were staying behind were introduced, and the Egyptians were told they were staying to find the people to take back on the next trip. If when the ships got back no way had been found for the Egyptians to harvest the gold in New Zealand then they would get another 3 tonne harvested for them by the Orbseyns.

The Cruiser was now back for the final load, and it was time to leave! The passengers were loaded and sedated; it was time for the Leaders from Orbsey to load. One Aerocar was being left for the two men who were staying, but it was hidden so that they wouldn't be wrecked by intruders. Li hadn't been so sure it was a good idea to leave the Aerocar, but it had been promised so it was too late to change, this she said would give the two persons left behind too much power and they may abuse that power over the Egyptians. Orlos and Coreum before they left warned the two that they would be subject to the laws of Orbsey on the fleets return, so they should always defer to defer to the laws of Orbsey at all times.

The goodbyes had been said to the Pharaoh and his Court, then their two comrades who were staying, then the Cruiser lifted off they were on their way back home. On their way back to the freighter as a gift to Li the Cruiser drifted over her old home, and she had a few moments to look back and remember. There had been little change and Li could see where she had played when she was a little girl, she shed a few tears until Orlos reached over and kissed her, then she was ready to go home to Orbsey.

There had been little excitement on the flight back to Orbsey, the transfer from one Galaxy to the other was just as quick as usual and the flight to Orbsey uneventful. All of the Earthlings had been lightly sedated as the heavy affects had worn off and they had been told only they were traveling to a new home far away from Egypt. They were being fed in the usual earthling way and were quite content; they were now coming in for landing and floating down to the hanger on a cushion of air. Li could now see inside the terminal and it was deserted, they were now able to receive thoughts from the ground, and they knew the earthlings were to be isolated until they could be got used to their new environment. Special Staff had been changed and given mouths and ears so as not to frighten the newcomers, while they were being transported to new quarters from which they would be debriefed for as long as needed.

Finally it was over the immigrants had been unloaded, and we're all doing well, they were being left for the sedation to fully wear off. Li, Orlos and Coreum would have to help with the newcomers just by appearing they would be reassured, this was especially important for Li to be there because she was an immigrant and could reassure her compatriots they were safe and headed for a better life.

Li had to stay at the immigration office for 30 days by which time most of the newcomers were settled down and had even got used to the look of their new owners. There had been trouble until Li had told them they had been bought off the Egyptian Pharaoh for gold, but if they couldn't settle down in 10 years they would be returned to Planet Earth. This worked wonders they knew what slavery meant they had come from servitude, not always slavery but all had lived under harsh conditions. The Egyptians were the hardest to settle their religion dictated they had to die within the borders of Egypt to earn eternal life. Li's comment that on this planet they would live to at least 300 YOA gave them pause to think that maybe this wasn't such a bad idea after all. The total load had been 1200 adults plus children, but there was more children than adults so as far as the promoters were concerned it had been a huge success, the total of new immigrants bought back was over 2,800 including babies in arms. The gold also was valuable but not as valuable as it seemed to be on Mother Earth, all up it had been a wonderful and very prosperous trip. Li and Orlos were out of trouble with all of the govt credits now paid and a huge surplus of almost 5 million commercial credits from the sale of the gold, and the bonus from the Govt for each of the 1200 new persons that were bought back.

Li was back at work as soon as her furlough was up and Orlos had the money now to be a developer. He joined up with Coreum as a full and equal partner, in building high rise apartments and scheming about their next trip to Earth, it was most important to them both the new immigrants settled down and liked their new home, so they kept their earthling appearance and visited the new development that had been especially built for them. Their homes were much the same as they would have had at home on Mother Earth, and they had land so they could grow their own vegetables etc, but the meats were processed protein and given to them to be cooked, there was no killing of animals allowed on Orbsey.

The new arrivals were more curious than frightened, they had been reassured by Pharaoh and Li they were going to be safe so it had calmed the men down the women had been settled from the start. The children were no problem at all the average age was only six so they thought it was all an adventure? The babies all they were interested in was the milk from Mummies breast for the rest they knew nothing. On arrival then being held in a type of detention the men began to get restless, but they knew they had to wait until their new masters were ready to expose them to this new world.

The day they first saw the real Orbseyns they were terrified for a little while, but Li, Orlos and Coreum was with them so they were reassured. The next day it was all forgotten their new masters were a different race, but obviously couldn't eat them if they had no mouths, but then they also had no ears so how did they hear each other. This had been explained so they were fine with that also very quickly. The Govt Representatives were delighted with how well their new persons had settled down and accepted their new home, they had heard of slavery in their own history but that was at least 5,000 years ago, now all were free and equal, unless of course they messed up themselves now and again.

It had been decided that the newcomers could work out among themselves when and if they wanted to be fed and have their thoughts arranged like the Orbseyns there would be no pressure. The govt had agreed that if and when this group had settled down, another expedition would be sent with a full fleet to bring several thousand immigrants back to join their compatriots, but this would only be if the present group was a complete success. It was also decided that if after five years they wanted to go home to Earth then they would be sent with no hesitation and no questions asked. All of this had been told to the earthlings but already it seemed that 90% of them loved their new homes, the other 10% would never be happy anywhere and they were being ridiculed as idiots by the majority who could see a great future for themselves. Not least of the advantages was the idea of living for so long. The length of life they couldn't easily understand 300 years goodness that was a prize indeed, and amazing that would really be something to try to get. Even Li warning them they may be sick of life well before the allotted time span but they could be kept alive even if they had a serious accident.

Li had also warned them that the law was very severe on Orbsey and criminals were usually caught very quickly, she stressed that capital crimes were judged harshly and execution was quick if found guilty. The reaction to that was well on earth the law is immediate, and we were executed immediately without being really able to seek fair justice, so that wasn't new to most of them, but especially the men had seen beheadings before and were very servile when it came to that part of the new society.

When they were first shown their new homes they were very happy, and the cleanliness to the women was wonderful, the men were only creatures of habit anyhow and would soon settle down. The children had been especially catered to, because they were the real persons that would decide if they were happy or not, so a special effort was being made to ensure their happiness. Special schools were built for the children and teachers were found among the group to teach them as a few had been taught on earth, but then special teachers were arranged to teach about Orbsey. Then there was another program which was compulsory for the adults, this was strictly controlled by teachers who would give lessons about the history of Orbsey.

Within 12 months most of the earthlings had converted to the Orbseyn way of life and were settling in, all were on course to be naturalized, of them all there was only two who were holding out and declaring they wanted to go home. In another 12 months all had been converted except the same two still held out, they still wanted to go home, the problem was they were married men with children and they wanted to take their families with them in total there was 12 who may have to be repatriated. All of the others even the two families had settled in, but after three years these two still held out, they seemed to glory in the attention they were getting and after four years were still insisting they wanted to go home.

Li was bought in, the authorities had hoped she may have some way to convince the rebels they were wrong, she was given a free hand to speak to the two recalcitrant's in the group. After persevering for over two months, Li walked into their compound one day and said, "I have convinced the govt to send the two families home within one week so please prepare yourselves to leave there; is no going back the govt is sick of the intransigence of these two families so as you wish it shall be, you are going," Then she turned and walked out without any further discussion, but behind she left an uproar.

The two men had been basking in their notoriety as the only ones who had held out, but now it was time to go, they were terrified, because the wives and children were refusing to go with them, so they were going home alone. Li had called their bluff now they were the ones in trouble, they had no way to know it was a bluff, they didn't know there was no way the govt would send a ship just for them. The next day they were chasing around for Li, who had refused to come at first, but when they sent a message they had changed their minds she finely came with a very severe look on her face, "well what do you two want are you ready to go I can arrange a Cruiser for you now if you are ready." She said with no malice in her thoughts.

"No we want to stay now because we were wrong can you speak to the govt men and plead for us please, we are so sorry and will never play up again," they whine.

"I will only arrange the change if you sign now you are going to stay of your own accord there is no way then you can change your mind, so sign and we will have it changed, but only this once, any more of your nonsense and you will be treated as a criminal," Li said finally with a smile she had won again.

About one week after settling the dispute with the two Earthlings she arrived home one night to find Orlos and Coreum waving an official govt letter, they had been chosen to lead a fleet of freighters back to earth to bring back 50,000 new Immigrants, the last lot had settled in so well it had been decided to set up a full sized earth community.

They would be leaving in 12 months time and there would be backed by a full fleet with all of the necessary Aerocars and Cruisers to service the entire program.

New programs, greater responsibility:

Li quickly settled down at her job and was soon back to her old self, because she had no need to worry anymore about Orlos she was once again able to concentrate. Her work load was soon back to the previous level, but her superiors had been told she was to be part of an expedition to collect 50,000 Earthlings which may take up to 12 months to complete, that was a lot of new people to find and a lot of work on planet earth. There was no problem she was granted twelve months furlough on full pay because she was still working for a govt dept. of Cordiance.

Orlos and Coreum were very busy they wanted to complete all of the private work before they left for earth; they were very excited the credits for each person they bought back would be quite large and once again they were allowed to bring back one tonne of gold. They had got a better price than they expected for the last load of gold, so this time there would be a huge profit.

The development they were currently working on was 140 stories and there were 700 home units in total, all had been costed out properly and would just be finished if they added extra contractors to the teams that are already working on them. Li had already won two major cases of fraud and the conspirators were, now working for the govt.

The next claim of rape she got was an interesting one in that at first the victims were alleging rape then changed their minds and only claimed minor assault. This had happened several times and there was always the same procedure then the change from rape to minor assault, but now Li was getting suspicious what she wandered is going on, we have a serial rapist, but he is getting his victims to recant how is he doing this?

The next victim that came in Li interviewed the women and asked why she was changing her claim was she in some way frightened? The women claimed not to be frightened so there was no point but to just log her in with the other redirected claims.

Then one day a man she knew slightly came into her office and said, "you think I committed all of those rapes don't you earthling?"

Li was surprised and said, "I don't even know you why should I be thinking of you as the rapist, but now you are here did you rape all of these girls?" Li asked.

"Have they said I did?" the man asked, "and if they did do you believe them?"

"No they haven't said you or anyone else has raped them, but yes I think they have been raped but won't complain for some reason, but I will find out let me assure you of that," Li said with a smile.

"Well whatever they say it wasn't me because I can prove my innocence very easily so whatever they say will be all lies," the stranger laughed as he walked away.

During the course of the next months there was an average of two females coming in with rape complaints and then changing their minds, Li was totally mystified, so she asked for a police psychologist to speak to the next victim that came in and then changed their minds.

Within two days a girl came in with the same complaint, and the psychologist was called in o interview her, before she had gone away then come back and changed her mind.

"Now what exactly is your complaint?" she asked

"I have been raped by a hooded man but when he had finished he let me go and told me to go to the police and complain," she said looking very confused

"And did this man actually penetrate your body fully?" she asked.

"Yes he did, but he didn't seem to mount me it was all very strange, I didn't really know what to think," said a very confused youngster, "I am not an innocent but never had sex like that before, can I go now please?" she asked.

"Yes you can go but when this man comes and tells you he never had sex with you can you come back and tell me please?" said the police psychologist.

The next day the girl was back and said, "No he never had sex with me and he proved it so I must be mistaken, but I don't really know what happened sorry".

In reporting back to Li the Psychologist said, "These girls haven't been penetrated with his penis he uses some type of sexual instrument, this man is impotent and hates women, because he blames them for his condition. You will find he has told these women of his condition and warned them they will be made a joke of in court, that's why they are changing their minds. The thrill he is getting is from fooling you not from making a fool of these women, he just wants to see you struggling to prove your case."

Li then had to work out what she could do to stop this person who was trying to make a fool of the system, so the next women that came in she told her what was going to happen and when it did she was to say, "I don't believe you and I am going to continue to take you to court, this will frighten him and he will offer to give you private credits, but you are to say and what is that for. Then he will say I want to keep the police making fools of themselves, but you must say, no I want more credits than that I want 50 not 20 and he will agree."

Then if you come back to me, I personally will show you how he has molested you without you knowing. When the women arrived back at the station she confirmed what Li had told her was correct and the man had been able to prove he was unable to perform the sex act, therefore when they got to court she would be found guilty of a mischievous act in naming him for something he couldn't do so she wanted to withdraw the charge she had laid.

Li smiled and then proceeded to show the girl what the man had done to her, it wasn't an indecent sexual act but it was an invasion of her privacy, so a criminal act had been committed, not rape that was true but still sexual perversion.

The entire over thirty women were bought in and persuaded to press charges of indecent assault, the accumulated charges was enough to make the pervert have to attend one of the govt controlled neurology hospitals to have his strange perversion fixed then he had to pay damages to each women. The amount was quite substantial so in the end he wasn't laughing, but then neither was Li, she was just doing her job.

By then it was time to go once more to mother earth, she had no way of knowing her career in the police force was over.

A Planet like Earth in a different Galaxy:

The Scientists suddenly announced another Planet had been found that looked a lot like earth, but probes were being sent out and if they could they would land and find out what they more and give a better report. This Planet was three times the distance away from Orbsey that Earth was, and sounded much more developed than earth. The radio signals being picked up were definitely sent by beings of a more advanced caliber than maybe even Orbsey, so the probes would be very careful, but it was sure the technology was far more advanced than they had found on planet earth.

Suddenly the news broke about the new find, it had taken six months for the round trip by an advanced type of probe; they had landed for a quick reconnoiter but hadn't stayed long. This new Planet was very advanced not up to Orbsey standard but quite close, and they were a very warlike Planet.

The Scientists were perturbed at the thought of a warlike Planet within easy reach, they would have to send another probe to see if the weapons could be neutralized but also they would have to put a shield right over Orbsey to protect their world if need be.

Another two probes were sent out one to land and try to find the weapons first, and then to destroy them if they could. The other would stand by and be able to report back if the first probe was destroyed in any way. Finally both probes were back and reported they had failed in their mission, so the cover over Orbsey had to be decided and if necessary erected, but it wasn't an emergency just to be on the alert and send for more information. It was certain the tyranny of distance hadn't yet been beaten as it had been on Orbsey only one millennia ago, so it would take travelers from the new planet hundreds of years to reach Orbsey.

It wasn't such a big deal to cover Orbsey but there was some thought that the coming fleet being sent on the mission to earth should be held up for at least another 12 months. The leaders could only agree fully, that there was no use bringing back a load of Immigrants only to find they had been locked out by the shield, and had to float in space possibly to be destroyed by the aggressive neighbor.

All plans were put on hold until further notice, but even if they went in 12 months time they would still be four years earlier than promised. The development owned by Orlos and Coreum was continued at the higher rate of production but another one was taken that was a lot smaller and consisted of only 500 units, this one could easily be finished in one year in time for lift off, if it was going to happen.

There was a lot of controversy now in the govt. most didn't like the idea of a shield around the entire planet, it would stop the flights out into the stratosphere and ruin a lot of ticket sales that kept their huge fleet viable. The scientists would find out if there was some way the weapons of war could be nullified, another two probes were sent out with plans to try and bring an example of the type of weapons in common use, in the new Planet named by their peoples.

Within six months the Probes were back with a load of weapons they had managed to steal from one of the bases on Xalafeu and the scientists were immediately looking for ways to nullify the deadly potential of the strange weapons. It didn't take very long before they had worked out a way to nullify the weapons, but the question now became how many more of these warlike planets are there out there, Orbsey shunned war but what needs to be done to protect themselves in the future. So far they had found planet earth and felt it would be at least 2,000 years for them to develop any real weapons of war, they were still driving around with horse and carts. Xalafeu was a very different world it had weapons well able to destroy their own world and so presumable wouldn't hesitate to destroy another world. All Orbsey was interested in was peace they had no desire to destroy or even fight other worlds, they had been civilized for too long and the idea of wars between the planets, was really anathema to the leaders and the citizens alike. Wars as they were waged on earth were not really a problem they could only kill a few thousand, but Xalafeu were different they could destroy planets even ones as big and as advanced as Orbsey.

Decisions no matter how unpalatable had to be made, it was decided that a screen had to be developed that could be erected over the Planet Orbsey within three days. Scout craft would have to be kept on constant surveillance in deep space working with a Mother Ship and the craft would have to be able to warn Orbsey at least 7 days before an attack from another planet. The scout craft would have to be able to protect the Mother Ship while it raced for home and safety, then the scouts would come in. The shield would be kept open over Orbsey only for a few hours after the warning, enough time for the fleet to get home. A watch would be kept on Xalafeu to see if there was any chance to negotiate a peace treaty if not Orbsey for the first time in millennia would to be on battle stations and arms production, but they would never be the aggressor, in any war.

The population of Orbsey had no conception of war, and the closest they could get was to bring a big number of real warriors from earth and planning for that was underway. Li, Orlos and Coreum were ordered to appear before the grand council and had to report on the chances to get at least 20,000 hardened warriors from Earth, the question was could that number be taken and where were the best warriors. Li said the Romans were the best trained and could be taken from the camps all, over the Roman World. Orlos was more inclined towards the men from Carthage who were wonderful sailors, and Coreum voted for the people from the plains of China the Mongols. The three of them were firm however in the danger of taking on board such men they were all brutal killers, and would destroy any space craft they were put into. The only way to get such men was to capture them and put them to sleep for the entire journey, and when they woke up, they would still have to be sedated.

The idea was to bring warriors to Orbsey that could train the millions that were doing time repaying credits to the Govt, instead of menial tasks they were to be drafted into the Orbseyn military forces.

Such a mission to earth would take about three months and would be a lot more dangerous than the previous two trips, but the three who had been in charge of the previous mission were quite happy they could find the number of warriors that the Govt was asking for. The Scientists had now set up a radio connection with the two men on earth and they were able to get messages through. The number of men wanted for the next load was to be

20,000 minimum but on transfer they would be beamed direct up into the Space Freighters and kept unconscious for the entire trip. The Pharaoh they were told should be contacted and told what was needed; the men must all be battle hardened veterans.

The two men were requested to go to NZ and set up another 4 tonne of gold of which 3 tonne would be paid to Pharaoh for his help. Although the men were being abducted if they didn't want to stay on Orbsey they would be returned to earth, but if they wanted to stay their wives and children would be bought to them within 12 months.

CHAPTER 5/
NEW PLANETS:

THE FIRST FREIGHTER TO be leaving with Li, Orlos and Coreum aboard, with extra 10 staff men of their own, and the usual crew of four were aboard and they would signal how many warriors they had to bring back before the fleet left their base in Orbsey. There was one Cruiser and 3 Aerocars in the docking bay, but there may be a need to leave an extra Aerocar behind, so the men left on earth could travel to various countries and find the families of those they were taking to Orbsey. The lift off and flight to earth was quite uneventful and when they arrived on the ground in Egypt their two men were waiting for them, happy to see persons from home.

An immediate meeting had been arranged with Pharaoh and his entourage, who were all anxious to see the travelers; they hadn't been able to find a way to get the gold from New Zealand the Southern Oceans were just too turbulent for the Carthaginian boats to navigate safely, and the Egyptian treasury needed gold urgently. The Gold was ready but way to heavy for the Aerocars to carry, the cruiser would have to be sent down to carry the gold from New Zealand to Egypt and Pharaoh was keen to do anything the strangers needed to get that gold, his army hadn't been paid for two months.

The Orbseyn mission expressed the need for hardened warriors! Pharaoh suggested they take 20,000 Romans and he would be pleased to see them go, but the exercise wasn't just to please Pharaoh they wanted a blend of warriors including some Egyptians.

To keep Pharaoh happy the cruiser was ordered down and the gold that had been harvested for him had been transferred and one tonne kept to take back to Orbsey. The need for caution was important the men were going to be abducted, and they were prime fighting men, who would object strongly if they were not treated properly. It had been suggested by Li that a trial should be done with only one freighter probably 1,000 to 1200 men at most, then she suggested all of the problems with men of this type could be known before a fleet load were taken. It would also establish just how the men would react when they were again conscious but still sedated.

Li was turning out to be by far the best thinker of the team, and since female leaders were quite common on Orbsey her leadership was quite easily accepted by her fellow traders, for they were after all traders in the sense that they were stealing men and taking them to another life. It was true that Orbsey offered a far better and longer life than they could ever conceive of on earth didn't change the truth they were stealing human beings to Tran's plant into another world.

Li had decided to take a trip by Aerocar to New Zealand to check what the men had been doing and was surprised at the amount of gold that had obviously been taken, "What she asked have you two been doing, it looks to me as if over 8 tonne of gold has been processed where is the rest?"

Unfortunately even on earth they could read each others thought so there was no alternative, "we have processed the extra and sold it in India they confessed, but it's not stealing this gold belongs to anyone who can get it," they protested.

"Is that so well as far as I am concerned the gold belongs to us because we provided the facilities to get it, were it not so you would still be at home on Orbsey," Li smiled. Now she continued, "what other mischief have you two been up to tell me quick before I get angry, and remember my position in the police force, because you seem to be getting into a lot of trouble here. It is lucky for you we are on earth because was that not so you would both be in Court tomorrow."

The two were natives of the Cordiance State and were not intimidated by Li, at the start, but instead were inclined to be cheeky. "Well we were left here on Earth and not given any rules, the Orbseyn laws don't apply here they sneered."

"You were explicitly told you still came under the jurisdiction of Orbsey law," was that not so asked Li.

The two men refused to answer although their thoughts confirmed they were. "Now let me explain! If we lock you into laser chains and take you back that way you will think you have been hard done by, but I think that's just what we will do, now what do you think of that?" Li said with a pleasant smile.

Orlos and Coreum looked on in wonder, they hadn't thought of something like this happening, but they didn't dare to dispute with Li what she was doing. The two men were cuffed and beamed up the Space Freighter within minutes; they were now two very downcast looking men.

On the return to Egypt when asked where the two who had stayed on earth were, Pharaoh was told they were in jail for stealing gold, but he expressed no surprise except to say they could have sold all of the gold to us, who did they sell it to?

"Our laws are not the same as yours it doesn't matter who they sold it to it only matters that they are thieves and must pay the penalty, the next ones we leave won't be so silly and do that again."

But protested Pharaoh, "our agreement was we could take all of the gold we wanted, so really they were stealing off me not you?"

"No the truth is you can take all of the gold you want, but you must transport it here on your own boats, it's only when we carry it for you do we get paid." Smiled Li and that's what we have done transported to you 3 tonne of gold now we want payment. Even if you don't mind persons stealing off you we do, those men will be dealt with under our laws. Under our agreement we want 1,000 – 1200 warriors now and when we get back we want 22,000 more, but we will bring you another 8 tonne of gold does that keep you happy?"

Pharaoh was beaming with delight he had already forgotten the other two persons, he was thinking about 8 tonne of gold he already knew this was only a trial so he had to have the number of warriors, and to him that was the problem.

But when Li explained they were just going to take them and put them to sleep until they got home he was jubilant, why we have a camp with 10,000 Romans they won't we even miss what you take and the sooner you take them the better. Are you sure you don't want to take the lot he asked it would be a mercy for us!

"No we will take 8000 of them and 6000 Egyptians hows that and 8,000 Mongols," asked Li.

"Well I guess that's what it will have to be, but these accursed Romans are so hated here I would like you to take all of them, but I guess you can take some of my own troops as well, but they aren't as good as the Romans," he said with a last desperate try to persuade.

Li just smiled and said this is what will happen, "one of our big ships will hover above and we will pick out the men we want, they will be beamed up to our ship but will be sedated on the way, then when they are aboard they will be put to sleep for the journey home, it's really very simple and you will have earned your gold.

The loading operation was started the following day, much to the confusion among the ranks. Some leaders were taken with those from among the ranks, to ensure continued control when they were rehabilitated later in Orbsey. The whole operation was completed easily and quickly and within two days the warriors were settled and sound asleep in the Space Freighters and on their way to their destination Planet Orbsey.

There was little or no fuss on arrival at the space terminal, the warriors were semi awakened and allowed to walk off the ship, kept heavily sedated at all times. It was over a month until the new arrivals were left to become fully conscious, but even so laser guns were held by their attendants at all times.

Li had been in constant control of their settling in program, and even though to be controlled by a female was anathema especially to the Romans they had finally realized there was no alternative, they were in an Alien Planet and the old rules of home no longer applied. As time went by they became used to Li being around and obviously in control of them, but then they began the program that had been developed for new persons who were being settled on this strange place. When told that Li was almost 90 YOA and the average age on Orbsey was 250-300 years they were silenced from complaints for the present. When they were asked about wives and families of the 22,000 men in the total draft, 20,000 had families and when all added up the total came to another 50,000 future immigrants to be bought to Orbsey depending on how many decided to settle and stay.

It had been decided to leave again two men on Planet Earth to search for and advise the families what had happened but also to ensure they were looked after financially by the Orbsey treasury. The ease with which these violent men were settling in amazed the authorities and they put the success down to Li primarily and her two compatriots secondly. All assessment had been made and finally it was decided to send a fleet of 20 Space Freighters to collect another 40,000 new warriors to join their compatriots already in full training. The men had been told exactly why they had been bought to Planet Orbsey that their mission was to train the natives of this world to be the focus of old style war in this world. It was also explained that in the modern age whole planets could be destroyed, but that the aim of the authorities in Orbsey was to lower the level of war to what it was on earth which in a planet such as Orbsey was considered very low tech.

The two men who had come before Li in her position now of being high up in the legal chain were sentenced to 10 years in the military with a nominal monthly credits allowance. The money they had earned from selling gold to India was transferred to the controllers of the trip the three partners.

It was only a few days later that the order arrived elevating Li to a position never before held by any person on Orbsey she became the supreme commander of the fleet in the search for interplanetary immigrants. Hence forth she was to be in charge of all immigrants from any planet including planet Xalafeu, since it had been decided the best way to get to know that planet was to abduct some of their citizens and get the information they wanted that way.

The fleet was going to planet earth again and by time the full program was completed it was estimated there would be about 50,000 (plus families) Earthlings living in Planet Orbsey and hopefully settling down. The next trip as soon as the fleet returned was a trip to Xalafeu to bring back 1200 of their persons for processing, Li was to hold the position of being in charge of all of those newcomers to Orbsey. Because this planet was far more developed than earth it wasn't expected to be their people would want to stay unless like earth there were special reasons like the increased length of life and far better conditions than on their home planet.

The fleet of 20 Space freighters each equipped with a cruiser and an aerocar in their holding bays, and all especially equipped to deal with any troublesome warriors, but no problems were expected the trial load had been very successful.

The arrival back in Egypt was greeted with great enthusiasm by Pharaoh, no doubt boosted by the thought of the eight tonnes of gold his treasury was to receive, but a bit tempered by the number of men his people had to find.

First the gold had to be processed in New Zealand and then freighted to Egypt. Orlos and Coreum where now acting alone as agents. Li no longer had a position within their activities except to check that Orlos was doing nothing illegal. She was now a high govt official and couldn't afford to be worried about commercial sidelines. It wasn't certain they would have any involvement with the next job she had, bringing men from Xalafeu, but that was in the future and not on her mind just now.

They took their full team to New Zealand and within 2 weeks had processed 12 tonnes of gold, 8 for Pharaoh and four for Orlos and Coreum, they had been surprised that there was a good market for gold on Orbsey and they had both become very rich men. However the Govt had cancelled all commissions for fees on each new immigrant bought back they didn't need to pay that cost now they had Li as a govt official.

Pharaoh had got all of the men needed and the transfers were just as easy as before with no hassles what so ever. After arranging to leave two men behind and promising to be back within 12 months Li had assembled all of the crews on her command ship, ensured all was well and the fleet left immediately for Orbsey. The same timing was the same as the previous three flights and soon they were home again in Orbsey, but this time with a big load of mainly Romans.

The warriors were just as easy to deal with as the trial run, as soon as they heard their families could be bought to them and they would have at least a 250 life span nearly all were very happy. When the calculations were done for all of the families the final count was another sixty thousand to come as soon as possible, but only after Li had done a trip of exploration to Xalafeu. Three months after the last trip to earth the probe was ready to take Li to Xalafeu, this really was a dangerous mission and one that would set the three worlds on a peaceful path, as it had been on Orbsey for two millennia or one that could degenerate into war.

XALAFEU ANOTHER WORLD:

This was a far more hazardous trip than the ones to earth, and Li was very aware of the dangers. Her ex partners Orlos and Coreum had decided to go with her, they were very wealthy men now and had millions of govt credits in surplus held by the Orbsey treasury. They weren't interested in the profits unless they could find another bonanza like Kauri Gold for that's what they had named the trees that had made them so wealthy in New Zealand.

Finally the Space Freighter was loaded, it was a far longer trip to Xalafeu and would take from 30-40 days by time they passed through three different galaxies and then to their destination. By time they had arrived at Xalafeu it had been a long boring experience, but Li would go on far longer voyages during her career as the commander for aliens being bought either peacefully or forcefully to Orbsey and she would many times face life threatening situations with the equanimity for which she was becoming famous. During her long career she was to bring settlers from another six distant planets to her home base on Orbsey, hers was a new career but a dangerous one.

When they finally arrived at Xalafeu they stayed high in the stratosphere for fear of being detected before they could land and take on the shape of the local persons. Li when she had landed and changed herself to the shape and understood the communication that were used by the Xalafeuns, she was ready to start work. The first thing was they seemed to have an antenna protruding from their foreheads, their eyes were situated higher in the head were quite large and they had a mouth and ears, the first sign they weren't as far advanced as Orbsey.

Their bodies were very thin and looked almost malnourished, which later proved to be a fact. The govt of this world was only interested in war and were spending all of its resources to that end. The dream was that some day they would conquer space and the tyranny of distance and were prepared to have force other worlds submit to their will, these things the Orbseyns had been doing but lacked the drive to wage war on others.

The only reason for embarking on a program bringing the people of foreign worlds to Orbsey was to learn all about them and to be able to ensure their world was safe not living in a fool's paradise. Li went carefully into the city but was uneasy all of the time, the people seemed to argue a lot and had no love for their govt, and she soon found that the greatest need was food, for hunger weakened them all. There was prime land in abundance, but everything produced went to the govt for redistribution that's where the profits were made. Animals for slaughter, and fishing fleets bringing in their catch, but all food had to be sold through govt controlled markets. Li spent time searching out the armaments factories and found them as being far behind Orbsey but pushing ahead. They had atomic reactors and the ability to deliver bombs over a maximum 7-8,000 miles no more, so it all seemed to be pretty safe for Orbsey so far, but Li was well aware of what her job was.

Having spent enough time searching out information and being ready to do a full report for the Orbsey govt she decided to beam up 1,000 persons, and wait for the safety of home to interrogate them.

It was a long trip home during which Li wrote a full report for the govt, but Orlos and Coreum were totally bored and were relieved to get home. They had found no gold or other mineral they could take back to Orbsey so it for them was time wasted, but at least that was their own decision not one made by Li for Orlos. They had said that Xalafeu was not anywhere near as beautiful as either Earth or Orbsey.

The Xalafeuns were bought home sedated because it was a long trip and it was a lot safer that way. But as soon as they were taken off sedation at the hostel that had been specially created for Li and her immigrants they became aggressive so Li ordered them sedated again immediately. It took another two months for these persons to be controllable without being sedated, but after they came right they were model immigrants and settled in quickly, with them the abundance of food was the main catalyst, all could never remember not being hungry. The abundance of food was something they found hard to believe, in Xalafeu only the wealthy could eat like they were being fed on Orbsey. The problem was they had families to get and that would be another 1800 people, plus it was still problematic how many Xalafeuns the Govt wanted to bring in total. That decision would be left to the govt but at first reaction it seemed they wanted as many Xalafeuns as they had Earthlings.

Li's report was well received in the Parliament, and the Orbseyns were so relieved to find there was no immediate threat, but the intent was to make sure there would never be a major threat, now they were alerted to a future possibility.

The debriefing of the new arrivals was quite slow they seemed far more suspicious than even the Roman warriors had been, but once they had settled down became very friendly. Their world they confirmed was a very hard one compared to what they now found to be the case on Orbsey. The leaders on their world were fanatical in the belief that one day theirs would be a superior culture, and all must be prepared to make sacrifices for the good of that future. Their world only honored the strong and the weak were considered to be a liability, which is why there are so many malnourished in Xalafeu.

One of their Scientists had recently discovered nuclear power and now they were trying to find ways to harness the power of the atom, but so far the success had been limited. There were over one hundred different countries on that world, but all were controlled by a central Govt; found necessary because of the constant war and bickering over the centuries gone by. Like the other Planets Xalafeu was mostly water but with less fresh water, so that water shortage was a constant threat and ways to control the problem were underway. Desalination was being tried and it seemed as if the answer had been found to the problem.

All agreed that there seemed to be a better standard of living on Orbsey, but they couldn't settle until they knew their families were going to be bought to live with them. It seemed that would be a bigger task than reuniting the Earthlings they obviously had bigger families, so much so that to bring them back together there would be over 2,500 new immigrants. Unlike Earth the risks were far higher, because there was no Pharaoh on Xalafeu to help them in return for lots of gold; Li was still searching for what they could bribe the leaders with.

THE PLANET CORRDELOO.

The Scientists had announced another planet, this time a little closer to home a big one almost as big as Orbsey, but not as densely populated.

Li decided she was going to take a trip to the new Planet and reconnoiter before deciding what they were going to do; this planet was in a different Galaxy than the others. But she only had to go through one system to get there; her position was now such that she could order up whatever Space Craft whenever she needed to help do her job.

The new planet was huge, just as big if not a little bigger than Orbsey! But it was quickly recognized as obviously if anything a little backward compared to Orbsey, but well ahead of earth. There were many great cities built and high rises covered the great city centers, but nuclear development was still in its infancy. It was easy for Li to identify the nuclear powered huge Navel ships that were big enough to deal with the violent waters, but they needed the mammoth size that kept them afloat.

Li and her crew did a trip around the new Planet taking photographs and film of the entire planet. There were ice caps at top and bottom a huge area of tremendously raging seas with very few areas that could be seen to be relatively smooth, most and possibly all were just as wild as, or wilder than the southern seas of planet earth. The land area was also very large and densely covered with bush and trees, but there were big areas that were being cultivated using fairly ancient style equipment.

Having gathered a lot of information from the air, Li was landed and with one other crew member had gone off to check the appearance of the people and changed their own appearance to make themselves able to mix in easily. A device had now been provided to Li that meant she and her companions could move from continent to continent and from country to country without having to have an aircraft. It was a simple device which enabled them to go to wherever they needed without any fuss and not having to call for help from their craft floating above stationery and waiting to ensure help was available if they needed any.

The persons living on this Planet seemed to be a happy well fed lot, they quite resembled Earthlings and Orbseyns in facial characteristics they had mouths and ears plus the tentacles on their foreheads like the Xalafeuns, but were completely hairless, this was a characteristic they had to themselves, on the other planets the natives were quite hairy; similar to planet earth. Their torsos were large and muscular but the legs were very short, the overall effect was that they were about the same height as the people on planet earth with a similar friendly appearance.

There were at least 12 medium sized continents with very few island type small countries, but that could just be an oversight created because of the quick assessment that had been done by Li and her assistant. It was later found there were a few islands but the hostile seas made them unsatisfactory to be heavily populated, these weren't in general a sea going people, but that was natural considering the constant high winds and violent seas.

Li returned home knowing there was no immediate danger from any of the Planets so far found but aware of her Govt; desire to set up local Colonies from all new planets found so the populations could be studied and a peaceful future assured for all of the people's not just Orbseyns. After her report had been handed in Li decided it was time to spend some time at home with her mate, family and their friends. She could have become a celebrity of Orbseyn society if she wished but had no inclination for fame of any type, she loved her job but she loved her husband far more, he would have only had to say, Darling I want you to be at home with me and she would have resigned immediately.

But Orlos never did once complain about his wife being away so much, he was well aware of her work and envied her not even a little, he knew it was a hard grind and was amazed at his mate's ability to physically continue the continuous grind of her work. The years had gone by and they were both over 100 YOA now in less than 20 years they could now have their first child.

Orleb the brother of Orlos was in his own home now with a mate, but their Parents weren't so happy.

The average life expectancy had been lifted to 300 now and the retiring age had been increased to 250 so they now had to work an extra 45 years. They both professed to have become very tired and a little depressed at having to wait so much longer to be able to stay home and rest.

The law in Orbsey was the doctors could and had to keep everyone alive until 40 years below the registered average, after that anyone could choose to live on or pass away it was their own choice, many just wanted to pass away life had become too boring at that great old age.

It was decided some colonists from the latest planet found, should be bought to Orbsey for research and then no more apart from populating the colonist numbers to the same level as the ones they had which was already a wonderful success. After that no more planetary work was to be done for at least 5 years to allow the research on the colonies to be completed.

Li was in full agreement with everything they were doing, and she was pleased this Planet was as close to Orbsey as Earth was, so the trips weren't so arduous it was only a matter of time and they would have been incorporated another local colony. First she went out and just bought back a full load of people, she just loaded up her Craft sedated them as they were being loaded then had them put into an unconscious state and came straight home. They unloaded them still as unconscious persons, then Li left it to her Dept to do the rest she had a holiday to wait for the reports that would come in quite quickly.

The reports about the Coordeloons were very positive, they would fit in very well with the Orbseyns, just as well as the earthling did but it was essential to bring in the families and fully populate their colony for them to settle down. They had not caused any trouble and seemed quite content apart from missing their partners a natural reaction; they seemed to like the earthlings and the xalafeuns which was helping them through their loneliness.

Their planet was a peaceful one which was a lot more developed than Planet Earth, but they were a Democracy of a type that was being attempted by the Greeks on planet earth. Their system of exchange was through the exchange of valuable metals the main one being Silver and Bronze from which coins were being produced up to very high denominational values. The size of the coinage was being disputed and the Govts of the bigger states were looking for better methods than the big and cumbersome methods they had.

Coordeloo was a highly animal powered society which was beginning to change and become mechanized, the inventors had successfully pioneered powered flight, but hadn't yet developed the source for the fuels needed. There were no horses such as dominated on Earth but there were other animals that had the same strength and courage and could run equally as fast.

Li had seen on her trip around the planet animals that looked a little like a type of camel, but they didn't seem to have become domesticated and just ran wild in the hot areas of the various continents. This was a planet way behind Orbsey but ahead of planet earth much to Li's disappointment, earth was a long way behind all of the planets so far found and she had hoped to find one more lacking in development than her own home planet, but so far it was not to be.

Li and her guards left with a team of the natives to pick up the families as promised and they took again four natives of the area from whence they had taken the first lot, plus they carried extra staff to go searching for the families they had to find. This time the collection of the families was very quick, and within three days they were on their way home fully loaded with their passengers lightly sedated just in case, but they were back on the ground at home within a week.

The noise and cheering from the impatiently waiting family members was intense and the excitement when they came together made Li's job ever so fulfilling. But as ever it was back to work, now the teams would go back on a single freighter and find enough who wanted to immigrate, but this time she sent an extra team because she wanted this area of her work to be finalized quickly just for now. The thought of a five year break away from constant space travel and strange countries was exciting to her, work had worn her down she needed that break.

The report that the full number of immigrants was ready came all too quickly, and once again Li and her guards were back in a space freighter going to another planet, but Orlos could see his mate was exhausted and he worried about her, she had been a mountain of strength, but that strength was fast running out. When the fleet arrived over Coordeloons she barely left their stateroom, Orlos took her place and settled the fleet into loading stations as was needed.

They were on their way back with 40 fully loaded Space Craft now and when they arrived, Li was immediately beamed down and taken home to rest, Orlos did the entire job including having the terminal cleared again to allow all of the spacecraft that couldn't land immediately to beam down all of their big loads. There was pandemonium in the terminal as old friends met so far from home, with the ones who had been in Orbsey longer telling the newcomers what a wonderful new home they had been lucky enough to find.

Back to Earth and Egypt:
It was now time to return to Planet Earth to bring the families of the

Warriors, who were starting to languish from not knowing how their loved ones were getting on without them. Li had been in touch with the two persons on Earth and they were nearly ready with 90% of the families found they asked for another month to find the rest. In the meantime Li spent time with her fellow earthlings all of whom were curious about how an earthling could have risen to such a high position in govt service. They had many questions and were so keen to get into the training program that Li was setting up, that Li had to ask for an assistant to help her, because the work load was so big. The govt. didn't want to prejudice her time spent on other planets and their scientists were almost ready to announce other finds so the immigration from Earth had to be finalized as quickly as possible now. It was expected that by the time she was next back from earth there would be another world to visit and bring back settlers from.

Word now came through that all of the families had been found and all of them would be ready to be reunited with their husbands and fathers.

Orlos and Coreum were both going on this final trip, gold had to be found for Pharaoh and they wanted a final load for themselves, there would be no future windfalls on any of the other Planets because the Govt had realized just how commercially valuable some of what they may find could be.

The trip to Earth was really anticlimactic and while the immigrants were being assembled the men were off to get the last load of Kauri Gold for themselves and Pharaoh; Li had decided to visit China by herself. Pharaoh had as usual been delighted to see them and was anticipating his new load of gold, but he was saddened that his Alien friends would not be back, he had hoped they would clear the earth of all Romans, he even said he wouldn't expect any gold.

Li's nostalgic trip to China was a bit heartbreaking for her, she visited the graves of her Parents and Siblings, she was sad that she hadn't been blessed like all of the immigrants she had to reunite with families now. It would have been nice to have all her family on Orbsey with her, but it could never be now, she was too late and she had a new family whenever she was home Orlos and his family had stood by her proudly as she has so quickly risen through the ranks of Orbseyn society, an accomplishment rarely achieved in their memories, and this by an immigrant it gave them great pride to think of their little Li as commander of the immigrants and the special fleet.

On her return to Egypt the men were back and Pharaoh was looking very happy once again, but he wasn't happy at the thought his friends wouldn't be back for a long time except with smaller craft on scouting missions only. The setting up of an earth colony on Orbsey would be complete and they would now let it grow naturally. The next day the gathered families were all beamed up on the Space Freighters and loaded, but only semi sedated these people were happy to be going back to their men folk it was a happy time for everybody, only Pharaoh was sad at the prospect of no more gold. Even Li reminding him he knew where the gold was and how to refine it from the trees didn't reassure him, no he said we won't get there the seas are too strong for the boats of our friends, and anyhow if we did tell them they would only steal it all for themselves. And so it was they left Mother Earth not to return for several years and then only on a research mission.

The return and landing at the terminal was an exciting time for everyone, the new comers had been told all about their new home before they had arrived, but even so natives from Orbsey were kept away to allow them first to be reunited with their men. The men were all in the terminal waiting and cheering so loudly that their families could hear the noise as soon as they were disembarking, that had made the occasion even more exciting.

Finally the big moment had arrived and Li led all of her charges out into the huge palladium that was used on these very important occasions, there were squeals of children calling dad and mother sobbing at being back with their men, for Li the best trip of them all.

For Orlos and Coreum to it was a very good trip they had bought back 4 tonne of gold for themselves a fortune indeed.

Visiting the Earthlings compound a few days later Li found herself a celebrity, the men had told their families how she was the one who had held it all together while they had been getting frustrated and angry. Li just laughed the praise off but said, "well I have done my job now it's time to do yours, the training in full will begin in two weeks and you will finally all be back at work but this time for the govt of the country of Cordiance on Orbsey."

The response she got was a loud cheer from all assembled and listening to her speech. Li knew it was now time to move on and concentrate on the Xalafeuns, they had been neglected for a short time but now she was ready to deal with their needs.

SETTLING IN THE XALAFEU COLONISTS:

First it was time for a two month furlough well earned and for the first week she did nothing, she and her husband had a second honeymoon with their love life as strong as it was at the start. Though they had been forced to spend a lot of time apart there was that very strong bond that had endured the years and the time spent away on Govt; work. The intensity of their love had been strong at the start, but had grown over the years so that now it was really over different time periods they had to spend some loving time for each other. Their physical love had always been strong and now had developed into warm soft encounters within which both were entirely satisfied. Their love making had always been regular and passionate; their increasing ages had certainly reduced the frequency but not the feeling.

They had two wonderful months idling at home and doing nothing beyond making love and occasionally making the marital bed, but mostly that was just pulling their bed together after a night of passion.

It would be only 20 odd years now and they would be allowed to have their first child and 30 years after that the second child would be allowed, but that was it no more, not even for valuable citizens like Li and Orlos. Their two months furlough was a time that they also caught up on family and quiet gatherings with friends. Orleb and his mate had their first child a son and they were very happily being quiet Orbseyns, not wandering all over the universe like Orlos and his wife, there never had been any envy from friends or family. The fact the couple was now the owners of huge Govt Credits still didn't attract any feeling of envy.

All too quickly the furlough was over and it was back to work, Li to her position in the Dept of Intergalactic Affairs, and Orlos back to his partnership with Coreum, but neither partner were highly motivated developers anymore. Li started first to settle down to examine the reports about the persons from Xalafeu which wasn't being as successful as the earth colonists were, they were far more aggressive towards each other and had demanded all sorts of extras that were being refused.

The concessions they had such as being well fed and housed, greatly extended life expectancy, were simply accepted as their right because they were superior beings, far in advance of the Earthlings and at least on a par with the Orbseyns. Unfortunately for them the general opinion of the Orbseyns was that the earthlings although not as advanced in their technology were superior to all but the Orbseyns and taken in the age or development as far advanced as the Orbseyns had been at the same stage in their history.

As a result the Xalafeuns were unpopular even in their small group, and it was being debated as to whether they should be sent home. They could be treated so there was no memory of what they had experienced on Orbsey all that needed to be done was to drop them off and then forget them. Li decided to face them and give them the choice, they could be returned home as soon as possible or they could be increased in number and also bring their families to join them.

There was an immediate heated debate among them; at present there were only 1200 of them, and their families hadn't yet been even searched for. On top of that there was the proposal to boost their numbers so they had the opportunity to become quite an influential colony on Orbsey; the earthlings weren't mentioned that would only have enraged the Xalafeuns.

After a week they came back with a list of demands that Li unilaterally refused, and informed them they should pack their goods they would be back home in no more than two weeks.

This response from Li elicited shouts of anger at which point Li walked out of the meeting with the final instructions to pack or she would have them forcefully sedated and loaded on board a Space Craft and made unconscious when they regained consciousness they would be back in a paddock in their own country on Xalafeu.

The police were sent to serve official notice and the recalcitrant men were told very bluntly they were no longer welcome on Orbsey, but now the mood was changed. They asked for a meeting with Li, this she agreed to but had a full unit of police on hand to ensure her own safety.

Li started the meeting by saying the Xalafeuns were now persona none gratis on Orbsey because of their arrogant attitude, and that she really didn't care if they stayed or left. What she did say was that like it or not Orbsey was superior culture than any of the worlds she had visited so far, and that they left at their own loss not hers she just didn't care.

Suddenly these arrogant persons were groveling and apologizing to Li for their own foolishness they wanted to stay with no strings requested and they did want to see a full and successful colony such as the Earth colony was. I never agreed at that point she said she would have to reconsider their request, orders had been given for a forced evacuation and she would have to try and get that order reversed if she could, but she gave no promises. As Li left the meeting the persons from Xalafeu seemed a very dejected group.

Li immediately called a meeting of her senior staff and the thoughts of them all were correlated to, for or against the request to stay. It was only by a slim margin the Xalafeuns request to stay was accepted but they were to be warned that any future misconduct they would be sent home without any hearing.

The Xalafeuns were requested to nominate four men to be taken home and given the job to bring the families together in 5-6 small groups to be collected by the Orbseyn freighters further they were to collect new colonists to come to Orbsey for settlement in a Xalafeuns Colony. There would be two Orbseyns with each Xalafeu to ensure the job was done properly, and when all was in place a fleet of Space Freighters would be sent to pick them all up. They were also told the trip was a long one millions of light years away, and could only be done because of Orbseyn superior technology. Finally if any of the men who would be going on the trip tried to play up their memory would be cancelled of all events concerning their visit to Orbsey and they would be dumped somewhere on Xalafeu.

Li was going to ensure all the new colonists were gathered up properly, but she didn't expect to work with the groups, rather she was going to spend time in the capital cities by herself just to learn as much as she could about these people because she needed to know.

When she told Orlos what was happening he asked if he could come with her. He was he explained tired of being by himself, and wanted to spend the time from now on traveling with his mate; and retiring from his partnership as a developer. His partner Coreum wasn't surprised; he had no need to work any longer and was interested in getting employed within Li's Dept even for a menial job, hopefully also traveling from Planet to Planet with Li's entourage. Both men were given positions immediately as guards escorting Li while she was on duty, this of course necessitated them traveling on all Li's space flights to the other worlds.

It was time to go to find the families of the Persons from Xalafeu, the four who had been nominated by their peers to find their families and help find more settlers were ready, and the space freighter with a cruiser and an extra aerocar aboard with the usual crew of four was ready and keen to leave. There was an extra eight guards on board to accompany the four from Xalafeu in their search first for the families and next for the new persons to be abducted. It was probable the new colonists would only be randomly selected as before and the families collected later, that hadn't been decided until Li made a decision about how many Space Ships would be in the fleet.

On arrival over Xalafeu the search party was dispatched immediately, and then Li, Orlos and Coreum left to see if they could find an official such as they had in the Pharaoh on earth. That had made things a lot easier, yet really had cost nothing because the gold was collected from New Zealand all it took was a little time and work. Li was doubtful they would be so lucky ever again, but she was still going to try who knows maybe there were gold producing trees in Xalafeu, they would never know if they didn't check. They didn't need an aerocar but they took one anyhow, just for the memory, but in the end they were quite glad they had it. They had as well the new method of being able to beam themselves from place to place, just by thinking about where they wanted to be and holding hands before they left going from one place to another. They could make long as well as short trips and didn't have to keep concealing the aerocar which made life a lot easier. It was only if they wanted to take with them something or someone with them back to their space craft that the aerocar could be handy.

They were soon in the Capital City of the biggest and most populous State, but like the persons everything seemed to be rather spartan for a world that had seemed to be quite well developed in a technological sense. They soon found looks were misleading and the advances as pictured by the scientist back in Orbsey were correct this was a well developed economy. The capability to produce nuclear energy and use it for war or production was well advanced but way behind what had been achieved on Orbsey.

The people were starved of consumer goods because all of the planets wealth had been directed to the nuclear development program. The subjugation of all of the countries in this world system was complete and none could act freely without full permission from the Central Govt, and they who didn't obey were quickly executed, there were no jails in this world you either obeyed or you died and there were no exceptions, except possibly at the very top.

Li's group travelled extensively quickly and found an array of different countries all totally in subjugation to the one at the top, none dared to make decisions of any type on their own, and this created an enormous beauracracy all ruled by fear. There was no way anywhere they traveled that they could find any independence of thought, the ruling emotion was fear, the population of the entire planet were fearful.

Li soon decided the search for any assistance couldn't be found by outsiders like them, better to let the locals do the job and just take the number they wanted there was no doubt now there would be plenty keen to go. They would get enough just from extended families of those who were already in Orbsey, for the first time in their lives they were free of fear and yet they had still tried to extract better conditions, these persons would be good immigrants for Orbsey.

There was no use searching any further, Li had done her job thoroughly and now she was prepared to take a load and go home, then come back with a full fleet to gather a full contingent for the new Xalafeu colony on Orbsey it would be a job well done!

On arrival back at the Space Craft it was still about another week before they heard from the search teams on the ground, they had the families of the present colonists ready to go, and by time the full fleet returned they would have the full contingent of 45,000 ready to pick up. The ones waiting were bought up immediately. Before she left Li warned they must only use thought communication as radio may be picked up and if found they would be executed as spies immediately, no question asked and no quarter given. In this way there could be no communication by radio from Orbsey, they should work to a program of the fleet being in place in six months, because Li wouldn't be using radio to give out any information which could put her own staff at risk.

The Xalafeuns when they had all been beamed up from the Planet below were very quiet and subdued. They weren't surprised or intimidated by the Orbseyns, they had been well exposed to their countries ambitions to be a leader among planets by bringing others into bondage, so another planet getting there first didn't surprise them.

They all appeared to be vastly relieved to be leaving and finding their male folk again, it had been desperately hard without them and they had been interrogated for months with fear of death if the males didn't return soon. The arrival in Orbsey terminal once again loaded with families was Li's triumph, and was a pleasure to see these tough males crying over their families was a deep pleasure to Li and her guards, but it was a long trip they would have a month off before they left again.

The trip back to Xalafeu was uneventful if long, but Li understood that without their unique thought propulsion they would never be able to travel so extensively like they did, so she was grateful for the speed in which they were back. As soon as they were within thought communication distance she was in touch with the ground crew, and very relieved they were all ready to load and leave, in their words this Godless world of death.

There was no time wasted as soon as they arrived the groups were beamed up and settled into the Space Freighters and they were on their way with one day they were heading back for Orbsey all 40 Freighters fully loaded and already into the next Galaxy, in other words out of reach of any retribution from the cruel leaders of Xalafeu. The arrival back in Orbsey was far slower as only five of the huge Space Freighters could land and unload at once, but suddenly Li sent out the order to beam them all down, and she had the terminals cleared of all other traffic it was that way all over in hours and the second colony was in place.

It took a further three months to settle the colony down, but that was up to her staff, Li had completed her part and glad she was off for a short rest at home.

CHAPTER 6/
LI PROMOTED:

THIS WAS TO BE after the two new colonies were fully settled to a similar size of the one containing all earthlings. The scientific community needed the time now to assess the future needs of Orbsey and in what direction Govt; policy should take. Should they just set up colonies similar to their native planets from which their newest immigrants had been taken of which the earth one was first, and really flourishing or should they just go into isolation and build defenses such as a nuclear proof cover over Orbsey and leave it at that?

The scientists and the politicians had disagreed so the military, small as it was were asked to contribute their thoughts, but they only added to the chaos. For the first time in two millennia there was confusion on Orbsey, so they decided to scrap all of the rubbish and allow the usual plebiscite to decide the future.

The decision confirmed that there would be no more planets from which colonies were to be developed for at least five years to allow the ones they had to settle down and their home planets to be properly researched as the planet earth had been. During that time the Orbsey foreign colonies would be bought up to the size of the earthling one and a new govt division had been created and would be responsible for working with them and settling them down.

Meantime the Scientists were to continue searching for new Planets that were peopled with beings similar to those already found. Each planet found the only work done would be an observation by Li or her staff. Li's work had been incorporated into the new division and she had been, with her own agreement, given the top job of Managing Commander responsible only to the Plebiscite of Orbsey based at Cordiance. Li was empowered to staff her division and ensure the usual schooling program was put in place because the future governance of space colonies was vital and must be fully catered too by people trained for the job over their entire life. This was the usual approach in Orbsey, when a new govt need was found outside the norm it had to be catered for at the present and schooled for the future by those who had the hands on knowledge to pass on.

Li certainly had the hands on knowledge, but so far she had had no problems since she had eloped from her little village in Central China, she had never been shaped in the stress of problems. Orlos had been her mentor and only lover from a very early age in Orbseyn time, she would have to prove herself in the stress of trouble in the future, but that was over twenty years away. At this stage of her life she seemed as if she just couldn't make a mistake, but she was still young with another 120 years of working life. She had been promoted rapidly because she had been the only one who really understood how to deal with the colonists and her career in the police training academy had been outstanding. But she hadn't done the years of training usually expected of those in high office in Orbsey and although she had been brilliant she was still very young.

But now her strength had run out the batteries needed to be charged up the Doctors insisted she take six months leave of absence and allow her staff to do the work. The three planets now had functioning colonies and they all had govt jobs she could pass the work over to Orlos and Coreum for those six months.

The report that came back from the Doctor was that Li had heart and kidney problems and she would have to be set up to have her body initiate the replacement of those sick organs and she would be laid up for 12 months. Medical procedures had to be initiated and the replacement organs must be started up to grow as quickly as possible because her old organs were well on the way to complete shutdown. This was because she was essentially of earthling origin and her vital organs had simply grown old. The new ones now being grown would see her through easily for the 200 years she still had to live. Even in her own body she was preparing the way for the doctors to know what they could expect from persons that had been brought in from distant planets, but it was a painful process as her own organs shut down and new ones were grown. Even on Orbsey the pain of kidney problems had never been beaten except by replacement.

By the time Orlos got home from unloading and settling down the new arrivals Li was in extreme pain and the growth hormones had been injected into her body so that the new organs could start to grow. Her old organs had expired from old age and would soon be removed, and then she would go on artificial help until the new organs could take over. She didn't need to go into hospital because there was none anyhow, but a day nurse would look after her and if necessary a night nurse would also be supplied. All other domestic help would be supplied but must be deducted from Li's govt credits; she and Orlos had far too many credits to qualify for free Govt aid. It didn't matter how high her position at her job was this was basic Orbseyn law and Li knew it all well as did Orlos, but Orlos cancelled all but professional medical help, he would nurse and care for his mate himself.

Within six months Li's new organs were working but were assisted for the time being artificially, the advice the doctors gave Orlos was that within another three months and she would be fit and strong and well able to work. They had now learned what had to be done to strengthen the bodies of the new Colonist so their organs would last for the full period without failure. It was well within medical knowledge to deal with the problems early and ensure that on the whole there would be few problems with aging organs in the future.

As the Doctor had predicted Li was back at work in another three months as fit and as energetic as ever, much to the relief of her family and mate. It had seemed to them for a while the earthling wasn't strong enough to live the life term of 300 years as was average for Orbseyns, but once again she had beaten the odds and won. Not only that, but she had set the example of how the newcomers needed to be treated because none of the planets so far found had an average life span of no more than 160 years.

By time Li had got back to work the three Alien Colonies had settled down and had each been separated to different parts of the state, and they each had different functions. The earthling were there for the training of the Orbseyns in basic military tactics, The xalafeuns were settled into Industrial developmental work and the coordeloons were settled into agricultural developmental work all meant to help in the further advancement of Orbseyn well being.

ANOTHER COLONY FROM PLANET EARTH:

While the preparations were being made for the trip to TeKahanui to pick up the new colony and the visitors Li decided to take a freighter to planet earth and pick up the new settlers as per the instructions that had been given her by the Plebiscite. She knew they could go and just take what was needed and then go back for the families, but she decided to go with one freighter and then order the full number of craft needed to bring back the full number in one trip. They were also taking fifty mixed men and women from the colony on Orbsey so they could go out and arrange the new settlers and their families. Once a full load was ready there would be forty space freighters needed to bring back the full load in one trip, the inter galactic flights was beginning to strain the fleet resources, so another ten new craft of maximum size were being built. The trip to earth wasn't so bad because it was a fairly short one, but trips in the future like going to Xalafeu with a six month return time would soon create problems and there were two planets of equidistant still to be explored by Li and her team so the new craft were desperately needed. Meanwhile the scientists had been instructed to go no further out than the distance they had gone, because beyond that the time and stress on the fleet was going to be just too much. Further they had been instructed that only another two from the ones they already had would be considered for the setting up of colonies. The trio had been asked to try and negotiate with the planets they had colony's with for leadership discussions, such as was being set up with TeKahanui.

The trip would collect gold which this time would belong to the state, Orlos and Coreum didn't care about that anymore they had both accumulated huge numbers of govt. credits which they couldn't use up anyhow. The privilege of being ambassadors for their planet was now more important than gold, and the two males were very happy with their positions most of which they knew was because of Li.

They left Orbsey two days after Li had decided it was time to go, they had the team of earthlings aboard. The agenda was that they would first beam down the earthlings to wherever they wanted and wait for them to signal they would be ready within one week. At this point Li would order forty space freighters to come to earth as soon as possible. In the meantime Orlos and Coreum would go to New Zealand in a freighter to pick up the gold, and spend some time with the tree spirits, and report on the wonderful progress of the kauri seedlings now growing strongly on Orbsey.

Li herself was staying aboard she was feeling tired, but also had work she wanted to do because at home there seemed no time for doing extensive reports, so she was going to work on that while Orlos was away. All of the earthlings now had the gift of languages and thought communication, and as well they all had the beamers to be able to move freely whenever and wherever they needed to go. It was almost a month until the new colonists were ready, by which time Orlos and Coreum were back with their load of gold and happy talk of their visit with the tree spirits. It took only a few hours after the fleet had arrived for all of the newcomers to be beamed up, and just to be certain all of them were lightly sedated for safety sake only.

Their arrival in Orbsey this time was just business as usual, they were met at the terminal by a lot of earthlings who obviously had relations coming and once again there were wonderful scenes of family reunification, which brought tears to Li's eyes.

It was decided by the trio to take another trip to earth before Li went into her two year period off work; they were going to take six earthlings with them to see if some form of representation could be bought from Earth to Orbsey. There was a need to get some form of agreement for earth to join the proposed federation of planets; there was a lot of doubt about that being successful, earth was the closest planet and yet the most backward, what was to be done. They were also taking a team to milk the trees for gold and to buy as much silk as they could? The VIP cruiser was being used and would now reduce the trip to six instead of seven days, the plebiscite was keen to have earth as a member because it was the closest to Orbsey.

When they arrived they went straight to New Zealand to the kauri plantation, Li stayed while the earthling and Orlos and Coreum went off to Egypt to start the search for leaders. They were also to arrange to buy any silk they could find the demand and value of both on Orbsey had sky rocketed very high. So far earth was the most backward in its development, but the only one that had sent products of great value to Orbsey. The kauri plantation was considered to be a great treasure in Cordiance and was already getting millions of tourists from all parts of that planet every year, the future when they were fully grown they were projected to earn millions monthly from tourists.

The persons that had been sent to get gold were hard at work, but Li was talking to the tree spirits much to her distress she was to hear a very sad story. The tree spirits were able to take on human form if they had one planted in their memory from previous visits an image such as for example Li had left an imprint in many female trees, but that was because she was human there was no imprints left by her companions on that last visit they had been Orbseyns and left no imprint.

The spirits if they had such an imprint could manifest at any time and could travel freely anywhere, as a spirit before manifesting in the shape in this case the young girl tree had Li imprinted on her memory. One of the young female tree spirits only 500 years of age had gone off to China and the taken on the image of Li; this was fine for a while, until she had fallen in love with a young man and so there was a tragedy in the making. The young man had also fallen in love and wanted to marry her which of course was impossible, but he wouldn't accept that and he wouldn't believe she was really a tree, all he could see was the women he loved and he insisted they be married. Sadly the spirit had to admit she loved him too, but that didn't change the truth she was a tree spirit and could never be a real human.

The couple was really upset, even though she was 500 YOA in kauri tree terms she was younger than her lover, it was all a real disaster but she could never be a permanent human she could only stay in her shape for twelve months at a time, then she had to come back and look after her body the huge tree that she really was. Then she couldn't manifest as Li again for another twelve months, she could keep doing this living a double life but her human lover had to be without her every other twelve months. He was insanely jealous and didn't believe she was really the spirit of a tree he believed she was going off with another lover and was causing a lot of problems for her. At this time she was in China with her lover, but the twelve months were nearly up and she would have to return any day soon. In China the tree spirit who had kept the image of Li was with her lover and they were trying to part as she tried to explain once again that she was an alien.

"But my daring I have now told you so many times I am an alien and have to return every twelve months to my tribe far away, why can't you understand and accept that? I have no choice I have to go and you just have to believe that I will be back in another twelve months, look let me show you I will change for you now and you will see its true what I have been telling you," so saying she manifested and became once again just a spirit.

But Yuan had seen this many times before even though she now became Li's image once again he just ignored that and still kept insisting she stay, "I love you so much and I cannot live for twelve months without you, if you leave me again I shall kill myself and I won't be here when you come back, I don't believe you, there is someone else and you only come to drive me crazy with my desire for you. Oh my darling I love you, I love you, I love you and I cannot live without you, life is terrible without you I cannot bear it again it's just too much, leave your lover please and stay with me, I beg you stay with me, what does he mean that I don't can't you see how I feel? Yuan was prostrated in his grief and she was so sad, but there really nothing she could do. If she didn't go in a week she would be taken away anyhow, by the other tree spirits, but worse they would be very angry with her, because her tree body would suffer gravely if she didn't appear of her own accord. There was absolutely nothing she could do she was really a kauri tree spirit and that would never change probably for at least another 2,000 years.

Being a little more firm she now said, "Yuan I have always told you the truth I am an alien from another world, I have to spend 12 months out of every 24 in my own country why cannot you accept that? I have always told you the truth. I love you deeply my love it's not my choice to go it's my tribes, but there is none other than you, and it will always be that I can only be with you for the time I am telling you. I love you I really do and I would never be unfaithful to you in any way but you have to know that when I go it's me as well as you that hurts and that will always be so. I am just as hopeless as you if only you could come with me and stay with me while I have to live as a spirit, but it is far away and I cannot take you, then you will see that all would be well with us if only you could get there, but you cannot. You must always believe that I love you dearly and if I could I would give up my other life just to show you just how much I love you?"

"Why can't you just stay with me and forget that being a spirit, they can do without you, but I cannot, if you go I am going to kill myself because I cannot wait for a year, it's just torture here wondering how and where you are oh my darling I love you so much my life isn't worth living without you?" Yuan cried again.

"If I don't go the tree for which I am a spirit will suffer greatly, its body reaches to the stars higher than you can imagine, but after twelve months it starts to suffer. Perhaps next year when I can get away we should try to find our way to our country then you could be with me all of the time, what do you think of that my darling? We should have done that this year but we were too busy thinking of ourselves so now we have to wait. But the trip will be dangerous, do you want to try? It is a long trip to the ends of this world and the seas are dangerous but with me guiding you we can make it, what do you think shall we try?" she asked.

"Yes I will gladly try but first I have to get through this twelve months that will be harder than any long trip, oh I love you , I love you, I cannot live for another twelve months without you it's impossible I shall just kill myself to get out of this misery. I know you must go and that you are really a spirit and have no choice, but that still means I shall be alone for twelve months, no its better if I finish this misery my love, but just remember I will always love you wherever I am."

The next morning when she awoke she couldn't wake Yuan up he had swallowed some type of poison and seemed to be dead. As she was trying to wake him she got a slight groan and knew he was still alive but only just. Using all of the spirit skills she knew she was able to bring him back to life but he was horrified, "why didn't you let me go he cried I don't want to live, I will wait until you are gone and just do the same thing again, oh my god I just love you so much I will not wait another 12 months I will do it again just as soon as you are gone?" The spirit was at her wits end what shall I do know she wandered there was no use arguing, so she left and did the journey to were the trees were so she could draw up a map, then she returned to Yuan.

"If while I am away you have a map to where I am do you think you could find me?" She asked "because if you can we can be together forever." Finally looking at the map Yuan brightened up, "I will follow you to the ends of the earth if I know we are going to be together forever. I love you so much I would do anything and if I die trying to find you it will have been worth it, just having that dream makes it worth everything my love for you is so strong."

And so it was settled she went back to her kauri tree and Yuan started to plan his trip to New Zealand which would take more than 12 months anyhow. When the spirit arrived back in New Zealand she was surprised to find Li there and her team from Orbsey they had just finished milking the trees for gold.

The spirit confessed her problems to Li and said her lover was trying to find his way to the kauri plantation which would take him over twelve months anyhow, but eventually he could live in the forest and know she was always near. Li agreed it was a real good solution because she couldn't change into a human since she had run out her quota, she offered to pick Yuan up but the spirit declined he would only be fretting for me every day, better he should spend the next twelve months trying to find his way.

Li had agreed but promised she would track Yuan from Orbsey, and if he got into trouble would have one of the Orbseyn colonists chase him and keep him safe.

The spirit was really happy with that because she knew it was all her fault she shouldn't have let the situation gets out of hand. She was after all a spirit that would live for over 2 -3,000 years the situation had become ludicrous, but it was too late now she really loved this common human being who at best would only live another fifty years. The next day the cruiser was loaded and they were ready to leave, there had been no possibility of leaders with enough power to speak for the entire earth, just before they left Li had an idea.

Going to the forest of kauri tree spirits she asked if they were able to travel to Orbsey and keep a human form, they agreed they could and would be happy to go there if only to see how their seedlings were getting on in their new planet. Li said no more but said we may be back in a couple of months to take about 50 of your spirits back to our world for about a month, she stressed they would only be away for about 5 weeks at most, with that the trio and the crew left for home.

True to her word Li kept a trace on Yuan and monitored his progress which didn't seem to be going very far, but he was trying very hard.

Li had decided to carry on with their plans to have their first baby, and if there was to be another trip to earth the Orlos and Coreum would lead it without her, for her it was time to be a mother and nothing was going to change her mind now. She had decided there was no reason she shouldn't keep a track on Yuan in his efforts to find his way to his hopeless love, she knew it was hopeless but she wanted him to arrive and not to lose his life in his efforts.

Yuan had walked firstly down thru China and slowly found his way to India, and was trying to find his way down through the subcontinent. He had serious problems trekking down through China but he was having far more trouble in India, first he had been attacked by Muslims, then by Hindus, but still he managed to make record time. Then he got down to the Indian Ocean and after that would have to deal with wild South Pacific, it was a daunting prospect but it never dimmed his memory of his love. All he could ever dream of was his lovely spirit day and night he kept himself going by saying to himself, oh my daring I am coming I will find you either that or I will die in the effort.

Oh my darling I love you so, I am coming my darling day and night her image was in front of his eyes he dreamed of her every night and woke up whispering her name. And so it went on he had now been travelling for six months but had only walked to the Indian Ocean, but how now he wandered how I shall get over this ocean and then the rest. Finally he had worked and managed to save enough money to buy himself a boat, even though he had never been in a boat in his life. He watched the boats coming and going until he figured he knew what he was doing, and after thinking for two days of his much loved spirit girl he launched himself into the sea in his flimsy craft.

Since he was still alive after two days he considered he was doing well and Li thought so as well as she watched him sailing along the coast, but he will never get to New Zealand she thought. Taking pity on his poor efforts Li then contacted one of the leaders of their colony in Egypt and directed him on how to find Yuan and propel him secretly to the shores of New Zealand. But she asked he be taken to the bottom of the North Island so he would have to walk right to the top; and would arrive just about when the twelve months was over.

This was done and Yuan thought he was being propelled by the gods, and then when he was shipwrecked on the shores of New Zealand he was certain the gods had saved him. He had arrived in New Zealand down at what was one day to become Wellington, in June, the weather was cold and he had almost one thousand kms to walk, but he was in heaven he had made it to the land in which his loved one lived. He had been traveling now for ten months soon it would be time and his love would be with him and they would part never again would she have to leave him to go back to her tree, because he was going to live at the base of that tree and be with her evermore.

He began his long walk northward ever northward dreaming and thinking every day about his lover and knowing he would soon be with her. But he didn't make it on time and his love came out of her body, the kauri tree and she went looking for him. She went back to China he wasn't there, then she followed his tracks all the way to New Zealand but she couldn't find him, then one day Li up in Orbsey looked down and realized what had happened, but she didn't worry because she thought Yuan is safe they will find each other soon but she was wrong.

Yuan was close but he still had to go through a mighty gorge he was only

200 kms away, and his love was close behind him when he got lost in that gorge, but he wandered for days until he collapsed in exhaustion still thinking of his love.

Still as he lay in the underbrush he was thinking of his beautiful tree spirit, and he kept whispering oh my love my love am I to die now I am so close to you? I have wandered far and the gods have brought me here. Am I to die here my love but if that be the case I will die happy knowing you are so close, and remember my love when you find me my last thoughts were of you? And so she found him only two days later he was really dead this time there was nothing she could do, but bury him where he had died.

She buried him after two days of being with him then she went back to her body the kauri tree only 200 kms further north and for many years she thought of her human love and every year she went to where he had died and stayed with him for a while. And she always remembered and said, oh my love you will live with me in my memory for thousands of years you will never be forgotten, while I still live I love you so if only you could have waited, but my love you would only have lived for fifty years, but you will be with me for thousands of years.

Meanwhile in Orbsey Li and Orlos were celebrating the birth of their first baby a son they named him kauri, in honor of their friends in New Zealand.

Great Kauri trees of NZ for Orbsey:

Li had read the report about the spirits of the kauri trees in New Zealand and was intrigued, so much so that she was considering going back to earth in a small cruiser to see if they could get some of the seedlings for transplanting on Orbsey. Her investigations about how the silk farming was going encouraged her thoughts greatly, that industry had taken hold and was flourishing. They had bought silk back on their final voyage and the ladies of fashion wanted more in fact all they could get, but it would be another two years until the industry was in production, and a hundred years before they had enough to satisfy the market. The production of pure golden rings and other adornments had also caught on in the shops so a full load of gold would quickly be sold out, now at far higher prices.

An inter galactic cruiser could bring back about six tonne of gold and silk as much as they could get, which wouldn't be that much weight even if they managed to buy the full seasons crop. The markets for all consumer products were very strong on Orbsey and credit values high if they were not controlled by the state govt. which both of these products weren't. Li had passed her thoughts on to Orlos and Coreum and suggested a private voyage could be profitable if they cared to do the investigation she would support a private trip, but they would have to hire a cruiser and pay all credits that would be due to the govt.

Within a few days Orlos and Coreum were back both very excited at the prospect of a trip to earth, the cost of the trip had been confirmed and they had managed to pre sell the entire cargo so it was a very viable proposition. They would take a team of ten including the flight crew of four plus themselves, and three extra men to help with harvesting the gold and silk.

The hiring of the fully equipped cruiser was arranged and they had been lucky enough to get the best in the fleet, which would be able to do the trip and carry back the gold easily. Li was going because she wanted the seedlings of the kauri trees, and she wanted to meet up with and talk to the tree spirits, that had been so well described in the report she had received. Unlike the big spacecraft the cruiser could be landed on its cushion of air wherever they wanted so they had gone straight to New Zealand and landed within walking distance of the trees. The crew had left a guard on the cruiser and come with the party to see these giant trees; they were all greatly impressed by the forest giants.

Li, Orlos and Coreum had left soon after to go to China and other Asian nations buying silk and silk worms all they could get, but the worms were too difficult for the smaller cruiser to transport as well as the gold so they managed to buy only the silk material, but got quite a large quantity much to the men's delight.

So now it was back to the trees and collecting seedlings for the govt; which of course what Li wanted, but she also wanted to spend time with the tree spirits. Because she had read the reports Li knew what she was listening for, and sure enough when evening fell the tree spirits came down and were talking as the previous team had described. Li sat and listened for a while, but she soon understood they were talking to her so she answered them, "we are she said of the same race of persons that spoke to you just a few months ago, do you remember we are back again as you know collecting more gold?"

"Yes we do remember and we are delighted to see you, for how long are you staying this time and how much gold are you going to collect of us?"They asked. All of the Orbseyns had gathered around and all could communicate with the tree spirits, for the spirits could read thoughts just as fluently as the Orbseyns could, "why we are staying for about one week, but we want to know more about you great trees. We want to take some of your seedlings back to our planet for we know they will grow there just as well as you are doing here. I want to know how to look after the little ones so that they can grow to be huge like you are, but we want you to give us advice so that we nourish them properly and put them in the right area?" Li said.

"Why that's wonderful we are so happy that some of our young will grow up in a new environment we have been here for so long, the thought that they will have a new home is a dream come true for us. Do you know we are the oldest living of any species on earth except rocks and I have no doubt our species on your planet will be just the same, the longest living by a long way? Some of us here are over three thousand years old, but we the oldest are getting weary now and our hearts are starting to wear out, you can tell which of us are getting weak by tapping on our trunks and it will sound hollow, that's because our hearts are wearing out inside. One day a heavy wind will come and I will fall over said one, but my spirit will move to one of the new trees and the cycle will start again, so it has been for five hundred thousand years.

"Well why don't some of you manifest as beings looking like us as you did last time and we can enjoy some time together it will be so nice, do you have some girl spirits this time they can manifest to look like me," said Li with a laugh. All of a sudden there were over a hundred tree spirits standing around half looking like a variety of the males that were watching and the other half all identical to Li. "Well here we are they all laughed half of us are male the other half are females, the world thinks we have a boring life just standing here immobile but it's not true, what is seen are our bodies our spirits can only be seen when we want to be seen as we are to you now," they all smiled in unison just to show they were happy to have bodies even if foreign ones just for a little while.

That evening and late into the night they all had a wonderful time, the Orbseyns had musical instruments and the spirits loved to dance and showed they had a great sense of fun. The Orbseyns always loved to party so they had all had a wonderful time for many hours, but gradually the eldest of the tree spirits grew tired and one by one vanished, until they were all gone and the party was over.

The next day when she could hear the tree spirits once again Li started a conversation with them by herself the other persons were off collecting gold. "How long will it take our seedlings to reach maturity or at least full size?" she asked first. "Provided the conditions are right they will be mature in 100-150 years, but the soil must be right and there needs to be plenty of rain as we have here," was the reply.

"And will they travel all right in our space ship, do we have to do anything special to allow them to travel easily?" she asked.

"You need to take plants that have matured and have their young spirits, without that they will wither and die quite quickly, we live for at least 3,000 years so there is nothing if we don't have a spirit to relieve our boredom of standing in one place," they replied. "But it's best if we choose seedlings for you we know the ones within which their spirits have grown well." "There are thousands of your species here how big a colony must we have to start with?" Li asked.

"We need at least one hundred healthy seedlings to be together spaced the way we are here, as you see there is no room for other life around us as we eat up the entire nutrient in the soil and none is left for others. Because your people have the gift of languages you trees will flourish and in time you will have a wonderful colony of trees, but you must not over milk the resin for gold. You cannot take what you do here for a long time, here there is a huge colony of very old trees we bleed anyhow, so from us you are taking nothing," was the reply.

"I notice there are huge quantities of solid nuggets on the ground here, why cannot they be turned to gold, is there a process we could follow because really you are gold producing trees?" Li finally asked.

"No we aren't not really what you are harvesting to us is just our normal life cycle, we bleed constantly this resin you call gold, its only that your tribe has accidentally found how to convert it to gold, we didn't know that ourselves until your first group did it. Normally the resin just bleeds out of us and flows to the ground then makes lumps, everywhere which gradually gets buried with time, the same as we ourselves get buried after we die it's all just a matter of time." LI finally asked, "Are you all happy here as you are now, or would you like to have a different lifestyle?"

"To be honest you have shown us a new lifestyle, we can go anywhere and take on the characteristics of the people surrounding us and join in the fun if they are having fun, no we are indebted to your people you have shown us a new way of life. After all if they try to hurt us all we need to do is change back into our spirit and move on, we are looking forward to trying everything. One day we can be Romans, another day Egyptians, thanks to you and your kind we will have a great time," and they all cheered for Li.

Li was incredulous what she wandered had they set loose on planet earth, a host of spirits from thousands of these giant kauri trees all the original natives of New Zealand. Over the rest of her life Li never forgot that night celebrating with the tree spirits as they did that night, but little did she know the future chain of events she was to set loose on the planet earth, not to distant in the future. Nor could she know that in less than 2,000 years her wonderful trees would be destroyed by man while her seedlings on Orbsey had become millions of protected giants that were marveled at and loved by the citizens of Orbsey, but not for their gold. Li had allowed the secret of how to make gold die, neither she nor her mates wanted the trees to be used as gold making giants, they loved the NZ Kauri for their majesty not their gold.

The trip back to Orbsey was by now just routine and nothing special happened, but they had a very valuable load the men were triumphant that their first cargo from a foreign planet had been so fruitful. They quite forgot it had been Li's idea in the first place, but she didn't care she had what she wanted 500 seedlings complete with their baby spirits for replanting in the state of Cordiance on the planet of Orbsey. A huge area of land ideal for the growing of these massive trees was set aside and the 500 trees planted Li had enough land so that in the future there was room for over one million of these magnificent trees to be growing in that one big plantation. They were on this planet forever more, to be known as Li's trees never was there such a wonderful memorial to one person, a true pioneer for her planet earth.

The two males found their silks sold out in no time with the persons of stature and credits clamoring for more and the gold bought them both enormous credits sitting in the treasury of the state of Cordiance treasury, but sadly for them earning nothing they had to find ways to spend their credits but how?

Li had settled down and was busy dealing with requests from her migrants who thought of her as their mother even the xalafeuns wanted to know if they could see Li the earthling. The colonies were all doing well especially the earthlings and the corrdeloons; the tendency of the xalafeuns to distrust everyone was destructive and tended to isolate them even from the Orbseyns. Li quickly found these peoples were best left to their own devices unless they started to cause trouble then she would interfere with and warn them they could always be sent home. That threat always shut them up for a while until they started to forget and get obnoxious again, finally Li called a meeting with them and gave one final warning, and she had decided that they weren't worth the trouble they caused. She told them if they didn't stop causing trouble they would be all sedated and sent home and they would have no memory of where they had been or anything about Orbsey it would all be cleared out and forgotten. They all knew that on their planet that could mean death for all of the men, so from that time they had started to behave sensibly, but their previous behavior was never forgotten by Li and she filed her full reports to be on record for her successors.

The earthlings were doing very well with their military training program for the Orbseyns, but they were just a trifle to physical and were having to lighten the training schedule. The antique weapons being used were a source of much hilarity even to the Romans, but the program was achieving what the govt; wanted a toughening up of a big group of their citizens so they would be ready if ever needed. There was now over 1,000,000 Orbseyns in training, but the aim was to have close to 5,000,000 so there was a long way to go, and possibly a lot more earthlings needed unless Orbseyns could be used as trainers, but at this stage this option seemed not hopeful. The earthlings had called for another 250,000 trainers from somewhere not necessarily earth but of a similar hardy type that would help reach the govt target.

With families this would mean at least another 600,000 immigrants, not a real problem now but only the Plebiscite could decide that many so quickly, even if it was only a small number by Orbsey standards. The following instruction came down to Li! She was to double the earthlings by just taking what they wanted from the battle grounds of earth, and she was to settle full families into the earthling colony. She was to follow up with just searching the other worlds the scientists had found to see if there were warrior types they could take and bring to Orbsey, when the scientists were ready to process more immigrants on Orbsey. If she could not find what was needed then the corrdeloons were to be transferred to working with the earthlings. Time to complete the program was given at five years.

Li looked at the diagrams of the three new planets that had been found and decided to take a month's break to think about the planets and study the profiles she had received from the scientists and their probes.

Working with the colonists:

New Govt Dept. of Colonists affairs had been created; and so far the only members were Earthlings and Orbseyns. In spite of the immense gap in understanding, the two groups seemed highly compatible; maybe a sign of the millennia ahead during which earth's technology might develop very fast.

The groups were made up of little fellas up to 10 YOA then from 10-20 and 20-30 when they all went out to their first 45 years training jobs. Orbseyns were encouraged to bring their young people and in this way help with the integration, it was explained the dept. would help both ways the Colonists to get to know Orbseyns and the Orbseyns to get to know them. Very quickly clubs sprang up all over the state wherever the Earthling Colonists were living and they quickly became a great success.

Every facility for the young was provided by the Dept. and of course being young they started to get to know each other very well. Obviously it was the mothers who spent most time at the club, because the fathers were working very hard and only came when they had work breaks. Very quickly the little ones were playing and getting along beautifully, the older group was taking more time but it was working quite slowly. The oldest group where more inclined to want to hang around and flirt with each other, the mothers tried to break it up but they didn't get very far. The Orbseyns and the Earthlings found their respective opposites very attractive, and it was obvious that in the years ahead there would be a lot of mixing. This wasn't frowned on by the authorities nor parents so the future for social integration looked positive.

Naturally because the level of social understanding was so much higher on Orbsey, special classes had to be held for the earthling parents, so they could have a better understanding of the culture they were now part of. It was always stressed that they could go back to earth at any time and they would be treated properly, the only thing was they would have no memory of Orbsey. What they had learned would be in their subconscious and would occasionally keep popping up much to their own surprise. A new education program was being set up for the graduation of pioneers of the future. The first period would be the study of the planets and travelling with the space craft just as spectators, but bringing back comprehensive reports of all the planets they visited.

The second term would be managing the affairs of Orbsey when it came to trading with the new planets in the distant future; these would be the future diplomats of the planetary system. The number of the young in the close to thirty age group were applying to join this new program were quite a surprise several hundred including earthlings had applied. The rule then came out that all who wanted to join this diplomatic core would have to become naturalized Orbseyns, and in the case of colonists that would include their entire family. The idea was to enrich Orbseyn society gradually obviously there was a big gap in the educative quality of the earthlings compared to the locals but that would be rectified quite quickly as the education system kicked in to the advantage of the young earthlings.

Very quickly the earth colonists were applying to be naturalized, the parents in the hope it would be great for their children and grandchildren. None were turned down they were a very healthy bunch of people and Li and her team were so happy to see their program turning out to be such a success.

As was expected a lot of romantic intercourse soon developed, 99% of it was across the planetary divide, one young couple both 30 YOA in particular made it plain they wanted to enter into the Orbseyn style of marriage immediately. The girl Desha by name was adamant she wanted to be married and wanted the Govt payment to buy their first home. This was refused on the grounds that her husband to be, Anthony the son of Roman parents, wouldn't be eligible for two years. Desha and her parents where extremely hostile to the govt. decision Anthony and his parents as Colonists decided they were best to keep out of the argument, they just agreed to the union between the two.

Desha's parents where quite prominent in their community and she was determined to create the maximum fuss about their refusal. The govt maintained Anthony had only been in Orbsey for 10 years and naturalized for only three. Since the law said they must both have been citizens for five years before qualifying for the money, she had to wait for another two years to qualify. Desha asked when the law had been written into the constitution and it was admitted it was only going through parliament now and would be law within 6 months. Then the real fuss started because 10 young couples stepped forward wanting the same as Desha was asking for. All of the proposed unions had been propagated by members of the clubs that had been set up, and as a joke they became known as marriage clubs as more and more interested in permanent unions became obvious.

The normal age to even contemplate marriage on Orbsey is 30 YOA when the first serious career job is started and schooling is finished. Until this age the young normally live at home with their parents, until it's time to set up their own home, but if no union is being considered then the young stay at home with their parents. The young cannot cavort around and try to keep secrets from the parents, because the truth is at this time hard to hide all the usual signs apply whether for Earthlings or Orbseyns, daydreaming, from the peaks of joy to the depths of despair, being obtuse without meaning to be, and all the new communications of a highly developed society constantly being used by that one member of the family.

A sure sign that there is an interest between youngsters is when they suddenly start blocking out their thoughts, they will normally do this to several of the opposite sex in their own group, this is so the interest isn't to a particular party isn't so noticeable. If the interest is mutual then it quickly becomes obvious to the two involved that there is a growing attraction and the two start to get closer. At this stage the only one privy to each other's thoughts are the two involved, if it has developed this far a full scale romance is quickly in full bloom. In this world of romance the earthling parents are of no use to their children all they can do is sit and watch, but the Orbseyn parents are well aware of what is going on, and are fully involved. The mating up with earthlings is attractive, because although they are backward they are obviously extremely virile and will strengthen any family's gene pool. The Orbseyns are so far ahead of the earthlings, they know the effect of the interbreeding and they know the only reason the two peoples are different is the enormous period of development that has advantaged them. The earthlings on the other hand no nothing, all they know is the lustful mating that is the norm on earth and they think of little else.

When Desha first saw Anthony at one of the clubs of integration she knew she wanted him for her own, she didn't want him to know that so she blocked her thoughts to all but her parents. Then she kept watching him to see if he understood her world at all or if they would be misfits, she was delighted to find he was quite knowledgeable in the Orbseyn ways, and well integrated.

Next she integrated herself to a group he was in and pretended she hadn't noticed him, she kept her thoughts locked up, but Anthony didn't understand all these feminine wiles and his thoughts were quite open. Anthony was thinking, gee she looks nice, but she wouldn't look at a colonist like me, she is one of these charity types who want to help us integrate, I wish she would go away she is distracting me very badly?

Desha was delighted she went to two more meetings and locked up her thoughts, and just kept reading Anthony's thoughts which of course were very unfair, but she was a woman, after all. Anthony was thinking wish that woman would go away she is distracting me way too much and I can't think properly. So finally Desha let her own thoughts free, but Anthony wasn't trying to read them, so now what was she to do? In the good old fashioned way she made a pass at Anthony, and at the same time she was thinking gosh he is nice wander what his name is.

Suddenly Anthony caught on and was reading her thoughts, it was on at last girl meets boy and they like each other. From then on they were inseparable they couldn't see or feel enough of each other for the next three years they were never out of each other's sight. Both lots parents could see there was true love in the air and were happy, now Anthony's six siblings became a nuisance, the only big families on Orbsey was Colonists, but in their turn they would be restricted to only two children. At all times night and day the young couple would be in touch with each other, as soon as they woke up their thoughts would link, then what they were at work they were linked with each other by thoughts, this was fine so long as it didn't interfere with their jobs, then they were forced to switch off their thoughts immediately and stay off until the end of the day.

They were constantly seeking privacy and going to small intimate wine and dine restaurants which seemed funny to Anthony since Desha only had to think of the menu to have what she wanted, but there was always an intimate corner for dancing to the modern band. Then they both turned 30 YOA and decided they were getting together, they both had good jobs and Desha couldn't see any reason why they couldn't get the Govt grant. For a while it was a lone journey as only Anthony and Desha kept chasing the Govt for the money on their own behalf until quite unexpectedly there were others wanting to do the same thing. All of the earthlings were in the same position as Anthony having completed their education and now in their first careers, some with big families some with small but all naturalized for over three years.

There was an immediate reaction on the intermedia networks that led to an uproar Orbsey wide, why the people were asking are these people being discriminated against. We stole them from their homes now because their children want to intermarry with ours they aren't good enough. On and on it went the argument developed huge proportions, the people couldn't be stopped and the govt was being pilloried daily for its insane insensitivity.

Polls were held and most showed at least 70% in favor of the young couples being allowed to get the money and go through the Orbseyn style marriage immediately.

The earthling parents were really surprised at how quickly their young were becoming integrated into their new home, but the parents themselves felt lost it was just all too much for them. One minute the fathers were in the military on earth where life was so cheap now they were living a lifestyle that seemed like it was all a world of fanciful dreams. Each morning father awoke to find himself lying in a bed beside his wife, and his wife would awake and for a few moments wander who this bloke was in her bed. From sleeping in tents almost always in full battledress to sleeping in a proper bed it was unbelievable, and before now seeing his wife maybe for a week each year thy now actually lived together. All of the earthlings loved their new home but couldn't help but wonder how long this new life would last, all felt it was only temporary and the Orbseyns would send them home.

The debates stormed on and on, why bring these people here if we don't want to look after their children same as our own, if they aren't good colonists send them home, but don't create second class citizens of their young. Finally one of the earthlings who had been of a high rank in a Roman Legion spoke up in exasperation. I can understand he said that we the parents aren't great settlers, it's just too much for us to grasp and we feel lost, but our young are integrating as we could never hope to do, and we are grateful for the better life choices they have been given here on Orbsey. It would be better to be full citizens of earth than second rate citizens of Orbsey so our family suggests you send us home and provided we don't get executed for desertion let us go back to our old life. He stressed he was speaking for his own family only, but he was aware that many colonists felt the same way, either treat us as equals or send us home.

This really set up an uproar, why is this happening people were asking is it true we stole these people against their will from their planet earth, sedated them and bought them here, do we really now want to treat them as second class citizens? What are we going to do with them now and how do we get them back safely? The uproar was really amazing, and the govt was being challenged for its lack of concern for these people who they had bought so far from their home planet!

Finally after 12 months of controversy the Govt agreed to release the funds to the young couples of mixed heritage just as Desha had asked for. This was a belated victory for Desha and Anthony, who under the old conditions now had only nine months to wait anyhow, but they celebrated with hundreds of other young couples all of whom now qualified for the govt money, and all who were of the earthling half; now felt they were real citizens of Orbsey.

Now that the young of the earth colonists were finding their way, it had become obvious the parents were unsettled, so because the earth settlers had in fact been stolen and then persuaded they were safe and had a new home for ever. They now had to be encouraged and somehow made to feel safe and made to understand they really did belong and would never be let down. The problems were many but all reasonable, 90% of them couldn't feel as if they belonged, everything was just so confusing.

The transition from an ancient culture to a highly developed one was for most of the parents traumatic. At home they didn't even have radio, now they had instant access to all the wonders of an ultra modern technological age and most were still apprehensive of what they were being shown. Their youngsters who were up to 20 OA when they arrived had adopted very quickly, now in their early thirties, they were totally assimilated and most were marrying Orbseyns of the opposite gender.

The younger ones were totally at home and comfortable, as far as they were concerned this was their home and earth was just a distant memory. But Mum and Dad well they were totally overcome, it was just too much for them to conceive of, back home their fastest locomotion was a fast horse, now they had cars which only the bravest would drive and only their children seemed willing to even try and learn. This in spite of the cars being self driven, all that had to be done was sit in the vehicle, enter on the control board where they wanted to go then sit back the car did the rest, but for those who had only ever ridden a horse even this was frightening.

When they had first been abducted and sedated for the journey their emotions were just too unsure of what was happening, then when they were put to sleep it was easy that's all they knew, until they were awoke on arrival at the Intergalactic Terminal. It was such a fright to wake and find beings working on them and asking them to get up and walk off the huge thing that seemed to have bought them to this new place. Apparently they were now prisoners of some type of being and even though these beings were far lighter in build they seemed to be controlling their prisoners easily, but they were also very friendly. The instincts of the men were naturally aggressive, how could they escape from this bondage, but when they first got sight at the real Orbseyns they were horrified. No mouths no ears how could they hear and at least they had no mouths to eat them.

Then when they were finally in their especially built compounds until homes were available, they had a group of visitors, the leader a woman looked Chinese and she had some men with her that look like ordinary earthlings, quite encouraging. During their period of being sedated they had seen these people, but now the images weren't blurred by the drugs and they could see and understand quite clearly and so they listened closely to what they were being told. First they weren't prisoners or slaves they were free and in a free society, and they could go home if after staying for a while they didn't like their new life. The Chinese woman Li, explained she was from Central China and had been living on Orbsey for almost 120 years, this bought a gasp of amazement but how old are you and how long do people live on this world, they asked.

"In Orbseyn terms I am now 144 YOA and my husband (pointing to one of the men) is 160 YOA we will both live to be 300 YOA unless we want to die sooner, that is our choice?"Li said.

The visitors, taking turns, then went on to explain where they were and what their condition was, all stressed they could go home if they didn't like this new world they were now in, and they would be landed were they had been taken from in the first place. The visitors agreed they had been stolen, but in recompense they would get a new home and vehicle as well as all the furniture needed, and if after five years they still wanted to go home then that wish would be granted without question. The visitors stayed for three days until there were no more questions being asked, then after explaining how to make contact with them they left with a very friendly attitude being expressed to and from all of the colonists present.

But here after some twenty odd years there was the need to reassure the colonists they were indeed and wouldn't be forcefully and in fact couldn't be forcefully sent back to earth because they were now naturalized Orbseyns, which didn't seem to be understood by 90% of the parents who came in for counseling. The clubs were now providing a full counseling service to answer any and all personal questions asked, and were staffed by older more understanding staff. All of the Colonists were now adept at communicating with thoughts so the meetings were normally quite quick and easy, the ease of understanding was very simple and there was no time wasted trying to find out what the other party meant. The main problem was with the men, why they asked are we teaching these modern people the old arts of war as we know them what use will it be now or ever.

Well the truth is our men have become too soft and we need to toughen them up, and we also want to introduce a way of forcing these men who owe money to the state to work off their debt and become worthy citizens. Our aim is to set up a system that will continue on even after the earthlings have graduated to other jobs, we hope you leave a base behind for the future when the system will be run by Orbseyns. Did you not know that all of your inductees are heavily indebted to the state; this is how we are hoping to improve this class of men and turn them into worthy citizens of our planet.

This was enlightening to the men and they felt much more able to contribute to their new society which of course made them happy and by extension their wives a lot happier as well. Gradually over the years with a lot of understanding and encouragement the earthlings were making a place for themselves in Orbseyn society; it was hard work but as deeper understanding of what their new lives meant gradually all of the earthlings were settling in and becoming as one with their Orbseyn friends.

We need only remember how backward earth was in comparison with Orbsey to realize why the parents would have such a difficult transition, they went from a horse and buggy lifestyle to being able to travel at supersonic speed any time they felt so inclined.

CHAPTER 7/
THE ORBSEY DEBT TO EARTH.

THERE HAD BEEN QUITE some discussion within the Govt of Orbsey because it was known a large credit account in favor of planet earth had been run up and the difficulty was how to pay the bill. There had been the young kauri trees that had been bought and a new plantation started the silk worms and mulberry plantation which had created a new fashion on Orbsey for the wealthy, these mainly from the pacific rim countries. Recently there had been spices from the Indus Valley and India and of course gold unrefined from New Zealand.

Now suddenly the Spirits of the kauri trees were asking for some type of payment, not cash but ways that could be used to benefit earth and help them advance as a planet with a future. So far earth had been in every way except virility, far behind all of the other planets, which made them easier to be used and little given in return. The tree spirits were only speaking out because the realized there was nobody else from Earth who could do so except Li and they were asking for her help.

When Li explained there were already discussions in the Orbsey parliament about the problem and how to help earth without doing any environmental or any other type of damage, the trees were happy, but when she asked for suggestions they had no quick answers either. The main suggestion was education of the young, but how were they to do that without causing a fuss among the leadership of each area.

The idea was not to take the young too far ahead but to keep the education at an acceptable level, but any attempt to get too close to the young of any group of people would be rejected. Certain groups of people understood education, like the Jewish sects had educated their children for many years; the Egyptians were quite good as were the Mexicans or Mayans. The Chinese were considered too brutal, as were the Romans and the Greeks who were the leaders in educating their children.

A lot of conjecture followed about just taking school age children to Orbsey educating them for two years and then sending them home. This sounded quite a good idea but they would lose all of the memories when they were sent home anyhow, and what about those who didn't want to go home the whole idea sounded good, but had to many ifs and buts. Memories of their education would be in the unconscious state and pieces would keep emerging that would make these children different, in the end the whole idea was abandoned until some way could be found to help Planet Earth. The major way was education but how? That was the big question and even the oldest Tree Spirit had no answer to the problem, Li had several meetings with them and they couldn't find an answer.

Finally it was decided to approach the Romans, the Egyptians and the Chinese to ask if they could set up one major school in each area, they guaranteed the teaching wouldn't be subversive to the leadership of each area in any way, and it was stressed they were Australians with advanced teaching techniques that they wanted to share with the world. When asked where Australia was they told all who wanted to know it was a huge continent far away, but that the teachers had the means to travel back and forth. When they asked how much they were to get for allowing the land and building to be built, Li simply said we are here to help your children and in so doin help you why should we pay you gold as well.

In the end it was agreed that if the schools worked within two years they would pay one tonne of gold for each school and that would allow them to run the schools for 20 years without interference. But if they didn't work within 2 years the project would be disbanded and the Australians would leave without paying anything.

Finally it was all agreed between the parties although on earth back in 100 AD the idea of contracts was unknown, only a shake of the hand was made by Li and her fellow negotiators to seal the deal. Not such a great idea for the Orbseyns but quite normal for the Earthlings.

Li had come to earth on her private VIP Aerocar specially fitted for her and Kauri, but he had stayed at home to study he had ambitions that one day he would have his mothers job which he thought was real easy, one day he would find out the truth when his mother was worn out and his father wasn't far behind Li's job was one of the toughest on Orbsey, the only one who couldn't see that was her son.

Li went home to Cordiance and met with the govt; she explained there was a way to pay the earthlings but she needed a Colony of 50 Orbseyns plus their families. Li went on to explain everything that had been set up on earth and also said she had called the Colonists Australian so there would be no trouble with aliens. And she also stressed the 20 years of teaching would mean that the debt to earth would be fully repaid, further she confirmed she had had forensic accountants check the figures and she had signed confirmation from them that all her forward projections were correct. She also stressed she was still trying to find a way to grow the Indian spices somewhere on Orbsey so far the future for that industry wasn't good, but her dept; would keep trying. She noted the Indian spices were very popular on Orbsey, again only amongst the wealthy.

It would not take long to set up the temporary colony for earth, this had become a favorite subject among the local Orbseyns, especially when they were told there were four periods of five years each they could sign up for whatever term they wanted from five to twenty years. Before sending the colony to Australia Li sent Coreum and Orlos to see how the construction of the schools were going, they reported back things were progressing quite well and there would be five schools ready within one month.

It was now time to move the teaching staff and their families into place, there had to be administrators, recruiting agents, a team to set up the homes for the Colony on earth, gardeners to bring the dessert around their new home into full production.

All of these details had to be attended to by Orlos and Coreum while Li watched closely from Orbsey the many pieces falling into the jigsaw puzzle until in her view all was ready. Finally all of the pieces were in place to the standard LI set so it was time to go, and the loading of a giant space cruiser was ready. The starting team consisted of 1,000 teachers, 500 other trades and 250 set up team. Li and her assistants believed this number would need to be doubled within 12 months and that would be the entire commitment to pay the debt to planet earth, certainly it was the only way Li could see to clear the debt.

Everything was going very well now, the teachers were all approved by the Orbsey dept; of education, and a type of delayed program had been developed for the ancient culture of planet earth. It meant the teachers all had to dumb down to what to them was a very low level of education program. In many ways this was far harder than teaching at home in Orbsey and it took a lot of serious discussions for some of the teachers chosen to really get the hang of what they were trying to do. The idea was trying to introduce the concept of school for the children of the poor not a particularly popular concept at all on earth in those days. Education was only for the sons of the wealthy who had no entitlement to an inheritance or some members of the churches who were again manly scions of the wealthy with no inheritance chances.

The schools had been going very successfully for two years and the fee of one tonne of gold for each school had been paid. Unfortunately the idea of educating the Sons of the poor was difficult for the aristocracy to accept, from the start the schools were for girls and boys, but this had created uproar and had to be changed now it was boys only. The rulers in the different areas were soon asking why the wealthy weren't included in the rolls, and soon they began insisting they were to be included. This demand was quickly refused on the grounds that the schools were owned by the Australians and they had paid pure gold to run the schools the way they wanted to for the next eighteen years which was what they intended to do.

The Roman reply was they would do as they were ordered to by the Senate or they would be moved out and the schools burnt to the ground.

The Australians replied that they would seek redress from the Senate because of the Emperor breaking his word, and if they had to they would try and defend their own property.

Li had met with the tree spirits and explained the new problem that had come up, and they had told her they would field for defense only 200,000 troop to defend the school properties. And how she had asked are you going to do that what happens if they are all killed in the fight? This created a great deal of laughter among the trees, and how they asked are they going to kill us we are spirits, we cannot be killed nor can we kill we would only be there as a bluff, but if someone calls the bluff it will all be a big laugh.

And so it was all set up The Romans sent out a small legion to destroy a school, but when they arrived there were over 200,000 troops waiting for them showing not one iota of aggression but looking to defend the school if need be. Looking rather shocked the leader of the Romans sent back for more troops but instead was told to withdraw until further notice.

One of the Emperors warrior sons then came to the school and asked, what are you people doing do you intend to refuse entry to the Emperor.

Yes if he is going to destroy the school after all we paid him a tonne of gold to be here now he wants to evict us is that Roma justice if it is then we don't want to be part of it, because that's not justice especially after he gave his word. A week later the envoy was back with a message that the Emperor had realized his mistake and his word would be honored, there would be no more attacks on the school. There were no problems with the Egyptians or the Chinese they never wavered from the agreement even though their aristocrats and the Egyptian priests caused trouble.

There was a school in an area controlled by Germanic Barbarians and this school was the most successful of the lot, the parents were keen to see their sons educated and they had no aristocrats. Finally there were the Mongols they turned out to be a heap of trouble in every way, first as soon as the school was built they wanted the tonne of gold, they wouldn't allow the school to start until they got their gold. Li refused to pay until the two year start of point as agreed was reached so the school sat there unused for about 20 months. After that they wanted the school to pay the parents the right to teach their children, Li was indignant in her refusal and accused the Mongols of having no ethics which they thought was very funny. Finally the school got started and then they threatened to close it down again, so once again Li called on the tree spirits to bluff their way through for her or at least try.

On the day designated to take the school over there suddenly appeared 200,000 troops outside the school grounds in a defensive formation. When the Mongols arrived with 5,000 troops they were totally shocked, but that was only a small part of the shock they were going to get that day. There was a quick withdrawal and then they were back with 100,000 cavalry troops ready for a fight and they attacked immediately. It was almost funny every time they killed one of the tree spirits they simple popped up again and kept fighting, soon the Mongols were completely dispirited what sort of enemy is this they asked we have killed 50,000 of them but there are no bodies on the ground and no blood. There are more of them there now than when we started to fight them and they seem to be getting more, we kill one and it just goes pop and there he is again what are we to do?

The Mongols called for a halt to the fighting and asked to see the leader of the school forces, what is happening he asked as soon as they arrived, the more we kill the more there are what does this all mean. Well the truth is we are protected by our Gods because your leadership has been unfair, you may kill us all but we will still all be there and able to fight it may take us a long time but we will kill you all in the end because you are wrong and have tried to beat the work of our Gods so it's up to you, keep it up it doesn't bother us just know, this you cannot win?

Well what can we do asked the Mongol leader?

Just withdraw and leave the school in peace and we also will leave, then in eighteen years time you will have the property back, and we will take our school somewhere else, but we will never bother you people the Mongols again. Remember this of the low numbers we have killed of your people and the high number you have killed of ours, the blood out there is only the blood of your dead not ours, because ours aren't dead. Now the choice is yours let us know because we want to go home, not stay here protecting a school set up for your children.

Without further hesitation the Mongol leader said yes we will withdraw, you are right and we have been unfair so you Gods are protecting you goodbye. The victory was complete and as agreed there was no more problems from the Mongols, the Romans now anyone else for the balance of the years that had been agreed would clear the Orbsey debt to Earth. When the time was due to finish up with the schools, at the request of the various leaders the Orbseyns stayed for another twenty years. After that it was left up to the teachers to decide what they wanted to do, but transport was provided for many years whenever there was a five year repatriation of staff home to Orbsey and another team going out. The whole program was an entire success thanks once again to the little Chinese girl Li and her fellow ambassadors Orlos and Coreum.

The tree spirits were delighted that was a wonderful success they told Li even if it only advances earth by six months it will help to improve the lot of the poor people. One of the older spirits predicted Earth would be in two millennia equal to most of her peers except those at the level of Orbsey. Meanwhile for the present as another put it, earthlings will continue to kill each other in big numbers, even if only with sticks and stones, best they not have all of this modern technology, they would wipe out their entire civilization very quickly.

Li decided to take one more trip to Earth to visit the tree spirits to see if there was anymore Orbsey could do for Earth, but they were all very happy. You have done a great job for your home planet they all chorused in unison, but earth needs to stand alone now all you need do is ensure a proper accounting of any products taken and any credits Orbsey has due to it in the future, this way a future will grow as earth develops. They will never know how much help they have had but so what? The future will tell the story, but don't forget to visit us now and again for the sake of what we have done together and also letting us know how the Kauri plantation on Cordiance is getting along.

Xalafeu: chapter 8/
Religion and Politics on the Planets:

I I GAVE INSTRUCTIONS THAT as far as possible it was time to work out the different religions and political systems practiced by the different planets.

She knew that on discussing this topic with most of the different peoples that this was a vital subject so she determined to do what she could to facilitate unity for all, but she was very careful not to support any radical ideas such as what she discovered was the case on Xalafeu.

This was a culture that worshipped animals each State having a different one they worship above all others, but they place the animals worshipped in other states further beneath the ones their home state worshipped. Animal rights were practiced in huge pavilions and the animal belonging at the head of that state would be worshipped as if a true God.

But the religion or worship of animals came down to a religion based on fear, if the crops failed or some disaster happened it was because that god was unhappy and person sacrifice was made to appease that god. Each State has a male animal of magnificent size that was at that time the living God, when that animal died there was one to take its place, but it must have been sired by the animal that had died.

Even if the new animal was but a calf it was still worshipped as a god and must be sacrificed to if it showed any signs of displeasure. The priests decided if a god was unhappy and chose the victims for sacrifice, these were normally beautiful young virgins taken straight from their homes to be prepared for sacrifice by the priests. The entire planet was under this strict religious code and the annual sacrifices were numbered in the millions. The monthly attendance at worship for these animal Gods were compulsory, but rotated so the worship sessions were actually weekly.

As well as giving up their young for sacrifice a monetary tribute had to be paid, this money was to pay the priests for looking after their living Gods. Any that didn't pay could be certain they would be required to supply a sacrificial child or self, very soon after not having paid their tribute.

There is one country that has defied all others and believes in one in one true God the creator of all things, this faith only survives because it has been in existence for thousands of years and none are prepared to deny its divinity. Most of the countries on this planet are Dictatorships but they must answer to the plebiscite that apparently has the final say there is no voting for this parliament and the leader is there for life. Only when the leader dies is there an opportunity that an outsider may take their place. That leader also controls all political practices, but like all of the Federation members they have the Eye in the sky which is all pervasive and it is hard to say who really controls this planet.

Within the agreement that was signed by all of the planets was a codicil that no human sacrifices may be made in the cause of religious or political agendas so at the time Xalafeu had agreed to stop all sacrifices of any type, and to control the priests who were so destructive towards the people.

EARTH:

There are a lot of different religions but none controlled by an entire planet philosophy; this was probably because there was no single world power, such as is the case on planet xalafeu. There was a great power the Roman Empire, and there was the Chinese, Russian's and Indian's but none have an all embracing spread, because there is still a lot of that world unexplored or only slightly developed. There were many different types of religions, Pagan, Jewish, Animist, Shinto, countries like Egypt, China, India, Sth America, had lots of, different religions some of which like the Aztecs could be called one which dominated the state similar to Xalafeu.

There were many instances of the people being held in thrall by religion, but life was cheap anyhow on earth and couldn't be just be blamed on religion, the overall concept was the state and religion were separate, but in many cases religion was perhaps more influential than the state.

A new religion was starting to find voice a breakaway from the Jews but its founder had been murdered and his followers were being persecuted by the State. The Jewish faith has survived for thousands of years in spite of persecution, many breakaways had occurred over the millennia, but they survive in spite of this because they are strong in their own faith. There are many different types of leadership but war generally decides who or what is in charge in the different countries.

ORBSEY:

Orbsey is a planet where freedom of religion is law strictly enforced over the entire planet. There some simple rules that are applied at all times and disobedience is harshly punished on any who would break the Freedom of religion is guaranteed but gatherings larger than 20,000 adult persons are forbidden big meetings are deemed to be gathered for the intention of bringing together a mass for religious or political intrigue; this applies to private as well as any public place.

The law of sedition applies if there are any who aspire to be leaders of any groups over the number of 20,000 members and would have political or religious ambitions. It is illegal to work with more than one group of persons with a particular religious or political ideology. If there are any problems for persons with a grudge against State, Country, Continent, of Planetary at any level there is a special dept created to hear such problem.

All individuals male or female have equal right, up to the International court of appeal, and if found to have a genuine problem all such actions religious or political are free of charge. Any actions taken deemed to be frivolous is liable to severe penalty, by way of deductions from the Govt. Credits. If no credits are held then they will be deducted against the nearest relations.

If there are none from whom fees may be collected then the person will be automatically transferred to Govt employ and his future credits garnisheed. If the present employer objects then the fees so demanded will be automatically transferred to the said employer. Orbsey is in a class of its own among the members of the group, but again it is hard to decide who really controls the planet the Eye in the sky or the plebiscite. The laws are rigidly enforced even the death penalty when it is the penalty the sentence is carried out normally within at most seven days.

CORRDELOO.

This huge Planet at this early stage is thought to be bigger than the size of Orbsey but has only a population of 8 billion persons. The freedom of religion applies in general but in some of the least populated states there are strict local controls and country religion is enforced within those countries.

The priests try to imprison the population into a type of religious bondage, but the state does monitor what is happening within their population and no religion is allowed to dominate. There is a pantheon of different gods all with a great canopy of priests trying to find adherents to their faith, but most are obviously very self serving. Collections are taken continuously to nourish the priests and keep the gods happy, but many feel it's to nourish and keep the priests happy.

The politics are a great mixture of differences throughout this planet, but there is a central govt; which controls any disputes within the different countries. In spite of being so big there is an air of goodwill among the inhabitants and they have no fear of priests, and other often malevolent forces such as on some of the other planets.

There is a huge unused land mass, not because its poor quality but there are just not enough people to get out and develop it so there is plenty of opportunity. Many have advocated an increase in population by all means possible, but most Corrdeloons like their planet just as it is, and see no reason for change. This was especially before they were in danger of attack, but now they had a fleet of 150 nuclear war craft closing in for the attack; at this stage their self confidence were badly shaken. But when it was announced the attack fleet had been destroyed by defense missiles from Orbsey the effect was, dramatic the whole population were in strong support of the Federation that had been the vehicle that had saved them from takeover.

The omnipresent Eye in the sky is here too but because of the huge land mass doesn't have quite so much influence as it has on most of the other planets.

THE PLANET TEKAHANUI:

This planet had been waiting for Li's attention until after the five year break was over, but now it was time to move ahead again, it had been a nice break with no interplanetary travel and the team were all now rested.

This planet named by its peoples TeKahanui was bigger than Orbsey and had been evenly populated, it would take about three months to reach, and from appearances was highly developed with all the evidence of nuclear energy being used but not for weapons.

The persons were rather squat in appearance with big trunk very short legs and arms with quite a large head. The head looked strange with a fish like appearance of the mouth and eyes and they appeared to breathe through their very large ears, because they had no nostrils. Although they had strong antennae protruding from their heads straight up, so perhaps that was the source of their breathing? The planet seemed to be very heavily populated and there was an abundance of obviously farmed animals that looked similar to the animals seen on planet earth.

It appeared the first planet for Li to go to would be TeKahanui mainly because of its nuclear capacity; the Plebiscite of Orbsey wanted an extensive report as quickly as Li could travel, there and back. She had decided to take the biggest Freighter in the fleet because she was going to bring back a full load even if only to get a true picture of their planet, but if it worked out then they would set up a colony just as they had already done with the three other planets.

They had a cruiser in the load out bay plus two Aerocars so they were well set up for exploration, they could have once again dropped off and could use their beamer to move from place to place. Orlos and Coreum were of course going as security for Li, but they were hoping to find products that they could sell just as they had from planet earth for them it was just business, but for Li it was her job, and she would do it to the best of her ability as usual.

It had been a long boring trip to TeKahanui but finally they were there and Li and her two escorts were ready to be beamed down to the planet, they were floating really high because this was a nuclear powered planet and they must be careful, they had to be sure not to upset anybody just yet anyhow.

As soon as they had been beamed down the three of them noticed the big difference, the air was clearer than any of the other planets they had been on including Orbsey, Li's first thought was how is this done it's like a clear spring morning on earth. They quickly found some of the locals and changed themselves as well as getting some quick practice with the language. They had landed in a paddock just outside of what seemed to be a medium sized city, and they were quickly right in the hub of the busy area which seemed to be a business one and they were highly intrigued. These were certainly the ugliest of the persons on any of the planets so far with their fish like features and strong antennae on their heads looking very different. As they looked at each other in their changed form it was hard for them not to laugh, Li thought ugh but said nothing. Orlos and Coreum were not so polite they both burst out laughing and said, "my goodness thank god we won't look like this for very long!"

Orlos pointed at Coreum and said, "gosh you are so ugly mate have you had a nightmare?"

Li decided they should go to another country and into the centre of a major city to get a real look. They bad arrived within seconds and found the situation there the same as in the smaller city, persons bustling to and fro but not seeming to achieve or do much, so again they left and went to a farming community.

This was far more interesting the animals were much like those found on earth it was obvious they were used for domestic purposes and also killed for eating. There was what appeared to be cows and horses as well as sheep and goats, there were even chickens and turkeys, they were all different in shape and look than the animals on earth but the similarity was very plain to see, Li of course was delighted.

From there they went to an industrial complex, from which they soon learned the prime source of power was solar and nuclear energy, all of which they were able to walk around quite freely there were no locked gates. Li wanted to go back to one of the cities because she hadn't noticed the solar complexes in the high rise buildings, but they were there every building had its own power source, and when they had a look in the suburbs they found every home was solar powered.

Li had made up her mind she just wanted to take a freighter full of the local persons find out more and then decide if they should set up a colony, but these people sure were ugly and may have trouble in their world, but who knew. They signaled to the freighter to be beamed aboard then they simply beamed up from a military establishment 1200 men sedated them and started the long trip home immediately. The men were kept unconscious all of the way, they looked to ferocious to take any risks with until they were back in Orbsey, if nothing else they could question the men and if necessary send them home again, but Li was in for a few surprises with this lot they weren't at all of a temperament that they looked like. She was about to realize they had some of the most intelligent persons ever and the most versatile.

When they finally touched down and the first few new comers had been revived the first thing they did was change their appearance to those around them. The next thing was to listen to the thought language of the Orbseyns and they immediately started to communicate with them fluently. Then they listened to Li as she deliberately spoke in her Chinese mother tongue and they understood and replied in the same way, it was all very exciting.

Li then asked if it was safe to bring the other back to consciousness, this was greeted with hilarity by the TeKahanuins, we are a peaceful people they laughed we may look ugly to you but to us we are beautiful, but they will all change immediately to look like you, why don't you try. Just as they had been told as soon as the rest had been bought to consciousness they changed and started to communicate by the thought language of the Orbseyns.

Every person at that awakening was just amazed, it was as if a new happening had arrived and the new arrivals really charmed everybody. Li for her part was very happy but at the same time disappointed, there would be no way she thought any of these new persons would want to stay on Orbsey, but she was pleasantly wrong.

When the blaze of notoriety they had started had calmed down Li had a meeting with them all, at the govt facility. It turned out that before they made up their minds they wanted to know more about this planet that wanted nothing but peace, because the politics of their own planet was exactly the same. If this was true they wanted to be ambassadors to their own world, because for many years a philosophy of peace to all peoples no matter where they lived had been taught, and the belief in eradicating all war was a professed aim of all countries within their planet and it was all starting to work.

They had been given the information they wanted and within 32 hours had asked for another meeting with Li. They were they said very impressed with Orbsey it was obvious this planet was far ahead of their own and they wanted to know how they could work with Li and her dept to bring an agreement between their two planets. The first thing however was to bring back to Orbsey their families and while there try to start initial talks between the two planets, they could barely contain the feelings of excitement that pervaded them all.

Li decided to start her discussions with the Orbsey Plebiscite and get permission to start discussions at top level of the govt. in teKahanui when they went back to collect the families. She had been warned their own govt would want to have a colony of Orbseyns settle in their planet, but that would be at this stage only a supposition on their part. Li had the full permission to speak for Orbsey and accept the exchange of colonies if that was required, but naturally they weren't to offer the exchange unless asked for. It was also stressed that first she must be certain that the planet teKahanui was a peaceful one that would be a good partner in a future league of planets that was now being considered by the Plebiscite that ruled Orbsey.

Before she left the members of the Plebiscite asked for a meeting with Li, they wanted to make it plain to her what they were starting to see as a possibility. First they thanked her for the wonderful work she had done then they asked if she was happy with her job, after all they knew she could earn three times as much in private industry. When she replied that credits were of no interest to her she worked because she loved her new country Cordiance and her Planet Orbsey, even if they paid her nothing she would still want to do her job to the best ability she had.

Having been reassured by Li's answer they proceeded to tell her they now had ambition of setting up a league of planets to ensure peace for all. They believed theirs was the most advanced planet and as such, were in a position to negotiate with others and to be the promoters of such a program. They wanted to have a league with ten different planets and Li was to be their initial approach to the leaders of all of the other planets, but another two were to be appointed to work under her management while negotiating for Orbsey.

Li's answer was that she had two business persons who she would like to work with her, Orlos and Coreum, she pointed out that these two persons had been to every planet and understood them just as well as she did, whereas others would have to be trained from the start. She also guaranteed they would do the work for the planet not for the credits they could earn, that would never be important to any of them.

After three days Li got a letter from the Plebiscite agreeing to the appointments as she had requested, but seeking guarantees that any commercial profit opportunities would be allocated to the govt. treasury. This was agreed to by Orlos and Coreum and contracts were signed with the Cordiance govt ensuring that any commercial profits that could be earned from any planetary activity would be owned by the state.

And so it came about that the three originals that had started out as a triumvirate in that long ago trip to earth were now joint ambassadors for the planet Orbsey. Before they left the two families celebrated together their future work for the betterment of all in the planets and the hope the work would be good for all peoples of any race.

Before they left the trio met with the teKahanuins and asked if they would all like to be taken back to their homes, because they were quite happy to take them, but much to their surprise all expressed a preference to stay on Orbsey. The group offered to send with the trio some representatives of the group who would happily introduce the Orbseyns to their govt representatives and help find their families to bring them back to Orbsey when they returned.

They took with them a group of four teKahanuins who would first make the introductions and then while the trio settled down to negotiate a peace and cooperation treaty the four would arrange the families to be ready to go when they left.

As soon as they arrived over teKahanui the seven were all beamed down and now the reverse happened they all became as if they were teKahanuins both in appearance and speech. They went immediately to the govt. buildings in the biggest country and asked to be allowed to meet with the senior politicians because they were aliens from outer space, but the four locals introduced themselves as citizens of the planet TeKahanui.

A quorum of officials was quickly assembled and was very keen for extended talks with the trio from Orbsey, but they wanted the top govt officials to be in the meeting. For that reason they asked if the strangers would enjoy their hospitality for two days while the leaders were bought from other countries to ensure all were in agreement. Li had presented their official papers from the Plebiscite of Orbsey so the officials of any and every planet would know they were authorized to speak on behalf of the planet as a whole.

They were given two guides and were also given complimentary accommodation for as long as they stayed, and because the guides couldn't be beamed everywhere as the trio could they were also supplied with govt. vehicles that were similar to the Aerocars of Orbsey. For the next two days they had a wonderful time travelling through the country they were in quickly and efficiently, and anything they asked to look at they were welcome, there appeared to be no secrets even from aliens such as themselves.

They were impressed with how developed the country appeared to be, they had nuclear and a lot of solar power that was sourced from two suns that appeared to be in the sky almost perpetually. Like Orbsey they had a 32 hour day, but only 6 hours of night which was very well lit up by the number of moons that circled the planet 32 hours a day.

The cities had plenty of light and there was lots of entertainment for which the persons all seemed to be addicted so that even when the suns were down there were lights the entire city was all lit up. They visited farms, art galleries, museums and lots of industrial complexes including the ones generating nuclear power, which according to the guides they had had for several hundred years. But all too soon the call came to attend the Parliament the next day and so it was time for work, the lovely but too short holiday was over.

They were greeted in the hall of assemblies very formally by the prime minister and introduced to all of the senior politicians of the country. They were given the respect they were entitled to as representing the Plebiscite controlling the planet Orbsey and then they all got down to serious discussion.

Li was the first speaker as leader of the trio from Orbsey, and she stressed they came in peace; theirs was a peaceful planet looking for partners who also wanted to develop peace in the various galactic spheres. Li spoke of the high level of development on Orbsey, but that the big advantage they had gleaned over the last millennia was to defeat the tyranny of distance. They stressed that although TeKahanui was millions of light years distant from Orbsey and that even travelling at the speed of light it would take thousands of years to travel the distance between the two planets, they had just done the trip in three months as their own people could attest.

There were gasps of astonishment when Li made that statement, but smiles of encouragement when she outlined the truth that Orbsey had no weapons of war, not even hand guns were produced anymore on Orbsey, only relics from a bygone age were still around. After Li had spoken for about two hours, Orlos took over and explained the agricultural economy and then Coreum spoke of the industrial achievements of their planet. All told the trio from Orbsey spoke for about five hours by which time it was time to break for lunch, and they would resume in two hours time.

The food on teKahanui was very palatable to the Orbseyn palate so the trio ate heartily and well, they were at the table of the prime minister and his deputy and a most convivial pair they were. The thoughts of the trio was all complimentary to their hosts, but they had forgotten all at that table had the capacity to read minds and their companions were just as complimentary to them, so it was a well satisfied group that reentered the assembly hall after the meal and drinks had been enjoyed.

The minister for the economy spoke first, and he outlined the country's economy but then also outlined the planets products and how well the countries worked together for the common good. Then the minister for the interior spoke and he gave a detailed outline of the different continents and island countries on the planet, the total population was the same as Orbsey just a little over 16 billion, but the planet was a little bigger with a greater mass of saline oceans and plenty of fresh water. The minister of finance spoke as well as several other important ministers and at the end of the meeting the trio was given literature setting out what they had heard. They in turn had to beam up to the freighter to get as much data on Orbsey they had with them, but they promised that next time they came back they would bring details the same as they had received. The meeting was then adjourned until the next day at the same time!

The following day Li led off by being again the first speaker, this time she asked to be allowed to set up a colony of teKahanuins on Orbsey and offered to set up a colony of Orbseyns on their planet, this was greeted with enthusiastic applause. But when she offered to take some high ranking officials to Orbsey show them the entire planet and then return them home, her words were greeted with hearty acclimation. She finished up by saying they would be glad to take their officials anytime and asked for the right to set up a colony of 50,000 teKahanuins and to return with a colony of 50,000 Orbseyns within 12 months.

Orlos and Coreum merely confirmed Li's offer and thanked the assembly for their kind attention. The prime minister then stood and accepted the offer to set up a colony on their planet and also one on Orbsey, as he said this would cement the ties of friendship. He further pledged that the next time they came back a tour party would return with them to Orbsey and in so doing confirm the first Inter Galactic peace treaty that had been agreed to in the last two days. He then wished the Orbseyns well and hoped radio communications could be set up by the scientific persons of both planets as quickly as possible. Finally he pledged they wanted only peace and would work with Orbsey to ensure those aims could be achieved.

For Li it was a major triumph she had led the first such meeting of the type ever known on two galaxies and she was so pleased to be taking home such good news.

The persons to be taken back to Orbsey were ready for loading the next day so they were all beamed up and within a few hours they were ready to leave. The last meeting was with the PM and his deputy and they assured them both they would start to set up radio communications immediately, and they would be back within twelve months excluding travelling time which meant in reality about 18 months. They would be bringing with them a full fleet and would have on board 50,000 new colonists for teKahanui and would want to take back 50,000 to Orbsey or a few less say 48,000 to take back. They would also be ready to take the official visitors and return them.

CHAPTER 9/
THE FIRST COLONISTS

THE TRIP BACK TO Orbsey was uneventful and boring for all on board, but the Trio tried as much as possible to keep their new colonists happy. The children in particular had to be catered for with games and all sorts of ways to keep them quiet, they had hundreds of movies that were constantly playing but with almost 2,500 aboard it wasn't easy. The trio then agreed it was better to sedate the travelers because the trip was so long and boring, but eventually it did come to an end, and they were being greeted by a lot of men happy to have their families with them once again.

The trio had a week off then reported in detail to the Plebiscite of rulers of Orbsey, but they had been joined by over 100 politicians from Cordiance who were all excited to hear details of this latest inter galactic trip, they had already read the thoughts of the trio so they knew what a big success there had been. When the data from TeKahanui had been copied and also flashed onto a screen Li started to give her thought report. She was followed by Orlos and Coreum, and at the end there were resounding claps of acclamation for the travelers, this time there was a real breakthrough and they all knew it was a wonderful moment in their history.

The new colonists were now given over to the charge of Li's dept heads and she and the trio had a month's well earned holiday. Coreum who was a single man still couldn't be bothered with a holiday, but Li and Orlos enjoyed themselves immensely they stayed in bed practicing to make their first baby. They only had another five years to wait and then Li would be made fertile so that the big day was now very near. Their physical attraction for each other was as strong as ever, even after 85 years of constant practice, they only had to be alone for a little while to be looking for a bed or table or anything on which they could come together it was still as good as the end of that first week so long ago.

Back at work the TeKahanuins were more popular than even the earth colony, their happy disposition made them the most lovable of persons, and Li could never get over that those who were naturally so ugly could be of such a happy disposition. The govt psychologists said it was because their home planet was so abundant in good things and the persons were all so open with each other this made the general demeanor of its population one of being always cheerful. She was told that if she had a good look at the native Orbseyns they were of a similar attitude, and that was because their planet had it all they had good reason to be happy. To Li's reaction and an open mind she agreed that the psychologist was right this in general was a happy planet with the right intentions, sure there was crime, but that was fairly natural with the size of the planet and the number of people living on it.

The radio communication network between Orbsey and TeKahanui was now in place and better relations were being established daily. The scientific communities of both planets were in mutual agreement about how clever they all were, so much more intelligent than the ordinary folk. A group of one hundred was going to visit as offered by Li. A mixture of scientists, academics, politicians, beauracrats, and others would be coming and there was a hum of excitement, this was going to be the first meeting of two planetary leadership, and all only possible because Orbsey had beaten the travel problems.

The trio was at this stage setting up the colony to go the TeKahanui, this time it was real, and even though the Orbseyns thought the TeKahanuins were very ugly they had been rushed by potential colonists. Most however wanted to keep their looks as Orbseyns, the trio thought it very funny, the TeKahanuins had also preferred to look like Orbseyns, they must realize how bloody ugly they are the trio laughed together in private.

Apart from checking up on the new colony of earthlings the job for the trio was now complete, and it was almost time to leave for TeKahanui to take a colony of Orbseyns and pick up a colony and bring back the visitors. A cruiser that had been designated to carry back the visitors had been especially equipped with radio communications and entertainment especially for them; this included a lot of information about Orbsey and its countries. There was also information about the colonies settled on Orbsey from earth, xalafeu and coordeloo, and everything possible to make the VIPs comfortable.

The cruiser was a lot faster than the freighters so the VIPs would be leave one month after the freighter because they would make the trip in two months not the three months that would be taken by the heavily laden freighters. The travel plan of the cruiser was timed to arrive at about the same time as the freighters, and the VIPs would be on board with Li as their companion. Orlos and Coreum would stay to ensure the Orbseyn colonists were well settled then load up the TeKahanuins for the journey back to Orbsey. By the time the freighters arrived in Orbsey it was intended the VIPs would be there to greet and reassure the colonists of the goodwill between the two planets.

Everything had worked as planned and Li on board the cruiser had arrived one day earlier than the fleet of heavily loaded freighters. There had been a round of VIP greetings with Li as the host and every courtesy possible had been extended to the visitors, so that there was a strong feeling of goodwill between the two groups. There were representatives from the various disciplines that had come such as politicians, scientists etc; so that all was going very well by the time all of the newcomers had been beamed down from the fleet of freighters.

The newcomers were assembled in the great palladium at the terminal and were officially greeted by the politicians of both planets. The persons that were already there were happily greeting their kin and others; it was a great day the first one when two planets welcomed the citizens that had come to settle as representatives of their own planet. The both sets of leaders expressed the hope this day would be the first of many in the efforts to bring together a league of planets, for the good of all of the different countries and their populations.

Li had to be the host for the entire different events that had been prepared for the visitors and as such received a great many tributes and thanks from the many dignitaries from both planets. This was especially so when one of the members of the plebiscite explained she was an earthling who had come to Orbsey very young and whose mate was an Orbseyn.

The visitors stayed for a month during which time they were shown around the entire planet of Orbsey and peace pledges were signed between the two planets.

It had been a very useful visit especially for all of the political and scientists of the two groups and the future for a close relationship looked very secure, but both planetary members recognized there may be harder times ahead as the more warlike planets became involved. The two planets were well advanced with their nuclear technology, and agreed that they wouldn't pass on any scientific information to planets that had a bias towards war.

The two planets agreed to set up a trade delegation within each other's main states and would also set up mutual ambassadors. But since Orbsey was the only planet that had the technology to defeat distance, until that position changed Orbsey would be paid for all intergalactic freight between the two planets.

Li was among the send off party at the intergalactic terminal as were thousand of Orbseyns and a few of the new TeKahanuins, it was a gala event appreciated by the dignitaries of both planets.

THE PLANET KANUITEPAI:

The next planet Li had looked at had been named Kanuitepai and was almost as far away as xalafeu was, it appeared from the probes photos to be about earth size and heavily populated. There appeared to be a lot of military activity, but there was no nuclear capacity apparent although such weapons may have been hidden the photos were unclear. Close up photos of the citizens showed nothing unusual they were just two legged two arms etc; differences were merely facial or that's how it seemed and their bodies may have had some extra parts that weren't obvious from so far away. Its size was almost identical to earth with similar land and sea areas.

This was to be a six months return trip, but Li had decided to take the biggest cruiser in the fleet and bring back only 250 persons on the first trip, this would reduce the time to about four months. The cost in time had now become too much for Li who had so many other duties at home as well as the approaching time for the right to have their first baby. Li and Orlos had agreed they would settle what had to be done with the two planets as yet unexplored by Orbseyns then Li would retire while Orlos and Coreum carried on. They would be given an extra person to work with them, either setting up political agreement or just taking colonists and looking for agreements later on when Li was back at work.

The flight was as usual uneventful and boring, but it was worth the trip for on arrival all agreed that this was by far the most beautiful of the planets so far seen, and now to be explored. The two men went down first while Li waited on board for their initial report which would indicate if they were just going to abduct a few persons easily, or try to have discussions with some parliamentarians.

The first thoughts coming back from Orlos was that this was just like planet earth and the people were identical, but the planet unlike earth was highly developed, his thoughts were that this was what earth would be like about two millennia into the future. They had a world govt. controlled by a plebiscite as on Orbsey and it was obvious that Li needed to talk to the leaders and try to set up a radio connection back to Orbsey. Orlos was thinking he and Coreum should try to open the way for Li and only after talks had been arranged should there be further thought communication to decide what to do. Li agreed but warned her assistants to be careful, because if they were a fully armed nuclear planet talks may not be feasible. If there appeared to be any danger at all the two of them should just suddenly beam themselves up to the cruiser, and they would decide from there what to do.

Later the same day the thoughts from Orlos again indicated a meeting had been arranged for the morrow, but these people aren't as hospitable as the TeKahanuins had been and they would need to be careful. However they were friendly enough and seemed interested to talk about anything to do with space travel, they had nuclear power for industry and for weapons, but were aware of the destructive power and not disposed towards nuclear war. Orlos and Coreum then beamed themselves up to the cruiser after confirming the meeting the next day with their planetary ambassador and themselves. Orlos was all smiles as he thought about the meeting on the morrow but Coreum was far more conservative, these persons he predicted are real hard heads and won't come to the table for serious debate quickly or easily.

Coreum proved to be correct, the meeting the next day started off rather coldly, as Li introduced themselves and their planet to her silent audience, the only thing that caused a small ripple was when she explained how they had defeated the tyranny of distance and time. They were also interested when Li spoke of the exchange of colonies, but their main interest was how to conquer travel times the rest to them was uninteresting. Then Orlos and Coreum spoke again with little reaction, so much so that the trio as agreed all had their fingers on their beamers ready to leave, and watching for any aggressive signs.

Suddenly when Coreum stopped speaking there was huge burst of applause, the trio were confused what does that mean they asked each other, they soon found out. A speaker from the audience then came to the podium and offered a vote of thanks to the trio from Orbsey and then proceeded to reply to the delight of the trio. They were all he said very impressed and grateful that they had been included in a visit from representatives of a planet so far away. Overnight their scientists had briefed him it would take them at least a million light years to reach the region around Orbsey, if in fact they could even find that planet, so the enormity of what their visitors had said was well understood.

He explained that he was the leader of their planets controlling plebiscite and as such welcomed the trio to their world if however briefly. They were invited to accept their hospitality while they were there, instead of sleeping in a space craft, no matter how comfortable that craft may be. He agreed to the exchange of colonists, but stressed that since they had not defeated tyranny of distance the transport would have to be left to the Orbseyns. Further he asked if a small number of politicians could be given transport to Orbsey and back so as the further cement a possible league of planets as Li had outlined because they would certainly like to be a foundation member of such a league.

He explained that Orlos and Coreum had outlined what Li wanted the day before which is why they had met the night before and now he was able to reply in such a positive manner. He finished by asking for travel for twenty, ten politicians and ten scientists, and they would have a total as requested of

50,000 colonists, and they would be ready to accept 50,000 Orbseyns and set them up fully as a self contained colony. Another two speakers stood and welcomed the trio; they were both members of the plebiscite and would be happy to visit Orbsey, at any time possible.

Li was the final speaker and she suggested first they could take up to 100 visitors perhaps of different disciplines and she promised to return them all well fed and happy. The meeting broke up with mutual courteous hand clapping!

The trio as offered stayed at the best hotel in the city and really enjoyed the hospitality of the ten members of the plebiscite that night, and for another week. An immediate radio connection was set up with Orbsey that got the scientists happy and working together and then Li gave them all an agenda to work to.

The cruiser floating in the heavens above would be loaded only with the visitors Li and Orlos and they would return to Orbsey, just as soon as the Kanuitapai visitors were ready to leave, arriving two months later. Meanwhile Coreum would stay back and arrange the new colonists that would be going to settle in Orbsey, and have them ready to load as soon as the freighters arrived.

When the fleet was ready in Orbsey, Orlos would help load and prepare the colonists that were to settle in Kanuitepai, and travel with them back to Kanuitepai. The order had already been sent to arrange the colonists so they should be ready by time Li arrived with her visitors, and the fleet booking for 40 freighters had been made, but there were many complaints from the space freighters dept. Li was keeping them working to tight schedules and the full fleet had to be fully serviced to be able to cater for this enormous increase in planetary travel.

Li would return with the visitors from Kanuitepai and wait with Coreum until the fleet arrived, this would fulfill all of their obligations at all times as the ambassadors for Orbsey, and the visitors will have been well catered too. The visitors to Orbsey were ready in a week so the cruiser was landed to take them all aboard as VIPs, with Li and Orlos as their hosts, but no one can stop the boredom of space travel hard as they may try. This was the same cruiser that had been specially set up for the previous group of VIPs but two months with little to do is tough unless the passengers are used to that life and these VIPs certainly weren't. By the time they had landed at the intergalactic terminal at Orbsey Li and Orlos were exhausted, but their passengers were now all smiles.

The visitors were given time in the best hotels to recover and then it was down to meetings and discussions, the scientists and politicians were hard at work within a few days, but Li opened the meeting in the great palladium that allowed media as well as all others with a vested interests to be able to listen to the discussions from the gallery. Li introduced the gatherings of VIPs from both planets, expressed her hope that the discussions would be fruitful then left them to their talks; so she and Orlos could enjoy a well earned rest.

The meetings and trips around Orbsey to any part of the planet took four weeks then it was almost time to leave again. In the meantime there were millions of applications to emigrate and the process was almost ready to select by ballot, another week and they were ready to leave the fleet was loaded and left a week before the VIP cruiser. The VIP cruiser arrived back in Kanuitepai three weeks before the fleet so Li stayed in a hotel until they arrived; she had inspected the lists of colonists going to Orbsey so that all were ready to leave as soon as the fleet arrived. Coreum looked a bit flustered he had been under pressure all of the time Li had been away and was happy to see her back but would be even happier to see Orlos.

The fleet arrived and the colonists were all beamed down to the air terminal which wasn't big enough to hold any of the giant freighters, but it was all dealt with efficiently. The arriving Orbseyns were beamed down and within two hours the fleet was ready to receive the Kanuitepai'ns on board so they were all beamed up in groups, over two thousand per freighter.

There had been an agreement reached to send a load of dehydrated meat back on the cruiser as a trial shipment of protein and the first planet to planet actual sales at govt level. Because no killing of animals for food was allowed on Orbsey they had to manufacture protein, the Orbseyns had products the Kanuitepai'ns wanted and they were happy to send products in payment the meat was a trial shipment of ten tonnes. The entire visit was almost an exact duplicate as the visitors from TeKahanui including the departure celebrations, the Kanuitepai'ns were far more reserved, but in the end the program had been just as successful.

The members of the plebiscite invited the trio in for a meeting and congratulated them on another new local colony on both planets, and a great job well done, there were now at least three members of the hoped for league of planets that included Orbsey and the three ambassadors were recognized for their major efforts.

When the fleet arrived back in Orbsey Li left all of the program details to Orlos and Coreum, she wanted to plan her last trip before she was medically treated to become fertile, she thought it quite funny at 118 YOA to be preparing for their first baby.

The load of dried meat had been a huge success, and a repeat order for 250,000 tonnes had been placed by radio ready to be picked up within 12 months and an order for five space freighters had been accepted with delivery of the first one within 12 months. There would have to be a team of their pilots sent to Orbsey for training of at least three months, and a team of buyers would be sent to Kanuitepai to investigate any other protein or supplies they could buy.

This planet was to become a major supplier to Orbsey in the future, in a way a little like planet earth but in this case there was no problem with the inter trade payments system it was meant to be quid pro quo and left to the trade missions to settle any differences. Orbsey of course had the technology to supply what all of the planets needed and in return there were a lot of products that could be bought for processing or retailing within their entire consumer base which was very large but evenly spread. Looking at the future for trade between the planets the plebiscite on Orbsey had every reason to be pleased with what Li and her team were achieving for their home planet.

THE PLANET TEPAKEHA:

The last of the three was the planet named Tepakeha and was really a long way off it would take at least 6 months to reach, the probes had returned with quite clear photos and this planet looked very nice. It was smaller than earth, but heavily populated with over 8 billion inhabitants so that even though small they had a far bigger population than earth.

There appeared to be a strong well disciplined military and the beginnings of nuclear power, but for industrial power not weapons of destruction. The people looked to be exactly the same as earthlings and even the homes seemed similar, this was an agricultural society but the beginnings of industry was starting to show in several of the countries.

The same technique was to be used the trio would go on a fast cruiser and should arrive in four months, then Orlos and Coreum would make contact at the right level and try to arrange for Li to meet with their govt. In the meantime they would all catch up with their reports during the trip ahead. They were travelling in the VIP cruiser so they had all of the luxuries, but privately they all wondered if one day they could just beam across space and be on these far off planets in seconds, it was a lovely dream when contemplating 4-6 months in space just filling in time. The three of them had bought their reports up to date and radioed them home within a week there was still a mighty lot of time to fill in. Li and Orlos were ok they were still busy practicing for that baby that was now only two years away, but Coreum was soon bored silly as he put it. There were hundreds of movies on board, a pool table and plenty of booze, and music, but no females on the crew, Li had agreed to ensure that female attendants on the crew for dancing partners were a part of future facilities to help break the tedium. They finally arrived at their destination and once again this was a beautiful planet, they circled around it once then the two males beamed themselves down to the surface, a matter of seconds was all it took. Keeping their thoughts on contact all on the cruiser could tell straight away that it was a very pleasant city they were in, but they still didn't know if it was the capital, or even if the planet had a controlling parliament.

The first thing was to find the seat of planetary power the next was to try and arrange a meeting for Li to address. Within minutes they were at the parliament for the entire planet and soon after they were in discussions with a member of the parliament. He was startled but soon recovered his poise and very quickly had arranged a top level meeting for these two self claimed aliens. Both Orlos and Coreum at this point had their beamers firmly in the hands ready to leave, but after two hours they were becoming comfortable again.

It was correct the persons here were very much like earthlings and although suspicious were friendly, and gave no signs of being aggressive. The meeting was recorded and the two aliens were asked to explain exactly what they wanted and why they had come? When they were satisfied they understood they were invited for another preliminary meeting in two days, after which their members of the parliament would decide if they wanted to talk. It was obvious quickly these persons were only beauracrats and could make no decisions, plenty of talk but no answers so as requested Orlos and Coreum agreed to come back at the appointed time. Just to ensure they were being taken seriously, the two Orbseyns said they would beam themselves up to their space cruiser immediately and return exactly on time in two days.

When they returned as promised there was a full group of about 20 persons waiting to receive them, and the procedure was gone over again just explaining what they had come for. The apparent leader thanked them for their patience, but asked if they could return in another two days while their leader was properly briefed and then he would meet with Li.

Orlos and Coreum declined this invitation by saying their leader wouldn't come unless an agenda had been first approved it was pointless without that. Orlos and Coreum offered to set up radio contact with their scientists and just leave it at that if they preferred, they thought about that then decided that no they would like to meet the ambassador from Orbsey. It was just that their leaders were away on holiday and had to be brought home for the meeting, but first they had to find them. Orlos then said it was just as easy to come down to see how it was going in another two days but he stressed they would be considering leaving, it had been a long trip and they didn't need to waste anymore time. He didn't say they would be taking 200 of their citizens with them.

Back on the cruiser the trio discussed the situation then decided they would next time down at the parliament building, advise the reps that they had to leave in seven days, without failure then if they weren't ready just pick up some men sedate them and start on back to Orbsey. They would simply set up a colony the old way and to hell with their govt!

The next time down there was still no leaders so the message was given they would be leaving in seven days and they wouldn't be back, well not legally.

On the sixth day Orlos and Coreum went back and the leader was there but didn't seem all that interested so he was told they were leaving the next day. That sparked a change in attitude and they were invited to return the next day for a meeting of the top leaders only and they would then decide their interest if any. Orlos was a bit insulted by the comment if any, but kept his always volatile temper and agreed they would come with the ambassador the next day.

Promptly on time the trio was there ready, but the leaders were ten minutes late which boded badly for any good results with this planet. But they duly arrived and with full courtesy invited the trio into the board room and then settled down to listen to what these strangers had to say.

Li wasn't at all fazed by the long period of messing around and expressed why they were there beautifully, then Orlos and Coreum spoke as usual then the trio sat down and waited.

After seeming to be thinking about what had been said their main speaker stood up and said that he was surprised they had come so far, was there any ulterior motive such as a takeover of their planet?

Li was not surprised but stood and said, "No we are not a warlike planet we want to set up an alliance of peaceful planets war isn't on our agenda, but if that's on your mind its useless to talk more, we might as well leave and visit another planet on our way?

This finally bought a spark of interest, "do you they ask know of another planet close to us?"

"Of course we do I have already told you we have beaten the tyranny of travel and know of several planets we can visit, why should we waste more time with you"? Li said with a chuckle in her voice.

"But we haven't asked you to leave you decided that yourself, we are happy to have you here you cannot blame us for being suspicious. You arrive here from a big planet over a million light years away and then wonder why we are being careful be reasonable, if what you say is true you are living miracles," he said now with a slight smile.

"We have offered to give your scientist the coordinates to find our planet and speak to our scientists by radio they can explain all of this, but all you have done is mess us around?" Li answered him now very sharply.

"This isn't correct madam we have been trying to check out your credentials nothing more if we didn't do that we should be sacked from our jobs, and I am surprised at your attitude. We are interested but if you have the technology to beat the distance then you must have the ability to beat us up very easy and I think that's fair comment don't you?" he said now with a real smile.

"That's true but you will find no weapons of war not even hand guns on our planet, but what we can do is lock any invaders out with a nuclear shield over the entire planet and neutralize the enemies weapons, we are for peace not war so if your philosophy is war then yes we are wasting our time?" Li said but still sharply.

"And how do we know what you say is true?" He asked.

"Simple if you want we can take you back but it's a four month trip, but we have a luxury cruiser up there that can do the trip in four months, the big freighters will take six months, you can see it all for yourself and bring 100 with you, the trip costs will be on us there and back," Li said with a laugh.

"What and you will show us your whole planet with nothing hidden?" he said again but now with a disbelieving look on his face.

"What Li asked do we have to hide you don't have the ability to beat distance it would take you a million years to attack us and then you would only bounce of the shield anyhow, so of course we won't be teaching you any of that really high tech stuff we aren't that silly," Li said now with a soft smile

"Ok we are interested when we go?" he asked.

"Tomorrow" Li said now with a big laugh.

"Ok" the leader said, "we will be ready in the morning do I need to bring a shaver?" Now it was his turn to laugh. "What say we get a team of 100 together and we will be ready to leave in a week is that right with you?

"That's fine and no you don't need a razor this is our VIP cruiser all set up for dignitaries like you, but remember it's a long boring trip".

And so it was that four months later the cruiser was landing at the intergalactic terminal with 100 VIPs from planet Tepakeha.

It was becoming standard procedure for the Terminal to be shut down and ready for the visitors, and flights for normal travelers transferred to another terminal. The Orbsey leaders and scientist were waiting once again to greet the visitors, and were all very excited They had been advised these politicians were far harder to negotiate with than the other two planet leaders because they were so suspicious, but at the terminal it was nothing but friendliness, quite in contrast compared to what the trio had had to face.

Li was on hand to introduce the leaders she knew; the others introduced themselves, but she was quick to notice that there were a lot of scientists and politicians in the group. The visitors had kept themselves far more isolated during the trip choosing not to mix with the trio and showing little interest in the data about Orbsey. Li had heard one of the visitors confirming how unbelievably quickly they were moving through the various galaxies and how completely dumbfounded they were, the comment was we have no conception of how this is done.

Li had sent coded messages back to Orbsey setting out details of her suspicions, but admitting she may have been influenced by her reactions to their first meeting and the lack of real hospitality after the trip had been arranged. She admitted that she and her fellow ambassadors where somewhat pessimistic about this group, but far more they were highly suspicious.

The Orbseyns where somewhat reserved at the terminal, but in true Orbseyn tradition offered full hospitality to the guests in top hotels with guides to show them around. They were offered an open door policy to see anything except highly classified secrets such as thought power and the neutralizing of weapon, although they were shown examples of the techniques that kept Orbsey way ahead of all other planets they were aware of.

The politicians now settled down to discussions about the Orbsey ambitions to set up a league of planets, but only within certain boundaries. Beyond that the scale of time and distance was just too much even for the Orbsey fleet, and until the times could be improved their planet was on the outer reaches of how far they would go. Li sat in as an observer and noticed that the visitors were still just as ignorant now as they had been back at that first meeting with Orlos and Coreum. She began to wonder if that was just the way they were, and now realized the trio should have just abducted some of them first and got to understand them a little. It was a mistake she would never make again in her long career in the planetary services!

The meeting were going moderately well, but making little progress on the question of their planet joining the future league, the main objection being; they didn't have the knowledge to travel so far so quickly and until they did it was pointless. They were quite happy to set up a colony of Orbseyns in their capital state and happy to provide a colony to live in Orbsey, but suggested the colonists be changed every ten years as a gesture to the colonists that they weren't leaving home for ever. Finally the visitors suggested that perhaps a fleet of Orbsey freighters be sold to them, fully staffed and that a license be granted for them to copy the technology.

The Orbseyns expressed themselves ready to sell freighters when a league of planets had been set up, but they stressed the power to move through galaxies wasn't in the freighters alone, that power source was always from Orbsey and at present that couldn't be changed. When and if the change could be made the travel times would be reduced by at least 100%, but that technology was at least ten years away.

When the change in times were expressed there was a gasp of surprise from scientists present, that would make us almost neighbors they said, and for once there was a ripple of laughter from the visitors.

The Orbseyns said that if a league of planet were set up, the members would be sold freighters, cruisers and the nuclear covers over their planets, that couldn't be pierced by nuclear power of any type. They would also be able to buy the ability to neutralize all weapons way down to hand guns, any fighting even internally, could only be done with bows and arrows; this statement was also greeted with a laugh.

Does this mean the leader of the Tepakehas asked that all of the planets will be hostage to Orbsey technological superiority?

Not at all the idea is peace and trade; we will have systems to sell and we presume you will have products to sell to us. But it cannot do all of this until we really beat the problem of time and cost for space travel, we aren't there yet, we are about half way to the goal. If you have had a look around this planet you will see there are no nuclear weapons, but there is a nuclear shield that can go up in three days, that's our safety net. There are way too many planets out there that have big populations; our aim is to set up security against being invaded by such planets. And if one of our members is being attacked then we have the facility to quickly arm and counter attack, but we will never attack we don't have to its others out there we fear. We aren't the only ones with the technology we have, although we haven't found any yet we are sure they are there and we want to be safe, and with us a group of planets.

"And how many planets do you have now that may join?" they asked.

"Two possibly five, we want to have ten and then will leave it at that, but we would want to set up agreements on a wide range of issues, trade, technological exchange, currency a wide range of issues that can be negotiated to everyone' advantage. We do have another two planets but we want to slow down and sort out what we are doing, then carry on to ensure we have eight partners, before we start to negotiate the final agreements?" the Orbsey leader finished.

"Well provided our territorial integrity is assured and we have eight members around the table with heads of govt and their advisors we would certainly be ready to join such a group. We would be silly if we didn't; but while we fully accept your integrity we would also have to be happy with the other members, that their integrity is indeed as stable as your own. Now we are quite happy to sign a letter of intent with the provisos and securities in place we would want, and may I say in closing we thank the planet of Orbsey and its representatives.

You have been well represented on our planet by your ambassadors we look forward to their visits at any time. But for now Orbsey will have to supply all transport, but of course we will pay our way in future. In the meantime let's set up the reciprocal colonies and the radio contact between our scientists and the hope the future works out as we all hope.

The discussions were then formally ended by the leader of the Orbseyn plebiscite, a ball for the guests was held that night hosted by the trio and the next day the cruiser was loaded the visit was over.

Coreum stayed behind to set up the colonists to go to Tepakeha, and the fleet would leave again when Orlos confirmed he was ready with a load to pick up in Tepakeha. Li would travel to the planet and come back immediately loaded with some of the first colonists and wait in Orbsey for the fleet to arrive home fully loaded with colonists from Tepakeha.

It was now time for Li to be treated for fertility, and when Orlos got back she would be off work for two years, with no more planets to settle in until she was back at work. The colonies in Orbsey would be slowly bought together, and the efforts of Orlos and Coreum would be to try to create unity between them all. They were to go to earth, but only to bring back gold, spice and silk and to try and find an earth leadership, they could bring to Orbsey for talks.

The next need was to bring the different local colonies together in an effort to try and create unity, none of the groups had been placed too close together because the Orbseyn Dept for the Colonists were aware there could be trouble makers among the groups much as there had been with the Xalafeuns. Again the idea was to get the children to unite with their peers and Orbseyn children as an important part of that process.

Li had instructed her Dept; to do an individual report on all of the groups except the earthlings, the rate of marriage or union between Orbseyns and Earthlings was very high and the settling down of the parents was now excellent, Li had no need to be involved with her own kind any longer they were settling in nicely, and nothing would be gained by further development.

XALAFEUNS:

The children of the Xalafeuns were very aggressive like their parents, but once they were bought into line they became quite settled. None of the age groups were as attractive as some of the other groups from the various planets, but gradually and slowly they settled in with their Orbseyn peers.

The Xalafeuns were obviously a dour people with a very poor sense of humor and the tendency for verbal aggression, at the slightest provocation the children would break into verbal attack and it was difficult to get them to desist. This was difficult when mixing with Orbseyns who were a mild happy go lucky people as were their children, the years for them of being aggressive were over centuries ago and all they wanted now was peace.

The exercise of bringing them together lacked the attraction for the marriageable aged Orbseyns because there was little cohabitation amongst them once they left the clubs they didn't mix. It would take many years for the Xalafeuns to remove from their memories some of the atrocities they had lived through on their own planet, and even after this period of being on Orbsey with its super abundance of food they tended to hoard food away in the most amazing places, so it couldn't be found, because some day they may once again be starving.

These children like their parents were very intelligent, and were way out in front with any combined schools exams. They were diligent workers and would study any subjects given to them for hours until their results as a group were exceptional.

The small antennae that the Xalafeuns had on their forehead was simply an extra device that allowed them to know whoever was coming up behind them and if there was any danger. This didn't make them appear ugly at all but it seemed to strengthen their innate suspicion of everything and everyone around them.

CORRDELOO:

These children were a happy lot and this applied in all age groups, like their parents they didn't get upset easily and they loved having a good time, the lack of hair didn't detract from their appearance in fact for many Orbseyns it enhanced them. They mixed well and easily with all of the other groups and the Orbseyn young found them attractive, which was very important. They came from a planet that had the best of everything that life could offer but were totally unspoilt, many were farmer's children and loved animals they particularly loved the fact that on this planet animal's weren't killed for food, but of course missed the taste of a good steak occasionally. Orbseyn food was pronounced as very good but very bland especially the imitation meat, chicken and turkey.

The children had heard their parents at home talking about trade agreements between the planets and all hoped that Corrdeloo meat would one day be imported to Orbsey, quite forgetting this meant that many more animals on their own planet would die.

Romance among them and the Orbseyns began to flourish among the eldest group and in the future marriages would be quite the norm.

The older Corrdeloons were very romantic as were there parents and as soon as they were getting close to thirty YOA were looking for partners among the Orbseyns. The Orbseyns found the females very feminine and the males very virile so the future for mixed marriages was very strong.

TE KAHANUI.

The children of the TeKahanuins were a delight to work with their complete lack of any pretensions made them the favorites of all. Their natural linguistic abilities was a pleasure to listen to, but their appearance the same as Orbseyns may have made their integration a lot easier, no doubt if their natural ugliness were seen they might lose that popularity.

They were the most popular kids at schools and clubs they surpassed even the earthlings in their popularity with all of the other groups. But they were newcomers and would take quite a few years to settle in to their new home. These children loved food and had no difficulty showing just how much they loved to eat, the Orbseyn food was a bit bland, but they didn't care they loved all food. It was when they were eating they were at their happiest, they only problem was they seemed to be hungry all of the time.

They weren't good students in the sense that they wouldn't work, but they were naturally very bright and did well without any apparent effort. The families were always happy and quite happy with their own company but at the same time were glad to mix with all and any who were around them.

These children tended not to mix romantically with any others, perhaps because they knew that in their natural state most others found them very ugly, whatever the reason it was obvious they would be no integration through marriage within this group.

KANUITEPAI'NS AND TEPAKEHAS:

Although these two groups were very reserved, once their reserve was breached they became very friendly, and soon became well liked by the Orbseyn young of all age groups. They appeared to have very little sense of humor but this wasn't true it was just that they were totally pragmatic and had two see the point in everything before they would react.

As their peer groups got to know them they realized it was more that they hated to make mistakes, and in so doing make themselves appear foolish

TRADE AGREEMENTS.

The Orbseyn Govt had decided it was time to set up the federation of planets immediately before any more planets were invited to join, and each one was asked to have a delegation ready to come to Orbsey and they would be picked up by the special high speed cruisers, and returned home after the conference was over. They were asked to send delegates who had the authority to sign the agreement so that the federation in this early stage would be binding and all could continue on to get the program underway. The earth by Li's suggestion would send a none voting observer delegation who could speak for their planet but wouldn't be able to vote on any of the binding agreements because they would be there as a protectorate of the Orbseyn govt for the foreseeable future.

Because Orbsey didn't want to let the other leaders get a glimpse of earth and realize how backward it really was Li was sent to invite the tree spirits to send a delegation for which she would be personally responsible for their safety, none except Li understood what a grave responsibility it was she was taking on. The tree spirits were delighted to be going as observers from earth and promised they would do their best to be good ambassadors for planet earth. It had been a momentous meeting lasting several days and at the finish the earth delegates were asked to speak on behalf of their planet. This was unexpected by all of the leaders of the other planets who had understood that earth was a protectorate of Orbsey and that any costs related to earth would be paid from the trade accounts between the two planets.

The leaders had sat as if mesmerized by the delegates from earth (three) who spoke, how they asked could this backward planet put up speakers with such powers of speech and persuasion and such understanding of what was being done at this conference, when the last one sat down there was a rapturous round of applause from the whole chamber.

Now that the legislative agreements had been signed it was time to set up the administrative arms so that there could be immediate moving ahead on the actual trade agreements.

Reciprocal political representation had been set up on every planet that was signatories of the trade agreement except earth which had only had a defacto representation at the signing. It was considered that earth wouldn't be ready to join any such agreement for at least 2,000 years, if then. The full signatories to the agreement were, Xalafeu, Corrdeloo, TeKahanui, Kanuitepai, Tepakeha and Orbsey.

Orbsey had agreed it would supply all space craft including a license to operate the special energy resource only available through Orbsey, the technical knowledge to erect the nuclear zone over their planets, and the equipment to stop the use of all and any explosive devices that were being used by outside planets to attack them. It was further agreed that Orbsey would take mainly food products in exchange for any products they supplied including the license agreement to break through the tyranny of distance. Orbsey reserved the right to license any planets that had the productive capacity and could assist in the production of some of the products ie she might have one of the industrialized planets build Aerocars for consumption on Orbsey.

This would allow Orbsey production to concentrate on high tech products, to help the planets to pay for their purchases without too much hardship on their budgets. The Ambassador and his trade staff were there to ensure each planet was able to produce a product that would help their budgets not drag them down. The following list was the first real orders between the planets and Orbsey.

From Earth 10 tonnes of gold per year plus spices and silk in return for education but there was no formal agreement.

Xalafeun: I million Aerocars per year in return for 12 Space craft over 12 years fully licensed a nuclear shield over their planet, and the ability to control all explosive devices that had been built for the purpose of war. This planet was a full signatory to the agreement as were all of the others except earth, the basis of the agreement was with Orbsey and with the other planets as well.

Corrdeloo: 250 million tonnes of dried beef per year, for a minimum term of twelve years, in return for twelve spacecraft including a license for the extra energy, a nuclear shield over their planet and the equipment to stop all explosive weapons selectively as required to prevent war.

TeKahanui this planet also was to be licensed to provide one million Aerocars to Orbsey per year in return for twelve fully licensed space craft a nuclear shield and the equipment to destroy all weapons of war.

Kanuitepai and Tepakeha: had the same agreement as each other, their order was to supply dried fish, chicken and turkeys as required, in return for twelve spacecraft fully licensed. Also to be supplied was the nuclear shield over their planets, and the ability to control all weapons of war right down to handguns.

On top of these orders Orbsey had to ensure its own fleet was kept up to top quality standard which required about five new spacecraft per year. The local population on Orbsey had started to complain because the price of joy flights had become far more expensive, because interplanetary needs were now such that the spacecraft weren't available for these flights anymore. The Govt had undertaken to guarantee these special low cost flights would be restored when their fleet had been increased and was able to do the job, but in reality that was going to take 10 years if not more before that would happen. This could turn out to be a problem for the Orbseyn govt in the near future, these flights were very popular and had been for many years, it wasn't going to be easy to dramatically cut off the availability of these space craft.

The Orbseyns gave guarantees that if any of their member planets were attacked by outside planets they would go into missile production and within two months would be able to launch retaliatory strikes against the enemy from their home base at Orbsey. The capacity was there but only to be assembled if needed. This had been proved and the strike accuracy was proven over millions of light years away, much to the delight of the members many who dreaded that someday an advanced planet such as Orbsey would attack them then they could be in trouble.

The ambassadors and the trade leaders were kept very busy as they searched for different products the planets may buy, but at present they were quite happy to have signed up the agreements they had done it was all to everyone's advantage. All of the Ambassadors especially the ones on Orbsey were really busy all of the time, it was a big job to suddenly have to coordinate trade agreements and at the same time work together with the ambassadors on each planet.

PROBLEMS AHEAD.

The trade agreements had been working beautifully for over ten years when the Orbseyn scientists gave warning there was a fleet of spacecraft heading towards Corrdeloo, and all were heavily armed. Within days the Corrdeloons scientists were confirming what the Orbseyns had first spotted these craft and quickly verified they were craft only suited for war and probably armed with nuclear warheads.

This fleet was still about eight months away from Coodeloo so something had to be done quickly. A request went out from Orbsey to the member planets for the right to produce 150 unmanned nuclear missiles which could be completed in less than six months. This approval had been given now the missiles were in full production, and a dangerous looking sight they were as they began to line up ready to be fired.

When there were 100 of the missiles ready to fire, the scientists on Orbsey asked that the Corrdeloo military make contact with the incoming fleet to ask what their intent was, there was no answer.

Another question went out and it asked if the incoming fleet was bent on war, because if it was there were 100 nuclear armed missiles that never miss their target being prepared to target them, this got an answer.

Where and how they asked is this planet going to get so many nuclear armed missiles when they had none the last time they had been inspected by our spies, and in a type of sneer they said, we will if necessary blow this planet to pieces. But they stressed they didn't want to do that all they wanted was to takeover and resettle this planet with their own people, to live side by side in peace and harmony with the present residents. All of the member planets had been kept well informed about what was happening, and were watching with awed interest what was soon to happen.

There was 150 craft coming into the attack and it looked as if Corrdeloo was quite unprotected, but the first 100 missiles on Orbsey were ready to fire they had been targeted on the attackers and they wouldn't miss the targets. So now the attackers were twelve days out from Corrdeloo the order was given and the missiles were all fired, while all of the members watched what happened with avid interest. Four hours later the second lot of fifty was fired also targeted on individual craft, so it was too late to stop now the missiles were on the way and there was no way they would miss the target.

The attack craft were now only ten days away and almost celebrating their victory, when simultaneously throughout the fleet 100 were totally destroyed. While they now tried desperately to make peace with Corrdeloo suddenly it was too late the final 50 were destroyed, there was no more talking, the invasion fleet was destroyed and its crews were all dead.

The messages of congratulations came in very fast especially from Corrdeloo, the extent of Orbseyn power had never been demonstrated because the agreement was she would only arm missiles in defense of her members, but now they had all seen just how effective that defense was and were happy, now they knew their defense was real and any who dared to attack them would be destroyed. Corrdeloo was totally grateful they had been the ones to first see the real power of Orbsey, and they had no doubt now their future was secure under the cover of their agreement with them.

The cost of the defense was shared among all members including Orbsey as they would for any defense mounted for members, but the sleeping deadly giant that was Orbsey went back to normal and were glad to have been of service to one of their members.

Lifestyles had changed on all of the member planets, they all now had spacecraft of varying sizes and their staff had spent time in Orbsey leaning all about the operating procedures and how to break the tyranny of distance, and all were delighted at how much more they could travel. The only problem was the cost of these machines and how much they cost to run, while it bought all of the planets up to a far higher standard, their citizens had to pay the bill which the leaders thought reasonable, but the citizens thought expensive. But now with the easy demolition of the 150 attack craft against Corrdeloo they had other thoughts.

The leaders called for a summit meeting at Cordiance, they were seeking reassurance that those missiles would never be used except as defense tools. They said they now realized how important the defense strategy was, but wanted to be sure those deadly missiles would never be used in anger against them. What asked the Orbseyns do you want us to do, if we agree to destroy that defense capacity then what happens if another attack occurs as happened on Corrdeloo? The Orbseyn Govt was prepared to give greater guarantees of good intent but what more could they do. Then it was suggested that the colonies on each planet were to be doubled and in this way there would be too many of their own people on the planets, while more immigrants to Orbsey would help create closer relations between them all, which they did quite quickly.

The subject was then bought up by the Orbseyns that it had been a mistake to destroy the entire fleet of aggressors because now they had no way of knowing who they were and whether they would try again. It is now imperative they said that all planets have their scientists constantly watching the skies to ensure there was enough time, to produce the missiles and allow them to be launched in time to counter attack. There would be the initial confusion when the leaders of any attacking fleet crashed into the nuclear shield, this would hold them up until they realized there was an invisible shield that had to be destroyed, and that would take about two weeks if they were nuclear armed. If they weren't nuclear armed they would never pierce the shield anyhow so they could be warned of their impending destruction, and that they would be a lot safer to withdraw and go home?

It was best if the time allowed could be three months to produce the missiles and then the time taken to reach the planets, they all had the systems now so were well aware of the time needed. The meeting broke up with an expression of confidence in Orbsey and its right intent towards all of the members. They were told that it was planet earth that was considered the most endangered, but that Orbsey would protect that planet at its own cost, because it would be helpless against any attack easily invaded and the entire population destroyed.

Li heard the news when she had just given birth to her first child so she was glad it wasn't going to be her bringing home the new immigrants, she would stay as far out of the way as possible and let Orlos and Coreum deal with this massive extra workload. But she appointed an extra two new Ambassadors to help them and then she settled back to have some quality time with her child.

Once again the entire fleet had to be put onto this special duty, much to the anger of the overworked factories' and the production managers struggling to meet almost impossible deadlines. It didn't take long however until the moaning was over and the new groups were being transported from Orbsey and then returning fully loaded. No new earth Colonies were to be set up because the new intakes from the other planets still didn't give them as many immigrants as the earth had already sent, or that had been stolen whichever was the more appropriate phrase.

The Orbseyns sent out word to the other planets that they wanted to find another four members to make up the full group of ten planets in the consortium, but that none would be accepted without the full vote of the current members in favor of the new applicants. It was stressed that costs were too high for their little group to cover and that the Orbseyn economists felt prices to buy and sell could be reduced by at least 10% with the greater inter planet trade. The Govt stressed they wanted to see economic stability among its members as well as security from aggressive planets, and the only way to do that now was to be able to reduce costs to everybody.

There had been a huge amount of economic data now gathered up by the trade groups and they were able to show how costs could be reduced with the bigger number of members, and that even the cost of the spacecraft could be cut back substantially. When Li heard this news that they were going to be looking for four more planets her first thoughts were to retire because that was such a big job and she didn't know if she would be strong enough to keep up with such a demanding job any longer, but she decided to talk it over with Orlos, she was aware that there was no retirement before the stipulated age which was now 260 YOA and since she was only 122 YOA it wasn't likely that her resignation would be accepted. Rather she would be put on some type of recovery program so her strength could be renewed for the new work load.

Suddenly the radio system came alive with a planet enquiring about its lost fleet and whether anyone had any information about what had happened to it. The Orbseyn scientists were immediately busy trying to track where the message had come from, they were able to trace a planet some two light years away from Corrdeloo, so they answered a query with a query what was your fleet doing they asked?

It was searching for a new planet for us to shift some of our population to; we are becoming overloaded and need a new home for some of us.

And was the finding of a new planet supposed to be by negotiation or be conquest Orbsey asked?

As far as we are concerned by negotiation but they may have taken a war like stance just to bluff their way through.

Yes their bluff was pretty strong so in the face of their threats we had no option but to destroy them, just as we would any other aggressor who entered bearing threats. We regret to inform you your fleet was destroyed before it reached the target that it was verbally threatening, your leaders were given fair warning but obviously felt we couldn't do what we said we could so they are all destroyed and the crews dead, all killed by nuclear missiles.

An answer came back who are you we don't believe our fleet could have been so easily destroyed they were all nuclear armed and expertly crewed.

Whether you believe us or not is irrelevant to us if you can find them somewhere then good luck but lets us inform you once again every craft and their crews were all destroyed, they wouldn't take the warning and refused to pull back so we had no choice but to destroy them.

And who are you the aliens asked how did you get involved with this battle anyhow, and how do we find you?

We are one of a group of planets that work together you unfortunately attacked one of our group and so paid the consequences. We aren't a planet for war but we have the installations in place to deal with any that think they can do what they like with one of our members. We think the price you have paid is high enough and you might be better off not to know where we are. We can tell you the planet you attacked was one of our groups and if you persist we are quite capable of destroying your entire planet so it's best you desist.

The belligerent reply came back we will find and destroy you one day be sure of that, and when we do we will repay you for every one of our people you have killed.

You had best hope we don't come searching for you, as we have already said we are for peace, but you may not come into our region and attack one of ours just whenever you want to. Now as to your ability to destroy us let us say that you won't do it with the fleet you sent this first time they are all destroyed so you will have to build another.

If you would like to send us your apace coordinates once we confirm them we will be happy to send you ours. The communiqué was suddenly broken off and no further word was heard from the scientists of that group.

The Orbseyn scientists had quite quickly been able to track the radio signals received and were already sending out two space probes to check them out and they were already on their way, only thought communication was allowed no radio signals were allowed. The both probes were back within a month with full information about the planet, they only called X. It was a medium sized planet a little bigger than planet earth but with a huge population, this was obviously causing a lot of problems because the land mass had large arid areas they obviously could do nothing with so they had opted for conquest. The planet was fully nuclear armed and obviously very warlike, they were pushing ahead building a new fleet of fighter craft, they obviously hoped would be able to do what the previous fleet had not.

The Orbsey Govt immediately called a meeting of leaders to be help in TeKahanui in a month's time; the agenda was what to do about the war planet if anything. The VIP manned cruiser was made available and Li was called in to do a month's work. She had all of her ambassadors with her and the group included some of the leading scientists as well as Orbseyns top politicians but not the plebiscite members. The Cruiser was loaded with all of the devices to repel all explosive devices of war, that might be sent out aimed at the cruiser would be exploded fifty miles before they reached the target.

When the cruiser reached a high altitude over planet x a radio message was sent requesting talks of a peaceful nature to be held aboard the cruiser, any who would come would be guaranteed they would be safe and would be beamed up and down just as quickly as they wanted.

There was complete surprise on planet X where are you they wanted to know?

We are high above your planet and we are immune to any nuclear or other devices you may fire at us, we only want to talk peace for our group of planets, any others you attack is none of our business but there are ten of us you may not attack without immediate repercussions.

There was confusion down on the planet but eventually they agreed to let the cruiser beam up ten of their people the following day for peace talks.

As agreed the following morning ten of planet x politicians and scientist were beamed aboard the Cruiser, while Li introduced all of the Orbseyns then they introduced themselves.

Li started off the meeting by explain who they were and from where, but she didn't name the member planets because that wasn't her place to do so. She explained her job was as the chief Ambassador for Orbsey on matters of interplanetary affairs, but her job was normally only to work with members that's why she had in the group some scientists and politicians, all of very high regard in Orbsey. None of the other ambassadors had been included in the meeting because the visitors may feel overwhelmed.

Li explained Orbsey will never release weapons of war on another planet or their allies unless one of their own were under attack but she said in closing, your commander treated our threat as a joke not once but twice and when asked to withdraw flatly refused in the end it was either defend out member or look weak so what happened was inevitable under those conditions.

The politicians then took over and said, we haven't come here to talk war we only want to talk peace, we can tell for instance you have a massive overpopulation problem, if you want maybe we can help with that and try to take off your hands a couple of billion people.

At this comment the people from planet x started to listen more intently, tell us more about yourselves they asked.

Well we are a very old civilization and have stopped all wars on our planet over 2,000 years ago, we have also controlled our population problem yet our people have a life expectancy of 300 years, this means that by time they retire at 260 YOA they have given all they can and retire gracefully, what else would you like to know, oh yes we have beaten the tyranny of distance a long time ago and we can travel anywhere in decent timing. For example it took us a week to reach here and then we spent a few days travelling around your planet having a look.

One delegate from planet X then spoke up, and so what he asked does this mean to us do you consider us as being on a war footing with your group of planets.

Firstly they aren't our planets we work together for economic and security reasons but we do have closed shop trade agreements and guarantees to defend any that come under attack from outside, we are the guarantors for that, but we don't want war we want peace, and no we don't see us as being on a war footing with your planet.

You say you may be able to help us and could place maybe two billion of our population, is this an offer or a speculation.

Our group is meeting in two weeks time the maybe we can turn this from speculation to a firm offer what else is there we may be able to help with?

No it's the population problem that's so depressingly urgent, we have a population of 10 billion and room for only six, and we are at our wits end. Something should have been done years ago but our politicians were just too weak, now it's completely out of control and the people breed like rabbits. We have now put a maximum of one child per couple but that should have been done fifty years ago. We went looking for a new planet that had lots of room and that's when we decided to take over Corrdeloo as you know, but that was an equally sorry disaster, that's over now and we must move on. We appreciate your mission of peace and thank you for that, be sure we won't attempt to take over any of your members in the future.

Well if we can be of any help at all we will let you know, we will put it to our members including our own Govt to see if we can help, who knows if we can reach a none aggression pact what ways there could be that we could help.

The meeting broke up well with expressions of goodwill all around, and the Orbseyns promising to see what they could do to help with the population problem.

The group meeting in TeKahanui was one of goodwill all around, and the meeting came to order and settled down to work on the problem of planet X. the main problem overpopulation was dealt with immediately. Without any strings attached after the Orbseyns had made their points the following offers were received Xalafeu 1million, Corrdeloo 50million, TeKahanui 10 million, Orbsey 10 million, Kanuitepai 10Million and Tepakeha 10 million, a total of 91 million people to be relocated. The terms were simple there must be a peace agreement between the planet and the group, relocation costs would have to be paid for by the X planet, and the immigrants would have to be screened as to character etc before they left their home planet, and any trouble makers would have to be returned home very quickly.

But as far as Li's dept of interplanetary affairs were concerned this was a mammoth task and in fact almost impossible to achieve even with all of the fleets helping. Li had decided to leave the job to the men and gone back to looking after her baby.

Planet X had been in touch and expressed how grateful they were for the offer to take so many, but now they were looking at the logistics and realizing how hard the whole job was. In the end they thanked the group and declined the offer because it was just too hard, and they had been foolish to even consider the foolish attack in the first place.

Gradually the Orbseyn politicians began to wander if there was any other way they could help, such as aid by way of food, but it was decided to leave that for the present because they had their own group to care for first.

The shifting of over 250,000 people in and out of Orbsey was now well underway, most of the member planets had decided to do their own transport and save some money, but they also greatly enjoyed the sense of defeating distance, it took over twelve months but eventually the job was done and the teams at Orbsey were delighted. Finally they were back to producing spacecraft and once again the people of Orbsey were enjoying their flights into the heavens at reasonable price.

There was still a lot of transport required for the product that were being bought off other planets, so the craft were still being used to their utmost level, but these type of flights didn't need to have attendants to load and unload there were teams just for that purpose at their destinations and at home.

The ambassadors were still all very busy they bad to ensure that there were no problems with any of their people wherever they were, and many were pulled of the space flights because of insubordination to the member planets. There seemed to be an unfortunate tendency to think of Orbseyns as the master race and that wasn't to be tolerated from any of the staff no matter how menial their job they were expected to be humble at all times.

One day at a airport in TeKahanui, Orlos came across two Orbseyns telling a group of the locals why the Orbseyns were so superior. Orlos immediately slapped set of laser cuffs on both men and started to tell the gathered crowd why they were all equal, he then beamed the two men up two their cruiser was up above.

Then turning to the gathered crowd he said those men are now in the lock up on the ambassadors cruiser and will be dealt with by the courts when we get home, in the meantime I hope this teaches them a bit of old fashioned humility. There was a polite round of applause from the crowd who then all drifted of laughing at the two big mouths that had got themselves into trouble. Orlos experienced this type of stupidity often when away from home especially from tourists and it was always a pleasure to teach such people a lesson, but it wasn't always so helpful in the courts because of course the culprits denied the accusations, but now Orlos had taken to carrying video tapes to prove his point. The same applied to Coreum, he also loved his planet but he hated to hear people making fools of themselves and making scenes in front of foreigners, but mostly they both hated to hear people from home boasting about what Orbsey could do and how they came from the greatest planet in the heavens.

New settlers galore:

The new colonists were arriving steadily mainly on their own spacecraft and the Orbseyns going to settle were being sent out in the same craft. The craft from the various planets were distinctively marked and, were all beautifully maintained, but now the terminal at Orbsey was far more than just a terminal for people it had had extensions built so that craft just carrying produce were able to go straight to their terminal for unloading and get immediate attention.

The new area was huge and could hold under cover ten spacecraft of a full size unloading at the same time. The children from Corrdeloo were so happy now they could get meat from home and thought it was wonderful. The shops now had products from all of the different planets and the people loved to just go window shopping and see all of the new style products, but silks and spices from earth was still among the top favorites.

Li and Orlos often went out window shopping just remembering the places all of these goods were coming from and how it had all started, Orlos would hold his wife tight and whisper see what you started now it's just a self perpetuating avalanche of wonder full goods from planets we both got to know so well doing our jobs.

Li would smile enigmatically at her mate in the way of the Chinese and say no my darling you started it all when you eloped with me from my parents home that was the real genesis of all of this. They also often went out to the now huge park with rapidly growing Kauri trees and remembered these giants and where they came from, but they never tried to communicate with the tree spirits that seemed all so unnecessary at present but the day would come when they would play with the spirits once again just as they had done with their parents in New Zealand, but that was almost 100 years ago and neither felt like dancing anymore.

Li was now almost due to get pregnant with their second child and they had decided to make sure it was a girl, and then they would settle down to work the next 100 years until they were allowed to retire. This time both Li and Orlos had to have treatment Orlos was no longer as virile as when he was younger and the medical centre had to check out that he wasn't just firing blanks as was so often the case with the second child. He proved to still be fully able so Li was made ready to have her egg fertilized, which happened very quickly.

On Orbsey men got no special leave when their wives were pregnant but all pregnant women got two years leave of absence no matter who they were, it was all paid for by the govt.

It seemed to them both it was only a few days until the little girl was born and named after her mother Lisa. Her brother came to see her, he was a strapping 30 YO now and looking for a wife so he didn't stay around for long, but took off on his nightly hunting for a women.

Li settled down to mothering her baby girl and she loved every moment of the time spent with the child, but all to soon it came to an end and it was back to work.

Li no longer went out with any type of space travel, she was now the chief administrator for her dept and only went to see official leaders if they came to Orbsey.

Orlos had now taken the senior position on the inter space flights and his orders were to bring in another four planets to the group. It was a lot different now first any newcomers had to satisfy Orbsey but then they also had to face a full group of leaders from each and every planet except earth, before they could get final approval.

The scientists had found four planets and had Probe reports back about all four; she had selected the first one that was to be approached one named Zoa and so Orlos and his team was off again. The planet was three months away and they took a space freighter in case they decided to steal some of the people for observation purposes.

It was as usual a long boring trip but the two extra ambassadors helped to break the boredom, for Coreum especially since they were both females, but sadly for him they were definitely not interested in getting too close, both had boyfriends at home so poor Coreum missed out again, while Orlos just slept most of the time.

When they arrived Orlos and Coreum beamed down and had a look around, the people looked like themselves, but maybe a little taller and they appeared good natured in fact very friendly. When they asked where the parliament buildings where of strangers they were very happy to explain without asking any questions, although they obviously wandered why these strangers didn't know the way. Orlos and Coreum then beamed themselves directly to the parliament buildings and asked to see someone of importance; they were aliens from another planet and would like to meet some of the leaders.

Some men came out but explained none of the main politicians would be available for two days and if they would explain what they wanted they would pass on the message and they were sure their leaders would see them as soon as they could get back to the parliament.

The two Orbseyns presented their credentials and explained why they were there in detail, and then they said they would be back in four days to see if there was any interest in what they had been saying.

When they returned it was to be met by some men who seemed very suspicious and not overly interested in what they had to say, why have you come to see us they asked?

Because our scientists had traced your planet as being quite close to us, so here we are it has only been a two month journey, Orlos replied and we wanted to see if you might like to join our group of independent planets?

Is the any reason why we should want to join they asked?

Yes there are very good economic and security reasons to join us, after you come and visit us of course, we would like to take a group of 100 of your best Politicians, scientists economists back with us then our top people can explain to you all what we are about. This sounds quite interesting the leader replied can you leave the coordinates of your planet and we will have our scientists check out if it is safe for us to go with you.

After they returned in two days they were told their scientists had been talking to the Orbseyn scientists and now felt it would be good to send a delegation, and they would be ready to leave in one week from that day.

Orlos and Coreum assured them they would be free to look at anything on their planet, and they would have guides to take them anywhere they requested off the maps that they would be given, or could buy at any store.

The trip back was as usual dull and boring and the ambassadors tried to keep to themselves to allow the foreign group every chance to get to know a little about Orbsey. When they reached the now enormous terminal it was interesting for the visitors to see the different spacecraft with the name of their planets emblazoned on their sides.

They were met by the usual big crowd and at this point Li took over as the senior official and welcomed all of the visitors, to Orbsey. She then introduced their own VIP party and asked the visitors to name their own individual VIPs, politician first. The groups now started to mix together and very successfully it seemed, the visitors were given a week to do any tours they wanted to and they could go anywhere except to the hub of thought power.

The conference was started with the Orbseyns speaking first, to the delighted applause of the visitors once they had finished.

Then the visitors tabled a list of question they wanted answered, how they asked can we be sure your big planet doesn't want to swallow us up, Will we be free to do our own thing or will we be shackled to Orbsey, and a hundred other questions the other Planets had asked. In fact it was revealed the other planets would all have leadership teams arriving within a few days in their own distance defeating space craft and they would prove they were completely free and uncontrolled in every way.

The meeting was adjourned until the others arrived and then reconvened with all of the planets represented by five of their top politicians and two scientists to each team. Once again Li was called on to open proceedings, because she was the one best known to all of the different planets leaders having spent so much time with them on their first journey to Orbsey.

They greeted her with subdued but very respectful applause, and the meeting was then underway.

The individual leaders of each planets group spoke and between them answered all of the questions that the delegates from Zoa had asked, but each one asked a few questions of their own about Zoa which were meant to find out for sure that Zoa was for peace with no warlike ambitions. The Zoan delegates were then given copies of documents setting out all of the agreements between the planet group and allowed to take them away. Then they were allowed the freedom of once again go anywhere they wanted to, until they were ready to go home.

The Zoan group met once more with the Orbseyns before they left and advised they were keen to join the group and would have the documents signed by their Plebiscite leaders, while the VIP cruiser just waited for a few days, for them to get it all done. Meanwhile they would also arrange for a colony of their people to be sent to Orbsey and would be happy to receive a full colony from Orbsey. In twelve months time all of the colonists were in place, plus ambassadors and trade delegations, Orlos and Coreum had completed their first assignment it was time to move on to other work..

The dept for interplanetary affairs had become so big it was decided to split them up so that Li's dept now only covered working with the planets for any political reason, finding new members and helping them to get settled. The other depts. had been split off because it had become just too big and it was time to separate them into several different depts. The entire division had become huge and needed close attention from a new dept that had only one area each to rely on.

Li and her fellow ambassadors were called into the parliament inner sanctum and given awards for the services they had given to Orbsey. Li in particular was given the highest award that could be given to any individual on the planet.

In her reply of thanks Li demonstrated why she had been so successful in dealing with such a wide range of people, her speech was flawless and she was given a loud round of applause from every person present that day especially Orlos and Coreum. Both had worked with her for many years now and had so often heard her work her verbal charm on so many high placed politicians, all there agreed she had earned her award well and truly and they were delighted to see and hear her so honored.

The scientists had another two planets they had sent probes out to and were satisfied this could be another two members for the group. One planet was about two months away in a different direction from present members and was named by the inhabitants Kiaora. The second one was three months away in the same direction and named Rimutaka, neither of them had shown signs of nuclear weapons, but both were well advanced with nuclear power for peaceful purposes.

The procedures were the same as the previous planets had been, meet with them explain what Orlos and his team had the authority to discuss then invite them back to Orbsey which was all duly accepted. Orlos had taken the unprecedented step of picking up the VPs of the two planets, and he was very nervous about whether he had done the right thing, but the two groups got along famously, and it was a very successful trip with two new members signed up from one round trip. And so it was down to finding only one more member and they had the total that was wanted ten excluding earth.

They were all busy trying to work out which planet they would invite to be that tenth member, when a radio communiqué came in from planet X. No one knew how they had become aware of the last membership being available; probably one of the scientists had explained what was happening and suggested they should try to join because it would be to their strong advantage. Because the first connection with this planet had been war there was a lot of hesitation in political circles, but a lot of enthusiasm in scientific and economic circles. It was argued that there could be no harm to talk and that if there was a chance to convert this planet to peaceful purposes then there was at least the obligation to try.

Planet X was sent a message asking when they could have 100 top officials ready to be picked up, because a cruiser would be sent to pick them up and return them to their planet after top level talks in Orbsey. The other older members were all notified of the request from planet X and given an approximate date to be in Orbsey for the high level talks. The timing on all counts was very accurate and on the date predicted all of the delegates were ready to meet in the great hall of the parliament.

The cruiser had beamed the visitors up because Orlos had decided they wouldn't land this could be a dangerous planet for their craft to land on and he wasn't prepared to take the risk. But the visitors were very friendly a fact that he advised Li of, back in Orbsey so she had prepared a suitable welcome, as for a friendly state visit.

There was the usual welcome at the terminal with the big excited crowds;

the Orbseyns had become used to welcoming dignitaries and they always made visitors feel welcome.

After the greetings the visitors were settled into hotels, but they weren't offered the same freedom to visit anywhere they may want to go, perhaps later after the meetings, but for the present they were given the best of hotel accommodation, and feted by their opposite number in the Orbseyn administration.

A few days after they arrived the first meeting was convened in the Parliament and they were introduced to the other planet members, the Orbseyn members were surprised there was an immediate rapport with all of the leaders.

After settling down the delegates from Planet X were asked to speak first since they had requested the meeting, and the Orbseyns didn t want it thought they had in some way been complicit in bringing this meeting together.

The planet X members spoke well and articulated the reasons they had made the approach but they agreed they had inside knowledge on what was happening within the group and that there was only one spot left, so they had decided to apply in spite of the poor start they had had with the war on Corrdeloo. They then spoke about their population desperation and how they were having troubles with the new laws allowing only one child. It had been legalized that only one child was allowed and any extras that were born would be taken and raised by the state. The parents were to be put in house arrest for two years, but if it happened a second time they would go to a govt controlled labor center for ten years. They acknowledged that the attack on Corrdeloo was stupid in that even had it succeeded they still couldn't have shifted their problems. The whole idea was poorly conceived and then foolishly carried out by an egoistic general who would listen to no one, because had he contacted his home base with the threat, he would have been ordered to abort his mission, but he didn't and they all paid the price for his arrogance.

The delegates from X made it plain they weren't just blaming one man they were all complicit, but now they were ready to destroy all nuclear weapons and guarantee a weapons free future. When these delegates bad finished and sat down the received a strong ovation from the leaders of the other planets, then the others began to reply to the request from Planet X. Every planet was positive to this possible new member provided they could live within the agreement that existed between themselves. Only Orbsey showed some hesitation they wanted first to know the nuclear stockpile had been destroyed and that the people had really been forced to the population agenda in spite of objections that their Govt could force the law through a possible hostile parliament.

The planet X delegates then invited 20 delegates from each member planet to come to planet X and see the answer to the final questions the Orbseyns had.

The delegates all agreed they would go straight from Orbsey to Planet X to see if the promises that had been made by their delegates could really be forced through their parliament.

On arrival all of the delegates were greeted warmly by the local VIPs it was soon obvious this was a very well developed society, but evidence of degeneration was beginning to show everywhere. Much to the surprise of the Orbseyns, the start on destroying the nuclear weapons were already underway and the legislation had been passed through a parliament that wasn't hostile. The question was then asked how secure the Govt was; and it was explained that the govt was in power on the basis of reducing the population and no more expenditure on nuclear weapons, the people were 100% behind leaving nuclear warfare and the enormous cost behind. The group idea of one defending force meant their budget for weapons would be eliminated and was a very popular idea.

Acquiring a fleet of vehicles for peaceful means and able to beat the tyranny of distance seemed to be the answer to a lot of their problems especially if paid for on a quid pro quo basis. The members then met in private and all agreed it was a good move to offer planet Coresou full membership if they wanted to bind themselves to the same contract as all of the others, it was decided they would wait until they received an answer.

The answer came back almost immediately; it was in the form of the documents fully signed with full acceptance of all the terms. The delegates all joined in a quiet celebration, knowing now they had a full group or a Federation of Planets that would in the years ahead prove wonderful for all of the peoples and give political, scientific, security and economic well being.

The final advice to the planets was never to drop their guard, the Orbsey missiles could defeat distance but they needed time to set the production lines up and they were never to leave their shields down unless they had spacecraft coming and going. Each planet had private codes that they could use only to contact the defense center in Cordiance, and any incoming craft had private codes that applied only to that craft. It was again explained that he shield would stop all incoming craft and if they didn't know it was there, a stranger would crash when trying to get through. Also that the shield would take two weeks to breach with nuclear weapons, ordinary weapons would never be able to break through.

Back in Cordiance there was quite some reason to celebrate the final member had been signed up; and there was no more need to go out hunting for new members. Li had been working on this project since she was 75 YOA and Orlos since he was about ninety. Li was now almost 200 YOA and Orlos

215 YOA; they were both near to choosing their last term of work. Li chose to stay with her dept; for another five years then spend her last term as a judge of the high court. Orlos and Coreum had decided to spend their last term as developers and were again building high rise home units.

Lisa their daughter turned out to be a gorgeous girl as her mother had been, with her mother's nerves of steel and she was ready to join up with her first job as a first year apprentice with the Dept; of interplanetary affairs the same as her brother who was almost through his first term.

Both loved the work, but whereas he had a crush on one earthling girl who didn't seem to care a hoot for him, Lisa was constantly being offered marriage which she always refused and both Li and Orlos were getting tired of rejected hopefuls petitioning them for help with their daughter. But neither of them could have given any help if they had wanted to which they didn't Lisa like her mother had her own mind and no hopeful male would ever influence which way she would go when she chose a partner so the best they could all do was sit around and hope they were the chosen one when the time came.

Both brother and sister got on well together when they saw each other which wasn't often, and Orlos and Li loved their infrequent times when they and their children were both at home. The old times had gone now it was not often that children stayed with their parents until they married, this was a sad regret to most parents, but the young said it was all so modern. Living with mum and dad was now terribly plebian and only for those who had no ambitions of their own, which may have been quite right.

A BLAST FROM THE PAST.

Quite suddenly one day Li was asked to come for a meeting at the main headquarters of parliament house, it seemed that help was needed out at one of the planets and they needed her golden charms once again to calm things down. It was a trade dispute but needed a top diplomat not just some people from the dept; of trade to try and sort it all out so on that basis Li agreed to go, and she decided to go in her private craft to save time and she decided to take Lisa, much to the girls delight.

The dispute was between the Corrdeloons and the TeKahanuins, the claim was that some of the produce provided by the Corrdeloons was sub standard, and the TeKahanuins were claiming what the suppliers said was an unfair attempt to extort them for money. The buyers said such a claim was ridiculous and they were only asking for the quality they had been charged for. Li listened to both parties separately and then made her suggestion that would be applicable to all parties to the dispute. Li had asked Lisa to go to the cruiser and clean her teeth and her mouth thoroughly then she had both sides to the dispute prepare some of the grain each in a small bowl, then when Lisa came back she blindfolded her securely and taking the two bowls she asked Lisa to taste one then go and clean her mouth again and then try the other bowl to see how it tasted better or worse. After she had done as she had been asked Lisa thought for a while and then said, I think the first bowl may have been a little better than the second, but there is little difference. Then Li asked which the sample that is claimed to be inferior is, this she was told was the second sample the first sample was the normal supply. Then turning to the supplier she asked how it came about that the product is so inferior to the original, but the supplier professed being completely astonished. Then turning to the buyer she asked, well what do you want to do about it now?

Well we want a discount for low grade material we would like a 10% discount.

Wow said Li that seems a little high after all the difference in quality isn't that great, how would 5% satisfy you and turning to the supplier will you allow a 5% discount?

Yes they replied we could just manage that but no more we are only agents for the product and the profits aren't high in the first place, but we will try and get the money back from the growers.

Both parties expressed themselves as satisfied and both thanked Li and Lisa for their help in settling the dispute so efficiently.

And so it was back in the cruiser and on the way home again, Lisa was loud in her praise for her mother's negotiating skills, but she was telling her father and he was already well aware of Li's abilities in that area. He merely said you should have heard her in her prime dear there was none who could ever match her, why do you think she is so renowned at the dept.

It was ten years later and Li was almost due to be appointed to the high court as a judge when a report came in that earth was due to be attacked by beings wanting to take earth over, but they were still 6 months away and only lightly armed they obviously thought earth wasn't well defended if at all, so they were being rather careless for an invasion force.

Suddenly the radios started to squeal as Orbsey scientist cut into their communication, what they were asked is your intention towards earth because they are a protectorate of ours and we will have to ask you to desist if you have intentions to invade.

Who are you and why should we desist, there is no law saying you are in control of this universe.

Well to prove a point the Orbseyns said we will in ten hours blow ten of you fleet out of the skies, if you still refuse to desist we will destroy your entire fleet, now once again what is your choice we don't mind we have nuclear homing missiles aimed at you right now.

The commander came on the radio and said this isn't correct you have no right to interfere with us unless you are from earth.'

We have said we are the protector of earth and in fifteen minutes ten missiles will be fired, and once they are on the way they can't be stopped, so you have fifteen minutes, we don't want to have a battle with you, but we won't let you reach earth under any circumstances.

The line went dead and the communication was cut off obviously they believed it was just a scam so right on time ten missiles were fired, and were on the way.

In three days the missiles struck and there was pandemonium among the attackers as ten of their freighters were obliterated. The radios started to really squeal now as the fleet broke into pandemonium immediately, the commander spoke and asked have you fired more missiles or do we have time to withdraw, we can see now you have the technology to back up your threat.

We will give you five hours to turn around and go home if not rest of you fleet will be targeted and destroyed, can you do that Orbsey asked?

Yes we will reverse course immediately and you need never worry about us ever again, we know now what you mean when you say earth is protected goodbye.

The message was sent out to all of the ten member planets and the incident reported, but they were exhorted to watch their own heavens, we don't want some power getting through and causing havoc out in any of the member's areas.

Orlos and his family heard of the latest defense work and was suitably happy, their special love earth, were safe and that was very important to them.

Meanwhile their son was very depressed the girl of his dreams wouldn't even look at him and he was devastated, what am I to do he wailed to his mother?

You must do the same as she is doing to you ignore her and make believe you have found another, if she has any feel for you this will stop her antics, how old is she by the way his mother asked?

"She is thirty five and enjoys having all of the men attracted to her shall I really give her up?"

"Well it seems to me she is very immature to be so footloose with her attraction, I think she may be a very poor choice of mate and may only lead to heartbreak, you have to find out for yourself unfortunately, but from what you have told me I don't like her because she is just a vamp that is refusing to grow up, she is totally immature."

Her son left but was in a terrible state, what can I do wandered his mother but she could think of nothing so she had to let it slip from her mind, several hours later he tuned into her thoughts and told her he was out with another girl, not as beautiful but far nicer and he was going to forget the other one. Be careful his mothers told him don't just play broken hearts now just start to be sure of yourself and let it all work out properly. Meanwhile Orlos had come home from one of their developments and the old couple settled down to an evening alone in the quiet together they had met young and grown old together now in the last years they were totally at peace with no thought of being bored, such were there thought when their son broke into their thoughts. The girl of his dreams who had been his one love for so long was now trying to get him to go back to her, what shall I do he asked, I am becoming fond of this new girl and she responds to me the other never did, Mum what do I do?

Stick to the new one she advised she had been proving to be much more stable and that's what you want at present isn't it both Li and Orlos asked.

Bankers and others:

Bankers had been purged from Orbsey centuries ago when they were found to be trying to manipulate money for their own ends, the Govt had taken over all money and now only Govt and private credits could be used as currency with the values tightly controlled. But in some of the other planets banks were in control of all currency, and the formation of the Federation of Planets had created for them they thought a golden opportunity, they were busily trying to create an open market for all trade exchange and Orbsey was being attacked as the planet that was controlling all others and therefore paying any price they chose to pay for products bought and sold. Orbsey treated these statements with contempt as just money brokers trying to destabilize the values to force big profits for themselves. They made it clear their Govt credits were a fixed value and all other should value their own currency in line with that policy.

It was clear the Orbsey money of whatever ilk was backing all other currencies and if any weakened they would have to answer to the planets board of trade not Orbsey, but the battle with the bankers raged on, it was a standoff that only Orbsey could afford to sit back and watch. In the end Orbsey invited all of the planets to bring their bankers to a meeting to answer all of the charges of claimed corruption against Orbsey their govt control of the money for which they never moved the value either up or down and the bankers were charged to prove their claims or leave the meeting.

The bankers first claim was the money being fixed worked in Orbseyns favor and that the other planets were held in thrall by their very superior economy.

And what they were asked would you have us do, to which they replied float your money and let it find its own value.

And who would that benefit and where the profits from trading in our currency would go they were asked?

Why it would find its own level of value and the other currencies would also float to their real level which would mean there would be a free and open currency market.

And who would decide the real levels you so avidly support.

Why the traders they replied.

And where would the profits of your such avid support for the value of our money go to they were asked?

Why it would be the market traders that earn that profit they would win or lose according to their skill or if you like their ability to read the markets on a given day? They replied.

And what else would you have these masters of finance be able to do they were asked?

Well a free and open stock market should be allowed so business could also find its true level of value up or down on any given day; and business should be able to borrow freely so they could develop freely without Govt interference.

And so you want us to free our business markets so the banks could become the masters of our economy with all the extras such as of course little things like fractional banking and all of the cost traps that go with it. Now tell us if the value of a major company according to your stock exchange ideas was to go up what happens to the real value of the business that your experts and their bankers are so judging?

Why no it's the shares that are traded not the actual business that value remains constant unless something goes wrong, they replied?

And could that something wrong have anything o do with how the investors see that company or are encouraged by their advisors to see that companies trading results?

Well it does sometimes have an effect but overall there is a real open assessment of a company's true value.

Orbsey will shortly be reducing our prices to Planet members by 10%, so how would you suggest we do this or what should be done to ensure they all benefit equally.

We suggest you open your currency markets because the value of your currency will float down and have quite some impact on every member of this planetary group.

So if our currency floats down as you say who will be the beneficiary of such an action?

Why every planet will get an advantage and will be able to buy more

Orbseyn products, they replied triumphantly thinking they had scored a great advantage.

These are only simple examples of the questions that the bankers were asked, in two days of solid questions, many were asked to leave the forum for making misleading statements but at the end most remained.

In the final summing up the panel of judges said. This planet centuries ago was held in thrall by the bankers the most parasitic class of people we had, and our cost structures were always subject to the decisions made by bankers. We kicked them out and changed to the system we have now and this planet has never looked back, we have gone from success to success, but our success has been shared by our people, not monopolized by one class of privileged money grubbers who until then were in a class of their own, and all underwritten by the Govt.

This planet will never go back to a system of banking that we know so well, that is a fool's paradise and would be a world controlled banking system and you want to extend that to an interplanetary system so the what others cannot do with war you will do with money, this will never happen to us again.

Now our member planets may leave as many economist as they like to learn our system if they want to, but bankers and lawyers are barred, we have no need for Bankers and we don't need lawyers hypothecating about what is good or bad for us.

Now we intend to unilaterally reduce our prices by 10% to all of our members in three months time, but if we are advised by our Ambassadors of racketeering by bankers in any planet that 10% reduction will be cancelled and full prices restored. As for gambling with our currency that's not going to happen because our treasury is well able to withstand the costs of what we are doing, but unless the benefit is going to them people and not a class of people that discount will be cancelled. Any planet that wants to get rid of its parasitic system controlled by bankers we in Orbsey pledge our support even in a financial sense, we will help you get rid of this class of people.

Thank you one and all and we wish you a good journey home, but be assured there will be no more invitations for bankers to meet with us in any capacity, ever again in the future, nor will any Orbseyn officials travel anywhere to meet with bankers.

As soon as the meeting was closed and the Orbseyns had all left the chamber there was an immediate uproar among all of those from the planets left behind and shocked at what they had just heard. Some mainly bankers and lawyers felt it was an imposition on their sovereign rights, others agreed and were going to work with the Orbseyns as had been offered. But the bankers felt terribly threatened by the final summation, they knew now as a class they were being threatened, and Orbsey had proved they didn't need bankers in fact had done away with them many years ago, and had done very well without them.

The economists were amused and the politicians were confused, how they wandered can we change to a new system we have been for so long controlled by bankers, but if Orbsey could do it surely they could too. The politicians decided to ask the Orbseyn politicians for a meeting before they left just to get a better understanding of what it all meant, so a meeting was convened for the next morning, all were welcome to attend except the bankers who were left to their own devices the next day, almost secluded in their hotel rooms.

The Orbseyns were very open as to what they wanted and that was the wiping out of the banking class and they were will to give advice and financial support to try and achieve their goal. Records from the past were shown to prove just how much the banks had benefited from an economy in crisis when they had control of the money. Some countries had massive wealth others were desperately poor and millions saved to death. Huge sums of money was spent on weapons for war, and the needs of the starving millions were ignored, graft and financial crimes were endemic because the people could see corruption all around them, society was degenerating rapidly as families fell apart. Then they showed graphs of how things had changed since Govt controls had been established, the changes were dramatic and showed in every strata of Orbseyn society.

But it wasn't the Govt that had succeeded so dramatically it was the systems they had gradually put in place, it took over a hundred years to complete. The universities started turning out aspiring business people, and they went on to spend their first work period (45 years) as practicing apprentices, all working for the Govt. Then in the second 45 year term they could choose Govt or private and about 60% chose govt because of the rewards available to them when their second term was over then and only then could they become captains of industry, and as such they were a respected but not selfish class of people. Private business could go on and do whatever they wanted to do, they could get grants from the Govt but they couldn't borrow and no interest was charged on the Govt grants. The meeting lasted all day, but at the end there was a lot of far more knowledgeable politicians who had suddenly found the desire to break the banker's yoke that held them in thrall. They also had the guarantee that Orbsey would give help in every way including money and that by time it was all in place bankers as a class would be finished.

Naturally after the meeting the bankers were all agog as to what was happening, and loudly declaiming that they weren't a parasitic class but had helped build their planets up as much as anyone, but after the way they had been put down by the Orbseyns their claims suddenly sounded rather hollow.

The first planet to test the waters before getting rid of their bankers was Zoa, the politicians had on returning home made it plain that big changes were going to be made, they argued that with their big population the systems as laid out by the Orbseyns were very attractive. The bankers argued it couldn't be done so the economists were working to prove it could be done and a lot easier than it had been for the Orbseyns to do it because they had had to create the blueprint which they were happy to share.

The govt of Zoa worked quietly until they were ready then suddenly announced the nationalization of the banking system and the firing of all the leading bankers. Because the politicians had been very careful to cover all of the weak spots there was a minimum of disruption, and the people cheered what they considered was strong Govt; they were proud to support such a move. The huge private assets held by bankers in many location on their world were confiscated and taken by the state and turned over to the consolidated accounts. The bankers were put down and shut out they had no recourse to the media etc and any mention of their woes was answered by proof of their former grand life styles, and it was stressed that had all been at the cost to the people.

The banks were now fully under govt; control and the Orbseyn systems were being implemented slowly but surely. The Zoan Govt; now extended an invitation to Orbsey to send a party of observers to see what they had done, which they were glad to accept.

When they arrived there were a few minor changes they advised but on the whole they congratulated their hosts on how practical they had been in the ways they had used to force their legislation through, they predicted that within 10 years Zoa would be a changed economy and that in fifty years they would have beaten their overpopulation problem.

The Zoans were ecstatic they felt so proud that they had at last moved in the right direction, and they were quick to acknowledge it was all because of the Orbseyns.

The other politicians from the member planets were watching with interest, and most now were slowly but surely changing some of their legislation to allow them to make the changes that Zoa had made. Quite a bit of travel between Orbsey and Zoa by the politicians and advisors of the other planets were now underway and most of the bankers realized they were a class under siege because of the influence of Orbsey. Then the cost of all products from Orbsey was reduced by 10%, and those that had floating currencies and large trading accounts with Orbsey found the value of their currency flying at way higher levels than before. This was the final straw against the bankers even to save their own position they were unable to control the currency movements, and the planets all who now traded extensively with each other found themselves under siege and quite unable to control the banks.

Within ten years all of the banks on every planet had been nationalized and the Orbsey methods were being put into practice. Business was moving ahead beautifully on all planets and the savings were proved to be substantial as a none productive cost on the GDP of each and every planet. It was proved that after ten years using the Orbseyn system the none productive costs had been reduced by 50%, and the boost to the moral of the peoples on every planet became stronger as they began to understand what had been done.

At a meeting of the leaders of all the planets, it was asked how Orbsey had got their lifespan up so high and whether it was a good move considering the need to control the high cost of the aged care.

It was explained that the aged care cost was all factored into the reality to having a highly trained workforce that could be worked for a long period and didn't just die taking their knowledge and expertise with them. This was balanced by the highly controlled birth rate of only two children per couple, and the people could be kept very well for the full period of their lives with no reason to suffer from any illness because all health problems could be treated including the re growth of body parts that may fail and have to be replaced. All such problems were minor and the maximum period needed to grow say a new set of heart and lungs would be five months. The only part of the body that still needed hospital attention was the brain and special hospitals were still operational for all diseases of the head.

The retirement period of 40 years allowed the old people to die in comfort or whatever they wanted to do whatever they wanted with their last years many just wanted to pass away peacefully which they were allowed to do in spite of the medical system being well able to keep them alive and well. It was pointed out that the age limits could be increased if the people wanted that, but most felt that a limit of three hundred was enough and any that wanted to go on could do so by paying moderate fees for the medical centers to keep them alive. All of the leaders left that meeting completely amazed at how health was managed on Orbsey and how well some of the oldest workers looked; to them it was a miracle. But they could see this system would be the hardest to copy, they could do it over a long period of time on average they thought 200 years to get their facilities up to the right standard.

Orbsey was quite willing to pass on the health secrets to all of their members, but they warned the medical professional had been hard to convince that they could still do well working for the govt. The dental and pharmaceuticals had been the hardest to bring under control the drug companies in particular had been difficult to deal with. But as they saw the no nonsense approach to the bankers they had become more prepared to work with the govt especially when the govt; had agreed to underwrite the cost of research by 50% and even more. Medical attention at a medical clinic was free for the first 12 minutes of consultation but any longer than that, full fees were charged. Home births were the norm and there was no charge for any service of that type. The setting up for growing new organs were free, as was the period of care needed while the new organs took over from the old.

Dentists in particular insisted on their independence to treat whoever, however they pleased but the govt; refused to in any way subsidize dental care. This put them at odds with the govt; and made them pariahs of a highly sophisticated society so that in the end they also agreed to work within the health system.

When the planets had first examined the Orbseyn systems they thought it was to nationalized and totally govt; controlled without room for private enterprise, they found they were wrong and this was a totally business friendly system. It appeared to be overbearing, but it wasn't the lack of having to borrow money that stood out as excessive control, it was the way grants were calculated and the fact that every business was entitled to get those grants and there was the fact that no interest had to be paid ever nor did the loans have to be repaid unless the business closed down. Critics of the system had when they had been implemented forecast that excessive govt; interference would destroy the Orbsey business community.

These claims had been made by the bankers as they fought to win back the former positions in society, but as the systems all started to work so they were banished and their critiques were considered as being irrelevant.

Planet	Population	Lifespan	Working life	Appearance	Height	Disposition
Orbsey	16 billion	300 years	230 years	earthlike	6 ft	contented
Xalafeu	6 billion	120 years	90 years	different	5ft 10 in	dour
TeKahanui	16 billion	160 years	130 years	ugly	6 ft	very happy
Coresou	12 billion	120 years	90 years	earthlike	6 ft	dour
Tepakeha	8 billion	160 years	130 years	different	5ft 10 in	happy
Kanuitepai	5 billion	160 years	130 years	different	5ft 10 in	hard working
Corrdeloo	8 billion	160 years	130 years	solid	6 ft	jolly
Zoa	12 billion	160 years	130 years	different	5ft 10in	contented
Kiaora	5 billion	160 years	130 years	different	5ft 10 in	contented
Rimutaka	5 billion	160 years	130 years	different	6 ft	contented
earth	1 billion	60 years	40 years	humans	5ft 8 in	reserved
total	94 billion					

Chapter 10/
Final years for Li and Orlos.

ORLOS HAD NOW COMPLETED his last work period and Li was now 245YOA and had fifteen years to go. Both of their children were doing well in the interplanetary diplomatic core and had taken over from their parents, they loved their jobs and Lisa especially was a gifted speaker. Their parents had actively supported their rise in the dept, as a new dept it didn't yet have many employees doing their third term so it was still open to youngsters to be promoted quickly if they showed true aptitude.

Li had handed back to the immigration dept. her personal spacecraft when she left the but they were happy to lend it to her if she wanted it for some reason, and she and Orlos was wandering about one last trip to their old love nest on earth. They wanted to visit the tree spirits one last time to say goodbye go to where Li's home had been and just take one look at the schools they had founded so long ago, Li applied for and was granted twelve months leave of absence, both of their children were going with them too look after the old couple who were both rather frail now, even Orlos who had once been so robust was just skin and bones now.

Li because of her appearances in the courts still tried to look as strong as she could, but her diminutive frame was now so very tiny. When they left the old couple felt the thrill of space flight one more time, but they were soon finding it very tiring and wandering if they should turn around and go home but they persevered and in the end had enjoyed that last trip. The visit to the tree spirits was just so wonderful, even though the spirits could see their old friend's had almost run their course. They stayed for a week and then reluctantly said goodbye for the last time.

Then they went to Li's old home in central china which of course was no more the area was all rice growing paddies now.

A visit to all of the schools which were thriving and finally short trips to Rome, Alexandria and India and it was time to go home. By time they arrived back in Cordiance they were both exhausted but happy to have been able to say goodbye, to the tree spirits and the five schools which were thriving with loving care from the teachers and money from Orbsey.

Both were too tired to talk when they got home, but their children stayed with them until they recovered which took about a month. Their entire peer group thought they were wonderfully brave to even have attempted the trip, but to them and their children it was well worth the struggle.

The final journey:

On her last day as a judge of the high court, Li launched a scathing attack on the system for the aged in Orbsey especially term five. She said that over the age of 200 it was only forced labor to keep the people working artificially by medical, means and that the state was actually using its aged population as slave labor.

This was one final speech from a once powerful orator, and the media really gave it maximum coverage, there was still a free press on Orbsey but it was always cognizant of that all Seeing Eye in the sky. Li said that 90% of the aged workers only kept going because they had to the power in the sky demanded it and the health care ensured it, but they weren't in the least bit happy. The additional term that had been added had been the straw that broke the spirit of all of the aged, that final extra 45 years of work took away the hope for a little comfort in retirement. Li said she had come to Orbsey at the age of 24 and had worked a total of 236 years and she had loved every minute of it, but she and her husband now had only a few years if any to enjoy each other's company because they were both exhausted onto the point of death, and she doubted if they would have long together at all.

My Darling husband she said is 15 years older than and has been living day by day probably just to have a few final days together and this shouldn't be. Even our two children haven't been allowed time off work to spend with their father because that Eye in the sky says they must work.

That Eye in the sky she declared is evil it has gone over the bounds of decency every person has had their life polluted by this evil thing in the sky. The keeping of law and order by this omnipresent Eye is a great thing, but when ordinary decent people were being controlled mercilessly it was time to take another look. People she said don't become criminals just because they take a day off work without permission, and by treating decent folk in this way it is an abuse of state power that if it isn't controlled will lead to the downfall of civil controls and eventually to anarchy as the young begin to understand the pressure their parents are under. It is ludicrous for example for a child to get a lifetime criminal record for stealing some lollies from the candy store, and it was a terrible shock to the parents of any girl to get a report that their daughter is taking part in the activities of a common prostitute because she has been caught flamboyantly dressed in the company of a boy. Who says she is a prostitute that Evil Eye in the sky has decided all on its own that these children are guilty, and they are labeled for life by an Eye that never forgets nor misses anything.

The people are tired Li said of this control by a none living thing in the sky that just keeps getting tougher and tougher, and one day the people will revolt not because they want to but because they will have no choice. By the time she had finished speaking the old lady was exhausted and had to be taken home from work never more to return it was all over and she had said her last hurrahs in the manner that only she could.

The media were very loud in their praise for a great citizen of Orbsey who had done so much for this and the other planets during her long working life. She had been a leader and instrumental in bringing together the Federation of Planets and was highly respected on every one of them. The farewells came in by radio thick and fast so she was able to try to enjoy what time there was left, with her husband. They passed away together in their sleep, they both simply wished for the end, and the look of relief on both of their faces when their children found them made it so plain how pleased they were to go. Orlos was 300 YOA and Li was 285 YOA, but what a life they had both lived.

320AD EARTH TIME.

It had been a quiet period after Li and Orlos had passed away some 120 years had passed by, and everything from a federalist point of view had been progressing well. The planets had been working and trading together perfectly, to the advantage of them all, but the problem that was growing was the one annunciated by Li in her last message to the high court. It had started with small claims coming in and people refusing to pay fines on the basis that they had been unfairly adjudicated by computers.

At the start there had been only a few but the volume was growing slowly until finally the courts were being overrun with millions of small claims. But now there were a growing number of larger claims starting to join the small ones, which was what was spear heading what was becoming a revolt, and now reaching alarming proportions. There was no leaders creating trouble it was a simple peoples revolt and they were simply expressing their rights in terms of the Orbseyn Constitution, which allowed all civilians and others to object to the high courts, if they felt their rights were being ignored.

The essence of the complaints was that there was nothing, but an Eye in the sky controlled by computers that decided everything to control the way of life on Orbsey. As the volume of court challenges kept getting larger the confusion grew, the once close control of the legal system fell into disarray and the once orderly society that had been Orbsey began to crumble.

The argument quickly developed that the problem was that all control was now vested in the all Seeing Eye. What happened to the various levels of govt we elected the people were asking and what about the Plebiscite which was supposed to have the casting vote on everything, there were no replies?

It soon became obvious that any answers that were being given by the politicians were being over ruled by the all Seeing Eye, and any comments by politicians that weren't considered correct by the Eye, were simply being trashed and in some cases serious charges brought against the politician.

Very quickly it became obvious the political class had been shut down and any that remained where merely pawns of the all Seeing Eye. But what couldn't be shut down was the ordinary citizens, a whole new class was coming into being, and no matter how many were fined or even jailed the level of discontent was becoming huge and would soon reach uncontrollable levels.

The people were asking, where are our leaders and what do we have to do to get answers in the courts, all we are getting are legal documents written by some computer and that machine is controlled by the all Seeing Eye. This is no good how do we get control back from this system that allows us no rights.

Then the special police were bought out, these were robots and their instructions were tied to the will of the Seeing Eye so that in theory there could be no revolt in a final threat from the people. But there was no threat from the people just billions of unpaid fines, all that could be done was to fine them for late payment, the problem was that the courts were now so far behind in processing the original complaints that the system was almost at the point of breakdown. The special robot police could find no work to do since the fault was mainly with the govt; all that happened was to create fear among the population as they suddenly saw these robots taking certain duties over that had been done by uniformed police.

Then suddenly the old people rebelled and refused to work out their final 45 year term, on the basis of it was just too hard and they wanted the life span to be reduced to 255 years and retirement reduced to 210 YOA. There were still no leaders stepping forward to lead what could have been a revolt, just individuals mainly husband and wife that had decided they weren't going to work after they had reached 210 YOA.

Once again from a few individuals the numbers grew quickly and before long there was a full class of workers at risk, because they wanted their final work term cancelled. All that could be done was to order the special police to pick up these recalcitrant's and sue them in the courts, but there were no jails so all that could be done was to fine them, and keep fining them until again the courts got bogged down and no letters of demand were going out. There was little else that could be done as there were no leaders that could be charged with heavy offences, all there was was a lot of people over 210 years of age they could take action against when the courts became unblocked. But the courts were getting out of control as the elderly and the unpaid fines were now blocking up the system. The problem was the computers couldn't handle the problems that were now developing and there was a feeling that anarchy would soon break out, but how was this to happen?

None of the legal infrastructure was under attack and all laws except the last work term were being honored, but even here who would lead a fight against the Seeing Eye? None were coming forward because all were happy with their standard of living, they just didn't want to be controlled by computers in the sky, nor did they want to work until they could no longer walk.

As Li had predicted all of those years ago Orbsey had become rich on the tremendous work load it had inflicted on its elderly people and the system had to break one day as even the Plebiscite members found themselves as servants to the Seeing Eye.

LISA:

Lisa was now 155 YOA married with a Son of her own and due to return to work after having had her second child a Girl only two years ago. Lisa was now the Managing Director of all interplanetary development work, having carried the job on after her mother, and just as successfully. She was surprised to have an urgent request to attend a Plebiscite meeting on her first day back at work, and that the need was urgent.

Lisa was aware of her mother's last statement to the high court and she was also aware that what Li had said was now beginning to come true, but she was also aware that her mother's words were not hers and therefore wandered what was happening? She was soon to find out!

After giving an outline of what was happening in Orbsey, the leader of the Plebiscite then continued to explain the problems on their planet was beginning to take a hold on the other planets and creating problems for the Federation. Her job she was told was to visit all of the planets and taking her brother they were to find out what needed to be done to contain the problems from getting any worse. The Plebiscite members were all well aware that Lisa like her mother before her was held in high esteem with all of the leaders and she was expected to calm down any discontent that may be growing in the Planets.

While I understand what is expected of me, it seems that what I really have to do is reassure the members that Orbsey is working to settle its own problems, and will do everything possible to bring our own people to understand the responsibility to retain civil and legal order on its own population as an example to all of the other planets. I am quite happy we can do this and at the same reassure them all that the problems will be dealt with fairly and properly; as they always have been and always would be.

Lisa was finally told she was to try and strengthen the interplanetary ties, but also arrange a full members meeting for about twelve months after she arrived home.

The trip would take over 18 months so Lisa applied to take her latest child with her, much to her surprise the request was granted. Since her husband and brother were both official escorts, the trip was going to be bearable after all, but there were hard times ahead and she would be glad to arrive back home..

Earth was not being visited on this occasion, this planet was a special interest to Lisa's mother and father but didn't have any special place as far as their daughter was concerned, but they were being looked after anyhow and certainly wouldn't be affected by the problems on Orbsey at present.

A special room had been set aside for the baby, he was two years old now so had to be kept away from underfoot of the crew, but apart from that no special arrangements had to be made. The fleet had been upgraded since Lisa had taken over and a special VIP cruiser had been built for her to entertain aboard while she was on any diplomatic trips. But the passenger capacity was reduced to 120 including Lisa and her entourage. Many gifts were loaded in the special bay with the two Aerocars, which were only there for emergency purposes or back up transport if other means of short journeys became difficult.

The proto cols were vastly different than in the days when the travelers from Orbsey, had to work hard to get access to the leaders of each planet, now there was a full embassy plus Ambassador and staff, to arrange all meetings for them, Lisa was still the main speaker and leader of the deputation from Orbsey.

The first planet the team visited was Xalafeu, and a great banquet was arranged on the cruiser, with all including the Orbsey Embassy heads invited. After the initial bonhomie of greetings all round the first main speaker was Lisa who like her mother had been, was a truly gifted speaker able to explain the reason for the visit by the federal interplanetary team in simple terms. Lisa came straight to the point and laid out the problems that had bought her planet to almost gridlock, with a silent, leaderless none violent revolution going on.

The system she said had ground to a halt as people objected to the control over their lives by computers, through what was termed the all Seeing Eye, they wanted leaders from the people again not from the Eye in the sky which they had developed a hatred for. The problems with the fifth term old people were far more entrenched and were a group of people who had simply retired and treated the govt with contempt. Lisa closed her speech by saying our job is to explain what is going on and why, she said put simply the elderly felt their working age was too long and had downed tools and the Govt didn't know what to do. The other was rule by the people as it had once been not through an all Seeing Eye in the sky that had the final say on everything, and the people want that to be stopped and proper leaders be elected with real power not subservient to the State. The introduction of robot police was just the final straw and now the population was waiting to see what would happen.

The leader for the Xalafeuns now spoke and started by saying the federation of planets had been great for all members, and the Orbseyn economy had powered them all too great advances, but what now he asked? What was going to be done about the problem with the people who it seemed wanted their elected parliamentarians to run the country not computers? The problem was whether this would spread to the peoples of other member planets, and create disruption everywhere.

Because Xalafeu was a more authoritarian regime they didn't expect any follow on effect, because while the Seeing Eye was also very active on the planet, it was more controlled. Obviously they would have to be careful that control was obvious so their people didn't start getting the same ideas, as the Orbseyns and start a ruckus over nothing. The control of the old age people on Orbsey seemed to the Xalafeuns to be something that had little or no effect on them, because the high life expectancy of that planet was not on their agenda.

What was of far more concern was what effect there would be on the Orbsey commitment to the mutual defense agreement that is one of the key points in the overall security enjoyed by the members of the federation of planets. The other major part of the agreement is the supply of certain vital technical knowledge including the great air ships that have made the whole interplanetary system viable including the trade that has now become such an integral part of all our economies. Of course the real health of Orbsey is vital to the whole system and if the full cooperation of all of our group of planets was needed to back that continued health, then it is vital we all meet but maybe not in Orbsey.

It is a set back to us all if in truth our well being is falling into the hands of computers, and all necessary action must be taken to correct whatever has gone wrong. Maybe the truth is that Orbsey has become just so developed it as gone too far and its people have become anxious. We must help to rectify this situation because of course we cannot have computers with too much power playing games within their preset formulas and commands, and in this way running such a great planet.

The leader then left the podium and Lisa closed the formal side of the gathering, firstly thanking the Xalafeuns for their strong support and also explaining the full agenda she had been given by the Plebiscite back in Orbsey. After they had been to all of the member planets she and her fellow staff members would decide the best planet to have the meeting on, this was within the mandate they had been given before they left Orbsey.

Lisa also pointed out that perhaps the leader of the Orbseyn Plebiscite had deliberately given her the authority within the mandate to make the decision away from Orbsey, but perhaps she also was being affected by the growing sensitivity of the population in Orbsey, and beginning to fear computers herself

The reaction among all of the planets was much the same as Xalafeu, some with stronger opinions about different subjects, but all very supportive of the Orbseyn Plebiscite. At the end of the last meeting Lisa announced the full meeting of leaders would be held in Xalafeu in twelve months time, she had already confirmed this date with the Orbseyn leaders back home and all of the Federation leaders.

It was just over fifteen months when Lisa and her team had completed the full trip and they were all glad to be home, but there seemed to have been a greater deterioration than ever among the unofficial protestors. It was estimated the courts were now over three years behind in issuing summons to citizens who hadn't paid their initial claims.

But the real problem was there was no top level class as the old people just refused to work and openly defied the government to do anything they wanted too, but they had finished work. The courts had no senior judges, all divisions of society had lost their highest level of administration; and everyone was confused without the guidance of their most senior advisors.

If the situation hadn't been so serious it would have been funny, the last such strike action on Orbsey had been 3,000 years ago, so everyone just sat back and waited. The old people just stayed at home and made it obvious there was no way they would be returning to work, and it didn't matter what the govt tried to do, they didn't care they were just too tired to continue, and they weren't going to be artificially stimulated by the medical systems anymore. It was amazing the historians could never recall such dramatic problems on their planet and yet there was no violence of any type, of course the oldies were too old for insurrection they were a minimum 210 YOA, and those who were refusing to pay fines the govt had the problem not them.

The courts were blocked up and there were no magistrates or judges to issue the various summons so the backlog was becoming daily greater. The robot police controlled by the Seeing Eye were still wandering around scaring people, but doing nothing effective.

Meanwhile Lisa and Kauri were at loggerheads over them not having visited earth. Unlike Lisa, Kauri thought of Earth with the same affection as his parents had done and had been angry when she hadn't considered earth in any way, not even the beloved kauri plantations.

Why? He had asked his sister when she had waved a visit to earth aside without any thought at all. In the end she had recanted and they had gone straight to NZ, where Kauri quickly showed he had remembered all his mother had taught him when they used to travel between the two planets together.

The tree spirits were quick to manifest themselves many taking the shape and look of Li when she was young, and some taking the shape of Orlos also when he was young. Lisa was so shocked she had never seen all of this before and her reaction was shame at herself for having been so callous.

Kauri was really at home with his parents old friends, and took great delight introducing Lisa and her Husband, he had already explained the past to his family but now they were seeing it for themselves, never are memories of the past so vividly portrayed and the tree spirits were quick to explain how their parents and Coreum had been the pioneers for what was now a great Federation.

They spent a week exploring the huge kauri plantations and gazing in wander at some trees that were over 4,000 years old, but then it was back to work, they had to look at some of the work that was still being done on Earth before going home. Lisa's report was accepted by the plebiscite and the meeting in Xalafeu was duly confirmed by all of the member planets.

CHAPTER 11/
THE PROBLEMS ON ORBSEY.

THE PROBLEMS HAD BEEN steadily growing worse as the effect of the Term Five workers having illegally retired. That highest level of knowledge and administration being lost to the system was having a deepening effect in all sections of society. Meeting production dates gradually lagging behind as quality control and other finishing off, of products were being held up. As a result mass layoffs were being considered even though the sales books, especially for all sizes of space craft were full and now lagging two years behind. The same applied to all industries, and the future of food production was looking tenuous, especially special food for the peoples who were genuinely retired.

Finally the Plebiscite came together and convened a full meeting of the Orbseyn Parliament in Cordiance. They had no sooner come into session than it was deemed an illegal meeting by the Seeing Eye and ordered to be broken up by the robot police force. These numbered some 100,000 fully armed robots, but able to stun only their weapons weren't for killing.

Pandemonium broke loose as the members refused to leave the chambers and they were besieged by these robots controlled by the Seeing Eye, this was going to be it a show of strength, but where would the strength of the people come from, was there to be no answer to the computers that were controlling their lives, it seemed unlikely.

Suddenly to the surprise of all, a division of the army that had been set up and structured by the original earthlings had surrounded the robots and made it plain their mission was to destroy them. This highly trained and fit army now numbered ten, million permanent members and they were all trained to kill without mercy any target set by their generals. All of the generals were all well known to be pro republic and pro federation of planets, so this was a challenge to the Seeing Eye the entire population knew what was happening and applauding the army generals.

The robots stood firm and insisted this is an illegal gathering now disburse or we will force you all to leave, and we want this done immediately.

The army commander issued an order for the robots to leave immediately or they would be attacked. It really looked so funny the ancient style army threatening the ultra modern robots, but the looks were deceiving the robots only looked deadly, the army was in every way.

The robots seemed at a loss for what to do keep forcing the assembly to leave, or turn and face the army in this situation they were leaderless.

The army had no such problem, the order was given to attack and the fight was on, but again no one told the robots. When the first robot was hit with a lethal spear thrust it looked all so strange, the robot seemed to fall to pieces. There followed in quick succession over a thousand robots destroyed and in pieces everywhere, but they weren't answering the attack just seemed to be lost in this melee of strange men attacking them.

The army commander gave the order to completely destroy the robots so the attack was widened and over 20,000 robots were destroyed within a short time and then the army withdrew. The general in charge then entered the assembly hall and told the delegates that order had been restored and they could rest assured that unless there was another attempt to close them down by the robots the army would not interfere with politics again.

The entire assembly then settled down to work to try to rectify the mistakes within their legislation that had allowed the Seeing Eye to attempt a takeover of their planet, and even their ancient style army were in a position to take over had they wished.

There was hope engendered by the actions of the military, but shock at how much control the Seeing Eye had over the entire planet, the politicians swore they would work until there had been a full investigation and the passing of laws that would make impossible such a thing ever to happen again. It didn't matter how many laws were passed the high court was closed down for lack of staff and officials, so the position was dangerous until answers could be given on some way to start raising the officials from level four to have the responsibility of their former level five colleagues. This was difficult because all levels right down to level one were affected, and there was no way a quick fix was possible. Then the govt asked the level five retirees to come in and negotiate a deal for early retirement sanctioned by the govt; this they agreed to do, but wanted no pay for the period they had refused to work nor did they want to be paid to negotiate. All they wanted was to be left in peace and to somehow alleviate the problems they had helped to start.

After a month of talks the oldies agreed to working for 15 years only on level five in other words the work period had been reduced by 30 years, it was still going to be very difficult but at least the govt had a point to start. The promotion from level four to level five would have to be carefully assessed, and a lot of the work load formerly done by five would have to be changed. The other problem the Seeing Eye had been unable to deal with was quickly rectified when special legislation was listed that canceled all of the billions of summonses that had been built up and unissued. The assembly agreed and passed the bill, but of course now had to wait on the court to sign it all into law, over a trillion in govt credits had been forgiven.

A law was approved and passed the full vote unanimously that said that henceforth the army was answerable only to the full assembly of the politicians and could never be used by the Seeing Eye to achieve the takeover that it had almost done.

The army now became the heroes of the people and their founders were posthumously honored. Since most of these men were earthlings it was a great boost for the people from earth, they were heroes. Even though the army was based on the ancient art of war; that was all Orbsey needed. It was just an extension of their overall defense strategy the same as the nuclear armed missiles and the people felt good.

It was Lisa's job now to make personal contact with all of the federation leaders and inform them all problems had been rectified on Orbsey and the intended meeting on Xalafeu was cancelled. Lisa had had to move quickly, but had been able to reassure them all, and tell them the meeting had only been cancelled because of conditions at home having been stabilized. She did inform them all that the return to full production would take about twelve months, but the possibility of anarchy was now but a bad dream.

The level four workers were now being asked to take over a spread of new duties, but the increase was not really that onerous, level five had been the lowest producers by far and had always had a lot of workers just filling chairs and filling in the days. This wasn't the same now they were more active because they had only fifteen years to go, some even less and they were enthused again. The same with level 4 the change seemed to reenergize the entire system, it proved quite conclusively the last term of 45 years was just too much, and that the state could only get away with 15 years and no more. As for the silent revolutionaries they were all glad it was over, they weren't really happy to have been undermining what they knew was a great planet with the best conditions of all, for its people of any of the federation members.

The Seeing Eye efforts to close down the parliament and rule by its own decree were never an alternative they had the laws right and everything done was according to law, but they didn't have the versatility to deal with personal thought at such a huge level. It was estimated that the amount written off from the unissued and issued fines was in excess of one trillion govt credits, but the money would have taken five years to collect and cost almost that amount by the time all of the arguments had been considered and the judges given verdicts.

The robot police were deemed a joke because of the way they had been so easily destroyed, by weapons that on Orbsey weren't even seen in the museums. It was hard to estimate the damage that could have been done if that army hadn't been there and so quickly come forward in support of real law and order.

The politicians of Orbsey had been stunned at how easily the Seeing Eye acting as a guardian of the law had almost seized political control, they had been equally stunned by the ease with which their archaic style army had so quickly routed the much vaunted robot police force. In theory the robots should have beaten the army easily, but no consideration had been given to the sureness of command that had been just too much for the Seeing Eye to counteract. The high tech weapons had been of no use against the charging energy forcefully expended by some very fit men who just loved the experience.

Orbsey now went into a period of unprecedented growth and maturity, it didn't turn to the creation of a modern military but was proud of its powerful force so successfully built up over the many years, and elevated their status as the planets peace keepers with all of the original intentions preserved.

There followed a witch hunt amongst the computer giants that had put the whole system together. Because it was found suspicious at how the Seeing Eye had gained the power it did, and that suspicion gradually matured to a belief that the computer industry leaders were implicated in a power takeover attempt. The police force brightest and best, was given the job to trace the veracity of the claims. They quickly came forward with charges of conspiracy against over 100 of the planets leaders in the computer industry who had conspired to get control of Orbsey, and in so doing be able to control the federation of planets obviously to their own advantage.

The plan had been to get control first, then after having destroyed the elected govt to install a puppet govt controlled by them through the Seeing Eye. The computer systems would be upgraded to give the Seeing Eye more versatility and ability to deal with unusual situations such as had happened and this would have given real control to the computer industry.

The men were all indicted as charged and found guilty of a conspiracy against the state, with the intent to usurp the rights of every citizen of Orbsey. They were all found guilty, given the death sentence then all executed within seven days. The investigations were continued and given a broader mandate to find other conspirators.

Over the course of the investigation over 500 more were found who had been complicit in the failed attempt at takeover. All who were found guilty were executed just as the original group had been. All Orbseyns hoped there was a lesson in their somewhere for computer Geeks and their Backers to in future be far more respectful of the system, that after all over thousands of years they had created. But it was obvious to all that weakness would always be there as that highly sophisticated industry again reached for the heights, it could only be hoped the prompt executions may have changed their attitudes.

Lisa and her team were ordered to go back to earth and plant a colony of Orbseyn immigrants there somewhere in the hope that that someday these people would be able to do for earth the same as earthlings had been instrumental in doing on Orbsey. It was also ordered that a fully equipped space station was to be set up over earth with a full set of medical equipment and the entire crew, were to work five days off and five on so they could leave the station and visit earth as often as they wished. However they were not allowed to have any other than Orbseyns on board needing attention of some sort. The whole team would be replaced from Orbsey every twelve months and they would never be asked to return unless they applied to go again themselves.

Both Lisa and Kauri took their entire families with them this time to make sure they were acquainted with the great kauri plantations in NZ; they both wanted that area to be a continuing home for their families that they could refer to as the many years went by. They also took the families to the great kauri park in Cordiance and explained the park had been started with seedlings from NZ by their grandmother. The trees were now only 200 years old and only babes but one day they would be the pride of Cordiance as they reached the maturity of the ones on earth.

At 1500 years they would be fully grown but Li had been planting for years and she had over one million young kauris with planting still going on motivated by the city of Cordiance. The number the city had promised Li they would plant in the park was five million trees and they had every intent of fulfilling that promise.

The city politicians knew because Li had explained to them, in the far distant future maybe 1500 years this would be a spectacular park and people would come from all over the federation just to see them, then her dreams will have come true. A little bit of planet earth growing on her adopted home Orbsey.

TROUBLE THREATENED.

Lisa was surprised to receive an urgent call to attend a top level Plebiscite meeting as soon as she had landed; the message came to her cruiser when she was almost home again in Orbsey from planet Earth.

She was told the leaders had received a request from strangers from an unknown in Orbsey planet, to be received by the leaders at a meeting to discuss future relations between the two planets.

The leaders had agreed to a meeting but decided they wanted their interplanetary ambassador present, since she was the one most knowledgeable on planets affairs.

The meeting had been arranged with Lisa's presence, and the leaders were now waiting to meet with the visitors in the parliament buildings.

The visitors didn't look any different than one of the many groups that could have been assembled from any of the Federation planets, but they did appear to exude an air of importance and confidence.

The visitors were asked to be the first speakers since they had requested the meeting, so one of them the most officious looking of their group of twelve took the podium.

They were he said there on behalf of their planet to offer the Federation of planet led by Orbsey an opportunity to join their own group, and by so doing peacefully avoid a war with them that could see Orbsey destroyed which would be unfortunate and not what they wanted to have to do. The speaker went on to outline his own planet which he claimed was in every way more advanced than Orbsey with a superior in every way destructive capacity, which unless an agreement could be negotiated would be used to get what they wanted by force. The leader for Orbsey then took the podium to replay, which he did with some effort to hide his feelings, but at the same time obviously more than a little annoyed at what he felt was a sheer impudence by the visitors. I am surprised to receive a threat of war to be delivered in such a manner lacking in any respect, and it mattered not, just how important they felt they were. The sheer arrogance of what you are threatening is unbelievable; first of all they could at least indentify themselves and their planet, then they could produce proof of the authority for which they speak. Orbsey and its leaders were quite prepared to accept a declaration of war in a proper format and would reply in the same way immediately, but in the meantime the visitors were told to leave since they were uninvited emissaries of war and as such unwelcome.

An immediate order went out to trace the space craft that must be hovering in the stratosphere above and trace its origins if at all possible. The next orders that went out were for Orbseyn missiles to be put into full production as a matter of priority. Then Lisa was instructed to contact all of the Federation members and to inform them of what was happening and that Orbsey would do all that was needed to protect itself and destroy any such planet that was declaring itself at war with not just Orbsey but the entire Federation. Then the Plebiscite went into closed session to await further events as they unfolded.

This wasn't long in happening within one day there had been a declaration of war received from planet x and its group a total of five associated planets and the first attack would be within six months. This would give Orbsey the chance to produce at least 1,000 missiles fully nuclear armed, and to tighten up it's the defenses so that only nuclear arms of a high explosive capability could penetrate the defenses.

Lisa and her team had left on a trip to meet with all Federation members, including a team from Orbsey at Xalafeu as the most central point and easiest for all members to reach.

Top scientists and heads of the defense dept were included in the Orbseyn team, plus a group of hitherto unknowns who were in fact the heads of the secret service. Their sole job was to keep track of any subversive activities that could be destructive to Orbsey, but to always remain unknown to all but the very highest of officials in the govt. Theirs had been a very passive role for many years, but they had been reactivated into top alert from the time of the problems with the Seeing Eye. There were also the top army generals who had been bought into an area of importance, because they had now an army of almost eight million men fully trained in ancient warfare but who could now be quickly taught the art of modern war as accurately as it was known on Orbsey, which wasn't much.

The scientists of Orbsey had been able to trace the source of their antagonists and were now having probes investigate the five planets that Orbsey was now at war with. The reports were of five planets heavily armed and war ready, all with nuclear armed missiles aimed at Orbsey. The one problem they had was they had not yet reached the degree of sophistication that Orbsey had in defeating the tyranny of distance.

Their ability to defeat distance was only 50% as good as the Orbsey system but they seemed unaware of this weakness in their attack plans which was in a high state of readiness. It appeared as if the initial attack was to be 500 nuclear armed missiles led by 20 separate ones designed to destroy the nuclear shield.

This would be followed up with a fleet of huge carrier space craft, bringing in a team of robots to follow up with a ground attack of some sort. They appeared to have a fleet of about 100 of these carriers on which they would bring 250,000 attack robots that would be followed up by another 250,000 within 30 days of the first lot arriving, but only if they were needed.

A top commander had been appointed to be in charge of the coming defense of Orbsey, and a top secret team including Lisa had been appointed as his assistants. There of course was only the simplest of information released for public consumption; there was no intention to frighten the populace more than they had to be, but Orbsey was in full war mode.

It didn't seem possible that this group of planets would declare war with such inadequate resources, so it was presumed that the information gleaned from the probes was only a fraction of what they had, and would use.

The formerly very open approach of the Orbseyn defense system was now closed down knowing full well the enemy would have infiltrated the missile resources and it was the first time for hundreds of years that an attack stance from Orbsey could be launched at any time. The thought of being attacked with 500 missiles etc was considered only a weak joke, and the 250, 000 robots would be destroyed almost immediately so more information had to be found urgently. Manned probes were now sent out and they were warned the danger of this special mission was very high.

Then quite suddenly and causing a lot of surprise a request came in from the attackers for another meeting, after careful consideration the request was denied with the response there was to be no meetings until the matter of war had been settled. Further it was suggested by Orbsey there was no further time for talk it was time for action because war was anathema to Orbseyn thought; therefore needed to be dealt with immediately. If having declared war planet X didn't attack quite soon Orbsey would feel itself justified to go on the attack without further notice. No response was received but then none was expected!

ORBSEY ATTACK STRATEGY:

The big question that was being asked is why would the enemy announce their attack with such meager resources? The only answer there could be, was that they had a hidden attack team, but how were they going to coordinate such a strategy from five different planets. Unmanned probes had been sent out to all five planets, but the information that was returned was the same except there was a very big fleet of pre nuclear battleships about 2,000 that seemed to be mission ready for conventional war.

There was another 500 carrier craft also mission ready that could be used to transport in the infantry whether they be robots or just attack troops. The attack order wasn't available; the men from the probes had been unable to steal such information. The initial enemy attack would have to be nuclear because first they had to be able to destroy the nuclear shield that would be over Orbsey and would require major force to remove. But they would have to first destroy the Orbseyn nuclear missiles, which would be aimed against their missiles or their planets. The big unknown to the enemy was that the Orbseyn missile fleet air speed was twice the speed of their own.

The Orbsey nuclear armed missile numbers were now over 2,000 and production had been changed over to producing flying bombs. These carried no nuclear warheads, but were just flying bombs using the same carriers as the nuclear missiles they were a lot cheaper and quicker to produce, but just as accurate.

It was then that the strategy of the enemy started to make sense! They wanted the Orbseyns to attack with nuclear missiles and they would hope to see as many launched as possible. They would hope to intercept all of these missiles with ordinary bomb carrying craft and thus deplete the stock of Orbseyn nuclear missiles. Stage two for them would be to attack the nuclear shield with the most powerful of their nuclear missiles to force entry, then they would attack with flying bombs in the hope that Orbsey would use up the rest of their nuclear missiles, and finally be open to invasion, after they had been softened up with a barrage of some 500 nuclear missiles directed at the major cities.

The audacity of the scheme started to become clear, the combined powers of the enemy couldn't match Orbseyn missile power, unless attacks could be provoked that would deplete those missiles and create an opening. It also became clear the real enemy was an Interplanetary Bankers group looking to gain financial control of the Federation of planets put together by Orbseyn influence and power.

The weakness of the Orbseyn situation was they were not prepared for an aggressive war their entire structure was based on one of strong defense; their newly formed war cabinet were inexperienced, but thankfully not foolish enough to fall for the enemies trap.

It was decided to send out against the enemy 500 flying bombs 100 aimed at each of the five planets just as a challenge to see just how well the enemy could deal with the faster missiles. The Orbseyn attack missiles would be traveling at over twice the speed of the enemy's defense missiles and would test their capacity to even repel such a simple attack. The beauty of this approach was the flying bombs could be quickly replaced, and thus no depletion of the Orbseyn position would be created.

The attack was timed to ensure the bombs arrived at the different destinations at as close as possible the same time, and probes had been placed high above all targets to view the results of this simple strategy.

The enemy would have been aware of the attack launch immediately, but they faced a few problems. One was what type of missiles was on the way and whether they were nuclear armed. Second was they would suddenly be aware of the far greater speed of the incoming missiles and would have to launch their own defense to adjusted intercept timing that they had little time to calculate.

The reports coming in from the probes showed an orderly approach initially to the incoming missiles, which would take an average 12 weeks to arrive. It was when the calculations came in of the expected time of arrival that some panic started to show through, suddenly there were bombs due to arrive far more quickly than had been allowed for.

To expand the challenge 100 nuclear missiles were launched 20 at each planet these were twelve hours behind the bombs, and all aimed at the industrial heartlands of each targeted planet. To further create surprise the unmanned probes high in the stratosphere were armed with small but devastating nuclear warheads, they couldn't be stopped since they were in orbit way above the stratosphere and remained unnoticed. The probes were targeted to hit the main govt buildings just hours before the enemy would be ready to launch their intercept missiles. There would be some damage, but the confusion created would be immense and would again hold up the enemy for a little while. Manned probes would by this time be ready to take over the surveillance and would by thought control now keep Orbsey aware of how their attack was progressing.

The first reports were a surprise with a 30% strike rate being reported and a 70% intercept. This meant there had been 150 flying bombs that had reached the target, 20 nuclear missiles as well as the initial small nuclear probes that had signaled the start of the attack. The damage from the flying bombs could be bought quickly under control, but the nuclear explosions had caused serious damage on the five planets.

A retaliatory strike force had immediately been launched by the enemy, there appeared to be about 1200 none nuclear and another 300 nuclear armed missiles.

This was exactly what the Orbseyns wanted, they immediately launched 1500 flying bombs and twelve hours behind them they launched 300 nuclear armed missiles. The bombs had set targets which they wouldn't miss and the nuclear attack was aimed at the major cities of the enemy. Then 12 hours behind the first nuclear missiles another 300 were launched aimed at different cities.

The impact on the enemy was devastating; they were all now under heavy attack and even a 20% hit would mean 60 nuclear bombs being exploded on their territories.

Orbsey meanwhile had loaded up 200 space freighters with army personnel ready to be taken aboard; these would be the initial invasion force. The intent was to send out another 300 nuclear missiles just as soon as the strike rate had been confirmed for the current attack. A week behind the missiles the space freighters would take off and follow, but they would be going in for a ground invasion of the enemy, who it was hoped by then would be suffering from severe nuclear damage.

The reports had now come in from the probes and the enemy was severely damaged, they had received direct nuclear hits by 300 missiles and their attack fleet had been totally destroyed. It was estimated they still had 600 nuclear missiles and about 100 flying bombs, but the five planets would be struggling to launch the missiles because they had been severely damaged by the nuclear blasts they had had to absorb from Orbseyn nuclear missile.

The Orbseyns then decided to launch a final attack, 500 bombs and 500 missiles all travelling together and identical if the enemy wanted to intercept, even with a 100% strike rate by their remaining missiles, 300 of the attack craft would get through. Then straight behind the missiles the troop carriers would leave fully loaded and the full scale invasion would be underway.

The enemies leading planet was the one first to be invaded, if this was a success the others would be asked for a full surrender and if this was achieved they may not be invaded. The lead planet war capacity would be totally destroyed and repatriation payments for the total cost of the war would be charged to them. As soon as these payments were guaranteed and the war capacity destroyed the intent was the soldiers would come home.

As advised by the probes the incoming missiles from Orbsey had only been 50% intercepted by the enemy and the results were devastating over 250 nuclear warheads hit their target and the devastation was just a shame to see if it could be seen. The damage and nuclear dust that surrounded the five planets caused the invasion forces to be held back, they all had nuclear clothing and head gear, but it was decided that first the atmosphere around the planets had to be tested. If the results were considered too deleterious to the possible health of the troops they were to be sent home. After waiting for a week the invasion was ordered to continue, the protective clothing was considered sound enough for the troops to be safe.

The troop carriers couldn't land so the men had to be beamed down to the safest places that could be found, no enemy forces came forward to oppose the invasion. The damage that had been done was horrendous there were huge areas that had been completely obliterated by the missiles, but it was easy to see where the flying bombs had struck, this damage was nominal by comparasion. After a month it became clear that the five planets had almost been destroyed, at least on average 50% of their entire structures were no more and the people were all living like rats in sewers. The occupation forces from Orbsey were forced to bury millions of corpses, but millions had been disintegrated by the nuclear holocaust that had been inflicted on them.

It was clear most of the leaders had been destroyed as all of the major cities were no more, only the few who had left the cities to hide in suburbia would eventually be found.

Lisa and her team had been ordered to keep the Federation members up to date with all information. Now she was able to announce the war was over, but as she reported the whole thing had been a farce from the start. The would be dictators who had declared war had created a position whereby Orbsey had retaliated in full force, and this had been unnecessary. The result had been a holocaust beyond description and five planets that would take hundreds of years to recover.

A full meeting of Federation members was called to be held in Xalafeu in six months time at which time a full report of the war would be tendered and discussed.

Chapter 12/
War and Punishment:

THE MEETING IN XALAFEU was very low key; none of the delegates from Orbsey were keen to discuss the reasons and outcome of the conflict. After the meeting started and the leader of the Orbseyn team rose to speak there was a noticeably hushed silence from the assembly, but he continued in an unemotional tone.

Orbsey he said hadn't wanted war, but having accepted the challenge from planet X that simply was a declaration of war against Orbsey and that challenge from the five planets not just the one. Orbsey he said had accepted the declaration of war and had been certain there was a major challenge which they planned to meet with all of the resources she had. The investigating probes sent out had reported the enemy was not as strong as it seemed, so under the circumstances it was assumed they had hidden resources such as other planets which would join them. This had proved to be wrong therefore the nuclear attack had been far too heavy and the destruction caused was reprehensible for any civilized society to inflict on another, it was for this reason 2,000,000 troops would be sent to help in repatriation, of this number 1,000,000 were already there.

While Orbsey regretted the over reaction to the war declaration it made no apology for defending itself in the manner that was deemed appropriate at the time, but perhaps the use of nuclear strike weapons needed to be modified. The intent was to change over to flying bombs in future with the nuclear missiles always held back as a threat to intending attackers; especially ones that had declared war on Orbseyn territorial integrity. After explaining a few more of the details of the brief war the speaker returned to his seat, after inviting a speaker from the Federation to take the podium.

The leader of the Xalafeun delegation who was the elected Chairman of the Federation then stepped forward to speak, but again to a very silent gathering. I think he started by saying is we should all remember that war was declared not only on Orbsey but on the entire Federation, and under its agreement with the Federation all were being defended under the Orbseyn umbrella. Therefore if Orbsey had over reacted then they all had, after all in a time of war there isn't the time to call meetings and procrastinate in any way only action was acceptable, and this was precisely what had happened. While everyone including the Orbseyns regretted the holocaust that had occurred; none regretted the fact that they were all safe and the enemy of whatever caliber had been vanquished. The fact that the retaliation was over strong was a reality of war, and happens when one's own safety is threatened. There is no real obligation to the defeated territories, but there may be a moral obligation to try and help them get back on their feet but in thinking about that we must consider what they would have done if they had been capable of winning the war. Certainly Orbsey would have been decimated and the Federation would have received demands especially of a financial nature.

They would have forced us to pay for their war, then we would have had real cause for complaint, instead we seem to be sitting in judgment on Orbsey which is totally wrong and the truth needs to be understood. Planet X and its four associates declared war on a planet with far superior facilities and technological knowhow. Orbsey was entitled to believe they must have superior forces to be so positive in the declaration of war, therefore they reacted in the interests of herself and the Federation.

There is no legal or moral ground now to assist the former enemy, but Orbsey was doing this at its own further cost even though repatriation for war costs could never be paid. Orbsey officials have said they are considering increasing all of its prices local consumption and export and in this way the enormous cost of the war will be recovered over 20 years. This isn't definite at this stage as inflationary pressures will have to be worked out before a final decision is made.

After several speakers from all of the planets had expressed their concerns, but noted the future wars would be more cautious bearing in mind the real strength of the Orbseyn situation the meeting was closed, but members urged to move freely and have free and open discussions.

From that time for over a thousand years there were no further upsets within the Federation of planets set up by Orbsey. Orbsey committed to and assisted with the rehabilitation of the five former enemy planets, but it took them 200 years to recover to a point of once again having stable economies.

THE END BOOK ONE.

EIGHT SHORT STORIES

WRITTEN BY VINCENT HAVELUND.

Americans Galore:
1945 # 17

HEY SONNY GOT ANY sisters at home? We want some girls; the Yanks were standing outside the Freemans Bay hotel when they accosted Vince's ears, with their raucous shouts. Vince ever conscious of the chance to make a buck shouted back, yeah but whats in it for me?

It was a Saturday morning about 11.00 am and as usual at this time; the pub was filled to over flowing. There was an American base just over from the Bay, and very often they were to be seen enjoying their leave; with very little to do, but Freemans Bay was not exactly the place for them to find any compliant women. Ever since about 1943 New Zealand like Australia; had been awash with American service men, and naturally they were constantly looking for companions.

The war in Europe was now over, but the Japanese were still holding out all though their homeland was now being heavily attacked. It was the time of Americans their Rum and Coca Cola, and different type chewing gum, all of which were new to the land down under, as we were known by the Americans. The Kiwi men were not yet home from the war, and so the eruption that was to follow their return hadn't yet occurred! There was a strong objection by Kiwi service men, who when arriving home found their families, had been increased by a little half caste American.

When the battalions had arrived home from Europe, including the Maori Battalion there had been a final march down Queen St Auckland, in honor of the New Zealand armed forces, before being demobbed. A lot of Americans on leave had attended the march, and could be seen shouting and cheering the parade. All of the NZ military had already been on leave and discovered their expanded families; naturally there was a lot of anti American resentment. The sight of the Americans cheering for them was just too much for the Kiwi's especially the Maoris' they broke ranks and en masse attacked the noisy mainly drunk foreigners. The Maori Battalion was the main perpetrators of the attack, and as is usual with Maoris' they were extremely vicious, and many of the Americans finished up in the Auckland hospital emergency dept.

The Stephens Family were free of any such despoilment, but one women living fairly close by had been guilty of entertaining such parties, much to the horror of Mum Stephens. As usual Vince knew exactly what was going on, and thought it amusing but disapproved in his own boyish way.

Unknown to the rest of the family Vince had been at the parade, and had seen what had happened. It had been one of the periods when he was living with Clare, and had found the fight highly amusing, but had never told his family that he had been a spectator. He never spoke up because he knew his two uncles had been involved, and had seen Murray as usual, fighting like a threshing machine. The reason Vince never admitted to seeing the fight, was because our men had no reason to fight, since our family wasn't so polluted.

On the day when Vince had been accosted by the Americans his first thought was here is the chance to make a buck, the second thought was shit there will be hell to pay at home. Anne and Clare were at home with Mum, but the men were away at the football, and wouldn't be back for hours. When those Americans started waving $5 each in their hands at Vince, it was too much and worth the risk! He would take them to Sale St and go inside and tell Anne and Clare they had visitors out front, then go through the house and climb over the back fence and vanish. Anne he knew would be furious, but Clare would think it a great joke, and Mum would just think; wonder how much that ploomin Vince got off those Americans.

So Vince crossed the road took their money and said follow me I will find you some women. The Americans were drunk and laughing and joking as they followed Vince home, but Vince was earning $15 American Dollars. He had no idea how much the money was worth since NZ was still using pounds and the conversion rate was something he knew nothing about.

When they arrived at 37 Sale St; he said to his new American acquaintances, just wait here I will get the women for you. As he had planned he went in told the girls they had visitors then took off over the back fence! He never came back until he knew the poker game would be started, at that time there would be too many people playing cards including Anne, and she wouldn't be inclined to tell him off in front of the visitors. Clare would think of it as a joke anyhow; and they would all want to see his American money later the next day.

His plan was all wrong, as soon as he went through into the games room, Anne started up. And what have you been up to she screamed from the table, even though she was in the middle of playing a hand only Mum could hush her down and tell her to shutta up Vince was young he had just made a silly mistake. Lucky for Vince Anne was sitting next to Mum so she did shut up. Just as Vince had thought Clare took it as a big joke, which was fine. And as he had thought the next day all were curious about how much money Vince had got, and what Yankee money looked like.

The only thing was Vince had forgotten about Clare's husband Uncle George, he didn't look to happy, but never said a word!

Vince Fencing at Titirangi: 1944. # 18

THESE OLD SHEILA'S ARE no good to me, they are all yours old fella!
The war in Europe was still not over; the English had just taken Sicily and was on the way to taking Italy. The Russians had turned back the Germans from Moscow, and were rushing towards Poland, and then would go on to Berlin. Vince was still enslaved to a work regime that was very hard, because of that war; there were very few men of working age, who were available in NZ for general farm work. On all of the farms, boy's old men and women had to do all of the work on the land, and many farm boys such as Vince, in modern terms would be considered to be enslaved.

The girls on farms had to do all of the house work, while their Mums worked hard; all of the work still had to be done, even though their husbands were at war? Vince was almost ten years of age, and was responsible to look after twenty five horses, and the farm in Titirangi this included the repair of fences; over the entire farm. The orchard still produced the fruit that had to be gathered for mothers to bottle and make jam, but the trees were not at full production, because no pruning had been done for years.

Vince had a team of horses that were used in the riding school in Avondale, and his job there was to teach mainly children of the wealthy to ride a horse! Each week he had to bring a team of horses to the Avondale farmlet of only twenty acres, and then after the weekends work take them back to Titirangi. Vince was an extremely good horse handler, and he could lead ten horses on a string from Titirangi to Avondale on Friday, then reverse the drive and lead ten horses back on the following Tuesday. When the school was busy and he needed more than twelve horses; over the week end he had to make two trips, which meant a lot of extra work, the ride leading the string took him over two hours each way. If he needed to do the trip solo on his own horse named

Kino, the trip would take only one hour because most of the trip would be done at a fast canter. (Just short of a gallop) Kino was only about fourteen hands high, (56 Inches at the shoulder) but even though small was very fast at a full gallop.

Kino was a gelding (castrated male) and very fast, but he had a real hard mouth (refused to stop for the bit) which meant he couldn't be let out to learners. There were always two horses and Kino kept at Avondale, so that any rentals during the week; could be catered to and if Vince was away working at Titirangi, his stepfather would deal with the rental.

On the day we refer to here it was mid week, and Vince had ridden Kino to Titirangi to repair some fences, it had been an exciting ride. Coming up Godly Rd which was the one on which the farm was located, knowing he was getting close to home Kino had bolted. Vince had not bothered to try and pull him up just let him go, and sat on him enjoying the ride. At the front of the farm there was a 1.8 metre gate, and it was at the top of a slight rise about ten metres from the road.

On this day when Kino had bolted; and they were getting close to the front gate of the farm! Vince just sat and expected Kino to have to stop or crash into the gate, but the horse knew the farm so he was expected to stop, as they came into the turn, Vince had expected a slow down then a quick stop. Much to his surprise on the turn the horse sped up, came to the gate bunched his muscles and jumped right over, then continued to bolt up the front farm paddock. Vince just sat there thinking you crazy barsted go for it, you will get tired before me, and sure enough that steep paddock finished him, he stopped blowing and puffing, but looking very pleased with himself. To Vince Kino seemed to be saying, that proved you really can ride I won't bother to do that again, and I bet you didn't know I could jump like that did you?

Anyhow Vince was doing his work fixing a fence, when a girl he knew who often came to rent a horse at Avondale, rode in and started to talk to him. She would have been about 18 years old and had a good horse, she had obviously hired from his Stepfather. The girl stayed and talked to Vince for about ten minutes then left, on the horse, and Winty had thought no more of her visit, until he got home that night.

After he had arrived home, fed and let Kino loose he went into the house, to be met by a very angry Stepfather. Did you he asked get a visitor today, to which of course Vince said yes. And what was the big idea keeping her with you for almost two hours, what were you doing to her for two hours may I ask?

What the hell are you talking about yes I did have a visitor today so what? And she only stayed for about ten minutes why do you ask?

Well she came in two hours late and said it was your fault, you kept her for two hours so what were you up to for two hours?

Vince burst out laughing, so what he asked would I want with an old Sheila like that! She would only be for old geezers like you, too bloody old for me! You have gone red, so that means you were jealous of me! That's funny I don't want old birds like that, be assured they are all yours old fella; you are very welcome.

RIDING TRACK AT AVONDALE RACETRACK:
1945. # 20.

CRIKEY BACK THEN ON track Winty had ridden some of the best race horses in NZ, which would have included Australia.

Vince was riding Kino around Avondale one day, when he got off he in the village centre, which in those days was quite small, a girl in riding jodhpurs came up to him and started to talk about horses.

Because of how she was dressed Vince was interested to listen to her, even though she was fairly old to him at least 18 years old, and he was still only ten years old. The girl was employed at the stables of one of the trainers at the Avondale race track, but she had suffered a fall, and was having difficulty riding track work in the mornings, which was a part of her job. After talking for a while about horses in general and what Vince had to do with horses, she offered him a job doing her track work in the mornings. She could only offer ten shillings per week, and that was for six mornings starting at 4.00 am and finishing at 6.00 am. Winty loved the idea and he knew it wouldn't interfere with his own work, for which he wasn't paid anyhow, so he had accepted on the spot.

The next morning he rode his old bike down to the stables at the racetrack, to start his first ever paid job and was met by his new friend Linda, and shown around the stables. Linda's job was looking after all the horses the trainer had in work, normally about six horses most in the top stream of racehorses over varying distances, and like all thoroughbred horses vary high strung. Vince was quite used to riding this type of horse, because at least half of the horses he had to look after were ex racehorses that had been retired from racing for various reasons, but mainly because they just were not fast enough. What was different for him was riding on such a light racing saddle with such short stirrups, but that was just a small adjustment that was soon over come.

Normally on a morning Vince had to ride about three to four different horses, over varying distances at different speeds, depending on what the trainer Linda's boss instructed him he wanted, before each ride. Obviously the Trainer had agree to Linda substituting Vince riding track work for her, and he soon became quite popular at the track in the mornings. Linda was also very thankful that she had been able to find a substitute to help her, she had been having a lot of trouble with her lower back, the jarring was extremely painful and she had been very close to having to give up her job.

Vince was often finished by 5.00 am so was allowed to go home, but he often stayed until about 7.00 am helping Linda to muck out the horses stall and curry comb them so they always looked their best if or when their owners came to see tem, which they often did? Linda's Fiancée was a Jockey who rode for the same trainer, and when he first met Vince thanked him for helping Linda, and offered free entry to the races any time he wanted to come.

This gesture might have been of interest to some of his Family, but was of no interest to Vince; during the twelve months he worked with Linda he never went to the races. Both Linda and her Fiancée were like all professional horse small of stature, and he (Gordon) was especially so but very strong as are all Jockeys, they have to be to be able to control their horses during any race they were riding.

Vince loved the time he worked with Linda; and he liked the pocket money he was earning, he had to be careful not to let his Stepfather know he had money or else Percy would have insisted he hand the money over every Saturday which was when he got paid.

Each morning when the track work was finished, and all of the stables had been mucked out (cleaned) Vince often stayed to have morning tea with the Trainer, Linda and Gordon they all seemed to have taken a liking to him, just as he found he liked them. Quite often Linda came up to Vince's home, because she liked to spend time with the many horses he had to look after, and she loved to fondle them; but of course never rode one. She had no taste for his job of teaching what they both agreed were idjit kids, from wealthy homes who were often so pompous and sure of themselves. Linda was sometimes there when the boys and their mothers arrived, and shuddered as she heard their stupid comments, about their ability with horses and how good they thought they were at riding a horse.

One morning Linda confided in Vince that she was pregnant, and going to get married within the next month. She then invited him to come to her wedding because both she and Gordon both considered him as a real friend.

It was only a few days later that Linda asked Vince on behalf of the Trainer if he wanted to take Linda's job, but he explained much as he would like the job; my family would never agree to him taking a job, and would immediately demand that he give the job up. So it was understood Winty would finish up on the day that Linda finished.

Vince managed to get permission to go to the wedding, and it was a very nice day, as all brides do Linda looked beautiful, and Gordon looked in his mind like a little cock rooster who was finally getting hitched, he was twelve years older than Linda.

Vince watched Gordon's career in the newspapers, he soon after became a top jockey and was working in the Ellerslie Stables for the same trainer. Vince heard that Linda had a little boy and she had named him Vincent, after the young bloke who had helped her by riding track work for her.

Browne's Farm:
1951 # 21,

FROM CRADLE TO GRAVE Love are the greatest needs and the Kipa's have that in great amounts!

The night that Vince came home to find the home at Sale St burned down, the family had already moved into Browns Farm. This was a large property out at Papatoetoe, owned by George's employer; Hellabys meat works, the only condition was the children were not allowed to play; or even go into the surrounding farm paddocks. This wasn't a problem, because the house had a big area for lawn and play area, in fact it was better than Sale St. Vince had shifted out to live with Mum at Te Papa, but that was only for a short while, because he got a job on a farm at Helensville; and was soon gone for two years, until he went into the Army for compulsory military training. Mum by now had adopted little Arthur Ayers as her own, and he had taken Vince's place. The Kipa children obviously loved the freedom of the farmhouse it was so big, and finally there was lots of room for all.

As the eldest children grew up, there was the usual sports gear all over the place, Richard was a really good cricketer, but a popular all round sportsman. The rest all had their areas of sport, but Vince was not around to see that period. Richard as the eldest Kipa was closest to Vince in age, and therefore both had common memories of Sale St, Grenville did to but he was always very quiet and more reserved.

Sonia being the only girl among seven boys; naturally stood out and was/ is loved very much by the entire family. Clare had the two boys (Walter and Murray) with severe dermatitis; she had a real fight on her hands. The family had shifted out to the farm when suddenly Clare went down with T/B to the spine, and she was in real trouble. For over eight months she was strapped down and wasn't allowed to move, but she always had a nice smile for her visitors. It was then she proved without doubt her indomitable Spirit; and George proved what a real Father and Husband he was, and incidentally how much he loved his Wife.

George kept the house in and outside, in immaculate order; looked after kept and fed his five children, never missed a day at work, and only once unavoidably missed his nightly visit to the hospital to visit Clare. It was a superb effort and must have helped Clare so much emotionally, to know her family was doing so well. She would have known full well what was happening, because the family would have told her, the entire Stephens clan thought George was just the greatest, always did still do; although most are now dead!

During this period Vince was living in Helensville farming so most of his information is second hand, mostly gleaned from Mum when he came home periodically. Milking cows is a seven day a week job, so it wasn't often that Vince came down from Helensville, but Mum Stephens always updated the family news when he did visit on his rare day off.

When Clare did come home she proved she was right again by having another three Kids, all of the family admired that strength, even Murray and Darby thought wow what a girl. Anne and Clare were of course always very close, and Anne did all she could for her Sister, but there wasn't much anyone could do! Mum couldn't do much, she was already suffering from heart failure, and could only walk short distances, and then she had to stop while her breathing settled down. Vince knows now what was wrong with his beloved Mum, because at 72 YOA he has been diagnosed with severe heart failure, (SHF) but the hospital can now treat the disease; he has to have daily medication. Mum Stephens died at 60 YOA because at that time there was no medication.

Sonia was always the favorite of us all; strangely she never seemed to have got spoiled in spite of being the only girl in that tribe of boys. If there is anyone spoiled in that family it's Clare, George has spoiled her for their entire married life, they are a family that stands out in their love for each other. Mum and Arthur Stephens had a loving family as well, but first Arthur died, then WW11 broke the family up and created health problems in the boys, so that the closeness that was originally there, was severely curtailed.

On the few times that Vince got out to visit Browne's farm, because of his work he thought the place was wonderful. But he was used to living in a farm environment, and he loved that way of life. One day he happened to be visiting and Clare was by then fully recovered, when suddenly there was a great noise from the Kids, all of the young ones including Sonia were running to the house yelling Mum, Mum the Coppers are here, the Coppers are here. Because the family had no need to fear the Coppers, the adults thought it a great joke and kidded Clare, the Coppers are coming and they want you Clare. As it turned out the Coppers were only looking for directions, to find the neighbors, so the Coppers were coming; but looking for someone else.

As Mum got sicker she spent more time over with the Kipa family, I think she got comfort from the family and wanted to be with them, she probably knew she was getting close to the end. We had the odd game of cards, but the old days were over, we only played to give Mum a little pleasure! If we played it was only at her level, a top bet would be sixpence. The rest of her final days she spent playing patience all by herself. Vince was there the day the old lady passed on, he had been notified that Mum wasn't expected to last much longer, and he should come to Browne's farm. That was the last time he ever visited Browne's farm the pain was too much!

Victoria Park Football:
1950 # 22

R UGBY LEAGUE WAS BACK at that time a new sport to NZ, Theo Kipa had been a Maori Rugby Rep back in 1948-49, but the other side of the family was early converts to League. Owen Anne's husband and his brother Jack were both avid league players; and their Wives were strong supporters who attended every game. Anne true to her Maori heritage was very rowdy at the games, always yelling support for Owen and sometimes Jack as well. Anne never did like Jack anyhow, so if she did yell support for Jack; it was a rare moment only! Jack was a big heavy man all muscle when he was young

Owen was a rather lighter build with quite a quick acceleration to top speed. Jack was a forward and a very good lock breakaway, and Owen because of his speed played on either wing, he was quite a prolific try scorer in the team. Jack for his size was quite quick and was a good spoiler, if the scrums were close to the try line. Both men had little time for Vince, but he was then only ten years old, and didn't give a damn what the Wrights thought anyhow, he thought of them as big dumb and stupid. The real problem was that because of his experiences with his Stepfather, and the thrashing's he had endured, he didn't care how he appeared to the Wrights, and made it plain he returned their dislike in full. There was another brother Joe Wright, but he worked for the Stephens Family Company, both he and his Wife Leonie were rather friendlier with the Stephens Clan. There were three families rather closely related through Arthur Stephens, the Stephens, Wrights, and Jobe's, and one main family through Mum the Roberts families? All of these families especially the Roberts, were high breeders so that if a chart were to be done of the extended families there would be many hundreds of close relationships, up to and including second cousins?

Many of the games were played at Victoria Park just a five minutes' walk from the Kipa home in Sale St; so it was easy for many family members to go down and watch the games. League while it was quite new drew good numbers of followers, but their facilities were rather poorer than Rugby; and the numbers of followers small by comparison. Anne was the one of the four sisters most like their Mother. She was extremely fiery of temper if roused, but she was harder than Mum to annoy, and very quick to cool down. Clare had always been very even tempered as was Millie! Winnie was in a class of her own and kept to herself even when as a young girl she was at odds with Mum, which was quite often all she was interested in was boys, she was the promiscuous one of the family.

How well did Winty remember the football gear etc; at their home in Te Papa, and the sweaty bodies after the game when the men left the field and all stunk of sweat. George was more a follower of Rugby, and there was a lot of pride when Theo won his spot in the Maori All Blacks. There were some very happy parties at Sale St; to honor Theo but to Vince who thought Theo was an arrogant prick before he was an All Black, he was now insufferable prig. Theo worked in one of the Govt depts.; and even when he first arrived, seemed to think that he was better than the rest of us George included. Clare used to be revolted at some of his nasty habits, but she said nothing except to Mum, Theo after all was her Brother in Law?

Vince was still going to Seddon Tech at the time referred to, but rarely had the time to go and watch the games. Not that he would have wanted to, his attitude was bugger those Wrights Anne can have them all to herself!

Of course with League being a relatively new game in NZ the spectators were few and most knew each other! Every week there would the same old barrackers calling out for their teams and Anne was right in there yelling for Owen, every time he got the ball she would be yelling and cheering, not at all caring what others were doing or saying. Every week was the same, with the same people and Anne was always there, always as loud as ever in support of her husband. Once when Vince did go he left as soon as he heard his Aunt making such a big noise, he was far too embarrassed to stay and listen to the noise, as far as he was concerned his beloved Aunt was making a scene for that idjit Owen, and his goofy brother Jack.

Anyhow week after week it was the same, Mum used to tell Vince stories she had heard from the Saturday League games, and who had won what. Vince was not in the least interested in the exploits of any of the Wrights, he found them on the whole obnoxious. The only Wright he liked was old mother Wright, who was a full blooded Jamaican, and a terrific gentle lady. It was old man Wright from whom the Sons got their habits, he was a full blooded Pakeha, and treated his black wife as if she was just a slave to him.

One Saturday the League game was in full swing, and Anne was at her prime best yelling for Owen. Owen was out on the right wing, when the ball was spun out to him, and he had a clear run for the try line. He was running straight down the line when the opposing winger caught, and tackled him just before he reached the line. There was a groan of disappointment when Owen went down. Suddenly out of the crowd a person Anne was used to hearing insulting comments from, let out loudly a foolish tirade about Owen Wright and his ancestry!

This was just too much for Anne she went over and asked, what did you just say about my husband? The culprit a man; foolishly repeated his comments! Suddenly to every ones astonishment Anne, king hit the man with a closed, if little fist; and the man went down like a log. Anne then walked away; never again did she hear that loud mouthed man voicing any comments about her husband. Touché Anne.

THE POOL ROOM SHARKS:
1950 # 23

LIFE HAS MANY KNOCKS for the young growing up, but there are many lessons in life we must all face as we age.

Back in the days before Television, the pool rooms were a favorite place for young men and boys like Vince, who had no other entertainment except Movies and Sport. Vince was quite a good player, but not as good as he thought later events were to prove that. Because he hated college he often used to put a change of clothes in his school bag, go to the pool room and change then spent the school day shooting pool, with the men at the local poolroom. This was from July to Oct 1950 and he got quite good, he didn't really care if he got caught, because he was only waiting for his birthday to leave school, and would then be saying goodbye to them barsted's forever. He has never regretted leaving, but knows now he did just what the Pakehas' wanted him to do; had he realized nothing on earth, could have got him to leave. Vince loved playing pool, and it didn't take him long to work out the game was set up. He didn't care because he quickly let those on the inside know he knew, and they had better let him in on the scam, or he would blow their cover. They obliged by letting him win every now and again which was all he wanted, but he set the same scam up over the years for himself, especially while he was farming out at Helensville.

Those final days at the College had been very hard for Vince, the color problem then in NZ was very strong and he found himself, alone and with an intense dislike for the other students, he couldn't wait to get the hell out of the place. The only sunshine in his life was Clare, she seemed to understand his unhappiness, and never condemned him in any way, neither did Mum but she was too old to comprehend his problems. His early years of working on the farms for his Stepfather had created a problem; he only wanted to earn money so he could wash away the feeling of being dirty. Wherever he went and whatever he did he felt dirty and alone, Clare now had her life and her Family, Anne was married and Mum was just too old, all she wanted to do was play cards?

Vince knew that Uncle George had started work as a solo slaughterman at twelve years of age; and he wanted to be just as successful as George was. What a disillusion life was going to hand out to Vince, he was destined never to be as successful as Uncle George was. After many years wandering everywhere, he finally realized at 70 YOA that success is individual and only in one's own head. He had the only success he was ever going to achieve, he was the greatest failure one could ever meet, and once he accepted that he was successful.

The poolroom was the one place Vince could be an adult, and be on an equal with the other men; who had so much idle time to spend doing very little. Winty had bought his own special cue, which was weighted to his own feel and had been granted a place to lock it away, with the many other regular players. He has often wandered over the years what happened to that cue since he left it behind when he finally left and never went back.

When he had got to know his way around his new job out in Helensville, the first thing he went looking for was the local poolroom. It didn't take very long to find friends out in the new area, but the game most played out there was snooker and billiards, and there was no gamblers until Winty arrived. He quickly changed that because they did have a set of pool balls, and there were a few who wanted to play. The commissions for the owner of the poolroom were far higher with pool, so naturally they were keen to see the game gain popularity.

Vince did the same when he went into the army at Papakura, every night he and some of his fellow territorial soldiers (18 year olds) used to go over the fence at night after lights out; and would go into the townships local poolroom. It shows how lax the inspections after light out, because they never got caught but went AWOL (Absent Without Leave) at least 4 nights per week. Vince in his own opinion was beginning to be a poolroom shark and thought he could take on all comers; he had a big shock coming to him. Up until that time he had been playing with keen mugs, so naturally he was the master, but that was soon to change at the hands of one he has always loved so much.

One day he happened to be in a popular poolroom when his Uncle George came in, and wanted to play a game. Vince said yes ok let's play on this table, and was thinking he would give his Uncle a lesson on the pool table, but what a shock he was in for. The game started and Vince was rather condescending until George hit his first ball, Vince was so startled he lost his confidence immediately. His Uncle gave him such a beating he gave up playing pool for some time. But on the other hand he was proud of his Uncle, and if anyone was going to give him a hiding, he was glad it was Uncle George. They only played one game that was enough to teach Vince a lesson he has never forgotten, never be such a bloody big headed idjit, because someone may come along who is just too good.

A Bull and Horse trapped in the Bog.
1943 # 24

BRAINS WILL ALWAYS BEAT brawn; just ask the bull and the horse!
Vince's dad was annoyed, the weather had been really wet and the rain had been continuous for the last week. In an area like Helensville the ground when so wet pugs up, and Animals can get trapped and bog down, in quite small amounts of water that has pooled up. This happens only if they keep stamping the very wet earth, and gradually the mud gets quite deep. Heavy animals like bulls and heavy horses are at risk, and on this occasion a big black and white bull and a horse had both got caught. The rain was still pouring down, and the animals would have to be rescued as soon as possible, which was not a reassuring prospect working in the rain. The paddocks were all very wet; and even taking the tractors out to pull the animals onto solid ground, was going to be risky unless the chains were put onto the wheels to get traction, only then would the wheels grip.

Right or wrong Vince wanted to go with his Dad to see the rescue taking place; and he was very excited. His Dad had decided to take him so he could show his Son the difference between a horse (equine) and a bull (bovine animals) even though it was still raining heavily. Wearing heavy raincoats and leggings, quite usual wet weather gear kept on farms; it was going to be an uncomfortable night's work. Mum Stephens was going too because it may turn out to be very difficult; and she may have to help with the pulling gear and the tractor.

The difference between the animals was obvious from the start, the bull snorted in anger as if to blame the rescuers for his problem, while the horse started to nicker in pleasure, as if to say, oh thank you so much for coming I am in trouble here. The need is to get the animals roped either round the back or front legs, or preferably round the shoulders. It is an easy pull if they can get the rope down round the breast and up over the shoulders, then hitching the rope to the tractor for the pull, which when they got that far was easy.

Both of the animals looked as if they could be attached by the shoulders, but the horse was done first, Dad Stephens had no problem getting the horse attached because it tried to help, by shifting as she was told to do. With his Mum driving the tractor and Vince holding the lamp, the horse being pulled out was quick and easy. As soon as it was freed from the rope the horse came up to her rescuers, and was trying to thank them; but seeing they were now going to pull out the bull she left.

The bull was a lot more difficult to get the rope on, so in the end they had to attach him to where his horns had once been. He had enough horn stumps left for the rope to be caught to, but then the pull had to be exerted, but this one was far more difficult, he struggled against the pull and made the drag far heavier. Vince watched in amazement at the difference between the two animals, the bull bellowed and roared in anger, as if they were attacking him. Dad Stephens warned Vince that as soon as the Bill was freed, they were to leave the paddock quickly, because as soon as he was able to find his feet he would attack them. Vince knew better than to ask questions just now, because it was all quite dramatic, especially with the bull roaring angrily in the background. Mum Stephens knew she had to pull very carefully, although there was no danger to the bull, his neck was too heavy to be hurt, but as soon as he was free and able he would attack the tractor. This time it was a dead pull the bull never tried to help himself just roared in anger, as soon as he was free Dad Stephens took off the rope from his horn stumps, and they left before the Bull could stand up.

When they got through the gate Dad said let's wait and you can see what the bull doe's, so Mum just stopped and left the tractor idling, and the three of them sat and waited. Sure enough as soon as the bull could get to his feet, he came over to the gate bellowing loudly, he had to stop at the gate, but he stood there really menacing his rescuers. The family went home on the tractor, and Dad Stephens said to Vince on the way, so now you know the difference, the horse is far more intelligent than the bull. That bull would totally savage us if he could have got at us, but tomorrow it will all be forgotten and he will be the same as usual, but the horse will never forget, we have a life time friend in her.

By the time they got home it was 11.00 pm and because milking started at 4.00 am all was off to bed and asleep immediately. Vince couldn't sleep properly all night he was dreaming of that big ugly bull chasing him around the paddock, growling and roaring. The faster Vince ran the more the bull bellowed! Vince's dog Shep kept coming to the rescue and biting the bull's hind leg heels. That was no good the bull just bellowed even louder, so

Vince jumped on its back just like he did onto horses, then the bull stopped bellowing and galloped around the paddock like a horse. Finally when Vince woke up he felt grand, I had a great dream last night he told his parents, I was a champion bull rider?

Tragedy on the railroad tracks. 1947 # 25

LIFE'S TRAGEDIES CAN SOMETIMES be so unexpected that only time can heal the emotional wounds! If horses are an important part of one's life, lose them and the pain is unbearable.

It was Tuesday night at the riding school in Avondale that Vince managed, it was his night to take the team back to Titirangi, but he had been too busy so they were going Wednesday night instead. The team knew they were supposed to be going home, and because they weren't they were all restless. Horses are animals most people underestimate, they are just as intelligent as dogs if not more so, but because they are too big to be house pets the public don't know them, except seeing them at the races. Our senior horse was old Jima; he had been one of the horses that had been used on the milk cart, and he was now twelve years old which in human terms is 84 YOA. He was a fine cut of horse over 17 hands high or almost 6 foot high at the shoulders, a stunning looking gelded (castrated) horse and the favorite of all. Jima knew all of the gates on the property and could open them all; we didn't bother to tighten the security, which as it turned out was a serious mistake. The Riding School had been very busy on that week; and had heavy bookings right up until the Tuesday afternoon late, which was why Vince had decided not to take them on the usual night. Some of the learner riders had been very demanding; and Vince had been in an ugly mood as a result, it was never so much the learners it was the Mothers who always upset Vince. While they recognized him as a very good rider, he was a black Maori, therefore inferior and could be treated like an idjit. (Idiot)

The weekend booking had been very heavy, with twenty horses out most of the time! When they came in they had to be watered and fed, then brushed down to keep their appearance up to the standard, Stepfather insisted on.

Vince by now was twelve YOA and quite capable to deal with the rentals, the problem was the teaching that could be hard on his nerves. It was not unusual to have 4-5 learner's at once, which meant the same number of wealthy Mothers acting as Directors. Most were very nice, but boy when he got a bitch she was a real bitch, insisting that black kid was a useless little Maori. It was fine if there were several Mothers there the good would shut the bitch up, but if he got one like that solo it was a nightmare.

Vince's Stepfather would never help even though he was a fine horseman, he insisted that was Vince's job, and he had to deal with all of the horses, which by number was 25 but no more than 20 working at one time. Usually Monday was a light day and Tuesday very few; then Stepfather would take over and run two horses; while Winty transferred the other to the farm for resting and plenty of feed. Stepfather's job was to repair the saddles and bridles shod (new steel shoes) all of the horses as needed, there was no doubt the work was fairly shared, but Vince never got paid and his food and room was not very good.

Vince had never dreamed old Jimma would lead the team into trouble, but he was very wrong the old fella was a bundle of mischief. On the night of the accident Jimma the old rascal had nuzzled the front gate latch and opened it and the whole team left and was on their way back to the farm at Titirangi. The main line of the railway passed by the Avondale property, and the horses were all very used to the trains speeding by. The point was just where the train sped up and was moving at its top speed, it therefore took quite a long run to stop.

Vince was almost ready to go to bed, all was quiet and he was very tired from the day's work during which he had had several hard mothers to keep happy, and he was exhausted. All was very quiet in the night, when suddenly screams of horses in pain rent the night air. The way back to Titirangi went over a railway crossing, and the 20 horses were just walking over the crossing and ignoring the train; when they were hit.

Eleven horse's were injured unto death, five had to be destroyed only four of the team survived. The police came and visibly blanched at the damage done to the dead horses. The injured ones were crying piteously, and the four uninjured were walking around in a daze. A Vet was bought in and he put down the injured horses; so the death toll was sixteen and four alive, but the survivors were visibly shaken and actually crying. Vince took them home, but he himself, as was his Stepfather was totally shaken.

Old Jima had been killed outright; Kino Vince's horse had to be put down, and as he watched Winty swore he would never have another horse. Vince really loved Kino and the horse was only six YOA! Vince could not face the report on the carnage that was being called for and his Stepfather faced charges of negligence. It was perhaps unfair since the gates were locked, but none of us had allowed for Jimma's engenuity, he really had been a crafty old fella and all of the other horses followed whatever he did.

Vince decided it was time to leave, so he left within a week, and went to live with his Aunty and Uncle George at Sale St; City. He never returned to either farm and until now he has never thought of that horrible night, during which the team of beautiful horses died in tragic circumstances. Had that accident not happened Vince would not have left those much loved horses, he left with a broken heart. He has horses bought for his children only, but never bought one for himself.

Ngapuhi Meats Auckland:
78

VINADS HAD BEEN OFFERED a chance to buy 13 meat shops in many of the main suburbs of Auckland city and because his retail division was only three shops Vince was looking at it closely.

The butcher shops were owned by Wally Morris through his grocery chain Shoprite stores and were all immediately beside one of his groceries. Shoprite was one of the earliest no frills grocery chains in Auckland and Wally had decided they weren't able to run butcher shops so he wanted Vinads to take them over for no cost except paying a rent for the floor space.

Although Vince was no retail butcher, in the sense that he had never actually run a sole butcher shop he was well aware of what was needed, but with the shops he was finally getting in over his head. The need to control theft of money and meat and even shop supplies were suddenly added to an overstretched poor administration, the shops were a disaster from the start.

The retail shops were set off into another company Ngapuhi meats, which was the tribe into which Vince had been born, and the new company was 100% owned by Vinads Auckland Ltd; in its turn 100% owned by Vinads Christchurch. The shops were never managed properly because Vince never appointed a retail manager; he just preferred to run them himself which in itself was indicative of his lack of administrative knowledge. All except one in Grey Lynn were nice looking shops, and all being beside Shoprite high customer flow stores should have been a raging success. The Takapuna shop which had been the one Vinads had purchased first; after the new factory was built just a normal shop it was added to the Shoprite ones and managed by Vince personally.

The time Vince could give to managing his shops was minimal, most of the time he was busy straightening out problems with his very big wholesale business. His idea of managing Ngapuhi Meats was to perhaps go around and visit his managers once a month just to see if they were doing all right which of course they were, every one of them were stealing money from the cash registers except his Sister Aloma who managed one of the stores.

When the realization that Ngapuhi Meats was losing big amounts of money came Vince settled down and concentrated on the rogue shops but he couldn't find the main cause of the problems. He devised profit and loss week sheets, he did costing's but still there was a money drain he couldn't find, there was a major leak somewhere, but it was really well hidden. On the face of it the shops were all making profits, but Vince's instincts were very strong that there was something wrong. Not having a background in retail Vince should have understood the need to appoint a manager straight away, he had actually done this but that hadn't worked either. The manager he appointed was the person he had bought the Takapuna shop off, but in retrospect he was an older man and probably spent most of his time sitting at home with his wife drinking coffee. Then Vince decided to do a shop audit, all the stock was assessed and to Vince surprise he found that every shop had a large debtor list, how can this be he asked these are retail shops why have they all got debtors? His manager told him that many Maoris shopped at Ngapuhi Meats but most demanded credit because they were related to Vince, they were all of Ngapuhi Tribe and as such were entitled to free meat.

Vince went into a rage, how stupid he stormed that no one asked me who they were entitled to give credit too. The only credit customers were buyers through the wholesale division and they must be buying for a business and be able to pass a credit application. All retail credit was cancelled immediately and the Maoris all stopped coming, they would not pay they said that Stephens had everything from the white man's world he should share with his brothers. Vince found it amusing that it was always those who did nothing and were lazy who wanted to share, everything they had. There were also other reasons why he never trusted Maoris again and never wanted to be part of the Maori Race.

Although a big reason for losses in the shops had been found, another was still to come. By this time it had become obvious there was a problem in the overall Vinads business structure, it had become a large integrated business but there was still something wrong. Now that Vince was aware and had started hunting it wasn't long before he found the fault. The distribution manager had a brother driving one of the delivery vans, and between them they were selling meat from the factory to the shops on a COD basis. They had their own delivery book, and they would do a COD docket then they would share the cash each day of what they got from Ngapuhi Meats and any others who wanted to buy on a cash basis.

Vince had found out what they were doing but that was only the start, he found they had linked up with an outside team of wholesale butchers who had decided to send Vinads broke, they were loading out from the freezers at night and in terms of 2008 values over two million dollars worth of frozen stock had been stolen.

The culprits were caught red handed by the police and got eighteen months jail for stealing, but what good was that to Vinads. Vinads lost its insurance claim because the thefts were committed by their own staff.

The purchase of the 13 shops then the formation of Ngapuhi meats was really the nemesis of Vinads and the total group in dollar terms for 2008 the loss would have exceeded USD100,000 m, this is a minimum, the real estate involved would have had an equity at that level, and the business was unique.

W HEN THE FIRST FACTORY owned by Vinads had been opened in Christchurch it was fully equipped with really old, but still workable machines. It had been a very successful wholesale meat factory previously, and Vince had worked there so was well aware of how to use the place to its full capacity as it had once been. It was a serious mistake to set somebody up who not only knew how to do the work, knew the place, but also had a close relationship with all of the customers. Sadly for the wholesale firm which had sold Vince the property, they were not aware he also had the money, which of course was the final ingredient needed to make the wholesale meat business work. Rather they thought he had nothing which is why they thought it was safe to sell the property to Vinads.

It was a matter of some pride among Vince and his staff that their production was so high in that little factory, they used to talk about output per square inch not square feet.

The big order that came in from Birds Eye was almost too much, there was meat everywhere and the staff had been increased to 35 men where there was only working space for 25 at most. The decision was made to work around the clock with two 12 hour shifts 6 days per week, but the next problem was getting enough freezing space. The freezer was under so much pressure it finally gave up the ghost and the entire product was only half frozen at best when it was loaded out to go up to Birds Eye in Hastings.

Luckily the trucks were frozen and the pallets went straight into freezer rooms when it arrived at Birds Eye so they never realized they were getting half frozen meat, at least they never complained. It was probably because by time they got around to using it they had frozen the meat themselves.

We finally managed to rent a little vacant shop over the road and set that up as a staff room, and it was quite good, we even had a few good parties there. There was a house attached to the factory and it wasn't long before we were making holes in walls and moving into the house, we used part of it for an office and another part we turned into a room for rendering dripping.

That little factory was really a gift, no one could have had a better place to start in business than Vinads had it was complete in every way.

The factory in Auckland was everything the one in Christchurch was not, it was big had lots of freezer space, and the equipment was all new.

The mincer was so big it didn't need the meat to be cut up into smaller pieces it could take the whole quarters of beef in one go, it wasn't possible to feed it by hand it had an automatic hoist attached to the sides. The meat could be put through so fast it almost needed the boners and the trimmers to feed straight into the loaders. These machines had been especially imported from Germany by Vinads.

The blender mixed up 500 kgs every complete cut and the filler was totally automated, so that the rate of production was easily 2 tonne per hour finished product.

The factory itself was very big about 5 times the size of the one in Christchurch, and there was room for two boning lines. The pickle room was also very big and the order room for the processing of hams and corned beef etc was equally large, but then we had very large orders. For example the Auckland hospital was quite liable to order one tonne of corned beef as part of one of its orders, as well as 5,000 lamb chops and that would be for only one kitchen, they had four altogether. They also had another 11 hospitals so it was a very big contract.

There was a separate prepacking room for bacon, but only females worked in that dept.

The coolers were quite large, but the freezing rooms were huge, there was holding space for over 500 tonne of cartoned meat which was good but there were no snap freezers which we badly needed to be able to give perfect service.

The staff rooms had been all built as new, but it didn't take long before the staff had badly defaced all of the new facilities. This unfortunately led to industrial unrest, when because of the abuse of company premises all free meat was cancelled.

There was a petrol bowser to refuel the trucks every morning, the company kept five delivery vans going all of the time.

The loading bay for carcass meat was almost right out to the truck when it arrived so that unloading was very easy.

The factory was completely surrounded by asphalt drive that was in good condition and able to take trucks with 40 tonne axle weight.

The office space was more than adequate, with the most modern book keeping equipment available at that time as well as a modern phone system throughout the factory.

Out front there were parking spaces for ten office staff and the general staff had more than adequate parking on company property.

In spite of all the advantages the Auckland plant would never be as effective as the Christchurch plant because the sheer size seemed to create a higher cost ratio in Auckland. The Christchurch plant being so small was always the one that threw up the very big profits.